SHOOTING IRON

SHOOTING IRON

A Devil's Gulch Western

WILLIAM W. JOHNSTONE

AND J.A. JOHNSTONE

PINNACLE BOOKS
Kensington Publishing Corp.
www.kensingtonbooks.com

PINNACLE BOOKS are published by

Kensington Publishing Corp.
119 West 40th Street
New York, NY 10018

Copyright © 2023 by J.A. Johnstone

PUBLISHER'S NOTE: Following the death of William W. Johnstone, the Johnstone family is working with a carefully selected writer to organize and complete Mr. Johnstone's outlines and many unfinished manuscripts to create additional novels in all of his series like The Last Gunfighter, Mountain Man, and Eagles, among others. This novel was inspired by Mr. Johnstone's superb storytelling.

Special book excerpts or customized printings can also be created to fit specific needs. For details, write or phone the office of the Kensington Sales Manager: Kensington Publishing Corp., 119 West 40th Street, New York, NY 10018. Attn. Sales Department. Phone: 1-800-221-2647.

PINNACLE BOOKS, the Pinnacle logo, and the WWJ steer head logo Reg. U.S. Pat. & TM Off.

First Printing: November 2023
ISBN-13: 978-0-7860-4974-5
ISBN-13: 978-0-7860-4978-3 (eBook)

10 9 8 7 6 5 4 3 2 1

Printed in the United States of America

CHAPTER 1

Sheriff John Holt helped Deputy Marshal Wheeler haul the prisoner into the prison wagon with the others. The autumn morning sun cast harsh shadows of the thick iron slats cage across the faces of the five prisoners already inside.

To Holt, the rattling chains that bound Joe Mullen's hands and feet sang a sad hymn. A month before, Mullen had been the most powerful man in Devil's Gulch and one of the most important people in the territory. The town had rarely decided on matters of importance without first seeking Mullen's opinion. Now, he was nothing more than a common criminal. A man convicted of murdering an outlaw in cold blood.

Sheriff Holt might have enjoyed the irony of a killer murdering another killer if it was not all so tragic. And despite all the bad blood that had flowed between them, he did not enjoy seeing Mullen in chains. He was always saddened by waste and Joe Mullen's predicament was a waste. The rancher and mine owner possessed many talents that could have made Devil's Gulch the envy of the territory. Instead of using them for good, he used them to further his own greed.

Holt had expected Mullen to put up more of a struggle when the time came to get in the wagon, but he had been as meek as a lamb. He had once been a proud, boisterous man of means and property. He had the town of Devil's Gulch firmly in his grasp. But now he was just another prisoner crammed beneath a web of iron bars on his way to the Colorado Territorial Prison.

Holt remembered Doc Klassen determined that Mullen had suffered a conniption during his incarceration. The prisoner's entire left side had been paralyzed for weeks. He had only regained use of his left leg a week before. As he watched Mullen lower himself to sit on the crowded bench beside two other prisoners, Holt could see his ordeal had robbed him of more than just feeling in his leg or arm. It had robbed him of feeling anything.

The heavy iron door squealed as Deputy United States Marshal Dan Wheeler slammed it shut and held it in place while he padlocked it. Holt noticed how small the heavy padlock looked in Wheeler's large hands.

"Didn't expect this one to go in that easy," the big deputy marshal said as he walked back to the jail. "Heard he gave you quite a time when you first brought him in."

Holt took a final look at Mullen before turning to join Wheeler. He had been with Mullen constantly since before his conviction and sentencing the month before. He knew he should have felt some sort of remorse for him, but he did not, except perhaps a bit of sorry at who Joe Mullen might have been.

"He had more fight in him back then," Holt told him. "My neck is still sore from him trying to strangle me. Guess he lost all of the fight in him since."

"Conniption's what I heard." Wheeler nudged Holt with an elbow to the shoulder. "That's where we differ, John. I'd have killed him if he'd tried to strangle me."

Holt saw no reason to debate tactics with him. Wheeler was a big man. Nearly five inches taller than Holt's six feet, and much heavier. Most of it was solid, but less of it was with each passing year. He had the look of a man accustomed to getting his way and Holt was not in the mood to argue. "I'd rather see him spend the rest of his life in jail."

"And that he will, I promise you," Wheeler told him. "He's used to easy living up on that ranch of his. We'll see how he likes standing on a prison chow line eating porridge three times a day. I don't think he'll take to it. He'll be dead in a year. Eighteen months, tops."

But Holt was not so sure. Bitter experience had taught him that anyone who found themselves on the opposite side of Joe Mullen would do well to not sell him short. "He might not be able to make a run for it, but his mind is sharper than ever. You'd best not forget that in your travels."

Wheeler stopped outside the jail and took his time in looking over Holt. He did not seem impressed by what he saw. "That's strange coming from you. I've heard you're no one's idea of a Sunday social either."

"You've heard right," Holt told him.

The two lawmen walked into the warmth of the jail, where Holt signed papers granting the federal government custody of Joe Mullen.

Holt had made a practice of never telling another lawman what he should do, but he could not let Wheeler ride off without speaking his mind. "The man down at the livery tells me that your cook wagon is still being repaired."

Wheeler frowned as he folded the papers and tucked them in his vest pocket. "Threw a wheel right before we came into town this morning. The terrain in this part of the territory is hard on horse and haulers alike. The prison wagon is as solid as they come, but that cook wagon is as almost as rickety and fickle as the old man I've got driving it. Me and Bob got it back on well enough to bring us here, but it was slower going than I would've liked."

That was the part that bothered Holt. "But you're still planning on bringing these men to the territorial prison alone?"

"The government doesn't pay me to wait around," Wheeler said. "They pay me to bring my prisoners in on time and alive. I don't plan on waiting around just because my cook wagon is busted. I have a schedule to keep."

Holt decided it was time to break his rule about advice to lawmen. "I'd strongly advise you to wait for him, Wheeler. The livery says they'll have that wheel fixed in a day or so. Why take chances riding alone over rough terrain with a bunch like this? You're more than welcome to keep your prisoners here in my jail until your cook wagon is ready to go."

Wheeler tucked a cheroot in the corner of his mouth and struck a match alive off Holt's desk to light it. "That's awful neighborly of you, John, but I have to decline. Waiting here is the sensible thing to do. It's expected, which is why I won't do it." He waved the flame dead and tossed the match out the door and into the thoroughfare. "If it was just me, I'd be inclined to do what you say. But it just so happens that I've got a wagon filled with wanton cutthroats, thieves, and nasty individuals of every low human description. Some of them have ridden with some bad people. People who might be looking to break them out if I stay in one place too long. Got a fella named Hardt in there who has some particularly unsavory friends. The sooner I get them locked up behind bars, the sooner I'll be able to rest."

He tossed his thumb toward the doorway. "Don't let those blue skies fool you, Holt. You're new to this territory. You haven't seen how fast the weather can turn ugly out here. We could have a foot of snow tomorrow and ice after that, making the trail impassable. It's already plenty rough as it is. If I delay, I could wind up being forced to stay here all winter."

Holt did not see the problem. "That'd be fine by me.

We can always use the extra help and we'd see to it your prisoners were healthy."

"I couldn't care less about their well-being," he admitted. "But I do care about my schedule. If I need to winter someplace, I'd rather it be in my own bed at the prison instead of on a cot here in Devil's Gulch."

Wheeler tried a smile as he rubbed his right hip. "You're too young to appreciate this, but I'm not as young as I once was. The years and the miles seem to have piled up on me in the past few months. Guess it's made me lonesome for my comforts. The sooner I get there, the happier I'll be."

Holt was not trying to be difficult, but he decided to put a finer edge on his words. "I might be new to the territory, but I know a thing or two about weather. The snow is still a week or so away. The trip to the prison takes three days. You'd fare better on the road with two of you watching the men instead of just you."

But Wheeler was clearly not having any of it. "I've been transporting prisoners from one end of this territory to the other since I was your age. I know how to handle six criminals in a cage. Five and a half, given Mullen's condition."

Holt decided trying to convince Wheeler to delay his trip was useless. He had told the man his concerns and that would have to be enough. He could not force the issue. "Since you won't listen to reason, how about a word of advice?"

The marshal grinned. "Sure, young fella. Just what are you gonna tell me that I don't already know about hauling prisoners?"

"Gag Mullen before you hit the road," Holt told him. "His limbs might not work too well at present, but there's nothing wrong with his mouth or his mind. I've seen how convincing he can be when given the chance. He's more than capable of turning those men against you more than they're already inclined to be. You just might find yourself with something of an uprising on your hands before you reach the prison."

Wheeler took the cheroot from his mouth and flicked the ash on the floor. "He can talk to them until he's blue in the face. Won't do him any good. Want to know why?" He beckoned Holt to come closer, as if he was about to tell him a secret. "On account of me not giving them a chance to run. See, I don't plan on opening that door again until we reach the prison."

Holt pulled away from Wheeler. "Not even to stretch their legs or tend to their business?"

"Nope," Wheeler said. "There's more than enough room in there for them to spread out if they're of a mind to. As for their business, that's their problem. If they had wanted to be treated like human beings, they shouldn't have broken the law in the first place. Would've saved themselves, the territory, and me a whole mess and bother if they had. They put themselves in that wagon, Holt. Not me. They'll just have to live with the consequences."

Holt had heard some odd strategies from lawmen in his time, but this one took the prize. "It's liable to get mighty ripe in that wagon."

"Good thing I plan to keep up a good pace," he said. "I like to keep my prisoners lean and hungry with only hard-tack and water each morning. Maybe a mouthful of coffee at night if I'm feeling generous. In my experience, a hungry man is easier to bring to heel than a fed one."

A hungry man's also more liable to get desperate and cut your throat, Holt thought. But Wheeler had made it clear that he neither wanted nor needed his advice, so he kept his opinions to himself.

Instead, he offered his hand to Wheeler. "Then I wish you the best of luck on your journey. For all of our sake."

The two men shook hands as a man out on the street

called out Wheeler's name. "Hold on a minute, Daniel. I need to talk with you."

Wheeler frowned as he stepped outside. "That'll be Old Bob, my cook. He's going to take this news worse than you. That old man has been trying to baby me for years."

Holt joined Wheeler on the boardwalk in time to see a man with a long, tangled gray beard who looked to be in dire need of a bath. His skin and clothes bore the dull patina of a lifetime spent on the trail that Holt doubted any amount of scrubbing would remove. He doubted Bob would even try. Men like him never cared much for appearances or money. They lived off the miles they had traveled and the endless stories they produced.

"Just hold on right where you are, Daniel," the cook called out. Three yellowed teeth hung on for dear life at the front of his mouth and caused him to whistle when he spoke. But despite his ragged appearance, the Winchester he toted was spotless and gleamed in the morning sunlight. "I aim to go with you."

Wheeler shook his head. "Not a chance, old-timer. You've got to stay with the wagon until it's fixed. Says so in the regulations."

"Them regulations you're so fond of quoting when it suits you say nothing of the kind," Bob told him. "And that wagon will still be here when we get back in a couple of weeks if the weather holds out." He held up a canvas bag. "I managed to scrounge up enough supplies for us to make the trip there and back with nary a thought. It won't be biscuits and gravy every morning, but it's a lot better than you just wandering the wilderness by your lonesome."

Wheeler took the sack of supplies from him. "I won't be lonesome. I've got six friendly prisoners to keep me company. And in case you forgot, that cook wagon of yours is federal property. You can't just leave it here unattended. Like

I just got through telling the sheriff here, I can handle this on my own. I don't need you."

"What you need is a good dose of common sense." The cook looked at Holt. "Tell it to him again, Sheriff. He won't listen to me anymore. Thinks I'm worse than an old washerwoman with all my worrying. Tell him it's just not sensible for a man to ride off alone with a passel of murderers, even if they are bound and chained."

"I tried," Holt said, "but he's determined."

"Stubborn is what he is." Bob poked the deputy marshal in the chest with a bony finger. "You've been that way since the day I first laid eyes on you, and you haven't changed a bit. You remind me of an old uncle I had once. You could tell him a storm was coming, but if he was of a mind to stay where he was, he'd just sit there and let the rain soak him to the bone. Never got sick on account of it, either, until the day he caught the coughing sickness and died."

Wheeler shut his eyes. "You and your stories."

Bob went on. "You say you're concerned about territorial property? Well, it just so happens that you're territorial property, too, Dan. And I'll remind you that busted wagon back there is mine. The territory just pays me for the use of it. And you're more valuable than a pile of pots and provisions. That's why I'm going with you, and I won't take no for an answer."

The old cook decided he had done enough talking as he walked over to the wagon and started to climb up into the box. "I'll just bring us back to the livery and pick up some of the things I packed. Won't be but a minute."

But Wheeler took a firm hold of Bob's arm and prevented him from going any farther. "You'll stay with the wagon like I told you. My word is final."

Bob tried to pull away from him, but Holt saw the cook's arm looked like a broom handle in Wheeler's massive grip.

Bob gradually realized Wheeler would not allow him to

come along and reluctantly stepped away from the wagon. "This is just plain, old-fashioned foolishness, Dan. Blind foolishness, just like my uncle and the coughing sickness. Especially after I went through all that trouble of packing up what we'd be needing for the trail."

"Nobody asked you to do that." Wheeler handed the sack back to him. "You've got no one to blame but yourself for the wasted effort. You can unpack it just as quickly as you packed it. I've already got everything I need for the trip."

Wheeler was about to flick his cheroot into the thorough-fare but thought better of it and gave it to Bob instead. "Here. Puff on that awhile. It'll make you feel better."

The deputy marshal touched the brim of his hat to Holt before climbing up into the wagon. He might have said the years were creeping up on him, but he was spry for a man of his size. "So long, Sheriff. Keep an eye on Bob for me. See to it he doesn't get into any trouble. And don't let him have a jug either. Don't let all that gray hair fool you. He's a handful when he's drinking. Don't let him talk you to death. Just walk away from him when you get bored. He'll hardly notice."

The cook offered a crude response, most of which was drowned out by Wheeler throwing the handbrake and snapping the reins to get the four-horse team rolling out of town and on the road to prison.

"Well, if that don't beat all." Bob puffed away on the cheroot as he joined Holt in watching Wheeler go. "That man's still as stubborn as the day I found him. No way to reason with him when he makes his mind up to something. No, sir. Not him."

Holt imagined there was a deeper story there but did not care to hear it. "The livery told me you should be able to hit the road in a day or two. Maybe you'll be able to make up some time and catch him on the trail."

"No, I won't. Not him." Old Bob inhaled the last of the

cheroot and burned his fingers as he spat it out. "He'll push those horses and those men hard. Got it into his head that we've got some weather coming." He continued to grumble as Wheeler and the prison wagon rounded the end of Main Street and disappeared. "Stubborn is what he is. No other word for it. Reminds me of a fella I used to ride with when I used to do some scouting for the army before the war."

Holt was not in the mood for a story and saw no point in continuing their discussion. "If you need a place to stay, you're more than welcome to sleep in the jail. We don't have any prisoners at present, so it'll probably be quiet. My deputy took off on me, so I'd welcome the company."

Bob cocked a bushy eyebrow at Holt. "That young fella I heard about? The one who helped you stop Joe Mullen? Jack Turner, wasn't it?"

"Jack Turnbull," Holt corrected him.

"No good for a man to walk out on his responsibilities like that, especially a young one. What happened? You two have a fight?"

"That's the problem," Holt admitted. "Everything was fine until one day he was just gone."

The business still troubled him. Holt had arrived at the jail one morning the previous week only to find a note from Jack waiting for him on his desk. The young man's handwriting was nearly impossible to read, but from what Holt could make out, Turnbull claimed to have urgent business to tend to somewhere.

Holt could not imagine what business might require a teenaged orphan's attention, and he had not been given the opportunity to ask him.

Holt did not like it, but he had no power over the young man. And with Mullen in jail, he could not ride after Jack to ask him. But he would be sure to have a long talk with the boy when he came back. *If* he came back, he reminded himself.

Holt decided not to dwell on it. "You can have the place

to yourself most nights if we don't have any customers. Can probably count on sleeping the whole night through. This town's been kind of quiet with Mullen in here. Guess no one was particularly anxious to keep him company. Even the drunks have been behaving themselves."

"Disagreeable sort, was he? Mullen, I mean."

"Evil sort would be closer to the mark." Holt stepped aside and gestured Bob to enter the jail. "Feel free to look the place over first if you want. See if it meets your approval."

"No need for such formalities, Sheriff." Bob glanced inside the jail. "It's got four walls, a floor, and bars. Just like every other jail I've been to. I'm sure it'll suit me just fine. I've slept in worse places." The cook picked up his bag and waddled under the heavy load into the jail. "Like the time I was taken hostage by a band of Comanche renegades. Don't know if you've ever come across their like, Sheriff, but they're not known for their hospitality."

Holt might have been able to do without a story for every topic, but he was glad Bob had taken him up on his offer. Before coming to Devil's Gulch, Holt had always preferred to work alone. One less person to trust meant one less person to disappoint him.

But young Jack Turnbull had managed to change his opinion on the matter. He had just begun to grow accustomed to having him around when he took off. He was not so much hurt as disappointed. He thought Jack held more regard for him, despite the fact they had met while he took him into custody.

"Make yourself at home," Holt said as he walked inside and took his rifle down from the rack on the wall. "It's about time for me to walk the town anyway. I'll do my best to be quiet when I get back in case you're sleeping."

"Be as loud as you like, Sheriff." Old Bob tested the mattress for firmness. "I've never been one to sleep once the sun comes up anyway, but if I do, you won't be able to wake me. Always sleep like a baby indoors. Guess that's on account of it not happening too often. I spend most of my time out on the trail with Wheeler hauling criminals across creation. The stories I could tell you would make that dark hair of yours turn white. Why, there was one time I found myself in Golden City right after . . ."

Holt stepped out onto the boardwalk and pulled the door shut behind him. Bob was clearly a man who liked to talk. He was probably brimming with stories of men he'd known in his time. Places he had been. Outlaws he had killed. He imagined Wheeler featured prominently in most of them.

But John Holt had never been much of one for conversation. He always preferred to let his actions and his guns do his talking for him.

And although he had only been in Devil's Gulch for little more than a month, his guns had already said quite a bit.

The sheriff took his time as he began the long walk along Main Street. Joe Mullen might be on his way to prison, but there was still plenty of trouble to be had if a man went looking for it. And the people of Devil's Gulch were paying quite a sum to seek it out. He walked the boardwalks at least once a day at different times. It paid to let the people know he was around and keeping an eye on things.

His first few days as sheriff had resulted in quite a bit violence, more than Holt preferred. But the mood in town had calmed to a low boil in the weeks since Devil's Gulch had lost their mayor to one of Mullen's assassins and several citizens who had foolishly dared to test Holt's mettle. He intended on keeping it that way.

When he had first come to town several weeks before, Holt learned the Blue Bottle Saloon was the center of political life in Devil's Gulch. That first day, he had found Mayor Blair Chapman, Dr. Ralph Klassen, Joe Mullen, and Tony Cassidy in the middle of breakfast, discussing town business over plates of runny eggs and burnt bacon.

The town had changed since then. Mullen was being carted off to jail. Mayor Chapman had been killed and replaced in office by his widow. Doc Klassen took his breakfast at Jean Roche's café. The Bottle, as it was known, had lost its shine for the town's leading citizens.

But Holt knew that while Cassidy might not have had the influence he'd once enjoyed, he was far from docile or defenseless. The recent downturn in his fortunes had made him desperate to hold on to whatever power he had. Holt knew desperate men were often the most dangerous.

Which was why he had decided to make the Bottle his first visit following Mullen's departure. Cassidy and his customers needed to be reminded they no longer ran Devil's Gulch. That honor now belonged to Sheriff John Holt.

The strength with which he delivered that lesson would depend entirely on them.

CHAPTER 2

Holt pushed in the door to the Blue Bottle Saloon and found Tony Cassidy at his usual spot, perched at the far end of the bar facing the door. He was slouched over a mug of coffee. He was too thin for his frame and his deep sunken eyes made it appear that he had not slept in more than a week. One might be forgiven for thinking Cassidy was sick, but Holt knew better. He always looked like that, and he was all too capable for Holt's tastes.

His reddened eyes were lifeless when they fell on Holt as the sheriff approached him. Cassidy used to be sharp-tongued and always good for an insult. But on that morning, he looked ready to climb into bed and pull the blanket over his head.

"What do you want, Holt?" Cassidy sneered as Holt stopped ten feet away. "Did you come here to gloat? Because if you have, you might as well turn around and be on your way. I'm in no mood today."

Holt had no intention of gloating, but he would not be run off by the saloon keeper either. "I wanted to make sure you knew that Mullen is on his way to prison. The marshal just took him away a few minutes ago. I figured you should hear it from me personally."

Cassidy slid the coffee mug away from him. "What do

you expect me to do about it? Throw myself on the floor, prostrate in grief? Give you an apology for all I've done or all that you think I've done."

Holt shook his head. "Wouldn't make much of a difference if you did."

"Do you want me to go for my gun? Maybe get even for my poor friend Joe?" Cassidy stepped away from the bar and held his arms away from his sides. "Well, too bad for you that I ain't armed."

"I wouldn't care if you were." Holt smiled. "You'd never get the chance to pull it."

Cassidy went back to the bar and picked up his mug. "Sorry to disappoint you, Sheriff. Guess I'm fresh out of feelings for the moment."

"Fresh out of friends too. At least the type that you don't have to pay to be in your company."

Cassidy sneered at the insult to his profession. "Men are always going to find a way to entertain themselves, Holt. If I don't sell it to them, someone else will. That goes all the way back to the Bible. You'd have figured that out for yourself, if you'd ever bothered to learn how to read."

"I can read just fine," Holt said. "I can read the Bible. I can read men too. Want me to tell you why you're still alive?"

"No, but I have a feeling you're going to tell me anyway."

Holt did. "On account of you being smart. Or at least smart enough to never push me directly. You're not just a flesh peddler but an instigator. You've had a hand in everything that's gone wrong and gotten people killed in this town long before I came along. You were all too happy to just plant seeds in Mullen's mind and watch him throw his weight around for your benefit. Now, he's gone, and you and I are the only two left that matter. If you keep on being smart, you'll have no trouble from me. But if you or any of your friends try to be smarter than you are, I'll see to it that you spend the rest of your miserable life in the cell next to Mullen."

"I don't need friends," the saloon owner said. "All I need are customers and I've got plenty of those, despite what you or Ma McAdam or the Chapman widow try to do to me. So, until I either break the law or cross you, I don't expect to see you in here much and you sure won't be seeing me."

Cassidy sipped his coffee and placed the mug on the bar. "I heard you out and you've heard me. If there's nothing else, I'd appreciate it if you turned around and went about your business. If I never see you again, it'll be too soon."

But Holt did not move. "You'll be seeing plenty of me if you ever stick your head out of the hole again. You'd best remember what I told you when your pride starts gnawing at you late at night."

Holt noticed Cassidy hesitate before he brought the mug to his lips again. He expected the saloon owner to try to have the last word but was surprised when he simply drank his coffee in silence.

Holt slowly backed out of the bar. As he resumed his walk around town, he wondered if Cassidy really was as beaten as he seemed.

He doubted it. Men like that were never out of a fight unless they were dead. He was cooking something else. And whenever he decided to serve it, John Holt would be more than ready.

Cassidy kept his eyes on Holt as he backed out of his saloon. He hated everything about the man. The way he walked. The way he spoke to him. How he thought he was better than anyone else in town. How he was every bit as dangerous as he thought he was. No amount of disdain he had for the sheriff would ever cause him to take him lightly.

But John Holt was not perfect. And he was nowhere near as clever as he believed himself to be.

Tony Cassidy had never been good with a gun or a rifle. He was even more inept with his fists. He only considered himself fair with a knife, but he took solace in the fact that he had killed every man he had ever marked for death.

He learned from an early age that his talents were elsewhere. There were other ways to impose his will on his enemies. One of them was through influence. He gained influence by listening to them. As a saloon owner, there was always someone willing to share their troubles. He knew if you fed a man enough whiskey or beer, he would bare his soul to you. His hopes and dreams. His greatest fears and darkest secrets.

Tony knew men would tell him all about themselves by what they said and did not say under the power of liquor. And men always found a willing audience in Tony, who often swept up the hidden parts of themselves only to store them away for a time when it might benefit them.

Having spent most of his life in saloons either as a bartender or an owner, Cassidy had spent many years honing his craft to perfection. Lately, he had used his dark gift—and he did consider it a gift—on Joe Mullen. The boisterous rancher was more than willing to play the fool for him in the belief he was serving himself while furthering Cassidy's hidden aims. Mullen craved adoration and notoriety. Cassidy was content to let him believe he took the lead. All Cassidy wanted was control.

John Holt's arrival in Devil's Gulch had changed everything. And once Mayor Chapman had been killed, it became clear to Cassidy that Mullen could not resist the chance to go against the new sheriff. That left Cassidy with little choice than to put another plan in motion. A plan that would remove Mullen permanently for the safety of Cassidy's influence.

The first part of his plan had gone well. Joe Mullen was disgraced and bound for prison where he would spend the rest of his life behind bars. Now that he was gone forever, it was time for Cassidy to begin the next phase of his scheme. A plan that would be far more subtle than Joseph Mullen could ever be.

And if it worked according to plan, John Holt would be spending the winter somewhere far away.

From behind him, Cassidy heard his bartender—a brute named Simpson—clear his throat to gain his attention. At least the big oaf had been smart enough to duck out the back door of the saloon when they saw Holt out on the boardwalk and remain hidden until the sheriff left.

But now that he was gone, Simpson had returned bearing a message.

Cassidy turned to look at him. "You can come out now. The bad man is gone."

The bartender lumbered into the saloon and kept his voice low as he said, "Got that package you wanted me to fetch for you, Tony. It's in your office."

Cassidy doubted Doc Klassen would ever ask the bartender to assist him in a delicate surgery, but he was more than capable at carrying out simple tasks laid out for him. Such as bringing someone to the Bottle.

"Good man." Cassidy picked up his mug of coffee and walked back toward his office. "Send the rest of the pot in when you have a chance, Bob. And see to it that no one disturbs us. Not even Holt."

"Pot's already in there waiting for you," Simpson told him. "And don't worry. Holt won't be showing his face in here today."

Cassidy hoped the simpleton was proven right. For all he knew, he might be, for even a broken clock was right twice a day.

CHAPTER 3

After pleasantries were exchanged, Sarabelle Mullen folded her gloved hands on her lap.

"So good of you to come by," Cassidy gushed as he sat behind his desk, "although I wouldn't have blamed you if you put it off for a day or so. I'm sure today has been very trying for you."

"What makes today so special?"

"Because the Federals were here in town. They carted Joe off to jail less than half an hour ago by my reckoning."

Sarabelle's expression remained flat. "Why would I care about that? We sprung our trap on that scoundrel weeks ago. Carting him off to jail just seals it is all."

Cassidy laughed. "You're nothing if not practical, Sarabelle."

There was hardly a man in town who did not admire her beauty. Not even Cassidy was immune. She had a graceful elegance about her. She was tall and thin with golden hair and clear blue eyes. It would be easy to dismiss her as a pretty face and nothing more.

But no amount of fine clothes or manners could conceal her true nature from Cassidy's discerning eye. He knew she was a frontier woman to her core.

When it became clear to Cassidy that Holt was a bone

that Joe would never bury, the saloon owner focused his attentions to Mrs. Mullen.

She had been unwilling to betray her husband at first, which was to be expected. They had been married for almost ten years by then, and although their union had failed to produce children, there was a certain allegiance present. An allegiance Cassidy watched die when he told her of the many times her husband had been unfaithful to her in the upstairs rooms of the Blue Bottle Saloon.

At the time, he could tell that she had been aware of her husband's dalliances, but being confronted with them by a relative stranger was something altogether different.

Cassidy remembered standing in the front parlor of the home that she and Mullen had built together when he told her the news. He allowed her to rage at him, at least for a time, before he slowly introduced his plan. A plan that would not only remove Mullen as a liability but offer Sarabelle the vengeance she wanted and deserved. To Cassidy's benefit, of course.

Since having convinced her to testify against her husband in open court, Cassidy wondered if her conscience might have gotten the better of her.

He could tell by her blank expression at the news of her husband being carted off to jail that she felt no guilt for her actions. *Good*.

"Since you don't appear to be in mourning," Cassidy said, "maybe we should skip the coffee and drink something stronger to toast our new partnership?"

"Not until I know what our partnership is, Mr. Cassidy."

The saloon owner waved off the formality. "Call me Tony, please. It's the least you can do after all we've been through together."

"You mean after we betrayed my husband," she said, putting a finer point on it.

Cassidy decided the conversation might not be cause

for a celebration just yet. "After he betrayed both of us first. He betrayed you upstairs and he betrayed me out there. On the boardwalk when he could not see past his blind hatred for Holt. All we did was solve a problem that plagued both of us."

When she listed her head to the side, Cassidy decided he did not like the way she was looking at him. He felt like something being studied as opposed to someone she was speaking with.

"You're a strange man, Tony. You never go after something straight on, do you? You like to come at it when it's not looking or maybe even from behind it."

"A deliberate nature takes many forms," Cassidy said. "The way a man goes about doing something doesn't matter as long as that something gets done."

"Or a woman."

He gladly conceded the point. "In this case, yes. Which was why I was looking forward to our conversation today. Your husband and I were very successful in business together."

She offered a hint of a smile. "Behind every successful man there's a strong woman, Tony. You'd know that if you'd ever decided to take a wife of your own."

"Why, Sarabelle." He picked up his coffee mug. "I could be forgiven for taking that as a proposal of marriage."

Her smile soured. "Don't flatter yourself. The only arrangement I want with you is a formal one. I don't even like the idea of shaking hands with you, much less the notion of taking you as a husband."

"We agree on that much." Cassidy laughed as he drank his coffee. "I don't sleep well with one eye open, and that's how I'd have to sleep with you around."

"I think we make a formidable team in our own way," she said. "We succeeded in ridding ourselves of Joe and I see no reason why we can't work together in the future, provided we come to some kind of an arrangement."

It was music to his ears, but he kept his enthusiasm to himself.

"I'm not sure we need an agreement." Cassidy set his mug on his desk. "I liked working with Joe, sure. We had a good thing going until he went and started thinking he was better than he really was. I'll admit my take has suffered some, but I'm still making good money on my own."

"You sound quite content."

"That's because I am."

She slowly shook her head. "No, you're not. You've never drawn a content breath in your life. You do what you do because it is your nature. Same as me."

Cassidy shifted in the chair. He was not used to being spoken to this way. And he had never had such a frank conversation with a woman before. "Sounds nice but it doesn't tell me what's on your mind."

"My husband is on his way to spend the rest of his life in prison," she began, "and we both know he's never coming back. The empire we built together remains. I'll make sure all my men know that the Blue Bottle is the preferred place for them to drink while they're in town. Some will disobey me, as is their nature, but we'll do our best to keep them out of the Railhead. I know Ma McAdam and Frank Peters are your enemies."

Cassidy did his best to hide his displeasure. "That's a nice sentiment, Sarabelle, but regular customers from your mines and ranches were never the biggest part of the arrangement I had with Joe."

She drew in a deep breath and looked up at the ceiling. "I'm quite aware that you and Joe had this town carved up between the two of you before John Holt darkened our door. We have that idiot Mayor Chapman to thank for bringing

Holt here. The best thing that fool ever did was get himself killed."

Cassidy smiled. "Not a very good idea to speak ill of the dead, is it?"

"And we need good ideas right now, you and I." She tilted her head as she looked him over. "What about you, Tony? You're the one who invited me here today. What did you want to talk about?"

"A mutual problem. With the mayor's widow taking up his duties, you and I are in a poor position."

"I don't see why. Mrs. Chapman and I aren't exactly cordial, but I fail to see how she can harm my interests."

"She thinks Joe and I put up that miner to shoot her husband," Cassidy explained. "She knows the assassin was in here drinking his fill before he got it into his head to shoot the mayor. She blames me and Joe for it. And that means she blames you in Joe's absence. She can hardly touch you now, but if you start expanding, she can find ways to make your life difficult if she chooses."

"Elizabeth Chapman isn't a nice woman, but she's smarter than her husband ever was." Her eyes narrowed. "Has she shown Ma McAdam's Railhead Saloon any consideration?"

Cassidy shook his head. "She doesn't like saloons much, even though drinking is the biggest business in town. Well, when you add together all the saloons, anyway."

"And how many do you personally control, Tony?"

Cassidy began to have a new appreciation for her cunning. He wondered how much Joe had told her about their association over the years and how much he had kept from her. "I own the Bottle outright. Helped the rest of them get started by loaning them money before the bank opened here. I have small interests in the other saloons in town except for the Railhead. The interest they pay me isn't enough to live on, but I've got some say over how they run things. Why?"

"Think you could take them over one by one?"

He was beginning to see what she was getting at. "None of them are close to paying off what they owe me, so I suppose you could say that I own them now. Why?"

He watched Sarabelle adjust her gloves as she appeared to give the matter some thought. "Since saloons are the most popular businesses in town, sounds like we'd have a chance to help or hurt any cause we care about. Maybe it's time we work on undermining Mrs. Chapman and put someone we trust in her chair. Someone who's more of a friend to us."

Cassidy had done something similar with Blair Chapman's candidacy. The friendly haberdasher had never even thought of becoming a politician until Cassidy and Mullen managed to talk him into it. The two men had used their combined influence to gain support from the town's drinking citizens and he was elected to office unopposed.

He had done whatever Mullen and Cassidy had told him to do. He had turned a blind eye to the rash of crimes that benefitted Mullen and Cassidy. Without a sheriff, Mullen's Vigilance Committee enforced law, which only solidified their hold over the town.

Which was why Chapman's decision to bring John Holt to town had taken them by surprise and, ultimately, destroyed their plans.

Cassidy liked the way Sarabelle Mullen thought. It was not only a good idea that had worked before. It would probably work again. "The election isn't until next year. We can't pin our hopes on a bunch of drunks remaining loyal to us for that long. Why, in a few months, people will think she's been in office for years."

"Which is why we must act immediately," she said. "Joe and I still have many friends in the capital," Sarabelle said. "None of them had wanted to risk helping Joe during his murder trial, of course. That's to be expected, especially from a politician. But me?" She smiled. "I'm as much a victim of his shortcomings as anyone, perhaps even more. They may not like my husband, but they like our money. I'm sure I can talk them into supporting a special election here in Devil's Gulch. Especially since Elizabeth seized her husband's office without giving the citizens a say in her decision."

Cassidy had always thought he had more influence with Sarabelle and Joe than he let on. His wife had just said as much. "How quickly do you think you could get them to do that?"

"I won't know for certain until I ask, but I can send a telegram today before I leave town. They'll probably be relieved when they realize I'm not begging them to help Joe."

The more he thought about the idea, the more he liked it. "Having an election is one thing. Picking the right man to run is something different."

She did not seem to mind the closeness between them nor his hand on hers. "I was counting on you to pick a suitable candidate, Tony. Your share of the burden of our partnership."

Cassidy laughed again, only this time, there was no trace of humor in it. "Our partnership. I like the sound of that. Joe and I might've worked together, but we were hardly partners. He had the income from his ranches and his mines. All I ever got was the business from the Bottle and what I used to make from providing protection through the Vigilance Committee. Now that the committee is no more, I don't make nearly as much as you think."

He was glad to see the stone façade of her expression fade a bit. She had not considered a downturn in his fortunes once change had come to Devil's Gulch. It also had the virtue of being true.

"When you put it that way," she said, "perhaps I was wrong to think there was a way we might be able to work together. It seems like your prospects have diminished a great deal since Joe's conviction. Perhaps you're not as valuable to me as I had hoped."

Cassidy held up a hand in slight protest. "Don't try flattery so early in the negotiations, Sarabelle. It weakens your advantage."

"And I sense I am wasting my time." She began to rise from her chair. "Good day to you, Tony."

"Wait!" Cassidy barked louder than he had intended. He had not counted on her calling his bluff. He could not allow her to leave, for it would cost him twice as much to get her back to the bargaining table later. "If you walk out that door, you'll be making a big mistake."

"I have a feeling the mistake will be just as big if I stay here."

"Not so." Cassidy could tell the time for subtlety had passed. "You've become a woman of considerable wealth. You've got a thriving ranch and several mines that show no sign of being played out for the next few years, maybe even longer."

Sarabelle remained seated. "Joe told you quite a bit, didn't he?"

Cassidy did not see the point in telling her that, when it came to drinking, Joe was a lightweight. Some men wept when drunk. Some sought out a fight. Joe became talkative and grew eager to prove he was far more powerful than he already appeared to be. He had always found a willing audience in Tony Cassidy. "If you set aside our mutual faults, Joe and I were friends. And we helped each other, just like I'm willing to help you now."

"Other than removing the Chapman widow from office, it sounds like I don't need any help from you or anyone else."

"True, but the fact that you agreed to come see me at all proves you're after more than just money," Cassidy said. "If all you wanted was wealth and riches, you never have to lift a finger for the rest of your life. All you have to do is tolerate a visit from your husband's business managers a few times a year to sign documents and spend the rest of your life counting your money."

"You're not doing a very good job of convincing me that I need you, Tony."

"I didn't think I'd have to. You're a clever woman. Ruthless too . . ."

"Now you're insulting me."

"But Joe never allowed you to know much about his affairs, which means you don't know the first thing about business. That's not to say you can't learn, but such lessons can prove expensive. Lawyers and business managers may try to take advantage of your inexperience. Not at first, of course. Any theft would happen slowly over time, but eventually it *will* happen, and you know it. Before long, you'll be at their mercy, and after they think they've stolen enough from you, they'll attempt to buy you out or force you out at a mere fraction of what your holdings are worth. They'll leave you the ranch, but that won't be enough for you."

Her eyebrows rose. "What makes you think so?"

"Because if it was, you wouldn't have bothered coming here today. You wouldn't be interested in getting your own man elected mayor. You need me and you know it."

Her eyebrows furrowed. "My mama raised me to never need a man for anything in my life. You think Joe was the brains in our marriage? I was manipulating him for a long time before you got your claws on him."

"I know," Cassidy admitted. "And you did a wonderful job of it too. But the men you'll need to rely upon are clever. They see an opening to further themselves now that Joe is out of the picture. What Joe lacked in smarts, he more than made up for in brutality and reputation. A reputation I already have and can use to your advantage."

Her expression softened again, and she sat farther back in the chair. She was not entirely convinced but she was thinking about it. "Why couldn't I rely on, say, Ty Arbour to handle my affairs? He's honest and capable."

Cassidy slowly shook his head. "He's a backwoods lawyer who doesn't know the first thing about business. He only has a practice because he and his cousin have the court in this town sewn up between them. Lester Patrick prosecutes, and Ty Arbour defends. And if Arbour didn't steal from you intentionally, he'd still ruin you through incompetence."

He tried a smile again. "Just about the only thing I've never been accused of is being gullible. With me, you know where you stand. You know what I am so you know you can trust me."

"Trust an untrustworthy man." She laughed. "Hardly a wise decision for a woman in my position."

"An untrustworthy man who proved his worth when he helped you push your husband out of the way as soon as he became a problem. A man who honors his agreements when it benefits me. As long as my partners remain true to their side of the bargain."

She grew very still and her normally clear eyes clouded over in thought. She had heard everything he had told her and realized he was right. "Let's say that I take you up on your offer and hire you as my . . . what?"

"Advisor," he said. "We could even draw up a contract to make it all perfectly legal. We can even allow young Arbour to draw up the documents."

He watched an element of surprise appear on her face. She had not expected him to suggest such a thing. "Let's say I agree to have you as my advisor. How much would it cost me? And if you say fifty-fifty, I'll walk out this door and never return."

"Ten percent of all future profits." He had planned on first asking for twenty-five percent when he had first invited her here but now decided it would be best to start with his rock-bottom offer. "All profits that occur from this day forward."

"That's still a healthy sum."

"Ninety percent of something is more than Joe seemed willing to give you," he reminded her. "And ten percent is enough to buy my loyalty to you."

Cassidy enjoyed watching her think it over. Ten percent seemed like a lot on its own, but not when it stood next to ninety percent. "I admit that it sounds reasonable, but I'd like some time to consider your proposal."

He had no intention of allowing her to leave. Time to think would only serve to allow her to devise a way to dilute his interest.

"No. I've given you a fair price for my counsel. I didn't haggle and I wasn't greedy. I'd like to know your answer now."

She looked down at the gloved hands in her lap. "I'm afraid that's not possible, Tony. I'd like to take at least a day to mull it over."

He saw it was time to show her how far his reach spread. "To mull it over or ask Hank Lassiter what he thinks of the proposal?"

She looked up at him as if she had been struck. Her expression was a picture of surprise and anger within a delicate frame. "How in the world did you know about him?"

"Not much happens in Devil's Gulch without my knowledge," he said. "And what your banker friend has in charm he lacks in discretion. My men have seen him riding out to your ranch once the bank closes and accounts have been settled. And I doubt he's making the trip to give you financial advice. Smart move on your part. He's a fool, but a rich one."

She grew flushed with embarrassment and anger. "Who else knows about this? Has anyone else seen him?"

"No one else," Cassidy assured her. "Only my men. And I can promise no one else finds out about it either. But the

cost of your continued good name and the lack of scandal
will cost you the ten percent we talked about earlier."

She sat ramrod straight. "From this day forward."

He shot his hand across the desk to her. "Deal."

She surprised him by offering a firm handshake. "We do.
I'll leave it to you to have Mr. Arbour draw up the papers.
Once you sign them, have him bring them to me up at the
ranch."

"It'll be my pleasure. I'll talk to him later this afternoon.
That should give you enough time to send a telegram to your
friends in the capital about the election."

Cassidy felt dizzy as he got to his feet and opened his
office door for her. He bid her a good morning and gestured
for Simpson to go with her.

Cassidy shut the door and had to use the desk to steady
himself as he made it back to his chair. He had just struck a
deal that could make him more money than he had ever
thought he could have in a lifetime. The money he had made
with Joe over the past few years had been good. But earning
ten percent of the Mullen fortune just to protect her interests
was a dream come true.

And the beautiful irony of it was that it was mostly legal.
He supposed there was nothing wrong with that, provided he
did not make a habit of it. After all, he had a reputation to
uphold.

The political part of the scheme would be tricky. They
could not just put anyone forward for the office. Blair Chapman had been an affable man. People liked him and had no
problem voting for him despite his lack of experience.

The next candidate would have to be someone of integrity.
Someone who people could trust more than they trusted the
Chapman widow now.

Fortunately, he already had an idea.

He went back to his desk and poured more coffee into his
mug. He pulled out his private ledger from the bottom

drawer and reviewed his list of accounts. For these were not the books he kept for his saloon. These were items of a different sort. The list of men in town who owed him money. Money they could never repay in gold or greenbacks, but with a much rarer currency.

He tapped the name at the top of the ledger page. The amount next to it was still in red ink.

Tony Cassidy smiled as the simplicity of the plan fell into place. Yes, he was the perfect candidate indeed.

CHAPTER 4

"Walk with me, Sheriff," Mayor Elizabeth Chapman said to Holt as he passed by County Hall.

Holt fell in beside her as they walked together along the boardwalk. The acting mayor wore a beaver pelt stole and a black coat much too large for her considerable frame. She was a broad-shouldered and square-jawed woman who walked with a sense of purpose. Her dark eyes were set deep, which only added to her stern appearance.

He knew she had lost most of her possessions when her husband's haberdashery was set aflame the night her husband had been killed several weeks before. The fire quickly spread to her home behind the store and destroyed everything she had. The clothes she wore were borrowed from the other ladies in town and he wondered how long it would be until she received some of her own.

"I understand the marshals carted Joe Mullen off to prison where he belongs," she said.

"Saw him off about an hour ago," Holt said. "Deputy Wheeler insisted on leaving without his cook wagon against my advice. He should reach the territorial prison in a few days if the weather holds up."

Mayor Chapman frowned. "Dan Wheeler always was a hardheaded man. Always had a rather high opinion of himself too. That doddering idiot Old Bob talking him up all the time didn't do his ego any favors. I take it the two of them are still a team."

"He's a guest of mine over at the jail as we speak," Holt said. "The livery is working on straightening out the wheel his wagon threw on the way into town. I have to admit it'll be good to have him, considering Jack took off on me like he did."

The mayor acknowledged some of the townsmen who tipped their hat to her as she passed. "You never learned where the young man ran off to, did you?"

"His note was awfully terse, ma'am." Holt had not known the widow long, but long enough to know she did not like vague answers. "I don't know where he went."

"Don't blame yourself. There's no holding down a wild one like that. He was feral long before you decided to take him in as a pet. Can't begrudge him taking off without warning."

Holt remembered how the young deputy had stood by him when everyone else in town hid inside. "He risked his life for me, ma'am. I've come to think of him as something more than wild."

"That's the problem with you, John. You're a tough man and a stone-cold killer when you need to be, but you like to see the good in people. You're just like my poor Blair that way. He only saw the good in people, too, and look at where it got him."

She nodded down Main Street in the direction of the town cemetery where her husband was buried. "Gunned down by a Blue Bottle drunk in the prime of his life. Seeing the good in folks is a nice way to live but it can cost a man everything if he isn't careful. Me? I prefer to see people for exactly what they really are."

She shook off whatever thoughts were filling her mind.

"You were coming into County Hall just now, weren't you? Why?"

He was glad to get back to business. "Wanted to tell you that Mullen was on his way and to see if you had anything else on your mind."

"I do indeed." Her pace picked up some and Holt matched it. "We have a fox in the henhouse."

Holt did not catch her meaning as she could have been referring to any number of people in town. "That so? Who?"

"Sarabelle Mullen. That witch was seen going into that den of inequity that shall not be named. It appears that she and the swarthy demon who owns the place arranged to have a meeting."

Holt knew that meant Mrs. Mullen was meeting with Tony Cassidy. "How do you know?"

"Before assuming my husband's office, I was something of the town gossip," she reminded him. "I have a ring of spies throughout town who are all too happy to give me regular reports that would put the army to shame." She clearly enjoyed the confused look on Holt's face. "They're all old women, John. Just like me."

"You're not old," he said.

"Perhaps, but I'm not young, either," she reminded him. "Still, that doesn't change the fact that Mrs. Mullen and the flesh peddler are doubtlessly conspiring about something. Whatever it is can't be good. I thought you should be aware of the situation."

"I was just in the Bl—I mean, the whoremaster's place earlier on my rounds around town. I didn't see her there. Wonder what they were talking about."

"I'm sure whatever it is involves us and employs underhanded tactics. It's a shame you didn't have the chance to kill more Mullen men when you had the chance. I estimate she still has about a hundred cattlemen and miners at her command."

Holt might not have been a stranger to killing, but he did not like it being discussed in such a casual manner, not even by the acting mayor. "Most of them are just working men. They're harmless alone but could cause plenty of trouble in town as a group. I'll keep an eye on them. See if I can't head off trouble before it starts."

"That'll be a tall order to fill," she observed. "You'd still be shorthanded even if Jack was around. I know you said Old Bob is willing to pitch in, but that is of little comfort unless you intend on having him talk them to death."

Holt thought of other ways he might be helpful. "If they come to town as a group, I'll ask him to hang around the Bottle with them. Have him tell me of any trouble that might be brewing."

"That drunk is liable to join them," she said. "I wouldn't place much stock in his loyalty."

Holt did not know the cook well enough to defend him, but he did know something about Devil's Gulch. "Here's something you can put stock in, ma'am. This town's changed quite a bit since Joe got locked up. The Vigilance Committee is gone and it's not coming back. Ma McAdam has some good men working for her now."

He remembered they had all been outlaws from the Bostrom Gang before hiring on with Ma, but he saw no reason to remind her of that. "If any trouble comes from the Bottle . . . er, I mean the other place, they'll be more than happy to step in." Having to remember avoiding referring to the Blue Bottle in front of her was practically a full-time job.

"I take it your relationship with Ma and her men is still icy?"

"Not as cold as it is out here," Holt admitted, "but they won't be inviting me over for a game of cards anytime soon."

Mrs. Chapman pulled her stole tighter around her broad

shoulders. "Perhaps the time has come for us to arrange a thaw. Stop by the Railhead in the next day or so. Make sure you tell Ma about the Mullen woman's visit. She should be aware of what those two snakes are plotting. She might even be able to do something about it."

Holt did not think that was a good idea. "I've only just managed to get this town in line, ma'am. Having Ma and Cassidy snapping out each other could prove mighty hard on the peace."

"You're well paid to keep that peace, John. I have every confidence that you'll continue to do so. Like you said, this town has changed quite a bit since Joe was locked up."

He realized they were in front of Jean's café. "Do you have time for me to buy you a cup of coffee?"

Mrs. Chapman shook her head. "I'll let you and Jean have some time together. I may be a busybody, but never let it be said that Elizabeth Chapman stood in the way of young love." She rested a hand on his arm. "Talk to Ma, John. Talk to her today. Sarabelle Mullen might be easy on the eyes, but she has a stone heart. She's impatient too. Whatever she's planning with Cassidy will happen sooner than later and we need to be prepared."

He assured her that he would and watched her stride across the thoroughfare before Holt could offer to escort her. Not that Hold was complaining. Jean promised to make for much better company and conversation.

He was about to enter the café when, down Main Street, he saw a man stumble through the doors of the Railhead Saloon. Holt could not tell if the man was drunk or if he had been thrown out onto the boardwalk.

But he noticed the man was sober enough to get to his feet and sprint away as fast as his spindly legs could carry him.

Holt cursed under his breath and headed toward the saloon. His coffee and Jean would have to wait.

CHAPTER 5

"Put the gun down, Simon. No one needs to die here today."

Upon hearing these words when he reached the saloon, Holt pulled his pistol from the holster and stepped inside.

He found the former outlaw Charlie Gardiner in a standoff with a man by the roulette wheel. The stranger was holding a knife to a woman's throat.

Holt had never seen the man before but recognized the woman with the knife to her throat as Ma McAdam, the owner of the Railhead Saloon.

The stranger looked drunk and scared. "Anybody makes a move toward me, and I kill her as sure as I'm standing here!"

Holt noticed no fewer than eight guns and rifles pointed at the stranger. These were the men who had once ridden with Gardiner and the Bostrom Boys before Ma hired them on. He was surprised Charlie was the only one who hadn't drawn yet, though his hand hovered above the pistol on his hip. As the leader of the group, he was also the deadliest in the bunch.

"Put down the knife," Holt commanded as he walked toward the stranger. "Put it down right now and I promise I won't beat you to death."

The man pulled Ma with him as he turned to face Holt.

The frightened gambler's eyes flicked down to the star pinned to Holt's lapel, then back up to Holt. "Same goes for you, Sheriff. Have these boys put down their guns and give back the money they stole from me, so I can be on my way."

"No one cheated you, Simon," Charlie said. "You just had a run of bad luck is all."

Holt continued to advance slowly but steadily on the gambler. "Last chance, boy. I told you to let her go."

When Holt was close enough, the gambler slashed at him with the knife. Holt grabbed hold of his arm and brought the butt of his revolver down hard on his right temple.

Ma scrambled away as the man fell backward. He cried out when Holt pinned his arm to the floor as he wrenched the knife from his hand. He tossed the knife away and jammed his gun barrel under the gambler's chin.

"I told you to drop the knife, didn't I?"

The stunned man slurred a response before Holt slammed the gun barrel across his temple, rendering him unconscious.

Holt stood up and slid his pistol back into the holster. He looked around and saw Ma McAdam sagged against a post, trying to rub circulation back into her neck.

From what Holt could see, she had not been cut. "You hurt?"

"Only my pride. Thanks, Holt."

He saw Charlie Gardiner had not moved. Neither had any of his men. Each of them still aimed their guns, only they were no longer aimed at the gambler, but at Holt.

The sheriff looked at Charlie. "You going to tell your men to lower their guns?"

"When I'm ready," the former outlaw said.

Holt had made a career of recognizing a challenge when he saw it and he was seeing one now.

He slowly stood and squared himself to face Gardiner. There was less than ten feet of open space between them.

Holt did not know what Charlie had in mind and he was not a patient man. "Something you want to say to me?"

Charlie nodded at the star pinned to Holt's lapel. "You need to remember that thing is no good in here. We've talked about that. Whatever good it does ends at the front door."

Holt smiled. "We've talked about it, but I never agreed to it. Want to talk about it now?"

Charlie smiled too. "I thought that's what we're doing."

Holt's smile faded as he flexed the fingers on his right hand. "That's fine by me. Why don't you start?"

"That's enough!" Ma yelled as she stepped in between them. "We've had enough nonsense in here today without you two going at each other. Everyone, put your guns down like the man told you or you don't get paid this week. Go on!"

From his peripheral vision, Holt watched the men obey Ma's order.

She pointed at Charlie and another man behind him. "You two grab hold of that miserable crud and carry him over to the jail where he belongs."

Holt said, "There's a deputy over there who will help you lock him up."

Charlie beckoned a man to help him but took his time approaching the unconscious gambler. "Sounds like the prodigal deputy has returned after all. I heard Turnbull ran out on you, Holt. Showed me that the boy had more sense than I gave him credit for."

"He didn't come back," Holt said. "The man in the jail signed on to help me for a couple of days."

"Well, he'll earn whatever wages you're paying him for however long he's here." Charlie and the other man grabbed Simon by the arms and hauled him up until they shared his weight across their shoulders. "Hope he doesn't mind some chatter. This one's a whiner."

"Old Bob's a talker, so they'll get along just fine."

Holt waited until the two men had dragged the man out of the saloon before he spoke to Ma. "What was that all about?"

"Simon's harmless. He just drank more and lost more than he could handle. He's pulled a blade on me countless times. Always ends with him breaking down and crying when he gets to realizing what he's doing. Still, I'm glad you were here. Charlie was about ready to kill him."

Ma motioned to the bartender, who promptly plopped a bottle of whiskey and two glasses on the bar. "I know you don't usually partake, Sheriff, but can I interest you in one? My way of thanks for what you did just now."

Holt responded by inching the glass away from him. "I thought Frank Peters was supposed to be keeping an eye on things."

Ma poured one for herself instead. "Just about the only thing he's keeping an eye on these days is the bottle he brings up to his room. He's too busy feeling sorry for himself now that I've got Charlie and his boys around. I know I ought to kick him loose, but I don't have the heart. He was with me when no one else was and I think that ought to count for something."

Holt was glad to hear Ma thought that way. Frank Peters had been the sheriff before Blair Chapman offered the job to Holt. Peters had made no secret that he had fallen in love with Ma and would've done anything for the madam. His loyalty to her had cost him his job and now seemed to cost him his sanity. Holt had heard many such stories in several towns that he had worked, but that did not make it any easier to take. He'd always had the sense that Peters was a good man who had not been strong enough to give himself a chance to prove it.

"Charlie's got to do a better job of getting a hold on this kind of thing before it gets too far," Holt told her. "He's not an outlaw anymore. We've got rules here. Laws that need obeying."

"I wouldn't be too rough on Charlie if I were you," Ma said. "I've never been good at playing the damsel in distress." She shrugged. "Besides, he has other qualities I'm pretty fond of personally."

Holt caught the implication and imagined that was probably the main reason why Frank Peters had crawled into a jug. "So, it's like that between you."

"For now," she said. "Poor Frank's not taking it too well. I suppose he'll get over it."

Holt doubted he would. A man like Frank could fall into a bad habit of chasing a dream he would never realize. It got so that the pain became a friend as it was as close as he would ever get to what he really wanted. Ma's love. Holt did not doubt Ma loved him, but not in the way Frank needed her to. It made him pity the former sheriff and Holt thought pity the greatest insult for a man.

"The heart wants what it wants, I suppose," Holt observed.

Ma lightly poked his shoulder. "Don't you go getting all soft on me, Sheriff. If you turned out to be a thinking man, I'd lose all respect for you. It just wouldn't do, especially now that we've got this town trimmed down to suit us like we do."

Holt had always felt uneasy about the loose alliance he had been forced to form with Ma and her gang of killers at the Railhead. She and her outlaws had been the only ally he had back when Joe Mullen had made his last desperate grasp to hold on to power. She'd had Charlie and his men prevent the town from being put to the torch one night and now Holt felt indebted to her.

A debt he would honor but would not be happy doing it.

"This town might need some more trimming before long."

Ma was about to take another sip of whiskey, but there

was something in Holt's tone that made her stop. "That doesn't sound like good news to me."

"It might be something. It might be nothing. I won't know which for a while yet."

Ma shooed the bartender away as if he was a fly. When it was just the two of them, she said, "Don't hold back on me now, Holt. Tell me what's troubling you."

He wished he'd had more time to think about how to break the news to her, but life did not always work out the way John Holt wished it would. Telling her now was as good a time as any. "Seems like Sarabelle Mullen has thrown her lot in with Tony Cassidy."

"How do you know?"

"She was seen going in the back door of the Blue Bottle Saloon earlier this morning. It happened just after Joe got carted away."

She frowned down at her glass of whiskey. "Unless she's taken a job upstairs, which I wouldn't put past her, I'd say that means bad news for us."

Holt felt himself bristle at the notion that he and Ma were partners, but he let it go. "That's why I'm mentioning it. We ought to be ready for whatever happens next."

"Out with the bad, in with the worse," she sighed. "I hope you don't let that pretty head of yellow hair fool you. She's every bit as dangerous as her husband ever was. He might've been louder, but I always thought she was the real brains behind him."

"I'm not fooled by anyone or anything," Holt said. "But whatever she is, siding with Cassidy only makes her worse."

"That's not the only partner she has." Ma slowly turned the glass on the bar top. "She's got someone else sweet on her. Someone much more appealing than Tony Cassidy, but just as dangerous in his own way."

Holt had not heard that, but did not doubt it was true. "Mind telling me who it is?"

"After you tell me who saw Sarabelle going into the Bottle this morning."

Holt saw no reason to keep it from her. "Mayor Chapman's friends told her."

Ma grinned. "Serves me right for not having chosen a more domestic line of work. Washerwomen always have the best gossip. As for Sarabelle's new beau?" She looked around to make sure no one was listening. "It's Hank Lassiter, the bank president."

Holt knew the tall, well-dressed man who ran the Farmer and Miner's Bank. "That so?"

Ma nodded. "And that's not idle gossip either. He used to be a regular of one of my girls. When he stopped calling on her, I got curious. That's why I saw him heading out to her place several times after the bank closed. I made it a point to keep an eye on him until he comes back. Never rides back into town until after dawn. Guess he's helping sweet Sarabelle balance her books, if you get my meaning. He thinks he's a slick one, old Hank."

Holt did not doubt it was true. "I always thought he was too much of a dandy for such a thing."

"She's a beautiful woman in need," Ma said. "He's a widower and a rich one at that." Another shrug from her. "I've seen odder pairings in my time." She pulled her glass toward her and examined the contents of it. "Still makes me wonder why she'd need to meet with Cassidy, though. Lassiter I can see. He's a good match for her. Better than Joe ever was and Joe, for all of his faults, had plenty of money."

Holt did not know any of these people well enough to be able to gauge their motives. All he could do was watch what they did and be ready to react to it, hopefully before anything got out of hand. "Think you can do some quiet digging to find out what it could be?"

Ma took a drink before refilling her glass. "I've got some customers with heavy bar tabs who I can send over there to keep an ear open. Most of the boys who drink in the Bottle have big mouths. The bartenders especially. Come back to-morrow morning and I'll let you know what I hear."

Holt could not leave without a word of caution. "Just make sure you don't do anything before talking to me first. I don't want you sending Charlie and his boys into some-thing too soon."

She winked and held her glass up as a toast. "Discretion is my middle name. Besides, we're partners, ain't we?"

Holt pushed himself away from the bar. The mere thought of needing her was enough to turn his stomach.

But before he reached the door, Ma called out, "How's Jean these days."

He had hoped he could leave before she asked him about her daughter. Jean hated to talk about Ma and Holt made it a point to never talk about her.

But if he was ever going to get to the bottom of what Sarabelle Mullen was plotting with Tony Cassidy, he needed to remain in Ma's good graces, so he said, "She's doing well. Business is good."

"I already knew that." A hint of sorrow was evident in her voice. "Does she ever ask for me?"

"No," he admitted, "but you're always on her mind. I can tell."

He heard the madam draw in a ragged breath. "I guess that's something to hold on to. Thanks, John. See you tomor-row."

Holt was glad to be able to leave the saloon. And to leave Ma McAdam to the troubles of her own making.

CHAPTER 6

Joe Mullen almost cried out when the back of his head banged against the iron bars of the jostling prison wagon. The deep ruts in the road jarred his bones every time Wheeler steered the team into one.

One of his fellow prisoners got sick to his stomach from the constant swaying of the wagon. The other men had dry heaves. Their stomachs were too empty to get sick.

Mullen began to wonder if the lawman was doing it on purpose.

His suspicions were confirmed when the deputy marshal interrupted his endless whistling long enough to call back to his prisoners. "Hope you boys ain't too uncomfortable back there. The roads are mighty bumpy in this part of the territory. I suggest you find a way to clean up your friend's mess or learn to live with it. We've still got a long way to go before we reach the prison, but it's no skin off my nose if you don't."

Wheeler laughed and resumed his whistling as he guided the wagon into yet another small crater.

The prisoner to Mullen's left cursed before saying, "He's been doing that the whole ride out here. I don't think there's a hole he's missed yet. Gotten so that I don't hardly notice it anymore except for the particularly deep ones. I was the first one he picked up, so I guess you could say I'm used to it by now."

But Mullen was new and noticed it plenty. Every drop made him feel his insides rattle almost as loud as the iron bars of the cage that surrounded him.

He looked at the five other men in the prison wagon with him. Each of them was a sorry sight of pain and misery. The prisoner to his left was the thinnest of the bunch, which made sense since he had been riding with Wheeler the longest. The rest of them were in various stages of starvation and filth. He decided that trying to figure out how old they were was pointless. Their current states of despair made them look much older than they probably were.

Each of them bore the same ragged appearance of the neglected and dying. Yellowed skin that was as leathery as it was grimy. Long hair and uneven, matted beards speckled with white and gray. Filthy clothes and blankets so threadbare they gave little warmth to the men huddled beneath them.

The stench in the wagon reeked of decay and worse. The gentle rattle of the chains that bound their ankles and wrists mingled with the rattle of the bars to sing a forlorn song worse than Wheeler's tuneless whistling.

Mullen cleared his throat and kept his voice low when he spoke. "Why do you men put up with this kind of treatment from him? There's rules against treating prisoners this way."

The prisoner hunched across from him offered a raspy laugh. "Does Wheeler come across to you as a man who cares about rules? About decency? The only rules he cares about are his own and they change every day. We're nothing to the likes of him. Less than nothing. So long as none of us dies by the time we get to the prison, he never gives us a thought. Why, I've been locked in here for three whole days and he hasn't given us the chance to so much as stretch our legs. It was a little better when he had the cook to help him watch us, but we won't have it that good now."

Another prisoner added, "We can't even stand up in here on account of how he hits every hole in the ground he sees."

The wagon dropped hard again, sending up a collective moan from the prisoners.

The man across from Mullen continued. "See what I mean? Happens just like that when you least expect it. Can't even fall asleep until he decides to stop, which ain't often enough."

A prisoner at the far end of the wagon leaned closer to Mullen. "Just about the only good thing we had going for us was the food. But the cook wagon threw a wheel on account of Wheeler bouncing us all over God's creation and now we don't even have that. We'll be lucky if he gives us hardtack and water until we reach the prison."

The man opposite the prisoner chimed in. "And if you think it'll be better in that place, you're sadly mistaken. This'll be my second time in there. It's no kind of fun. It's bad enough to make us miss this trip. I'd consider doing something drastic if I could."

But Joe Mullen had been considering doing something drastic for weeks. He had put his time rotting in Holt's jail to good use. Most of the feeling had gradually returned to the left side of his body, though he had continued to play the cripple for Holt's benefit. Whenever Holt or the Turnbull boy went to bed, Mullen would spend the dark hours working his legs and arms to regain full strength. He was limited by what he could do in his cell without calling too much notice to himself but used the bars to pull himself upright dozens of times to rebuild the strength in his body. He felt stronger with each passing day and, with that, hopeful that he could take advantage of any mistake Holt or his young deputy might make when they came to feed him or empty his bucket. Surprise would be his only ally. His only hope for salvation.

Unfortunately, Holt had learned his lesson from Mullen's earlier attempt to strangle him against the bars of the cell.

He never allowed himself to get close enough for Mullen to make another attempt on his life. It was as though he could sense Mullen was healthier than he had let on, though there was no way he could have known that for certain. He and Turnbull had kept their distance until Mullen had been led into the wagon at gunpoint earlier that morning. He had not seen the Turnbull boy for more than a week, but Wheeler had provided more than enough of a deterrent from attempting an escape.

Joe Mullen might not have been able to do anything about it then, but there was certainly something he could try now. But if his plan had even the most remote hope of succeeding, his timing would have to be perfect.

"Time," he swore under his breath. Time was everything to him now. For every moment they failed to act took them that much farther away from civilization and deeper into the wilderness.

Farther away from the revenge he sought with every fiber of his being against those who had taken his life from him.

Mullen looked at the large man across from him. "What's your name?"

"My name?" The man laughed. "What difference does that make in here?"

"It makes all the difference, friend. A name makes you someone. It makes you human, not just a piece of meat rotting in a cage on the road to Hades. I'll start if you want. My name's Joe Mullen out of Devil's Gulch."

Mullen was glad his words seemed to put a little iron in the man's spine as he sat up straighter. "Name's Frank Geary."

The other prisoners followed suit by whispering their names as well. Marty Fraser. Al Lepine. Burt McCaffrey. Cecil Hardt was the last of them. A smallish man with cold eyes.

None of the names meant anything to Mullen. None of

the men did either. He did not care about their crimes, only that they were in the wagon together and that they could do something about it.

"I have a plan," he told them. "I don't know if it'll work and we might get busted up in the process, but right about now, I'd say anything is better than going on like this. And I think all of you agree."

Geary stole a quick glance up at Wheeler, who was too busy whistling while he steered the team to pay them any mind. A good wind was blowing in his face, making it even more difficult for the marshal to hear them.

Geary hunched again to rejoin their conversation. "I've been in this rig for days, mister. I've spent every waking moment trying to figure a way out of this mess. You haven't even been here a day, and you think you've already got it worked out?"

"I know I have." Another sharp drop rattled his teeth and those of the other men.

Hardt cursed as he spat out a loose tooth between the rattling iron bars.

Mullen pointed up at the cage. "And that's how we're going to do it," he whispered. "You've heard how this thing rattles and shakes. The bars are old. Loose. There's too much give in them. They're about ready to bust apart and we're going to make them do just that."

Mullen watched the hope drain from Geary's face. "Mister, I'm the strongest man here and I've barely enough strength to lift my head. I've already tried those bars plenty of times. There's give in them, sure, but not enough for us to free ourselves."

"And even if we did," McCaffrey said, "none of us are strong enough to run away before Wheeler catches us."

But Mullen's plan was already way ahead of them. "Since Wheeler's so fond of rough ground, we're going to use it to our advantage." He nodded at Fraser, who was seated closer to the wagon box from where Wheeler steered the team. "You think you could get a good look at the road ahead if you tried?"

Fraser considered it for a moment. "Don't see as why not, but why would I want to?"

"Because we're going to need you to keep an eye out for the next big hole that comes along. Left or right side doesn't matter. You call it out and just as the wagon is about to drop into it, we all rush to that side and turn it over."

He looked at each of the men in turn. None of them seemed to understand what he was saying, so he explained it further. "If the hole is on the right, we all get up and throw ourselves to the right side to pitch the wagon that way. If it's on the left, we all rush to the left side."

Mullen almost bit his tongue as the wagon dropped again in yet another hole.

Wheeler cackled from the wagon box. "That one'll sure wake you boys up!"

Mullen kept his voice low, glad to see the men finally understood his meaning.

And Geary did not seem to like it. "You weren't kidding before when you said there's a good chance we could get busted up, Mullen."

"Busted up," McCaffrey repeated, "and still in the same spot as before only worse."

But Mullen had already thought out that part. "This old rig is rattling so bad, there's bound to be some give in these bars. One good slam is likely to crack this thing open like an egg. Listen."

He held his finger to his lips to motion for silence so the men could hear it for themselves and realize Mullen was right.

"I can see the bolts at the top wiggling," Lepine said. "The sides too."

Mullen felt a pulse of excitement course through the men as they caught on.

Hardt said, "I've been hearing that sound for days and never thought much of it. It's been there the whole time."

Mullen continued to drive his point home before any doubt could creep in to weaken their resolve. "Five men would have a hard time pushing this rig over. But six of us working together? I know we could do it if we get the timing right."

Frank Geary looked at the iron door beside him. "Even if the bars hold, they might just loosen enough to make that latch pop open if these bars were pushed off-kilter."

Fraser jerked his thumb over his shoulder. "That's all well and good, but we still have to worry about him."

Mullen was glad he had an answer for that too. "There's six of us and one of him. If that door opens and we can get free, those numbers get a lot bigger." Mullen raised his hands and pulled the chain. "He'll be worse off than us if we can flip this thing. Our feet are shackled but so are our hands. All it would take is for one of us to get to him, wrap these around his neck, and we're free."

He was warmed by the fire of possibility he saw light up in their eyes. They knew he was not trying to sell them a bill of goods. He was risking as much as they were. And they knew his plan had a good chance of working in their favor.

Any indecision was wiped away when Geary asked, "When do you plan on doing this, Joe?"

"Right now," he told them. "We don't have a moment to lose." He gestured toward the prisoners at the front of the wagon. "You boys get up there and keep an eye out for as big a hole as you can coming our way. Look back at us when you see a big one, but don't rush it. We'll only have one chance at this, so make it count. Call out which side is deepest. As soon as we're about to hit it, we all dive for that side and throw ourselves against it. We'll let gravity do the rest."

Geary yanked Fraser to his feet and pushed him toward

the front of the wagon. The prisoner grabbed hold of the bars and pulled himself as straight as he could against the top bars. He pressed himself as far as he could into the highest corner on the right side of the cage and peered out at the road ahead.

Mullen's heart sank when Wheeler looked around and noticed him. "What do you think you're doing, convict?"

"Just stretching my legs as best I can, boss," Fraser said without taking his eyes off the road. "No law against that, is there?"

"It's against the rules and you know it." Wheeler turned in the box and glared at him. "All prisoners are to remain seated while the wagon is moving. You want to stretch, you wait until—"

"Right side!" Fraser shouted. "Right side! Right side, now!"

He had no sooner said the words than the men sprang to their feet and threw themselves against the right side of the cage just as the wheel dropped into a deep hole. The prisoners cried out as one as they felt the left wheels begin to rise.

Mullen knew his plan was working.

Wheeler cursed as he scrambled in vain to grab up the reins and snap the team to move faster, but gravity was already working against him. The sudden rush of weight on the right side caused the wagon to pitch farther to the side until momentum won the day.

Mullen cried out in victory and fear as he felt the cage lurch and the ground quickly rushed up to greet them.

The terrified horses screamed as the weight of the tumbling wagon pulled them off their footing and pulled wagon, iron, men, and beasts tumbling over the hillside.

Mullen felt the wagon begin to skid down the hill as he heard the chain that bound the team to the wagon break.

Iron creaked and wood snapped as the cage continued its

slide, gaining speed until it crashed against a rock, which caused the wagon to roll over its top. The prisoners rattled around beneath the bars as the wagon went end over end before it slammed down on its left side, then slowly slid to a halt.

Mullen felt a searing pain in his scalp and the familiar sting of blood in his eyes. He did not know if it was his blood or that of his fellow prisoners. He did not have time to care.

He shook the clouds from his eyes and tried to get his bearings as he looked around for the wagon door. He almost cried out in joy when he saw it hanging open.

The freedom that had eluded him for so long was finally at hand!

He scrambled over the bodies of the moaning prisoners and leapt through the open door. He landed face-first on the frozen ground, but for all he cared at the moment, it was as soft as a meadow on a warm spring day.

He was free. Finally free!

His joy was short lived as he felt a hand grab his collar and jerk him to his feet as though he were a rag doll.

He could not see the man but knew in his heart it had to be Wheeler.

"You hurt?" came the now familiar voice of Geary.

Now that he was upright, Mullen felt a sudden dizziness come over him. He took hold of Geary's shoulder before he fell over. "Don't worry about me. Where's Wheeler? Get him before he gets us."

Geary raised both chained hands as he pointed back up the hill. "Don't think we'll have to worry about him. He looks like he's busted up pretty bad."

Mullen used his sleeve to wipe the flowing blood away from his eyes as he tried to focus on what Geary was pointing at. He saw the marshal lying flat on his back farther up on the hillside. Flat being a sickening description. His arms were splayed out on either side of him. His lower body crushed. The ground around him had been dug up. It was clear that the wagon had slid over him on its journey down the hill.

But he was still alive. His eyes were open as he struggled to lift his head.

"Serves him right for what he did to us," Geary said.

Mullen had other concerns besides Wheeler just then. "Everyone make it?"

"Looks like Lepine is dead," Geary told him. "His neck broke when we tumbled over. Fraser thinks his hand his busted, but McCaffrey and Hardt are alive."

Geary took Mullen by the shoulder and shook him. "You did it, Joe. You did it! We're free!"

But when Mullen looked past his fellow prisoner, he realized their troubles had only just begun. He spotted the silhouette of a man on horseback.

"We've got a rider over there. And it looks like he's coming this way."

Geary turned around and looked at the rider for himself. He dropped to a crouch, as did Mullen. "What do we do now?"

Mullen had not anticipated a stranger stumbling onto the scene so soon after their escape, but it was clear how they could use this to their advantage. "The odds are still in our favor. Tell the others to stay where they are and keep quiet. Act like they're unconscious. If the rider comes close enough, we grab him and take his horse."

Geary ran back at a crouch to the others in the cage while Mullen dropped flat on the ground. He positioned himself so he could easily see the rider as he approached.

What happened after that was entirely up to the unfortunate stranger.

CHAPTER 7

Jack Turnbull was in the middle of practicing how he would explain himself to John Holt when his bay reared up as terrible screams filled the valley.

He held on to the saddle horn as the horse bucked and threw its head from side to side. He surprised himself by how he managed to remain in the saddle.

The screams were followed by the sound of a great crash and screeching metal. It sounded like he'd imagine a train would sound if it came off its tracks, not that he had ever witnessed such a thing. There were also no trains within a day's ride of where he was, so he knew it could not be that.

He reached down and patted his bay gelding's neck, trying to soothe him as the last sounds of whatever calamity had happened ahead of him died down. The animal began to fuss again as the ground began to rumble and he saw a team of four horses still hitched together speed up a hillside. They ran wild-eyed, their manes flying as they fled in panic.

Turnbull had never considered himself much of a horseman, but even he knew a runaway team was bad news. All it took was one of the animals to misstep to send all four to their deaths, especially as they were still bound together.

He brought his horse about and dug his heels into its flanks to chase after them. His mount was still fresh after a long night's rest and had no problem catching up to the winded animals.

He managed to easily overtake them and leaned to the side to grab hold of the lead horse's bit and slowly pulled back. He was glad they gradually slowed down until they stopped entirely.

He stroked the muzzle of the horse he had stopped, fearful the team might get spooked again and try to trample him.

When he thought they were as calm as they were likely to get, he rode around the team in the hopes he might be able to see what had caused them to run. When he got to the backside, he found a chunk of wood that appeared to have been bolted to a wagon. He decided their load must have tipped over the hillside, which would have explained the screams and other sounds he had heard only a few moments before.

He stood up in his stirrups to get a look down the hillside to see what had happened. He immediately saw the wreckage of a wagon on its side with twisted metal sprung up all around it like the tines of a ruined fork.

It looked like a wagon he had seen a sheriff use to transport prisoners when he was a boy. He had seen his father carted away enough to remember what one looked like.

Deciding the team of horses were too tired to run off again, he urged his gelding down the hill toward the wreckage to look for survivors. He saw one man who appeared to have been thrown clear of the wagon as it had tumbled down the hill. The wagon had obviously slammed into a large rock jutting from the hillside as it rolled.

Jack spotted another man closer to him on the hillside who looked like he had been staked to the ground. He was trying to pick up his head while his arms were splayed out on either side of him. He thought his legs must be broken and brought his horse to a gallop to reach him sooner.

He brought his mount to a sliding stop near the fallen man and leapt from the saddle to aid him. When he got closer, he saw the man was beyond any help Jack could offer him. He looked away when he realized the man had been crushed below the belt.

He took a knee beside the dying man and leaned closer so that he could see Jack was with him. "Rest easy, now. I'll help you any way I can."

He knew it was a stupid thing to say under the circumstances, as the man was clearly beyond all hope, but it was what Jack imagined he would want to hear if he was in his last moments.

The man's eyes grew even wider as he struggled to speak. Turnbull lowered his head and strained to hear him, but all he heard was the final breath escape from him.

Jack Turnbull's father had never been one for religion and had never been known to pray. Jack wished he knew a prayer or two now. He would have liked to have said some kind words over the stranger to help ease his passing. He had never seen the man before but decided few could have done anything in life to have deserved such a death.

He rested a hand on the man's chest. "Sorry I couldn't help you, mister. Hope you're some place peaceful now."

That was when he noticed the star pinned to his lapel. A deputy U.S. marshal's star.

He looked down at the wreckage with a new sense of caution. That was not just any prison wagon. It must have been the one that had come to Devil's Gulch to bring Joe Mullen to the territorial prison. He remembered Holt had gotten a telegram about it just before Jack decided to leave town.

And unless he missed his guess, Mullen would be among the men still in the wagon wreck.

Jack got to his feet and pulled his pistol in one smooth motion, just like Holt had taught him. He kept it aimed down at the wreckage, knowing he was too far away to hit anything at such a distance, but it made him feel better. He backed up to where his horse had stopped and pulled his double-barreled shotgun from where he had placed it in his bedroll. He had left town in too much of a hurry to outfit himself with a proper scabbard, so the bedroll had to do.

He tucked his pistol back in the holster on his hip and approached the ruined wagon at a crouch. He moved slow and steady, keeping a tight grip on the shotgun. He knew he was approaching a gang of hurt and desperate men. He may not have spent much time with John Holt, but he had spent enough to know such men should be handled with every caution.

He walked in a wide arc around the wreck and got a closer look at the damage. Its iron slats were broken and snapped in places. He kept his shotgun aimed at the man who had been thrown clear of the wagon as he stole a quick glance at those still inside.

All he saw was a bloody pile of humanity. One man gazed out at him as if asking for help. Turnbull quickly saw his head was at an impossible angle to still be alive. He moved even farther from the wagon as he neared the man on the ground.

When he drew closer, Jack recognized him as Joe Mullen. He had spent enough time tending to the prisoner to know him anywhere. And more than enough to know he was dangerous, even though it looked like his hands and feet were still shackled.

"Get up, Mullen," Turnbull called out when he got close enough. "I know you're still alive, so no use in acting."

He waited for Mullen to respond, but the man continued to lie in a heap.

Turnbull knew it was likely a trap and stopped walking. "Last chance, Mullen. Either you get up or you're already dead. Either way, I intend on squeezing this trigger just to be sure."

A great moan rose from the prisoner as he slowly raised

his head. Turnbull spotted a nasty gash just below his hairline.

"That you, Wheeler?" Mullen called out. "I . . . I can't see. Help me."

Turnbull remained where he was and kept the shotgun aimed down at him. "If you can talk, you can get on your feet. You don't have to be able to see to do that."

"Help me, Wheeler," Mullen called out again as if he had not heard Jack. "I can't get up. I think my leg is busted."

Turnbull peered around the shotgun. He could see Mullen's legs clearly and they looked fine. "They ain't broke. You can get up on your own. Do as I told you real slow before I cut loose with a barrel."

He heard the jangle of chains behind him too late as a prisoner dove at him from the wagon. He managed to turn his shoulder to absorb the blow, but the man knocked the shotgun from his hands.

Still on his feet, Turnbull grabbed for his pistol just as he saw a chain drop over his head before he felt himself being lifted from his feet by his neck. He forgot about his pistol and tried to wriggle free from the chokehold. The sky spun above him as his feet kicked wildly at nothing but empty air.

Turnbull's stomach turned as he heard the unmistakable sound of Mullen's familiar cackle fill his ears.

"Look at you, Geary. Free only a couple of minutes and you've already hooked yourself a fish. A minnow maybe, but it still counts as a catch."

Turnbull felt his strength begin to wane as he swung his arms and legs in a desperate attempt to get free. To breathe.

"He's fading fast," Geary said. "Won't be long now."

Turnbull could smell the stench coming from him.

"Don't be so hasty," Mullen said. "Set him down for a bit and let me introduce you to him. If you're not impressed by who he is, you can always kill him later."

Turnbull saw stars fill his vision as he was dropped on his

tailbone. A lightning bolt of pain shot through his body as he gasped for air. His pride began to hurt even worse as he felt other convicts gather around him.

He had only just begun to catch his breath when he felt a sharp kick to his kidneys.

"Cheer up, Turnbull," Mullen laughed. "We've got plans for you, boy. No one's going to hurt you." Another kick to the back of the head rendered him dizzy. "Not much, anyway. But first, we're going to have some fun."

The unsettling sound of their laughter carried him into unconsciousness.

CHAPTER 8

Jack Turnbull was jolted awake by the cold.

He heard the horse he had been slung across breathing heavy as the rider pulled it to a halt.

When he had first woken up back at the prison wagon wreck, it was already too late for him to try to get away. The convicts had stripped him down to his long underwear and thrown a blanket over him after they had bound his hands and feet beneath the barrel of one of the draft horses he had stopped from running away. He knew it must have been a draft horse because the animal was much broader than his gelding.

They had tied a filthy pair of prison shirts around his head to prevent him from seeing where they were going. The stench of the clothes, combined with the sweat from the un-saddled horse and hanging upside down, had made it impossible for him to sleep.

He imagined the smallest convict was now wearing his clothes. He figured the men had put him out front, probably on Turnbull's own horse. Anyone who happened to be riding past would certainly notice five men in striped prison outfits riding bareback on horses. But one rider out ahead of the others could make sure the road was clear before urging his companions to follow him.

At least, that would be how Turnbull would have done it.

Mullen and the man who had almost strangled him to death were too big to fit into his clothes, but the smaller man who had helped the others beat him unconscious might be able to wear them.

Mullen had done too good of a job wrapping the ragged clothes around Jack's head for him to see clearly, but he knew it was either sunup or just after. His suspicions were confirmed when he heard the muffled sound of birdsong and felt the warming rays of the autumn sun on his back.

His hips and shoulders ached from having been tied across the back of the horse and the blood roared in his ears from being slung low for so long.

He strained to listen to what was around him to understand the reason for why they had stopped. He doubted it was because they were tired. They were men on the run and could not afford to give in to weariness unless they had found shelter. A place to hide where they would not be spotted.

He thought they must have found a cabin or something, which would undoubtedly mean someone was about to die. And he cursed himself for being powerless to stop them.

He forced himself to grow still as he felt the rider of his horse drop to the ground. He heard the men talking among themselves in whispers and decided they must be coming up with a plan.

He heard boots scrape on the ground before a sharp blow struck him in the back of the neck. The rags around his head served to soften the sting some.

"You awake, junior?"

It was Mullen and Jack resented being called "junior" by anyone, especially him. He was about to tell him so, but quickly thought better of it. "What? I can't hear you."

He heard the men laugh as Mullen must have made a gesture.

That's when Mullen yelled straight into his left ear. "This loud enough for you, boy?"

Jack summoned all the energy he could manage as he swung his head hard toward the sound of Mullen's voice.

He heard the unmistakable sound of a nose breaking, followed by what could only be Mullen dropping to the ground.

The laughter from the convicts told Jack he had struck his mark, though he braced himself as best he could for another beating.

He was beyond caring what happened to himself at this point. During the night, he had resigned himself to the fact that he would not get out of this predicament alive. All he could hope to do was punish Mullen and anyone else who got too close as much as possible before they decided to kill him. He would carry the satisfaction of dying as best he could with him into whatever afterlife might await him.

He yelped as he felt the rags being ripped from his head, along with a good hunk of his hair. He forced his eyes open and breathed in deeply just before he felt the cold steel of a gun barrel pressed hard against the back of his neck.

"You want to play rough, junior?" Mullen spat. "Then we'll play rough. My way."

"Take it easy," Jack heard the one called Geary say. "You told us you had plans for the boy. Don't go spoiling it by killing him so soon."

Jack strained his neck to look up at Mullen. He was standing too close for him to see the convict clearly, but he was warmed by the sight of fresh blood on his overalls from his broken nose.

He had learned in his short time as John Holt's deputy that there was a point in every conflict when trouble could no longer be avoided. The best a man could do was rush at it and hope to catch it off guard.

"Go ahead!" Jack shouted with as much air as he could draw into his lungs. "Shoot me. Make sure whoever you're ambushing hears you coming. Give them a fighting chance!"

Jack felt the gun press even harder against his skin as another convict spoke to him. "The kid's right, Joe. If you shoot him now, that farmer and his family yonder will be ready for us. The only guns we've got are the ones the kid brought with him. The shotgun's no good at this distance and neither is that pistol he was toting. We've got to get closer."

"I can handle Wheeler's rifle," Mullen said through gritted teeth.

"With you being as dizzy as you are?" Geary asked. "I wouldn't chance it. And we can't risk you missing one of them and letting them get away to go for help. We need the horses that farmer has in his barn, Joe. We need new clothes. You told me earlier we can always kill the boy later and you were right. Once we've got the farm and his family, you can do what you want with him. I'll even help you do it."

Mullen swore in frustration as he quickly jerked the pistol away from Jack's neck.

Jack heard him stomp away as he joined the others. His life had been spared for now, but likely at the cost of the innocent people they were about to kill.

"Fine," Mullen said as he spoke to his men. "Marty, you're the one wearing proper clothes, so you go on and ride up there to put them at ease. Tell them you're on your way to Devil's Gulch and you want to make sure you're headed in the right direction. And when you get close enough, pull that shotgun and herd them all outside. Once you've got them corralled, wave your hat at us to come in. We'll be right on your tail. That much I promise you."

The one Jack imagined was Marty said, "Sounds like a

good plan, boss, though I'll be needing that pistol from you.
I'm wearing the boy's holster and they're apt to think something's wrong if I ride in there with it empty."

"You're right," Mullen said. "Best take off the gun belt
and hand it to me."

Jack might not have been able to see them, but he sensed
the first crack in whatever bond they had formed during
their escape.

"You're sporting two pistols," one of the men observed.
"That kid's and Wheeler's. Only makes sense for you to give
Marty one."

"I might be needing it if the father gets jumpy," Marty
added. "He's got a pretty daughter I've been watching out in
his garden. He's apt to be suspicious of strangers."

"Give him the pistol," Geary urged. "Won't do us any
good if Marty here gets himself killed. And there's no reason
to take the farmer lightly. One of them is the reason why I
got locked up in the first place." Jack was encouraged by the
brief pause that followed. "That is, unless you don't trust
someone else being as well armed as you."

Mullen cursed again as Jack heard him slap the gun in
Fraser's hand. "Don't be stupid. We're all in this together,
aren't we? But you'd better not be getting any fancy ideas
about running off on us because, as God is my witness—"

Turnbull might not have known much about horses, but
he knew how to make them run. And while the men argued,
he stretched his bound arms and legs as much as he could
before slamming his knees and elbows into his horse's flanks
at the same time.

The animal lurched forward and took off at a hard gallop.
Jack held on with his legs and arms as tightly as he could
while the large horse barreled through the convicts and away
from the group.

Jack shut his eyes and held on for dear life. He could not

control where the frightened animal was headed and had no idea where it was going, so he decided there was no sense in getting dizzy. His teeth rattled as the horse thundered through the grass. Small branches raked across his face and head. Flecks of sweat and spit from the animal hit him as he bounced along on its back.

Jack braced for the impact of a bullet from Mullen at any moment. He doubted they would let him escape and would sooner see him dead first. The shot might give them away to the farmer they were planning to kill, but so would a man who was tied across a horse's back.

He did his best to keep himself as flat against the horse as he could to avoid flipping beneath it. He knew he would be caught up in its legs, only to be throttled to death before it tripped and rolled over him. He did not want to meet the same fate Wheeler had suffered when he had found him on the hillside, but at least it was a better risk than living according to Mullen's whims.

When he chanced to open his eyes again, he saw that the horse had led him to some kind of a clearing. He soon heard a man yelling, "Whoa, there, big fella. "Whoa!"

The galloping horse slowed at the sound of the human voice, though it tossed its head and reared back some on its hind legs.

"Whoa, there, big fella," the man soothed again as Jack felt someone take hold of the reins. "That's it, boy. Just steady down, there. No one's gonna hurt you."

He felt a firm hand on his shoulder and looked up as a boy about his age—late teens or so—had taken hold of him. "You all right, mister?"

"Please, cut me loose," Jack said. "Do it quick. There's trouble coming this way."

"Trouble?" A man Jack took to be the boy's father repeated. "What kind of trouble?"

The words came faster than Jack could control. "Convicts.

Escaped. Five of them, I think. One of them is Joe Mullen out of Devil's Gulch. They killed a marshal yesterday and jumped me soon after. Sounds like they've been watching your place and are looking to hit you. Quick! You've got to cut me down and get inside where it's safe."

The boy produced a knife and knelt to cut him loose until the father stopped him. "If Joe Mullen's out there, just who might you be, boy?"

"Jack Turnbull," he told them. "I'm John Holt's deputy in town."

Jack was glad the boy cut his hands free as they both took hold of his shoulders and hauled him down from the horse. His legs hit the ground but were too numb to hold his weight. The father placed Jack in a bear hug while his son got busy cutting away the ropes at his feet.

"They've had me strung up on that horse all night," Jack said. "Can't feel much of anything right now."

"You'll be feeling the rope I put around your neck if you're lying to us," the father warned.

Jack willed his limbs to work through the numbness as the father and son carried him into the small farmhouse. He heard the wooden planks of the floor creak as they went inside. The room spun as they dropped him on his back on a bed. He felt pricks from the hay of the mattress poke through his long underwear but at least he was no longer upside down.

The roaring of blood in his ears began to die down as he heard a woman call out, "Will! What's wrong?"

"I don't rightly know yet," the father said. "I've been trying to find out for myself. Until then, you and the children better skedaddle downstairs until I do."

"I ain't going anywhere, Pa," the boy said. "I'm staying up here with you. I'm old enough."

"Haven't thought of you as a baby in a long time now,"

Will said. "Get your rifle and make sure it's loaded. Not much good if it ain't. Have your sister do the same."

Turnbull's stomach turned when he tried to lift his head to see what was happening. He lay flat again as he heard a great amount of commotion in the tiny house. He heard a door open somewhere and the complaints of young voices as their mother ushered them into what Jack could only assume was a root cellar beneath the house.

He heard gunmetal scrape across wood, which must have been the boy grabbing hold of his rifle from under a bed.

Jack's ears perked up when he heard a young female voice say, "I'm staying up here, too, Pa. I'm as good a shot as Tommy is."

"Didn't raise you to be a sunflower, girl. You've got a rifle too. Best grab hold of it."

Turnbull felt pins and needles begin to bristle throughout his body as feeling began to return to his arms and legs. He hoped he'd be better soon so he could help this brave family face down the fight that was about to darken their door.

"I can help," he said as he struggled to sit up. His head had stopped throbbing and his stomach settled some. On the second try, he was able to prop himself upright on his elbows.

And found he was staring down the barrel of a rifle.

The father was aiming a rifle Jack recognized as a Winchester down at him. "Best tell me that story of yours again, son. Best tell it real slow and same as before or you won't be long for this world."

Turnbull struggled to hold himself up despite the tingling in his arms. "The men who are looking to ride in here right now are a bunch of convicts who managed to kill a deputy marshal last night. Wheeler was his name. Dan Wheeler. I don't know how they did it, but they managed to flip his wagon. They jumped me, took my clothes, my horse, and my guns and threw me on back of one of the wagon team horses. The same one you found me tied to just now."

"So you say." Will thumbed back the hammer of the rifle. "But how do I know you're not lying? How do I know you ain't the convict who escaped from Wheeler?"

"Because I ain't asking you to trust me, mister. I ain't asking you to do anything except to watch out for yourselves and to keep a gun on anyone who rides onto your land."

He watched Will struggle with all that Jack had just told him. He did not blame the farmer for being suspicious. He only hoped he did not decide to kill him until he had the chance to be proven right.

"Pa," Tommy called out from his spot at the window. "I see a rider coming."

Turnbull saw the indecision creep into the farmer's eyes. Part of Turnbull felt guilty about putting him in such a position, but it had not been his choice.

He also knew they were running out of time. "Have your son keep a gun on me if you're of a mind to. Tell them to shoot me if I try to get off this bed, but make sure you keep two guns aimed on whoever that is riding up on you now. Please!"

"Rider's coming fast at a good gallop, Pa," Tommy called out again.

Will kept the rifle on Jack as he spoke to his daughter, "Emma, you keep an eye on this boy. If he moves off that bed, shoot him."

Emma levered in a round as she stared down at Jack. "Don't worry about him, Pa. He ain't going anywhere."

The father grabbed a handful of Jack's shirt and pulled him off the bed. "Just so happens I know Dan Wheeler. And if that's him coming for you out there, I'll kill you before he gets the chance to haul you off to jail."

Turnbull dropped back onto the bed as Will let him go and joined his son looking out the window.

"If you know Dan Wheeler," Jack said, "then you know that ain't him. Skinny fella, ain't he? About my size? Riding a bay gelding?" He stole a quick glance at Emma, who kept her rifle trained on him from the kitchen. "I know all that because that's my horse and those are my clothes he's wearing."

Will stepped away from the window and moved to the door. "I don't know who that is, but it sure ain't Dan Wheeler. That doesn't make you right. And if you're lying to me, it won't matter to you for long."

Relief washed over Jack as the farmer seemed to finally believe him. He only hoped that would be enough to save all of their lives.

CHAPTER 9

Jack was careful to remain on the bed as he tried to look out the tiny window behind where Tommy had taken cover. He recognized the convict atop Turnbull's horse and wearing Turnbull's clothes as he slowly rode toward the front door.

Jack felt a bit easier as he saw that Tommy stood to the side of the window, holding his rifle to his shoulder. He was not presenting himself as a target and would be in a prime position to shoot the convict if he had to. Turnbull decided John Holt would have been impressed.

He heard the convict's voice through the door as he called out, "Hello to whoever's in the house. Come on out. I mean you no harm."

"That remains to be seen," Will answered him through the closed door. "State your business or move on. We don't like strangers around here."

"Looks like you've got one among you right now," Marty Fraser answered. "You've got a prisoner who managed to run off from me up the trail a piece. A man who's wanted in two counties for murder and theft. I'd appreciate it if you brought him out to me so we can be on our way."

"We'll get to that," Will shouted through the door. "What's your name?"

"I'm the Deputy U.S. Marshal for these parts. That man you've brought under your roof is my prisoner. Jack Turnbull is his name."

Will and Tommy glared over at Jack, who threw up his hands and whispered, "I already told you that. Ask to see his star."

Will held his rifle tightly as he spoke through the door. "I thought Dan Wheeler was the marshal for this part of the territory. I've never heard of you before."

Jack had hoped the question would have given Marty Fraser pause but lying obviously came as easily to him as breathing. "We had wagon trouble. He's back there with the other prisoners tending to it as we speak."

Then Will surprised him by opening the front door. His rifle held across his body. "If you got a prison wagon with you, why was this boy hogtied over a draft horse's back?"

Jack sensed the silence that followed lasted just a bit too long for Will's taste. His sense was confirmed when the farmer quickly brought his Winchester to his shoulder. "You got a star, boy? Every marshal I ever saw had himself a star on his shirt."

Jack could no longer see Fraser, but he could hear him plainly enough. "Sure do, mister. Got it right here in my shirt pocket. Gonna pull it out nice and slow so you can take a look at it."

Jack's mind filled with questions. *Where could he have gotten a star from? Had he taken it off Wheeler's body?*

"See?" Fraser asked. "There it is. You can see it plain enough for yourself."

Will did not seem impressed by whatever Marty had shown him.

"If that's as real as you claim it is, why don't you ride into Devil's Gulch and get Sheriff Holt? If he comes here and tells me to hand him over, I'll do it and gladly."

Another hesitation served to make the farmer suspicious.

Tommy caught his father's eye and brought his own rifle to his shoulder. "Doesn't feel right, Pa," he whispered.

"Won't be any trouble for me," Fraser answered after considerable thought. "But it could be plenty trouble for all of you. See, Jack Turnbull's been convicted of taking liberties with women. I wouldn't think you'd want a man like that being around your daughter for so long."

Jack watched the broad muscles of the farmer's back tighten and felt the situation tilt in his favor. "How'd you know I've got a daughter, mister?"

Tommy fired through the window at the same time as his father shot from the doorway.

Glass shattered. Jack's horse cried out. Emma screamed.

And through the ruined window, Jack watched Fraser drop from the saddle. The horse began to fuss, but Will ran out to grab the reins.

Jack called out, "Grab his pistol and shotgun! I've got bullets in my saddlebags too!"

Tommy had taken a knee behind the broken window and covered his father. "I'll keep watch for you, Pa. No one's coming."

Will pulled Jack's horse to the porch post and wrapped the gelding's reins around it. "Emma! Come take this."

His daughter rushed outside and took the empty shotgun her father had handed her. He pulled the gun belt and pistol from Marty's corpse and pulled the saddlebags from the horse before ducking back inside. Emma shut the door and her brother helped her lower the heavy bar across it. It was plenty thick, and Jack was sure Mullen and his men would not be able to break in anytime soon.

Jack was glad to finally be able to do something, even if he still could not walk. "There's plenty of cartridges for the shotgun in those bags, Will. A few bullets for the pistol too."

"That's Mr. Henderson to you, boy. Don't go getting too familiar with me. You ain't clear of trouble yet."

Will set his rifle on the table in the center of the room and opened the pistol's cylinder. He checked to make sure it was still loaded before he buckled the gun belt around his waist.

"At least he was telling the truth, Pa," Emma said. She was no longer aiming the rifle at Jack. "If he hadn't told you about that man, who knows what would've happened."

"Mind yourself," her brother said from his spot at the window. "Pa knows what he's doing."

Will pulled open the flaps of Jack's saddlebags and began looking inside. He raised his voice so his wife could hear it through the floorboards. "Everything's fine, Maddie. Looks like our stranger here was telling the truth. Best stay where you are for now until we know what we're up against."

Jack was glad that most of the feeling had returned to his arms, though he still could not feel much in his legs. He wanted to help but did not dare push the farmer any further. He probably was not accustomed to killing and was likely not himself.

Will picked up his Winchester and handed it to Emma. "Make sure that's fully loaded. Bring your brother the rest of the box. We might be in for a long day."

Emma obeyed her father and disappeared into the back of the house.

Will cracked open the double-barreled shotgun and dumped out the empty shells. "This ain't a practical weapon, boy."

Jack was almost embarrassed to tell him. "I'm not much of a shot. The sheriff figured I should use something that didn't require accuracy."

"You any good with this thing?"

"As good as I need to be, I guess."

Will tossed it to him and Jack was glad he caught it. He hurled the saddlebags next to him on the bed. "Make sure it's loaded and keep an eye on that front door. Anyone comes in, feed them both barrels."

Jack dug out two fresh cartridges from his saddlebags and fed them into the barrel. "Don't worry. I will."

Jack sheepishly opened the other bag and removed a pair of muddy pants.

Will did not look pleased. "I thought you said that dead fella out there took your clothes."

"He took the clothes I was wearing. I took a tumble on my way to where I was going. Ruined my pants, but it's better than running around in my drawers like I am."

He pulled them on and grimaced when he realized they were still damp and stiff from mud. "Should've thought to bring another pair of boots."

"I'll pull them off your dead friend outside." Will got up and went to the door. "Ain't like he's going to have any use for them. Cover me, Tom."

"No!" Jack called out as he struggled to button his pants. "Please, don't go out there. It's not safe."

Tommy glanced at him from the window. "I've been watching the entire time, Pa. No one's coming."

"That's because they're up to something," Jack told him. "I heard them planning to send in Marty to get the drop on you while the rest of them rode in here out of sight. Since I put a crimp in their plans, they probably changed up things. They took to riding around back while Marty kept you busy in the front."

Tommy ducked lower beneath the window as he moved to the right side and looked out. "I know I didn't see anyone ride up behind him, but they could've moved along the brush in the western field."

"The others were riding four team horses bareback," Jack explained. "I escaped with one of them, so there's two of them on one now. They couldn't have closed in on you quietly in a rush, but I'd check the back. I'd be real careful about it too."

Will nodded to Emma, who went through the kitchen to check.

"They armed?"

"Got a pistol from Marshal Wheeler. Probably a rifle too."

"You heard that, Emma?" Will called out to his daughter.

"I heard him, Pa. I'll be careful."

"I'll do it," Jack said as he struggled to get off the bed. "This is my doing."

Will shoved him back onto the mattress. "My house, my family. Besides, your legs are shakier than a newborn colt. Don't worry. There'll be plenty of killing to come."

Jack felt ridiculous just sitting on a bed as helpless as he was. He began to gently punch his legs, willing feeling back into them. "Then at least let me go downstairs and keep your wife safe."

Will knelt beside his son at the window. "That's a good way of getting yourself killed, boy. Maddie's down there with a coach gun aimed up at that door right now. She sees any face other than mine, and you'll catch a mouthful of lead."

Jack stopped hitting his legs. "Maybe that wasn't such a good idea."

"Smart boy." Will finished looking over the front of his land and went over to the small hatch in the floor. "Maddie. It's me. Don't shoot."

He pulled up the door and, from his place on the bed, Jack saw Will's wife was, indeed, aiming a short-barreled shotgun up at the opening.

"How are the babies?" he asked.

"They're fine," she told him. "How are Tommy and Emma?"

"Proving to be a credit to their mother." Jack could have sworn he saw a hint of pride in the farmer's face when he looked back at Jack. "Looks like our friend here was telling the truth."

Maddie scowled up at Jack. "Brought trouble to our doorstep is more like it."

"The trouble ain't his doing," Will told her. "Still, it's better if you stay down there with the babies until we know where these men are. I'll be back in a bit."

He quietly lowered the door and winked at Jack. "Don't mind her. She's a spirited woman."

Jack was glad he had enough saliva in his mouth to swallow again. "Seems so."

From her spot at the back window, Emma shushed them and motioned for them to be quiet.

With enough feeling having returned to his legs Jack pushed himself off the bed and limped over to Will as he moved to the back window at a crouch.

Jack was glad there was no back door to the place. His time spent under siege at the jail had taught him that one door was much easier to guard than two. The windows were concerns, but it took longer for a man to crawl through one and he would be exposed the entire time.

"What do you see?" Will whispered to his daughter.

"Saw the thickets moving just now," she said without taking her eyes from the window. "Could've just been wind, but it's not windy out."

"Think you can keep an eye on them for a while?" Will asked her.

"Can shoot them too if they show themselves."

Will seemed satisfied with that and beckoned Jack to follow him back to the front room where Tommy was still standing watch at the window.

"Here's what we're going to do," Will told them. "Tommy's going to cover us from the west corner of the house while you and me go around the side. That way, if they hear us coming, Tommy will have a clean shot at them. Emma too. You and me will go at them head-on from the side. You'll be out front with that cannon you're hauling."

Jack lost his balance and leaned against the front door. "That's not a good idea, Mr. Henderson."

"I already told you this is my land, my rules, boy. What do you expect us to do? Just sit here while those men figure out a way to try to kill us."

Tommy added, "You said they were planning to shoot us before."

"Things are different now," Jack explained. "They don't have to kill you and now they won't even try. They would've done it when it was easy, but I put a stop to that when I got away. You've already killed one of them, so they're ready for that now. They know you won't go easy so they'll try to escape."

Will's eyes narrowed. "What makes you so sure?"

"On account of they fancied those horses you have in your barn. At least that's what I heard them say. Any clothes you've got drying out on the wash line too."

Will was barely able to keep his voice low. "Do you know what those horses cost me? I'm planning to use them for breeding. I'm fixed to have myself a decent herd to sell in a couple of years. I'm not going to let them just ride in here and take them."

Jack may not have been a farmer, but he understood Mr. Henderson's point. He hoped he could make him see sense. "We're behind a thick door and have solid walls between us and them. They're also armed and know how to use them, maybe better than we do."

He hated interrupting Mr. Henderson, but he did. "They saw what you did to their friend and they're probably just looking for a way to get out of here without getting killed. I say let them go, Mr. Henderson. It's not worth the risk of going up against men like this for a couple of horses, no matter how valuable they are."

The farmer's face reddened. "I'm not—"

Jack surprised himself when he grabbed hold of Henderson's rifle and pushed it down. "Think of your children, Mr. Henderson. Think of Emma and your wife. If they kill us, and these men are killers, do you really want them getting in here?" He glanced at the younger Henderson. "No offense, Tommy, but I don't want to go up against this sort and I've seen more action than you."

Will's eyes bulged. "I've got good saddles out there too. I don't aim to let a passel of thieves just ride in here and rob me blind. If you won't do anything to stop them, I will. Get out of my way."

He tried to push Jack away from the door, but Jack grabbed onto his arm as tightly as he could manage. The farmer was easily twice his size and even if Jack had full use of his limbs, he doubted he would be much of a match for him. But this was not about strength. It was about keeping this family alive.

"Joe Mullen is a dangerous and desperate man and he's running that bunch out there. We can get your horses back, Mr. Henderson. John Holt and me will get all of them back, I promise you. But a few horses, no matter how valuable, are a small price to pay for keeping your family safe."

Jack was glad to see some of the fire in Will's eyes die down a bit as his words hit home. The farmer pulled his arm free of Jack's feeble grip. "Just not used to taking a step back in front of a man is all."

"You're not taking a step back," Jack assured him. "You defended your family when you needed to and that's what you'll be doing now if you let these men ride on. Just for now until we can get them later when we're better outfitted and prepared."

"You sure of that?" Tommy asked.

"I'm not sure of anything." Jack touched the door at his back. "I'm only sure about this door being sturdy enough to keep them from getting in here. And you three being good enough shots to keep them from coming in if they try."

"There's no doubt there." The pride was evident in Will's voice. "Anyone who tries to get in here will die trying."

For the first time all day, Jack was sure of something.

CHAPTER 10

"I don't care what you say," Geary shouted as he struggled to get free of the others. "I'm going in after them!"

Mullen, McCaffrey, and Hardt tackled the bigger man into the overgrowth. Mullen whispered for them all to be still. The farmer had already killed one of them. He had no intention of losing another man when they were so close to getting what they wanted.

"Calm down! You saw what they did to Marty. Do you want to wind up with a bullet in your head too?"

"They've got guns in there, Frank," Hardt added. "You know I've never shied away from a fight, but they'll cut us down the second we stick our heads up."

"We have guns, too, you fool." Geary strained to pull his arms loose, but the three men had finally managed to get a good grip on him. "The pistol and the Winchester we pulled off Wheeler. We can't let them get away with killing Marty like that."

"And for what?" Mullen said into Geary's ear, trying to keep his voice down despite the effort of keeping the big man still. "Waste all of our bullets on revenge? Even if one of us gets in, or all of us, what do you think we'll find in there? A bag of gold?"

He shook Geary's head. "Think, man. Think! They've got

rifles in there and likely more bullets than we had. We'd be dead before our feet hit the floor. And even if we kill them, do you want to be out here on the run with empty guns? I know I don't."

"And what about Turnbull?" Geary seethed. "That weasel is in there right now telling them all about us. He'll tell Holt about us, too, if we let him live. I should've let you kill him when you wanted to."

Mullen knew Geary was right, but this was no longer a matter of right or wrong. This was about survival. "Someone was always going to know we escaped when they find the wreck. They'll know who we are as soon as someone wires the prison. The only thing we've got going for us now is our freedom. Let Turnbull tell them everything. It's too late to do anything about it now."

McCaffrey annoyed him by saying, "It was you who wanted him alive, Joe."

Mullen kicked him in the side. "I don't need you reminding me of what I want and don't want. Marty's dead and so are we if we don't get out of this prison garb." He pointed at the line full of drying clothes. "Wearing them will help us blend in a little."

"Don't forget the horses in the barn, Joe." Hardt added. "Those team horses we've been riding are just about played out. Mine's got a rattle in its lungs and yours is limping."

But Mullen was already aware of that. "All the more reason for us to quit arguing and getting on with what we came here to do. Get the clothes, get the horses, and get out of here without any more of us getting killed."

He eased up on his grip around Geary's neck and was glad the big man did not make a run for it.

"There. Now you're listening to sense." He motioned for the others to let Geary go and they did.

Mullen drew himself into a crouch and pointed at the back window of the farmhouse. "That wash line is just behind those bushes. They can't see me unless I stand up. I'll run out there, grab all I can, and dash back here. Once we're changed, we'll work our way around to the barn and grab those horses."

No one tried to stop him when he broke cover and half crawled, half ran to the clothesline.

Much to his relief, he was able to grab everything he thought might fit them without getting shot. He scrambled back into the overgrowth and the men changed into their newly stolen clothes. For Mullen, the father's shirt and pants because they were a bit big on him, but he was in no condition to complain.

Mullen had been the first to finish dressing and kept both eye and ear out for any sign of the family coming their way. The smart thing for the farmers to do was remain safe inside, but people could not always be counted on to do what was best for them.

McCaffrey and Hardt had taken the boy's shirts and pants, but they fit well. Geary was the largest of the bunch and looked like he might pop the buttons at any moment.

"Now it's time for us to grab them horses," McCaffrey said.

"Trouble is getting them," Hardt added.

Mullen knew waiting would not improve their chances any. They had to move and move now. "Follow me and stay low."

Mullen had already decided on the safest path to the cover of the barn. If anyone from the house took a shot at them, it would most likely be high and miss. Nothing was guaranteed but it was a gamble that Mullen and his fellow convicts had no choice but to take.

He threaded his way through the overgrowth as he made his way to the barn. The men followed without complaint. As he moved, he knew the branches above them shook and he braced for the sound of a rifle and kept moving. He was relieved when they made it to the barn without a shot.

When he reached the barn, Geary pushed on the back wall and cursed at its sturdiness. "No way of getting in this way. Looks like we're going to have to go around front."

Mullen had thought as much.

"Those farmers will have a clean shot at us from the house," Hardt said.

"Or they could pick us off one by one when we try to ride out," McCaffrey added.

Again, Mullen already knew that, but saw no other way around it. "I'll go first, and you follow me just like before. Stay low, get those horses saddled as quickly as you can. We ride low and fast when we're ready to make a break for it. Hitting a man riding away from them is going to be a lot harder than hitting someone standing in front of them."

Before the men could think about it, Mullen dashed around the side of the barn and to the front. He braced for the impact of a bullet with each step but made it inside without a shot. So did the others.

They quietly and quickly took down the bridles and saddles from where they were hung and slipped them on the horses, who fussed at the scent of the strange men tending to them. Mullen knew they were probably responding to the fear each of them felt.

"Quickly, men. Quickly!" he urged them as he moved as fast as he could. He was glad his new companions were comfortable around horses and did not need his help getting them ready to ride.

When four of the six horses in the barn were ready, Mullen climbed up into the saddle. He stole a quick glance outside and was glad he did not see any sign of the farmers.

He looked at the other prisoners to make sure they were set and, since they were, he dug his heels into the animal's sides. The stallion sped out of the barn like a shot and Mullen, who was more than an able horseman, tugged on the reins to bring it hard to the right and away from the house.

A shot cracked out as Mullen heard Geary and the others riding close behind him. Mullen stretched out low across the horse's neck as they rode toward the timber. He heard more shots ring out as he put more distance between himself and the barn.

He looked around quickly when he reached a clearing. A quick glance behind him proved the other three had made it. None of them looked as if they had been hit.

"We're free!" Geary called out. "We did it, Joe! We did it!"

McCaffrey and Hardt cut loose with whoops and hollers that echoed through the wilderness.

Mullen decided it was safe enough for him to sit upright in the saddle and let the horse keep its pace. It would do the animal good to get some air in its lungs.

Free air was good for both man and beast alike.

Jack Turnbull yelled at the Henderson men from the doorway of the house. "What did I tell you two about staying inside and keeping cover?"

Will lowered his rifle and turned on the young deputy. "This is my farm, son, and my stock they're escaping with. You don't get to tell me anything on my land."

Tom stood right beside his father. "Pa's right, mister. You'd do well to keep a civil tongue."

Turnbull's legs were still wobbly from his ordeal, but his temper remained intact. "You're lucky they were only interested in the horses."

"Lucky?" Will stormed toward the barn. "You call what happened just now luck? They rode off with four of my best stallions. I don't call losing them to a pack of murderers anything close to luck."

"And those stallions wouldn't do you any good if you

died trying to save them." Turnbull thought it sounded like something Holt might say. "And don't go thinking you're going to saddle up and ride after them now. They'll be expecting that. If they hear you coming after them now, you'll ride right into a bullet."

William Henderson looked like he wanted to say more, but quickly thought better of it as he continued to storm off toward the barn. "I'd better see what your friends were kind enough to leave us."

Tom joined Turnbull in watching the father walk away. "You'd do well not to talk to him like that, Jack. He's got a vicious temper."

The anger of the moment had passed, and Turnbull sank against a well in the front of the house. "I didn't mean to do that, Tom. I should've kept my mouth shut or said it better, but you don't know those men out there. Letting them go was best for your family. I promised I'd bring those horses back and I live up to my promises."

His own words reminded him that was not always true. He had taken an oath to be John Holt's deputy and he had shirked it the first time he felt he had a reason. It was the last promise he intended on breaking.

"Pa's a desperate man too," Tom said. "This land's not much good for farming and he was counting on having a herd to sell in a couple of years. He's not one to allow a man to take something from him without a fight." He kicked at the dirt. "He's been fighting this ground for five years now. And he'll be saddling up one of those horses to get back what's his."

Turnbull did not know William Henderson well. In fact, he did not know him at all. But even though he had only been on the farm for a short amount of time, he imagined what Tom said was true. "Well, if he does decide to go after them, he won't have to go alone."

Tom snickered as he looked Jack up and down. "You plan on going with him? Why, you ain't much older than I am."

Jack had never taken kindly to being laughed at. Not by his father. Not by the people of Devil's Gulch who had tried to kill him. And not by a farmer's son either. "What I lack in years, I make up for in experience. Believe me."

Tom Henderson did not look like he believed him, but at least he was not laughing any longer.

CHAPTER 11

From the bench in front of her café, Jean gestured across the street toward the sad figure of Old Bob, who was standing on the boardwalk in front of the jail. "I think your friend is part bird dog. He's been standing there, gazing down the street for ages now."

Holt sipped his coffee as he watched the cook standing in the doorway of the jail, looking in the same direction as where Wheeler and the prison wagon had headed earlier.

"The man's a strange one," Holt said. "I don't think he's used to having four walls around him or a roof over his head. He said he's accustomed to sleeping out under the stars in all kinds of weather. I guess civilization doesn't agree with him."

"Something to be said for that." She slipped her arm through his. "I'm just glad you were a bit easier to tame."

She enjoyed watching him smile, for she knew he did not smile often. "I spent enough time sleeping outside during the war. After it, too, come to think of it. I'll take a nice bed instead of the elements anytime. Besides, you make it easy to want to stay indoors."

She shifted herself as close to him as she dared in public. The night had grown a bit cooler after sundown, but not by much. She knew there would not be many more nights like this when they could sit together outdoors before winter settled over the town. She wanted to spend as much time with Holt like this as she could get.

"I saw you have a new prisoner," she said. "He the one who raised a fuss at the Railhead?"

"The very same. He seems harmless enough now that he's had time to think it over. Doubt Judge Cook will see it that way, though. He wants me to bring him before him the day after tomorrow."

Jean was glad to hear it as the town paid her to bring meals to the prisoners. That part of her business had been good when Holt had first come to town but had fallen off some since Joe Mullen had been convicted. She was glad to have picked up more customers in her café in the weeks since to help make ends meet. "So much for our hopes of you getting your evenings back now that Joe's been carted off."

"It's only a day or so," Holt assured her. "The judge will probably fine him and make him clean the streets for a month. Ma doesn't even want him charged. Said locking up her customers is bad for business, especially the ones who lose at the wheel as bad as he does."

She felt a shudder go through her at the mention of Ma McAdam. She usually did a better job of keeping John from seeing her reaction to her mother's name, but it was too late.

"Didn't mean to upset you like that," he said. "I should've thought before I said anything."

She put the best face on it she could manage. "You arrested that man in the Railhead. She owns the Railhead. Can't be expected to tiptoe around something just because of me."

He sat back on the bench and laced his fingers with hers. "Next time I'll think before I speak."

She did not bother to tell him that he was already the most thoughtful man she had ever known. She knew he did not like compliments. In fact, he avoided them whenever he could.

She waited until he had begun to drink his coffee before saying, "Glad to hear you prefer sleeping indoors, though. Makes my life easier."

She was glad she almost made him spit his coffee back into the mug. "Like most things, it's about the company you keep."

She giggled when she saw him blush. She had seen Holt in many dangerous situations in the short time he had lived in Devil's Gulch, but to the best of her knowledge, she was the only person who had ever managed to embarrass him.

She held his arm tighter. "Red isn't your color, John."

"Good thing it's getting darker earlier these days. Wouldn't want anyone around here to see I'm flesh and blood."

"Me too. Not everyone needs to see that. Only me."

She knew there were some towns that would have frowned on a Creole woman sitting on a bench with a white man, much less a sheriff. She knew some people in Devil's Gulch frowned on such things, though most of them had the common sense to keep their opinions to themselves. John Holt had a way of making people think twice before they spoke.

But Jean had never placed much stock in the opinions of others. She had never had the luxury of caring what people thought. Her father had been a miner and her mother was Ma McAdam. Pedigrees had not counted for much when Devil's Gulch had been little more than a mining camp. The town may had grown since and more people might be living there, but it was still the only home she had ever known.

"How are you and Mrs. Chapman getting along?" she asked.

"She's quite a woman." Holt sipped his coffee. "She's mighty opinionated about things." She watched his expression dim a bit as he seemed to remember something. "Have you heard any of your customers talk about Joe Mullen's wife being in town this morning?"

She had been wondering if he had heard about that. She had never lied to him before and she had no intention of starting now. "Some of them were talking about it. Don't know how much truth there is to it. Rumors around here often aren't worth much."

"In this case they happen to be true. The mayor's spies told her so. They saw Sarabelle sneaking in the back of the Bottle soon after I stopped by to put Cassidy in his place."

She had an idea of what such a meeting might mean for him. "Any idea what they were talking about?"

"No," he admitted, "but whatever it is, I doubt there's any good that could come of it. She's every bit as dangerous as her husband ever was. Maybe even worse, since people don't always know what she's up to."

Jean frowned as she straightened out her skirt. "In my experience, Sarabelle isn't subtle. She bats her eyelashes and throws a grin at you men, but she doesn't have any of us women fooled. I'd say you'd do well to steer clear of her if you can."

"She'd do just as well to steer clear of me. She should remember what happened to her husband when he crossed me. A jail cell door closes just as easily for a woman as it does a man."

Jean disliked the idea of John finding himself against Sarabelle Mullen. She knew how ruthless the woman could be. She had heard the stories that she'd had a hand in killing a miner's wife just to keep the rumors against Joe at bay. To Jean's way of thinking, anyone who would take a life over something as minor as idle gossip should be avoided at all costs. Even if it meant John's pride had to stand aside.

"At least you know she's up to something. That gives you an advantage you didn't have when you went up against Joe."

She hated seeing John frown as he looked over Main Street. "Yeah. Just another thing to keep me up at night."

She held his arm tighter again. "Not if I can help it."

She laughed when he blushed worse than before and decided he'd had enough teasing for one day. "Will I be seeing you later?"

"If you'd like." He nodded over toward Old Bob. "For now, I'd best go over and check on my guest. He's liable to forget he's standing out there and freeze to death unless I move him along. Got any food back there I can run over to him?"

"I've already got a plate warming for him and your guest." She reluctantly moved her arm out from under his. "You stay here while I go get it for you."

As she got up to go inside, Holt gently stopped her by touching her arm. "I need you to be careful, Jean. This business between Sarabelle and Cassidy might not amount to anything, but if it does, things will happen fast. I want your promise that you'll take care of yourself first, even if it means leaving me on my own. I can take whatever they might throw at me, but only if I know you're safe."

She smiled down at him. She wanted to take his face in her hands and kiss him and tell him how much she loved him. How he was the first man who had ever truly loved her for her. Not for how she looked or what she was, but who she was.

But she also knew such public displays of affection were frowned upon on the boardwalks of town—even among married couples—so she kept her urge to herself. "Don't waste time worrying about me, John Holt. I was taking care of myself for a long time before you showed up. Just worry about you and I'll be just fine."

He closed his eyes. "Just promise me. It'll make me feel better."

"I promise to look after myself." She gently eased his

hand off her arm. "And now I'm going to look after your supper. I'll be right back."

She went inside and stole a glance at him through the glass of the café door as she closed it. More cracks in his stoic veneer seemed to show the more they talked. She did not like thinking of him that way. As a human being. Because if he was just human, only flesh and blood, then he could be killed. And while the thought of his death always lurked somewhere in the back of her mind, Jean had yet been able to bring herself to face it outright. To do so might serve to make it a reality and she could not dare risk that.

She had waited too long for happiness to find her and now that she had it, she was in no hurry to lose it again. If something happened to him, she did not know what would become of her.

She wiped away a tear as she moved away from the door. There was food that needed preparing.

As he carried both plates of food across the thoroughfare to the jail, John Holt noticed Old Bob had not moved an inch in more than an hour. He had just stood in front of the open jailhouse door like a statue, thumbs tucked into the pockets of his denim pants, looking in the direction of where Wheeler had driven the prison wagon. He had not shifted his weight from one foot to the other. Had not even leaned against the building in thought. He had simply stood there motionless while he seemed to wait for something to happen.

There was an eerie quality about the cook that made Holt feel uneasy as he approached the man.

"Evening, Bob. Brought you some food for you and the prisoner. Figured you might be hungry."

If Holt had hoped the man would react, he was wrong. He kept his vigil looking down the street into the darkness of approaching night. "Thanks, but I ain't hungry. You can put it on the desk or give it to the prisoner. I might gnaw on it later if there's anything left."

Holt had never been much for humor but decided to try it in this instance. "I wouldn't do that if I were you. Jean's watching us from her café and if you don't eat, she's liable to think you don't like her food. I'd have thought a fellow cook would understand that."

The older man's eyes narrowed as he continued to peer into the darkness. "Fickle business, understanding something. Understanding men most of all. Most fickle indeed."

Holt brought the heavy plates of hot food inside. He placed two on his desk and the third into Simon. The prisoner had not stopped crying since he had been thrown into his cell and Holt ignored his pleas as he offered his plate to him.

With the prisoner fed, Holt went back outside to see to Bob. "What's the matter with you anyway? You've been standing out here for an hour at least."

"What concern is it of yours? I'm watching the jail like I told you I would, ain't I? The prisoner is under lock and key. That was our bargain. Ain't nothing against the law about a man taking the night air, now is there?"

"No, but you're just standing there gaping at nothing without a coat on. If I didn't know better, I'd think you were a bit touched in the head."

Bob blinked but did not move. "I sure hope you're right about that, Sheriff. About me looking at nothing, that is. I truly do. I hope this is just me getting old and letting my mind run away with me." He rubbed his right hand across his flat belly. "But that's not it. I just know it. I can feel it in the middle of me as sure as if something was sitting on my stomach."

"That's just hunger talking," Holt said. "I'd bet you haven't eaten all day. Come inside and eat. A full stomach will settle you down some."

"Food won't help me shake this feeling, Sheriff. I've been hauling prisoners all over this territory for a long time. Longer than any other man in the territory by half. Did it in Illinois and Nebraska too. Been handling bad men for almost forty years, near as I can figure. Got to be so good at it that the governor of Nebraska gave me a special pardon excusing me from getting drafted into the army. Said I performed too vital a service to the state to go and fight."

Holt watched the old cook continue to rub his belly. He felt something change in the man. A feeling that came off him like heat. Holt did not understand it, and he had never been one to trust that which he could not understand.

But he knew better than to interrupt him while the cook went on.

"And in all that time, this feeling I've got in me right now has never been wrong. Not once. Every time its ever struck me, something horrible has either happened or was about to happen. Guess I've always been good at knowing when bad things were headed my way. It's the only reason I have for why I've managed to live for so long. It's an aching that starts right here in my gut and spreads through the rest of my body. It's like a fever pain, only I'm never sick when I get it. Well, I've got that feeling now, and since I'm safe here in town, that means it must have something to do with Wheeler."

He took his hand from his stomach and pointed a crooked finger toward the end of Main Street. "Something's happened to him out there just like I feared it would. I can feel it in my bones as sure as I feel that night wind on my face."

Although he was standing next to Bob, Holt did not feel anything at first. Then a gentle wind reached him, lending weight to everything the cook had said.

He joined him in looking down Main Street, hoping for a glimpse of what Bob saw and felt. But all he saw were the flickering flames from the oil lamps he had gotten Mayor Chapman to allow hung up along the boardwalk to make it easier to see things in the dark.

The night did not speak to him as clearly as it apparently spoke to Bob.

"What do you think happened?" Holt asked him.

"These feelings I get are never that particular," Bob explained, "but they're never wrong either. I don't see visions or anything so fanciful. But I've ridden with Dan Wheeler for a long time. Kind of got attached to him in a way, if you can believe anyone can get attached to a man like him." His Adam's apple bobbed up and down as he swallowed. "He's lying out there on the cold ground dead someplace. I can almost see it."

Holt wanted to assure the older man that he was just imagining things. That a meal and a good night's sleep would make him feel better.

But Holt had known men in the war who had been able to sense when trouble was close. He had ignored their feelings at first, but after enough battles, decided to pay attention to their warning. He had known an old woman in New Orleans who often had similar feelings.

Life had taught him to listen to them when they warned about an ill wind blowing through the city. A wind that could not always be felt on the skin. Only in the mind. They had been right more than they had been wrong, though Holt could never be sure if it was just because they knew more than he did about the citizens of the city or if it was more than that.

Just about the only thing Holt was sure about was that he could not allow Bob to continue to stand outside all night looking for something neither of them could see.

He placed his hand on his shoulder. "If you won't eat, you

might as well come inside and get some rest. We'll ride out at first light if you want. Take a look around to put your mind at ease. If Dan's out there, we'll find him." He motioned up to the sky. "There's no moon tonight, so going out now would be pointless."

Bob stiffened as whatever trance that had gripped him seemed to leave him. He looked at Holt as if he was seeing him for the first time.

"I'm not crazy, Sheriff. Something's wrong."

"And we won't be able to make it right until morning." He pulled him back toward the jail. "Might as well get some rest. Sounds like we've got a big day ahead of us tomorrow."

Bob took a final look into the distance before he turned and shuffled into the jail.

Holt walked in behind him and bolted the door, just in case whatever was outside tried to follow them in.

CHAPTER 12

The sun had just begun to rise when Holt led the borrowed mare from the livery down Main Street. He had been surprised when the liveryman did not charge him for use of the horse and tack. He told Holt he was welcome to anything he needed free of charge if it was in the course of his official duties. He had never known a liveryman to be so generous.

He had expected to see Bob waiting anxiously in front of the jail, eager to get on the trail in search of Wheeler. He had not expected to see Frank Peters sitting on the steps, shivering in the cold morning air despite the fact he was wearing a heavy coat.

The former sheriff looked as if he had not slept in days. His face bore thick, dark stubble and his eyes were red. Holt wondered if he might be shivering more from a lack of whiskey than from the cold.

Peters got to his feet as Holt approached. "Morning, Sheriff."

Holt stopped his horses a few feet shy of the jail. He and Peters had never been cordial with each other. "Morning, Frank. What are you doing here?"

"I'd like to talk to you if you've got a moment to spare." He made a show of patting his coat pockets to prove they vere empty. "I'm not armed and I didn't come to cause rouble."

As far as Holt was concerned, that remained to be seen. "Then you shouldn't have a problem telling me why you're ere."

The former lawman shifted his weight as he looked round the deserted street. "It's kinda touchy and I'd feel a night easier about it if I didn't have to shout up at you like 'm doing now."

Holt decided the man meant no immediate harm, so he dged his horses farther before climbing down from the addle and securing their reins to the hitching rail. "Speak our mind and keep your distance."

Peters stepped up on the boardwalk, careful to make sure is hands were visible at all times. "I hear you might be iding out today. That you might be heading out to check p on Dan Wheeler."

At first, Holt did not know how Peters could have known hat, then remembered that he had talked to Jean about it last night in the café. There had been a few patrons around en- oying a late supper. It was possible that one of them had gone to the Railhead after and shared what they had heard here.

"What if I am?"

"Still got Simon in a cell?" Peters asked.

Holt did not like the direction the conversation was aking. Frank Peters was not impartial where Ma McAdam or the Railhead was concerned. "Judge Cook wants me to bring him before him tomorrow morning. Why?"

"Guess young Jack hasn't come back to help you keep n eye on the prisoner. To my mind, that leaves you without nyone to look in on him while you're gone."

Holt had already taken care of that. Lester Patrick, the own prosecutor, and Dr. Ralph Klassen were going to split their time at the jail watching the prisoner until Holt and Bob returned to town.

"I've made sure he won't be alone. Why do you ask?"

"On account of I'd like to pitch in if you'll have me," Peters told him. "I know how to do it and it wouldn't be a bit of trouble."

Holt had not expected him to volunteer so easily. "I don't think that would be a good idea, what with you working and living over at the Railhead and all."

"That's just it. I don't live there anymore. I quit last night."

Holt hung his head and let out a long breath. After his talk with Ma McAdam the previous day, he had been afraid something like that might happen. At least he had not been called to the saloon to haul away Peters's body after Charlie or one of the others killed him.

"Why'd you go and do a fool thing like that?"

"On account of me not being able to stay there anymore, John. I can't stand seeing her parade around with that outlaw in front of me like I was never anything to her. I gave up everything for that woman. My job. My good name. Why, I even got shot for her once or twice. And this is how she thanks me. By throwing me aside for that pup. All she does is feed me liquor and keep me up in my room to pout like some old dog."

Frank's expression grew dark. "I know you don't think much of me as a man, Holt, but I'm not an old dog." He pointed at the star pinned to the lapel of Holt's coat. "I lost that because of her and you wear it better than I ever did. I'm not trying to get it back and I'm not asking you or anyone else to forgive me either. I'm just asking for a chance to prove I'm better than she thinks I am. Better than anyone else in town thinks. I know I've done wrong. I just want to be able to show everyone I can do right for a change."

Holt's heart sank when he saw the man's lower lip quiver.

"Please don't make me beg you, John, but I'm so low, I'll beg if you make me."

Holt looked away as he ran his hand across his mouth. He had seen men at their lowest before, usually before a battle or right after. Men who were afraid of what they might do when the guns started firing. Regretting what they had done to other men on the battlefield. In New Orleans he had seen how low men could sink from too much drink and that last, desperate lunge at respectability when they realized they were about to go over the edge of sanity forever.

He sensed Frank Peters was at such a point right now. He had all but admitted as much. And although Holt doubted he could ever fully trust him, he did not want to be the one who cut him loose and let him be carried away on a tide of whiskey beneath which he would surely drown.

"Our road hasn't always been the smoothest, Frank."

The former sheriff used his sleeve to wipe at his eyes. "I know that and I'm not asking you for much. With Jack gone and no one else around, I'm just asking for the chance to keep an eye on Simon. That's all. Something small and something easy so I can prove I'm useful. To you and to myself."

Holt felt his objections to the idea crumble before him one by one. "When was the last time you took a drink?"

"Two days ago."

Holt was about to protest, but Peters was quick to respond. "Two days, John. I swear it. That's why I wasn't on the floor when Simon went for Ma yesterday. I was up in my room sick with the shakes. I'm better now and I haven't touched a drop since. You'd be able to smell it on me if I had, but I haven't." He held out his hand level for Holt to see for himself. "Steady as a board. I haven't touched the stuff and I won't either. Not if you help me by allowing me this small thing."

"He held a knife on Ma, you know. I won't have you looking to get even with a defenseless man in my jail."

"Simon's no bother," Frank explained. "He's done that lots of times. I won't touch a hair on his head. Just tend to him until you get back."

Holt looked him over and did not see any of his belongings with him. "Where are the rest of your things if you quit the Railhead?"

"Still in my room. Ma said she'd keep it for me until I found a new place to stay."

Holt knew he had always had a sense for sincerity, and he could sense it now in Frank Peters. "You won't have a gun or a knife and I'm not leaving you the keys to his cell."

"That's fair," he said eagerly. "I'm not asking for that."

"Jean brings over three meals a day and one for you. She's smart and she doesn't miss much. When I get back to town, if she tells me she thought she smelled any whiskey anywhere near this jail, I'll run you out of town with the clothes on your back. Understand?"

"Yes, John. It's just black coffee for me from now on. Thank you."

He was sure that he would come to regret his decision, but if he could manage to help turn this broken man around, it would certainly be good to have someone else working with him.

Both men turned when the jailhouse door opened and Bob stepped outside toting his shotgun. "Morning, boys." He looked over Frank Peters. "Good God. Is that you, Frank? I haven't laid eyes on you in more than a year outside a saloon. Why, you look worse than I feel."

Peters offered a weak smile. "Good to see you again, Bob. And I'm sure I look a lot worse than that."

Holt cleared his throat. "Frank here's going to help us keep an eye on the prisoner while you and me hit the trail. Said he's trying to turn over a new leaf. Figured there was no harm in helping him try."

"A new leaf?" The cook squinted at the former sheriff.

"Looks to me like you'd be better off burning down the whole forest at this point."

Holt had never been one to kick a man while he was down and felt a sudden need to defend his former enemy. "There's coffee on the stove, Frank. Best get yourself inside and situated. We're liable to not be back much before nightfall."

Peters thanked him again and ducked his head as he walked into the jail.

Bob joined Holt in watching him go inside. "You sure that's a good idea, John? Frank wasn't much before he took to the bottle. Always had too much of a weakness for that soiled dove over at the Railhead. Wheeler and me never trusted him then. Don't know if you can trust him now."

"Neither do I," Holt admitted. "But I figure he's just about as low as a man can expect to go and still be living. Can't hurt to give him a chance. Besides, I happen to need him."

"It's your town and your jail, Holt. I don't have a say. Just don't go expecting me to trust him. Not now, not ever."

Holt had no intention of ever trying to talk the cook into doing anything. After all, it was him who had convinced Holt to ride out in search of ghosts.

Two hours later as they followed Wheeler's trail, Holt noted that Bob had rarely taken his eyes from the ground and had not said a word the entire journey.

The old man had complained of creaky bones and pain back in town, but now that he had a track to follow, he seemed to be a man reborn. Holt knew Bob might have spent the better part of the last several years steering a cook prison wagon, but he looked mighty comfortable in the saddle.

John Holt had never been much for conversation, so he did not complain about the silence. And Bob was too focused on reading the ground to have heard him if he had.

The cook stopped his borrowed mare short, causing Holt to do the same a few feet behind him.

"What do you see?" Holt asked.

"Look there." Bob pointed down at what appeared to Holt to be the remnants of a camp just off the road. "Wheeler stopped them there for a time."

Holt was unaware how he could have known that much detail from such a distance. "How can you be sure?"

"I'm as sure of that being Wheeler's fire as I can be of anything," Bob boasted. "Look at the way those stones are stacked around it in a square. Then the sticks and such are piled up in the center. Wheeler's the only man I've ever known who builds a fire that way, even a quick one. Always thought it was silly, but that's how he did it, even if it was just a small fire like this one to warm his coffee by."

Holt looked at the same site but failed to see as much as Bob had. "How do you know it was quick?"

He nodded to a pile of droppings along the trail. "Only an hour's worth. If I can read anything, it's manure."

Holt decided to take his word for it.

Bob urged his mount forward and continued to follow the trail southward. Holt had always considered himself an adequate tracker, but men like Bob always seemed to be able to read the ground in ways that he could not. He had done his best to pick up a few things here and there from the scouts who had worked for him back in the army but he had never acquired the skill.

"Wheeler must've been needing a coffee and a smoke mighty bad to have stopped so close to town." Bob scratched his gray whiskers with a gnarled finger as he continued to think aloud. "He didn't have any coffee before he left. That could be the reason. Wonder if Bessy was giving him trouble."

"Bessy?"

"One of the lead horses on the team pulling the wagon. She's not as young as she once was, and I thought I heard a rattle in her lungs. I would've looked her over if Dan hadn't been in such an awful hurry to get moving again. Or maybe the wagon was giving him a problem. I was mighty surprised it didn't throw a wheel along with my cook wagon, seeing as how we rode the same trail and all. But your liveryman checked it over and assured us it was fine for travel."

Holt was glad he could finally contribute something to the conversation. "The trail Wheeler took is torn up pretty good. And, as I recall, that cage rattled something awful."

He watched Bob chew over his concerns as he rode ahead. "Speculating won't help us much, Sheriff. Let's keep riding a bit to see if we can figure out more to the story."

For the next three hours, Holt rode behind the man without saying a word. Bob was as engrossed in reading the trail as he had seen men lost in a good book on a cold night.

Holt had been conscious of the time the entire ride. He did not like being away from town for so long, especially with Sarabelle Mullen and Cassidy possibly hatching a plan. There was no one left in Devil's Gulch to keep an eye on things except for Frank Peters and he was busy with the prisoner. He seemed to be hanging on by his fingernails, and Holt wondered if he had made a mistake in leaving him in charge while he was gone. At least he was not armed and did not have the keys to either the rifle rack or the cells. He imagined any harm he might do would be minimal.

Holt had hoped Old Bob's concern about Wheeler would have been quelled after they had found the first campsite. But that had been three hours ago, and the cook was still searching.

Holt was beginning to think about the ride back. They had set off just after sunrise and if they turned back now, they would be lucky to reach Devil's Gulch before dark. If they delayed any longer, they might be forced to rest the horses and camp outside for the night. And since neither of them had brought blankets or provisions for themselves or the horses, it would be a miserable night for all concerned.

Holt was about to tell Bob of his worries when the old cook shouted, "There!"

He watched Bob pointing to a small rise ahead before spurring his horse to ride toward it.

Holt had to stand in his stirrups to see what Bob had been pointing at. It was a deep gouge in the trail next to a sloping hill.

He snapped the reins and caught up with his companion just before the old man steered his horse down the hillside.

This time, Holt could clearly see what had happened.

The right side of the ruts were deeper on this section of the trail. The grass had been gouged up and scarred all the way down the hill. He saw the wreckage of the prison wagon beneath a nasty rock that jutted out from the hillside but noticed something else had caught Bob's attention. He drew his horse to a skid and practically spilled from the saddle.

He had obviously found something.

Holt climbed down and wrapped the reins around his horse's front leg before scrambling down the hill to join Bob. The pitch was not too steep, but enough to prevent him from drawing his pistol until he got closer out of fear he might lose his footing.

He recoiled when he saw the mangled body of Dan Wheeler pressed into the hillside.

Bob was checking his friend's neck for any sign of a pulse, though it was evident that the man was long since dead.

"I'm sorry, Bob," was all Holt could think to say.

But the cook was too busy examining the body to accept condolences. "He's got no bullet holes in him. No bruising either. Doesn't look like he was jumped." He looked over the length of Wheeler's remains. "I'd say it looks like the wagon crushed him when it slid down the hill." He ran a hand over his bearded face. "By God, I knew something had happened to him, but I didn't count on this."

Holt knew there was nothing more either of them could do for Wheeler now, so he turned his attention to the wreckage at the bottom of the hill and the prisoners who might still be there. "You stay here with him. I'll take a look for survivors."

Bob remained with the marshal while Holt crept toward the wagon. His pistol up but held at his side. He doubted he would find anyone alive. If they could have gotten away, they certainly would have, but he had to be certain.

He had to know if Joe Mullen was alive or dead.

He stepped wide around the broken iron slats that sprang up at odd angles from the wreckage. As he had expected, he found the iron door at the back of the cage was open.

He raised his pistol as he continued to walk in a wide circle around the wagon. He found the body of one prisoner inside. At first, he hoped it might have been Mullen, but one look at the corpse told him this was a much thinner and smaller man. It looked like his neck had been broken when the wagon had tumbled down the hill. He and Wheeler had probably died at the same time.

A quick search of the area revealed little else except for the discarded shackles that littered the ground. The chains and clamps had not been cut, so they had probably taken the keys from Wheeler's body. And his weapons too.

Holt slid the revolver back into its holster.

Joe Mullen had escaped. The other prisoners had, too, but they did not concern him. Mullen was free and he had undoubtedly formed the convicts into a desperate gang.

He did not need to have Bob's tracking skills to know there was only one place they would be heading. The closest town, which happened to be Devil's Gulch. The only home Mullen had ever known.

And the only man standing in their way was Frank Peters, a drunken, half-crazed fool down on his luck.

Holt grabbed for his gun as he turned when he heard someone approaching from behind. He was relieved to see it was just Bob on horseback and he had brought Holt's horse with him.

"Time for us to go, Sheriff." The cook handed him the reins of his horse. "We've got criminals to catch."

Holt took the reins but was surprised Bob was in such a hurry. "Don't you want to bury Wheeler first?" He remembered they had not brought shovels with them, but he had dug graves with rocks before. Even with his bare hands. It would be hard going, but with the two of them working on it, they could get it done in reasonably short order. "You can't just leave him in the open like that. The animals will get at him."

"Vultures, too, I expect," Bob added. "But Dan Wheeler wasn't a sentimental man. He dedicated his life to locking up convicts and he died doing what he loved. If he was able to, he'd be the first one to tell us to get those men back in chains as soon as possible instead of wasting precious time putting him in the ground. By my reckoning, they've already got half a day's jump on us as it is." He looked up at the cloudless sky. "We've got a cold night coming on, so we'd best pick up the trail of those escapees while we can."

Since Bob seemed set on the matter, Holt saw no reason to argue with him. And he needed to get back to town now that Mullen was back on the loose.

He climbed back into the saddle. "We were taking our time reading the trail earlier, but now that we know where they're going, we can make decent time back to town if we ride hard enough. Should be able to make it back to Devil's Gulch before dark."

"We're not going back to Devil's Gulch, Sheriff. We're tracking those convicts. We're going wherever they went."

Holt heard a firmness in the older man's voice he had not detected until now. "We don't have to track them. We already know where Mullen's going, or at least I do. He's got a lot of enemies back in town and he's liable to try to get even with some of them. He's also still got a few friends in town who'll help him do it. If he's not in town, we'll find him out at his ranch. If you want to find your prisoners, our best chance is to ride hard for town."

"They might've gone that way, might not have. Your town will be just fine until we find them."

Holt heard the words, but he had a tough time understanding them. He began to wonder if Bob was not in shock over finding Wheeler was dead. "You remember I left Frank Peters in charge, don't you?"

"Frank might not be good for much," Bob agreed, "but I expect he's still capable of stopping a bullet or two if he goes up against Mullen. But we don't know for certain where those men are going. They're probably heading back to town, but they might just as easily be hightailing it out of the territory. I know I would. And I don't intend on losing track of them on account of a guess. We'll follow their tracks and go where they lead us."

Holt decided Bob was not in shock, just stubborn.

Bob continued. "Mullen's not my only concern here, Holt. The men who escaped with him are a violent, desperate bunch." He inclined his head toward the wagon. "That dead one over there was the weakest among them. Geary's a big man and a stone-cold killer. He'd cut a man's throat for a crust of moldy bread. The others with him aren't much better. The sooner we put them back in chains, the better all of us will be, including that town you seem to love so much."

Holt did not want to argue with him, but he would not be dictated to either. Not when he knew his duty. "I don't think you understand me, old man. I'm going back to town right now. You can either come with me or not. I've got no say in your decision."

He was surprised when he heard a crack that could only have been the hammer of a pistol being thumbed back. He was even more surprised when he saw Bob aiming that pistol in his direction from just above the saddle horn. Holt had not known the cook had one and decided he must have had it tucked inside his shirt.

"You might not have any say in my decision, Holt, but I've got plenty of say in yours. Dan Wheeler wasn't the senior marshal in charge of this outfit. That honor belonged to me. I only let Wheeler act like he was in charge because it made him feel good and easier to work with. He always needed to be the stud horse in the herd."

With his left hand, he dug out a brass marshal star from his shirt pocket and pinned it on his coat. "I tried not to throw my weight around because I know it irked him that I outranked him, and Wheeler was always easier to take when he was calm. I did the cooking and took care of the prisoners, but every time we rode together, the man responsible for the assignment was me. I indulged him once too often and it cost him his life. That's my burden to bear. But this here is a federal matter. I'm the one in charge and I've got every right to press you into service whether you like it or not. I'm exercising that right here and now. We're following their tracks, Holt. And we're following them now."

Holt's right hand flexed as he fought the urge to reach for his pistol. He did not doubt that he was faster on the draw than Bob, even in the saddle, but no one was faster than a finger. And the cook's finger was already on the trigger.

"I don't like this," Holt said.

"Neither do I." Bob nodded past Holt toward the line of trees behind him. "Those boys took the team horses and rode in that direction off the trail. I think they grabbed someone who happened to be riding by, but only time will tell for certain. We're going after them. If you ride off, I'll swear out a warrant for your arrest. Judge Cook is an old friend of mine. I'll see to it you're fined and put in jail for a year or more. But I'd prefer to have your word that you won't do that so I can put this thing away."

Holt did not see that he had any choice. "You have my word."

"Glad to hear it." He tucked the pistol back in his shirt, revealing a holster he had on the inside of his pants. Since he had always kept his shirt untucked, Holt had never noticed it before.

Bob traced the terrain through the overgrowth with a finger. "Looks like Mullen and the others rode through the timber. We'd best get after them so I can track them while the daylight's still good."

Holt glared at the man as he rode past him. "I really don't like this."

The old prison cook kept riding. "Then you're in good company because that makes two of us."

CHAPTER 13

T he sun had just sunk below the western mountains when Joe Mullen led the band of escaped convicts to the valley above his ranch. He was warmed with pride when he saw the glowing lamplight from within the large house he had helped to build with his own hands. And although he was still a good distance away, he could have sworn he smelled the smoke rising from the great stone chimney.

His pride was quickly replaced by the bile that rose in his throat when he remembered all that he had endured since the last time he had laid eyes on the place. Sarabelle's treachery had led to his conviction for murder. He had rotted away for weeks in Holt's dank cell while his wife went on with life without him. A life she was building on the ruins of his own.

"You sure this is your place, Joe?" Hardt said beside him. Even atop a horse, he looked small and younger than he should.

"It's mine, by God and by law," Mullen said. "It's as much a part of me as the blood flowing in my veins. Some of that blood is in that land down there. Sweat too. My land goes as far as your eyes can see from up here, gentlemen." He pointed toward the hills in the east. "Own a fair number of mines up in those rocks as well. Decided to build this place right next to my first claim. It didn't yield much, I'll grant you that, but that little mine is still my pride and joy."

Geary cut loose with a low whistle. "How'd a man with all that wealth and power find himself next to me in a prison wagon."

Mullen gripped his reins tighter and not just from the approaching cold air of night. "Deceit. Betrayal. Conniving."

"Ah," Geary said. "Sounds like a woman, then."

"Yes. A woman." Mullen knew the vengeance he had only dared to dream of for all these weeks was now finally at hand. But he had to be careful. Blind vengeance could get them all killed. "You boys see that bunkhouse off to the west down there?"

The men used their hands to shield their eyes from the setting sun but told him they saw it.

"There's no fewer than twenty men in there as we speak. Every one of them is willing to die to defend this place. That's why we'll wait here until dark before riding down there. When we do, make sure you ride as quiet as possible. Any sound will be enough to send them spilling out of there looking to kill us all. I didn't ride all this way just to get shot on my own property."

"Sure," McCaffrey said. "But what do we do once we get down there?"

For the first time in months, Joseph Mullen broke out into a broad grin. "Then, my grimy friends, we walk into my house and reclaim what's rightfully mine."

The men laughed together, with Geary saying, "Sounds like you've got quite a homecoming in mind for yourself."

But Mullen did not laugh. "Not so much a homecoming. More like as a reckoning."

It was full dark when Mullen led the men down through the valley toward his house. His *home*. He did not need light to see where he was going. He knew every rock and divot of the land as well as he knew his own face. He could have walked it blindfolded and barefoot without so much as stumbling.

He was glad the men had followed his directions about remaining quiet as they rode. Besides the gentle jingling of the bridles, they had not made so much as a sound during their approach. They were riding into the wind, which only served to help them go unnoticed and undetected by the horses in the nearby corral.

Mullen was the first to reach the great ranch house and quietly dismounted in front of his porch. He wrapped his reins around the hitching rail and waited for the others to do the same.

He was glad to see the place had not changed much from the outside. The rocking chairs had not been moved and heavy curtains still hung in the windows. Oil lamps burned steadily from somewhere within. *Awfully cozy, Sarabelle. Awfully cozy, indeed.*

He beckoned the convicts to follow him as he crept up the stairs and pushed in the door. He had never bothered to lock it. No one had ever dared to enter without his permission.

A wave of relief washed over him that almost brought him to tears. The large front parlor stretched out before him and still impressed him as much as it had on the first day it had been built. The furniture was dark and heavy but comfortable. The roaring fire in the fireplace still made the large house feel like a home.

He heard a dish break in the hallway leading from the kitchen to the dining room. He was not surprised to see Sarabelle standing there, her hands brought up to her face. Her mouth hanging open in surprise and terror. She looked as if she might scream had she been able to breathe, but all she managed to do was slowly back away from him.

He drank in her horror as if it were the fine whiskey he had once kept in his den.

"Hello, darling," Mullen said. "I'm home."

Sarabelle screamed now as she blindly backed away from him until she struck a wall.

He glanced behind him and told his companions, "One of you shut the door. The rest of you stand watch at the windows. It appears my wife has had something of a fright."

He took his time walking toward the hallway as Sarabelle slowly sank to the floor. Her eyes grew wider with every step he drew closer. Her screams even louder, longer.

"My dear!" came a man's voice from the dining room. "What's come over you?"

Mullen had just reached the hall when a man stepped out from the dining room. Mullen recognized him as Hank Lassiter. He did not give Lassiter the chance to recognize him before he fired a left hook that connected with the banker's jaw. He watched him collapse and fall backward. He was already unconscious when his head hit the rug beneath the dining room table.

Mullen looked in the dining room and saw no one else there, not even a servant. The table had only been set for two. Lit candles burned in the center of the table.

"Just the two of you for dinner?" Mullen said to his wife. "How romantic. Sorry for barging in like this, but I was anxious to see you. It's been a while."

Sarabelle scrambled from the floor and darted into the kitchen. Mullen laughed as he took his time following her. There was no need to hurry. There was nowhere for her to go.

She headed for the back door but must have seen the reflection of his approach in the glass, for she quicky turned away and made a blind dash for a knife on the counter.

"That's the spirit," Mullen mocked. "That's the frontier girl I married. Just look at that fire in your eyes!"

She stabbed blindly at the air in front of her like a mountain lion lashing out at prey. "If you come any closer, Joe Mullen, I swear I'll kill you!"

Mullen knew how dangerous his wife could be when cornered, so he kept his distance. Just as he had no intention of allowing one of his ranch hands to kill him, he did not wish to die in his own kitchen with a knife in his belly.

"You already tried to kill me once, my love. Remember?" He held out his hands away from him. "Now's your chance to do it yourself." He tapped his chest above his heart. "Come on. One thrust ought to do the trick. Get it out of your system before I lose my patience."

Out of the corner of his eye, he noticed movement from outside the kitchen door. He saw Bart Gamble, his ranch foreman, approaching the house with two other men. All of them had Winchesters at the ready.

Mullen opened the door and stood still until they gradually recognized him.

All three lowered their rifles immediately.

Gamble squinted at him through the growing darkness. "That you, boss?"

Mullen patted the beard he had grown since his incarceration. "It's me, Bart. Tell the men I'm home now. Home for good. Mrs. Mullen and I are just getting reacquainted. Looks like I gave her a start, showing up like this."

"Home for good?" Gamble repeated. "That true?"

"It's a lie!" Sarabelle shrieked from inside as she held the knife at him with two hands. "He's escaped somehow. Shoot him, Bart. Just shoot him now!"

Mullen knew Bart had always been a good worker, but no one would ever confuse his loyalty for genius. "Don't mind her. The law and I had a bit of a misunderstanding, but that's all over now. I've even managed to bring home some new friends I made in prison. Mind if I send them over to the bunkhouse in a bit? See if you can't get them outfitted somehow. Clothes, horses. Pistols. Rifles. That sort of thing."

Mullen could not blame the foreman for the odd look he gave him. Before his incarceration, Joe Mullen believed in a social structure where those who worked for him were far beneath him and his wife. His employees were not accustomed to him being friendly, much less asking their permission for something.

"Sure thing, Mr. Mullen." Bart was clearly still unsettled by the whole situation. "We'll be happy to. Send them down whenever you're ready and we'll see to it they get everything they need."

"I appreciate it." Mullen decided to add one more thing. "And Bart, make sure none of the boys go to town tonight. I want to make a formal announcement that I'm back, so I don't want any of them to let it slip that I'm home. I still have a few legal details that need to be ironed out before it's all said and done."

"I'll tell them to keep their heads down and their mouths shut," Bart assured him. "You can count on me, Mr. Mullen."

Mullen bid him and the men with him a good night and quietly shut the door. He slowly looked at Sarabelle, who had begun to sob in the corner of the kitchen. She still held the knife before her with two hands, though the blade was shaking much worse than before.

"See that, my sweet? Looks like they still think of me as the boss. You'd be smart if you fell into line with them. But we've got plenty of time to talk about that later."

He called out for Frank and stood smiling down at his wife until Geary came into the kitchen. "What's the matter, Joe?"

"I'll need you and the others to head over to that bunkhouse I pointed out to you on the ride down here. My men will get you better clothes and guns. See if they can't feed you while you're there. Tell them I want them to give you somewhere to sleep, but don't take one of their bunks. It'll only add resentment among the men and I need them happy for now. You understand, I'm sure."

"I understand." The convict glanced down at Sarabelle and grinned. "She doesn't look happy to see you, boss."

"Just an initial shock. She'll get over it soon enough." He had no intention of discussing his marriage with a man like Geary. He and the others had already served their purpose. They had helped him escape from Wheeler's wagon and had gotten him back home. Familiarity in such circumstances could only breed contempt, though he imagined they might prove useful again before long.

"I'll need you to keep an eye on the men for me," Mullen told him. "Don't let on too much about how we met and make sure none of them leave the property either. I want to make sure we've secured our position here before word gets out about my return."

One nod of his head told Mullen that Frank understood. The convict gestured down at Lassiter, who remained unconscious on the dining room floor. "What do you want me to do with him?"

"Leave him there for now," Mullen decided. "He might come in handy sooner than he thinks."

Geary went back into the main room to gather the others and bring them down to the bunkhouse. Mullen waited until the men had left before he turned his full attention to Sarabelle.

Despite her tears, she had managed to hold the knife, but now it sagged in her grip. She slammed it on the counter next to the sink and screamed in defeat.

He took his time as he walked to the hallway and looked down at the banker, who was only beginning to show signs of consciousness.

"Hank Lassiter," Mullen teased his crying wife. "Hardly a good replacement for me, wouldn't you say?"

"The only one who could replace you is the devil himself."

But Mullen disagreed. "No. At least that wasn't true before my trial. I might've run my affairs with an iron fist, but I always had a blind spot wherever you were involved. I suppose that's why you were able to wound me so deeply. I never saw it coming until you had me locked away and slipped all that I had built into your pocket."

"All that *we* built," Sarabelle spat at him. "You would've just been another cow puncher made good if it hadn't been for my prodding. My planning. I'm the one who pushed you into taking a piece of the tables at Cassidy's saloon. I'm the reason why you own the copper and gold mines. I'm the one who you made the old crows in town see as more than just another well-heeled bully."

She flinched when he pointed his finger at her. "Your ideas, my action. And I won't forget that it was your word that cast me aside as soon as you had your chance."

"Because you were growing weak," she told him. "Weak and stupid. Holt had you cowed, and Chapman and Klassen were eating out of the palm of his hand. You were a mighty big man when you were pushing around a bunch of farmers and miners who didn't have the sand to stand up to you, but when Holt came along, you folded just like a cheap parasol. You're nothing compared to the men who had the guts to stand up and fight him."

"And look where it got them," Mullen reminded her. "They're dead and I'm still here."

"You were heading for the grave and don't tell yourself any different," she argued. "I put up with too much for too long to let you just let it slip through your fingers over some lousy lawman. I did what I've been doing every day since my parents dragged me into this wilderness. I found a way to survive."

"By putting me in jail."

"By protecting my interests." She raised her head and pointed her chin at him. "You were already done. You just didn't know it. And I'd do it again if I had the chance because you couldn't beat Holt before and you still can't. No matter how many jails you break out of or how many killers you bring with you. Because it'll always come down to you and him and we both know you just don't measure up."

Mullen took a step back. The heat of her anger staggered him. He had never fully trusted her, but he had never thought she would seek to harm him. Not until the day she had testified against him at his murder trial. Even now, on the long ride back to the ranch, he had held out hope that seeing him again might give her a change of heart. He knew his chances of survival as an escaped man on his own were slim at best. He knew Sarabelle's cunning combined with his grit was the only way he could possibly hope to remain free.

But it was clear to him now that whatever heart she still had was turned to stone as far as he was concerned. He had been fooling himself to believe otherwise.

Whatever happened next, his conscience was clear. If he could not have her love, he would have his revenge.

"You know what, my dear? You've left me no choice other than to believe you. I suppose I'll have to treat you accordingly."

He dove at her when she grabbed for the knife on the counter. He stopped her just before she managed to plunge the blade into her own heart. He wrestled the handle from her grip and threw the knife across the kitchen, where it clattered to the floor somewhere behind them.

She did her best to try to get away from him, though despite his weakened condition, he was still too strong for her. She collapsed against him, racked by heavy sobs.

"That's it," he soothed her as he untied the apron from around her waist. "Let it all out. Holding in all that hate is no good for either of us. We'll need to be strong for the struggle that lies before us now."

She lifted her head as Mullen pulled her hands into the small of her back and quickly bound them there with the strings of her apron. She struggled, but it only served to make the knots even tighter.

"I'm afraid that's the way it'll have to be until I can trust you again. Can't expect me to get a good night's sleep if I'm worried about you cutting my throat in the middle of the night, now, can you?"

She tried to bite his neck, but he backed away before she could reach it. "You'll never be able to trust me again."

He smiled. "Then you'll be spending a lot of time being very uncomfortable. What a shame. You have such delicate hands."

He took her by the arm and pulled her away from the sink. He stopped in the hall, where Lassiter was groaning as he began to attempt to sit up.

A quick boot to the temple sent him flat again.

"Don't get up," Mullen mocked him as he pulled his wife past him. "I have plans for you yet."

CHAPTER 14

D r. Ralph Klassen sat alone at his table in the café and enjoyed his coffee. He had never enjoyed eating alone but, being a bachelor in a town with few single women, had become used to it.

As he digested his meal, he thought about how much his life had changed since the day Mayor Chapman had brought John Holt to town. Devil's Gulch had never been a quiet place. There had always been an element of danger swimming just below the surface. In many ways, life there had been like his time in the army during the War between the States. Long periods of boredom and tedium followed by flashes of violence and bloodshed.

The life of an army doctor was never without some degree of worry. Even quiet times between battles were filled with tending to the sick and the dying. There was an endless stream of sick and wounded who needed care. Broken bones that required tending. Fevers that had to be broken and infections to fight.

This did not count for the ever-present dread of disease sweeping through the ranks.

That was how Doc Klassen remembered Devil's Gulch before John Holt had come to town at the invitation of the late mayor, Blair Chapman. Although it seemed like that had been years ago, the doctor remembered that it had only been little more than a month before. The town was so much different now as most of his friends from the time before John Holt were gone. Mayor Chapman had been cut down in the prime of his life, only to be replaced in office by his wife. Joe Mullen was on his way to spending the rest of his days in territorial prison. Tony Cassidy had found himself once again at the mercy of Ma McAdam and her hired guns.

The players might change, but the object of the game remained the same as Doc Klassen watched it unfold from the edges. And of all the people in town who might be able to understand his unique position, he imagined only Earl Sibert could come close. Devil Gulch's undertaker had enjoyed a dramatic upswing in business since John Holt had come to town.

Not that the dead did not have it coming. Klassen had witnessed most of Holt's gunplay and had yet to see him kill a man without proper justification. But the effect of his violence had caused an uneasiness to settle over the town. People acted differently now. Drunks were less likely to fight out of fear John Holt might be called to put a stop to it. Arguments ceased before they even began lest someone complain to the sheriff about someone disturbing the peace.

Even the tradesmen in town—the butchers and bakers and other merchants—charged fairer prices out of fear that a customer might complain to the sheriff.

Yes, Ralph Klassen decided, John Holt may have been hard on the peace, but there was no denying that his influence had changed Devil's Gulch for the better. Even young Jack Turnbull had commanded respect from the wilder citizens when he used to walk the boardwalks on his regular patrols. He, like Holt, had been sad to see the deputy leave town suddenly and hoped he would return soon.

He pondered all of this as he set his cup back on its saucer because that day had been the first in a while where he felt a disquiet in town. John Holt and the prison cook had left on an errand, only to have Frank Peters watch the jail. It was a strange choice given the former sheriff's fall from office, but he had learned that Holt rarely made decisions without some degree of thought.

Still, it influenced the mood of the town. A relief of sorts, especially among the less law-abiding citizens in the way one is relieved when a boot is removed from a neck. Klassen noted the difference only a short time ago in the people he passed on his way to supper.

They cast an uneasy eye toward the jail and seemed either troubled or emboldened by the sight of Frank Peters at Holt's desk. He detected a slight spring in the step of more than one ruffian when they realized the sheriff was not there.

A mood had rolled through the town like a fog, which concerned Klassen. The cat was away. The mice were about to play.

He was mercifully pulled from his thoughts when he realized Jean Roche was speaking to him.

"Doc? Was the dinner not to your liking?"

He smiled up at the Creole woman. The proprietress of Le Café was much prettier, not to mention more pleasant, than Tony Cassidy and his brooding thugs at the Blue Bottle had ever been. The food was also much better, albeit slightly more expensive. Klassen gladly paid the difference without complaint. It was a small price in exchange for the recovery of his soul.

"The meal was as delicious as always," he assured her. "Just got lost in my own mind for a second. Guess I'm getting old."

"You're far away from old," she assured him. "And you're not the only one around here with troubles. John hasn't come back yet, and that nasty old drunk is still sitting at his desk over in the jail. Looks quite pleased with himself too."

He always enjoyed the frankness with which Jean expressed herself. "I saw him when I stopped by earlier. He seemed alert enough."

"Hungry enough too. He hasn't left so much as a crumb on the plate of any of the three meals I've brought over to him and Simon."

"Can't blame him for enjoying a good meal," Klassen said. "All he ever had at the Railhead is boiled shoe leather and stale beer."

"And his jug," she added. "I'm worried about John."

Klassen had been practicing medicine long enough to know that worry was a destructive and useless emotion. "Don't be. He'd be fine by himself, but don't forget he's got Bob with him. That old mule will be around long after the rest of us are gone."

Klassen was sad to see his assurances did not appear to ease her mind. "John said they'd be back before dark. You don't think they ran into any trouble along the way, do you?"

He offered his most confident smile. "If there was any trouble out there, it ran into the two of them and was quickly handled. I'm sure they're just a bit behind. They'll be back soon."

"I'm not as worried about John as I am about that old fool getting him into some trouble. It's not like John to break a promise."

Klassen had no choice but to agree with her there. Holt had made a promise to uphold the law in town and, despite all the risks to his life, he had done exactly that. He was as troubled by his unexpected absence as she, but in his role as the town doctor, it was up to him to provide comfort, not add to concerns. *First do no harm.*

"I don't think there's been a trouble invented that John

can't overcome." He rested a fatherly hand on her arm. "He'll be fine, Jean. Promise me you'll try not to worry."

"I will if you will." She bent to pick up his dinner plate. "Looks like you've got some things to worry about on your own. Someone outside seems awfully anxious to talk to you."

Klassen casually looked past her and saw a man waiting for him on the boardwalk. He recognized the tall, rangy man who looked just this side of the grave. His pocked-marked skin. His dark eyes that never stopped moving. When he was not watching the street, he was glancing into the café, checking to see if Klassen was still there.

And now that the doctor had noticed him, Tony Cassidy beckoned him to come outside. His rapid gesture conveyed a sense of urgency to his request.

Klassen's dinner suddenly sat uneasily in his stomach. It was nearly impossible to avoid seeing anyone in a town as small as Devil's Gulch, but the doctor had succeeded in putting a thug like Cassidy entirely out of his mind. He rarely thought of the man these days now that he no longer had to break bread with him first thing in the morning. Distance had allowed delusion about hoping Cassidy might forget the debts Klassen owed him.

Jean frowned. "What's the likes of him want with the likes of you?"

"Who knows with him?" Klassen hoped to play off his growing nervousness with a shrug as he finished his coffee. "I guess it would be impolite to keep him waiting, though. I'd best go see what he wants."

Klassen stood and dug into his pocket to pay the bill, but Jean stopped him. "No need for that, Doctor. You can pay me on Friday all at once just like you always do, remember? I won't need it until then."

He felt his face redden with embarrassment. Was he

really that nervous? "Of course. Forgive me. Too much coffee, I suppose."

They bid each other good evening as he took his coat from the back of his chair and put it on. He tugged on his hat and nodded politely to the patrons who greeted him as he walked to the door to meet the owner of the Blue Bottle Saloon.

The only man alive to whom Dr. Ralph Klassen owed anything.

Cassidy grinned as he tipped his hat to him. "Evening, Doctor. Sorry for interrupting your dinner like that, but it's a matter of some importance."

Klassen closed his eyes as he pulled on his gloves. "Don't try to talk like a cultured man, Cassidy. It doesn't suit you."

Cassidy's hoarse cackle grated on Klassen's nerves as the two of them began walking along the boardwalk together. "You're just cranky on account of me cutting your dinner short. You didn't have to rush because of me. You could've just invited me in to sit with you awhile. Would've been nice to meet in a nice place for a change."

Klassen shuddered and not just from the cold. "I don't even like walking with you in the open, Tony. What makes you think I'd want anyone to get the impression that we're friendly."

"Guess you're right." Cassidy shrugged. "We ain't friends, but we *are* partners, ain't we, Doc? Or have you gone and forgotten that already?"

Klassen tried to face him, but was stopped by Cassidy's grip on his arm, keeping him facing forward. "Glad to see you've still got that temper of yours, Ralph. That's good. I hate to see that fire go out in a man, especially you. You just keep walking normal like you were and keep a civil tongue in your head. If you sass me, I might have to backhand you.

Then where would you be? You're the only doc we've got around here. Kind of hard to treat yourself with a broken arm, isn't it?"

Klassen may have thought Cassidy was an idiot, but he had never doubted his cunning for a second. He tried to pull his arm free, but the saloon owner's grip was not easily broken. "I rue the day I ever laid eyes on you."

"I bet you're not sorry about all that money I lent you to buy your office back when you first came to town?" Cassidy reminded him. "Or the bets I took for you in your hopes of paying it back sooner."

But Klassen was sorry. He was sorry for having been foolish enough to see this fiend as anything resembling a friend. To see him as anything but a parasite who never does a favor unless he is sure to benefit in the end.

Such had been the case with Klassen when he had first come to Devil's Gulch. He had been long on memories of the war and short on money. He had found the Blue Bottle Saloon to be more appealing than the gaudiness of Ma McAdam's Railhead Saloon or the other, more run-down places in town.

Predators like Cassidy always sought out the weak in any situation, and Klassen imagined he must have stood out. He had drunk like a fool back then, eager to quell the screams of the wounded in his care and the stench of the dying who were beyond it. He had come to the territory with the hope of putting the war behind him but had brought little else with him. In fact, he had used up what meager sum he had managed to save while an army surgeon to bring him as far as the Gulch.

When Cassidy saw him, he saw a ripe opportunity for a steady stream of money. He had not only staked the young, battle-worn doctor to the money to buy his own office but offered him credit in the various gambling dens he controlled around town that might allow him to win back his debt.

In hindsight, Klassen now saw how much of a fool he had been. Cassidy had never been generous. He had never been a friend. He had seen an opportunity to put the town doctor on a financial leash of his own devising. And every day since, Cassidy pulled it harshly to make sure Klassen did not forget his circumstances.

"How could I ever forget what I owe you," Klassen said. "You've never been shy about reminding me."

"Men remember and forget what suits them, Doc. That's why I work so hard to make sure you don't decide to forget that I own you lock, stock, and barrel." He patted his coat reverently. "Got a signed contract right here that'll be upheld by any court in the land if you doubt me."

Klassen did not wish to be reminded of his servitude. "What do you want, Tony?"

"For once, I'm not asking you for money. In fact, I'm giving you the chance to wipe the slate clean. Erase your debt to me and cross your name out of my ledger for good."

The idea of it was enough to make Klassen stop dead in his tracks. Cassidy never spoke of money idly. In all their interactions over the past several years, he had never so much as joked about completely forgiving Klassen's debt.

Part of him was joyed by the prospect of finally being free of him. But the rest of him feared what that freedom may cost.

"You're not a naturally generous man, Tony. What do you need me to do? I already told you I won't violate my oath. I won't kill anyone or allow anyone to die."

Cassidy seemed to enjoy the idea. "Perish the thought, Doc. I'd never dream of asking you to go back on a promise. And if I wanted someone dead, you'd be the last one I'd call. Why, all I'd have to do is turn my head and spit and I'd hit someone who'd make a better murderer than you. Nope, what I've got in mind doesn't call for any violence. At least, not in the usual meaning of the word. I think it's even legal, if you can believe that."

"Coming from you?" Klassen asked. "No, I can't believe that. What is it?"

"It's your way to a new life, Doc. I'm asking you to run for mayor of Devil's Gulch."

Klassen backed away from Cassidy. The idea was insane. "Have you lost your mind? I'm not a politician. I don't know the first thing about governing a town."

Cassidy shrugged away his concerns. "Don't have to know much about it. Blair Chapman only knew about cuffs and collars before I gave him the job. All you have to do is put your name on the ballot and get enough people to vote for you. Don't worry about that because I'll handle that part of it for you. And when you win, you get to take another one of those oaths you like so much. I'd have thought you'd enjoy that, seeing as how you took one when you became a doctor."

Klassen laughed at the comparison. "Tending to the sick and hurt is much different from running a town."

"Both need care," Cassidy observed, "and care is something you definitely know about. You know how to listen to folks when they tell you what ails them, and you have to figure out a way to make them feel better. That's exactly what a mayor does, except there's a lot less blood involved."

Klassen wanted to shout at him, but remembered they were on the street, so he held on to his temper. "There's always blood whenever you're involved, Cassidy."

"Not this time, I promise you, though I will wind up with a pound of flesh before it's all said and done. Yours." Cassidy pulled a toothpick from his coat pocket, blew the lint from it, and stuck it in his mouth. "See, we don't really care who becomes mayor so long as it isn't Mrs. Chapman. Doesn't suit our interests."

"Our?" the doctor repeated. "We? Just who helped you cook up this crazy scheme?"

"That part doesn't concern you yet and never will if everything goes according to plan. The fact is there's no shortage of men in town who'd be more than willing to run against her with my backing, but none of them are men of your quality. That old woman has gone and taken her husband's office without nary a peep of complaint from the people. It doesn't belong to her."

Klassen fought to keep his temper under control. "It doesn't belong to you either."

"She's used to having her way," Cassidy went on. "Now, old Blair was a simple man willing to listen to reason most of the time. She's not and she has to go."

"Chapman did almost whatever you and Mullen told him to do," Klassen said. "Right up until the day he had the good sense to bring John Holt to town."

"And I'd say that cost him plenty, wouldn't you?"

Klassen tried to swallow but found his mouth and throat had gone dry. He had long suspected that Cassidy had a hand in the mayor's murder. Now the cold look in his eye confirmed it.

"I suppose I could always have someone just shoot her," Cassidy thought aloud, "though it wouldn't look good for the town. Having two mayors in a row get killed like that would raise a lot of eyebrows, especially since they were married."

Klassen began to reach for Cassidy's coat, but the flesh peddler shoved him down a narrow alley just off the boardwalk. The doctor had barely stopped from falling over when Cassidy grabbed him and threw him against a wall.

"Mrs. Chapman doesn't listen to anyone except herself and the town gossips she calls friends. I'm not telling you to like it, but you will put your name on that ballot. We need someone in that office who'll understand who really runs this town. If you refuse, I'll make sure everyone knows you've been working for me for years. Just how long do you think these people will smile at you when you pass when they know Ralph Klassen is nothing more than a degenerate gambler."

Klassen may have been bigger than Cassidy, but he knew fighting him was pointless. Instead of struggling, he found himself nodding slowly as rumors he had heard throughout the day came back to him. "You and the Mullen woman cooked this up, didn't you?"

Cassidy grabbed the doctor's lapels tighter. "I already told you that's none of your business. It doesn't matter anyway because you *will* put your name on that ballot. You don't have to want the job, Ralph. Why, you don't even have to do it after you're elected. But you're the only one who has a chance of winning, so you're going to run." He slipped the contract out from the inside pocket of his coat just enough for Klassen to recognize it. "And on the day you take office, I'll give you a present. This contract. I'll even let you light a cigar with it."

Klassen shut his eyes to try to quell the panic rising in his gullet. "She's a friend, Tony. I never left her side after her husband's murder. I tended her on her sickbed. I won't have a hand in tearing her down now. The whole town saw it. They'd never believe I'd do anything against her. Your plan is doomed to fail before it even started."

Cassidy's eyes narrowed. "The people will believe whatever I tell them to believe." He let Klassen go but poked a hard finger against his chest. "And they'll vote the way I tell them to vote, which will be for you. I put her husband in that chair and I can just as easily pull her out of it. You just do your part. I only told you about this so you wouldn't make a fuss when word got out tomorrow."

"Tomorrow?" Klassen felt like a fool for repeating everything Cassidy said. "When is the election supposed to be held?"

"A couple of weeks," Cassidy told him. "The folks in the capital already gave it their blessing. I want that woman out of office and you in it before she can do too much damage. I figure not even she can wreck everything I've done in such a short amount of time. But she's a determined woman, so there's no sense in discounting her. I'd rather be safe than sorry."

Klassen sagged against the wall. If anyone would be sorry, it looked like it would be him. Mrs. Chapman would never forgive him for this. No matter how it turned out, she would never look at him the same way again. Even when she ultimately discovered that Cassidy had not given him a choice, it would not make a difference. She would curse him for being weaker than her husband had been in his dealings with the likes of Cassidy and Mullen.

If anything, she would view Klassen's betrayal as an even worse offense since Joe Mullen had been sentenced to pay for his crimes.

The saloon owner's glare softened as he patted Klassen on the shoulder. "Don't let it get you down, Ralph. Cheer up. No one's asking you to do anything terrible. It's politics. Bad things happen to good people all the time in politics. It's the people who count." He leaned in closer as he lightly elbowed him in the belly. "But never forget it's people like me who count first. And if you make a scene about not running, she's out of office anyway. Either by ballot or bullet, understand? The choice is up to you."

Klassen watched Cassidy roll the toothpick in his mouth as he left the alley to resume his stroll along the boardwalk to his way back to his lair in the Blue Bottle Saloon.

Klassen tried to push himself off the wall but felt as if his legs weighed a ton. He had no doubt that Cassidy would be more than happy to back up every threat he had made. The saloon owner was not a boastful man. He was competent too. If he wanted Mrs. Chapman removed from office, he would see that it was done. He would see to it that Dr. Ralph Klassen replaced her.

Mayor Ralph Klassen. The mere thought of it was enough to set his teeth on edge. He had never liked politics, much less imagined that he might one day become a politician.

But Cassidy had not given him any choice in the matter. And Cassidy would see him in County Hall no matter what it cost him.

Or Klassen. Or Mrs. Chapman. He would sooner see her dead than remain in County Hall.

He wiped a gloved hand across his damp brow and set off for his office, fearing how much his life would change the next day.

CHAPTER 15

It was almost dark as John Holt continued to ride along the trail behind Bob, and he was reminded of why he had left the army. As a Virginian who had decided to remain loyal to the Union, he had always been looked at with a certain degree of suspicion by officer and enlisted man alike.

No matter how many men he killed or how admirably he had performed in battle, there was always a question about his patriotism. Was he feeding information to the rebels just over the hill? Could he be counted on to kill the enemy when the time came? Was he just biding his time for the right moment to sabotage his men?

Such suspicions had followed him throughout the war and all the way down to New Orleans. And he knew he would never be able to do enough to answer those questions to the army's satisfaction.

He had not fought to win medals or glory. He had not fought for rank. He had not fought to be popular. He had fought because he had taken an oath. Because he knew the cause was just and worth his life if necessary.

He may have been a soldier, but he was also a human being, and the constant distrust of his fellow officers and his men ultimately led to resentment on his part. So when the time for his reenlistment came, he chose to leave the army to forge his own path in this world. His way and according to his own standards.

He did not envision that path leading him to following a prison cook on the trail of desperate men. He did not like being pressed into service at the end of a gun or under the authority of a star. He imagined he still had enough of old Virginia flowing in his veins to brace at any hint of federal authority.

Holt had wanted to hunt for Joe Mullen on his own. His way. And although he could not prove it based on what he had seen back on the hillside, Holt knew Mullen had been responsible for overturning the wagon. He had not done it alone but had undoubtedly talked his fellow prisoners into following his lead. Mullen had a gift for being able to control the weak willed. His time in Devil's Gulch had proven that.

Which was why Holt knew Mullen was now in charge of the escapees. That meant he would eventually make his way back to Devil's Gulch or to his ranch. A smart man would get as far away from civilization as possible. Out of the territory, just as Bob had considered earlier. Perhaps make his way out west where a man's past was not held against him. Even murderers and manipulators like Mullen could find their place in the farthest reaches of the young country.

But Holt doubted Joe Mullen was thinking clearly now. He was not only a creature of habit but a vengeful, proud man. He had been embarrassed by his wife, who had testified against him; by the jury that had convicted him; and by Judge Cook, who had sentenced him to spend the rest of his life in prison.

All those days and nights he had spent locked in a tiny cell, forced to depend upon the good graces of the sheriff he hated, had burned a brand deep in his soul. Just like the constant questions about Holt's own loyalty had turned him against the army for which he bled, Joe Mullen's shame had changed him into something darker.

The law had a way of changing a man. Those who wore shackles. Those who wore a star too. Holt knew Mullen was more dangerous now than ever before because he was desperate. Not just for food or shelter, but desperate to avenge the injustices he perceived had been done to him. Desperate to reclaim that which had been taken from him. And desperate to make those who had turned their back on him pay for casting him aside.

Such desperation made him predictable, which was why Holt knew the best way to catch him was to head back to Devil's Gulch and wait for him to show himself. The men with him would follow willingly for they had nowhere else to go.

Unfortunately, Bob did not agree and as he had the authority, Holt had no choice but to follow him despite his better instincts.

"You still brooding back there?" Bob asked as their horses loped along the trail. "I can hear that mind of yours churning like an old paddlewheel in the Mississippi."

"Not brooding," Holt said. "Just taking stock of my present situation. Sir."

The prison cook glanced back at him. "No need to call me sir, John. I'm not your boss. I just need you to help me track these prisoners to wherever they're headed."

"They're headed for Devil's Gulch. I already told you that."

"If their trail leads back that way, as it surely seems to be, then I won't need your help. I'll thank you for your service and won't trouble you any longer. But if we catch them out here in the open, it'll take both of us to bring them down, especially since they're likely armed. Didn't find Dan's guns on him, so Mullen and the others probably took them with them."

Bob seemed to wait for a response but laughed when all he got was silence. "You wouldn't want a harmless old codger like me to be set upon by a passel of ruffians, would you?"

Holt gritted his teeth. "I'm warming up to the idea."

"That's the trouble with men like you," Bob observed. "You would've insisted on coming along with me anyway, even if I hadn't pulled rank on you. Your conscience wouldn't have let you just ride off to leave me out here by myself. You would've known it was your duty to help me. You just don't like that I pressed you into doing it. That's your pride barking, son, and you know it."

Holt's pride did spark. "It's more about common sense than pride. Let's say we do find them, which is doubtful now given how dark it is. But let's say we get lucky and stumble upon them out here in the woods. Just how do you expect the two of us to corral five men without ropes to bind them or shackles to keep them from running off? They'll slow-walk the whole way back to town and try their best to get away the first chance they get."

"Let's hope that's a problem we need to consider."

Holt rolled his eyes. He could not even pick a fight with the man. "I already know where they're going. If we'd headed back to town when I said we should, we could've stopped them before they get there."

"And if Mullen took them to his ranch?" Bob asked. "Can't be in two places at once, now can we. Or do you figure on pushing exhausted horses farther if you're wrong."

"The livery's got fresh horses."

"Possibly," the cook conceded, "but there's something else you've missed while you've been sitting back there stewing in your own juices. I've been reading this track and I've learned they found themselves another horse along the way."

It had since grown so dark that Holt was having trouble keeping sight of Bob, who was only a few yards ahead of him. "How do you figure that?"

Bob pointed at the ground. "On account of one horse is shod different than the others. The gait is different too. I ought to know, seeing as how I took care of those horses like they were my own kin. Shod them myself back at the prison before we set out. This other track is made by the kind of shoe your liveryman uses in town. I know because they're the same sort of prints we've been leaving behind us all day."

Given the dying light, Holt had to take his word for it. "Could be older tracks."

"Could be," Bob allowed, "but the droppings don't lie." He pointed at a fresh pile as he rode past it. "You can see the difference in them. Most of them are dry. Those'll be from the team horses that were tuckered out from the effort back at the hillside. The fresher piles are from a horse that's been tended to recently, probably as early as this morning. Been well watered and fed too. Grain's my guess. You'd most likely have seen that if you'd been paying attention to your surroundings instead of pouting."

Holt felt his grip on his temper begin to slip. "The only thing I see is you and me being forced to sleep on the cold ground tonight. It's getting so dark we won't be able to see our hands in front of our faces before long. And these horses need rest."

"Then I suppose we're fortunate that we've found civilization." The prison cook pointed through a clearing in the woods toward a farmhouse a fair distance away.

The sight did nothing to quell Holt's annoyance. "We got lucky is all."

"Luck had nothing to do with it. We followed the trail and

it led us here." Bob pulled his pistol. "We're too far away to tell if Mullen and the others are still there. We'll wait until full dark to get closer. I don't want to take chances on—"

Holt stood in the saddle when he saw someone step out onto the porch. He was still too far away to see the face, but he could tell who it was by the way he moved.

"Put that thing away, old-timer. We're among friends." He dug his heels into the horse's sides and rode around him. "That's my deputy up there."

Jack Turnbull and William Henderson eyed the two new arrivals as they hungrily spooned soup to their mouths.

"You should've been more careful riding in here," William said. "We've had our share of trouble today."

Holt had not realized he was hungry until Mrs. Henderson placed the bowl in front of him. "When I saw Jack on your porch, I knew we were safe."

Jack elbowed the farmer. "See, Mr. Henderson? I told you John's smart."

The older man did not seem convinced. "Those escapees could've been holding us in here at gunpoint."

Bob pawed at the soup soaking his beard. "Wouldn't hardly make sense if they were to allow young Jack here walk around as free as a bird if they did. To hear Holt tell it, Mullen doesn't think too kindly of Jack. All those bruises on the boy tell me he's right. Mullen would've had him hog-tied in the barn if he was still here. You and your son too. You should be grateful he only took your horses."

Holt saw Jack brighten like he usually did when he had been proven right. But a glare from Henderson made him think better of it.

"Grateful?" William Henderson sat straighter in his chair. "It's those convicts of yours who ought to be grateful this boy here talked me out of putting them down. We might be farmers, but we're not sheep."

"Will!" Mrs. Henderson chastised him from the kitchen. "Mind your manners. These men aren't only our guests but are men of the law."

"Men of the law are still just men," William said. "They're as capable of an insult as anyone."

Holt did not want bad blood to ruin his meal, especially in another man's home. Besides, disagreements at mealtime always affected his digestion. "Nobody meant to insult you, Mr. Henderson. Bob was just talking about the evil nature of the men you fought off today, not about anyone here. Your family ran them off and put one of them in the ground. That's to be commended. We're just glad none of you got hurt in the bargain."

Tom Henderson spoke before his father could. "Did you arrest all those men yourself, Sheriff Holt? Bet you whooped them good when you did."

Holt used his napkin to wipe his mouth before answering. "I only arrested one of them. A man named Mullen. The rest were part of the prison wagon run by the deputy here. Can't say as I knew anything about the others, but Joe Mullen is a dangerous man."

William frowned at his son's interruption. "Jack told us all about him. I would've been happy to put a bullet in him for you, but young Turnbull here advised caution."

"I'm glad you were wise enough to listen to him, Mr. Henderson," Bob said between spoonsful. "Holt's right about Mullen being dangerous, and he's the nicest of the bunch. The big one you mentioned earlier is named Frank Geary. A judge convicted him of beating three men to death with his bare hands about a day's ride north of here. All of them were armed when he did it and, well, let's just say those men he killed weren't often seen in church."

Henderson did not seem to appreciate the comparison. "Haven't seen the inside of a church in quite a long time myself."

Neither Holt nor Bob saw any reason to carry on the discussion further and turned their attention on their soup.

But young Tom Henderson still had some questions. "What were the other ones like, Deputy? The men who escaped with Mullen and Geary. They sure seemed like rough characters."

Bob looked toward the kitchen at Mrs. Henderson and her daughter, Emma, before saying, "They're less than admirable men, son, but don't press me more. It's not fit conversation for the dinner table or mixed company."

Maddie and Emma laughed from the kitchen, with the mother saying, "Don't worry about our delicate ears, Deputy. I doubt there's anything you could tell us that would offend us. We rode up here from Fort Worth. Any notions we had about the refinement of the human condition were taken from us long ago. Tom there might be young, but he's not a boy anymore. He and Jack are about the same age. Anything you tell him or Emma would be more along the notion of an education than an offense."

Bob grinned at Holt as he gently nudged him. "Why, I think that's the most elegant way I've ever been put in my place." He fixed Tom with a stare. "The one you killed out front was a thief and a rustler named Marty Fraser. Killed a couple of old folks for a plow horse that died a couple of days later. I already told you about Geary, so I won't waste time repeating myself. The other men who escaped with him were known violators of women and were set to hang because of it."

The prison cook shifted his gaze to William, who looked sickened by the news. "That's right, Mr. Henderson. You might not have known it at the time, but Deputy Turnbull there gave you sound advice about staying away from them. All you lost was a couple of horses. Fighting for them wouldn't have done you any good if you were dead."

Holt realized Bob's words had not done much to quell the fire in the farmer's belly, so he added, "All the horses we find will be returned to you as soon as we find Mullen and the others. You'll get them back as quickly as we can manage it. That much I promise you."

William Henderson slowly stood up from the table. "Those stallions weren't taken from you, Holt. They don't belong to you. It's my responsibility to get them back and that's what I'm going to do. With or without help from either of you." He beckoned for his son to get up also. "Best leave these men be and get your rest, son. You too, Emma. The sun won't rise any later and the chores don't stop just because we have guests."

The children reluctantly obeyed their father, bidding everyone a good night as they moved to their beds elsewhere in the house.

Before he left, William said, "We don't have any beds to spare for you boys, but you're welcome to stay out here where the fire's warm. I'll be ready to ride with you early right after I tend to my animals. The one I still have, anyway."

Bob began to tell him that would not be necessary, but Holt spoke over him. "We thank you for your hospitality, sir. All of you have been most kind to us."

Henderson grunted his acceptance of their gratitude before he, too, went off to bed.

Mrs. Henderson moved to a chair in the far corner of the room and began her knitting. "I hope you'll accept my apologies for my husband's lack of manners. We don't get many visitors out this way, and this has been a trying day for all of us."

"No need to apologize, ma'am," Bob said. "We understand."

"Understanding a thing and excusing it are two different things. Unfortunately, William has never been one to tolerate stealing or thieves."

"Can't say as we abide them either, ma'am," Holt said. Now that he had heard the woman speak, he thought he recognized her accent. "Am I mistaken or do I hear a bit of Old Dominion in your voice."

She looked up from her needlework. "You do indeed, sir. Do I hear it in your own?"

Holt smiled. "I guess you never know where us Virginia folks will wind up, do you, ma'am."

"You certainly don't. I'm from just outside Falls Church myself, but my husband is a Missouri man through and through. I'll admit there's times when his toughness is an asset, but he's not always as willing to listen to reason as I'd like. I've managed to wear down some of his rougher edges over the years, but he's still as stubborn as a mule when he makes up his mind."

Old Bob cleared his throat. "Even a mule can listen to reason if the carrot's enticing enough. I'm asking you to talk to him, Mrs. Henderson. Make him understand that going after these men isn't up to him. We'll get back those horses for you, but his place is here."

She lifted her head. "I assure you that William Henderson is a most capable man, Deputy. If he decides to ride with you, you may rest assured he'll prove to be more than valuable."

"And if we tell him we don't need him?" Bob asked.

"Then I'd advise you boys to bring shovels with you when you hunt those men. They'll be needing burying after William finds them." She rose and put her needlework back in the hollow of the chair beneath her seat. "And with that, I'll wish you a good evening. There's more soup waiting for you if you're hungry. Just leave the plates there. We'll tend to them in the morning." She mussed Jack's hair as she passed him on her way to bed.

The boy reddened as he flattened his hair down again.

Holt had never seen his deputy blush before. "Looks like you're right at home here."

He shrugged. "They're nice people. Good people too. I know there's a difference."

"I can see that," Holt said. "You hold any sway with the father?"

"Can't say as I do," Jack admitted. "He blames me for letting Mullen and the others take those horses. The rest of the family knows I was right, even Tom, though he'd never admit it."

"I thought they'd never leave." Bob picked up his bowl and tipped the remaining contents into his mouth. "Never had much use for spoons or table manners. Food is meant to be eaten, not poked at like that woman's needlework."

But Holt did not care about Bob's opinion on proper etiquette. He was still focused on Jack. "I figure now would be a good time for you to tell me where'd you run off to, boy."

Jack reddened again, only much deeper this time. Being embarrassed by Mrs. Henderson was one thing. Falling under questioning from John Holt was quite another.

"My mother died."

Holt did not believe that. "You never made mention of a mother to me. In fact, you always talked about your pa instead."

"I guess she wasn't really my mother," Jack admitted, "but she might as well have been. Raised me like I was one of her own, at least until Pa took me away from her and moved us out into the woods."

Holt was willing to go with it. "How'd you find out about her passing?"

"A man in the Railhead told me what happened two weeks ago. He said he'd ridden through my hometown on his way out here. She owned the dry goods store and when he saw it was closed, people told him she'd died from a fever. I thought it was only right I pay my respects."

"Nothing wrong with paying your respects, but it's just as wrong to ride out without telling me."

Jack looked around the table as if the right words might be found there. "I didn't want to think too much about it out of fear I wouldn't want to go. I knew I'd be sorry if I didn't go, so I just up and left. The sun was coming up anyway, so I knew you'd be at the jail soon. Mullen was still sleeping when I rode off, so he didn't need anything."

Bob stopped drinking his soup long enough to ask. "Were you riding back to town when you came upon Wheeler?"

Jack nodded. "Heard it happen too. When I saw that overturned wagon off the hill, I rode down to see if anyone needed help. The marshal was still alive then, but only barely."

Bob set his bowl down. "Did he say anything to you before he passed?"

"He tried but couldn't manage it. He was in a bad way."

"I know," Bob said. "We saw him for ourselves."

Holt did not want them to dwell on the gory memory. "I guess that's when Mullen and the others grabbed you."

"Sprang up at me like a nest of rattlers," Jack explained. "Before I know it, the big one had a chain around my neck and about a foot off the ground. You would've found me out there, too, if Mullen hadn't told him to let me go. They didn't kill me but kicked the hell out of me instead. They threw me over the back of one of the wagon horses and set about attacking this place. I waited until they were distracted before I set it to running."

Holt was far from happy. "You could've been killed. For that crazy move with the horse. For riding leaving town alone. Did you ever think that fella in the Railhead could've been working for Mullen? That he could've been lying to you to set you up to get grabbed and held against me?"

Bob made a great show of smacking his lips and patting his belly. "Yes, sir! That woman sure can cook. Not enough to make me consider taking up farm life myself, mind you, but enough to make me appreciate it just the same."

Holt was beginning to think the older man was losing his mind. "Keep your full belly to yourself. Jack and I are having a talk."

Bob acted as though he had not heard him. "I do appreciate a good meal from time to time, and appreciation is no small thing. It's a notion that's wasted on young men such as yourselves, but when you get to be my age, it takes on a fair amount of meaning. You come to understand that you might not have all the answers and never will, but answers ain't important. The only thing that's important is what you've got right in front of you, not how it got there. Or where it was. Or why it's there."

Holt understood the old cook's meaning. "Guess we're not talking about her soup anymore."

Bob placed a hand on Holt's shoulder as he pulled himself up to his feet. "Who cares why he left, John. He's young and the young do stupid things sometimes. The only thing that counts is that he's back now. Back safe and sound despite what Mullen tried to do to him. I wish I could say that about Dan Wheeler, but I can't. You'd do well to appreciate what you have now and be grateful that he's alive."

Jack pointed at the deputy. "You ought to listen to him, boss. He's right, you know."

But Bob was not in the mood to accept validation from Jack. "Appreciation goes both ways, youngster. You had a good friend in John Holt here. He's not an agreeable man, I'll grant you. Nor particularly pleasant either. He's given to brooding and a sour disposition that ruins—"

"Enough," Holt said.

Bob stopped his teasing. "Holt's not perfect, but it sounds to me like he gave you a home when you needed one.

Sounds like he was a friend to you when you didn't have any. You'd do well to remember the people who were good to you every bit as much as you remember the men who slight you. Good friends ain't so common that you can just forget about them when it suits you. Just like you stick with them even when they disappoint you."

Holt looked up at the old prison cook. "You a preacher too?"

"Nope. Just born with more common sense than either of you. Now, if you girls could set aside your difference until morning, I'd like to appreciate this fire a spell and get some sleep. It has been a trying day." He hitched up his pants and headed for the front door. "But first, I've got to go hunt for some bandits."

Holt and Jack watched him step outside and quietly shut the door behind him.

"Bandits?" Jack asked. "But he didn't even take his guns."

Holt dropped his head in his hands. It was times like this he remembered just how young the boy really was. "That business about the woman dying true? I don't care if you lied before, but I'll be angry if you repeat it now."

"It's true," Jack said. "I didn't tell you on account I was afraid you might try to talk me out of it."

"I probably would have," Holt admitted. "But I'd like to think I'd have heard you out first. I might've even ridden there and back with you. Not when you left, but after Wheeler took Mullen away. She'd already been gone for a while and the wait wouldn't have mattered much to her."

"I hadn't thought of that." Jack hung his head. "I'm sorry."

But Holt did not want him to be sorry. He wanted him to listen. "You're my deputy, Jack. I count on you to be around when I'm not. To help me handle whatever the town throws our way. I know you're not used to people relying on you, but those days are over. Mullen and the others aren't going to just let us catch them and bring them back to prison. It'll likely mean killing. And I need to know the town will be in good hands while I'm doing it."

Turnbull traced the grain of the table with his forefinger. "Gee. To hear you talk, I might be forgiven for thinking you missed me."

Holt had not thought of it like that. "Guess you're like those mosquitos they had down in New Orleans. It got so that I didn't even realize they were there until I rode north. And then, I just noted their absence. Doesn't mean I missed them."

He watched the boy's eyes water and his lip quiver before he surprised Holt by getting up and coming around the table to throw his arms around his shoulders.

"Sorry."

Holt was not accustomed to receiving affection and he had not been expecting it. But Jack was still a bit young to control all his emotions, so Holt tolerated it. He patted the boy's arm. "Don't be sorry. Just don't do it again."

The boy released him and stood upright. He turned away from him as he dried his eyes with his sleeve. "Guess I ought to go hunt some bandits, too, before I turn in."

Holt called after him as he left. "Just don't wander off again."

Holt was glad to be left alone with the fire. He allowed his mind to wander as he watched the flames dance high above the logs.

He wondered if Mullen was out there in the dark somewhere, huddled over a campfire planning his next move. He wondered if Mullen had already made it. He had been given plenty of time to plan his revenge while he rotted behind bars. He had probably already struck.

Holt hoped it was at his ranch and not the town. At least his ranch did not have any innocents around.

He was glad to have Jack back. He was glad the boy was

safe. He hoped he would be strong enough to live through all the trials that stood before them.

For John Holt knew Joe Mullen would not be placed in chains again quietly. It would most likely mean the end of one of them.

And Holt knew it would not be him.

CHAPTER 16

The sun was just beginning to rise when Holt woke with a start in the chair. The sharp pain in his back and shoulders immediately reminded him of his poor choice in sleeping arrangements. He had not intended to fall asleep in the chair. He had planned to spend the night on watch while he thought about how he would catch Mullen. How his plan depended on where the convicts were hiding. He hated how so much of what he did next depended on the whim of a desperate man.

If Mullen was camped in the open ground, it would be easier for Holt to catch him and the other escapees. If he had gone back to his ranch, catching him would be difficult, but not impossible. The open spaces around the ranch house made it nearly impossible to approach him in daylight. Mullen was said to be a good shot with a rifle. Holt had no choice but to assume that the convicts with him were good as well. Even if Holt could scrounge up a posse to ride out with him, hitting the house during the day would be suicide.

He doubted hitting the place at night would be any easier. He would probably have some of his men standing watch. Holt might be able to use the darkness to get close to the house, but he would still be outnumbered. Not outclassed when it came to shooting but against that many bullets, they only had to be lucky once.

Holt decided the worst situation would be if Mullen retreated to one of the mines he owned in the hills around Devil's Gulch. They were honeycombed with mines that tunneled deep underground. Since coming to town, Holt had heard local gossip that claimed all the mines were connected somehow. It might have only been idle gossip, but if true, Mullen could easily evade him for quite some time.

Hiding in the mines would have been Mullen's smartest move, but knowing the man as well as he did, Holt doubted intelligence was playing any role in his decisions. He and the other convicts had come upon this farmhouse—directly in the path of Devil's Gulch—and kept going. He had sacrificed one of his men to get what he needed.

Mullen was driven by a need to avenge all that had been done to him. To get back what he had lost and to get back at those who had taken it from him. His wife, Sarabelle, was his most likely target, which meant he might already be at the ranch house. From there, he could make his plans in comfort and security.

All these thoughts had been coursing through Holt's mind as he had been looking into the fire. Sleep had snuck up on him at some point in the night. Now it was just after sunrise and pain radiated through his back. So much for an effective brooding session.

He stifled groans as he pushed himself to his feet. Someone had added more wood to the fire, for the flames burned higher and hotter than he had last remembered.

"Good morning," Mrs. Henderson said from the kitchen. "I see you slept in."

"Sleep in?" He squinted at the weak light coming in from the windows to judge the time. "It can't be more than six in the morning."

"I reckon it isn't, but that counts as sleeping in on a farm, Sheriff Holt."

It was one of the many reasons why John Holt had never seriously entertained the idea of becoming a farmer. "Am I the last one up?"

"You are, except for my two youngest ones," she whispered. "The rest of us had chores to do."

Holt had been called many things in his life, but no one had ever accused him of being lazy. "I'm no slacker, ma'am. I'll be glad to pitch in and do my share. Just tell me what needs doing and it's done."

"There's not much for you to do," she said. "Besides, Bob suggested that I let you sleep on account of your rank and all. He told me you needed your rest because of all the big thinking you'll be doing over the next couple of days."

Holt shook his head. Even while he was sleeping, there was no end to Bob's teasing. "He likes to talk, doesn't he?"

"Talked enough for both of us. I wouldn't be surprised if he does it in his sleep." She poured a cup of coffee from a pot and handed it to him. "Drink this down. You look like you could use it."

He thanked her and took the coffee with him as he stood in front of the fire in the hope that the warmth would dull his aches. "Your husband still planning on going with us?"

She frowned. "William Henderson isn't a man to give up on an idea just because he's wrong. When he gets something into that thick head of his, a team of mules couldn't pull it loose."

"Yeah." Holt sipped his coffee. It was strong, but good. "I was afraid of that."

She set the pot on the table. "I think you might be able to talk some sense into him, though. Bob might have more years than you, but I don't think he'll be able to talk Will out of it. He's probably anxious for a new audience to hear all those old war stories of his, not that my Will's ever been much for listening. Jack holds no sway with him on account of him being so young, not to mention a bit scared of him."

Holt sipped more coffee. "Jack has more grit to him than you think."

"The only one who might be able to stop Will from going is you. I'd be awfully grateful to you if you could at least try, Sheriff. His place is here with his farm and his family, not on the trail of Mullen and his kind."

Holt could not argue with her. And there was something in her voice that told him she was not accustomed to asking favors of anyone. "Where is he now?"

"Outside with Bob and Jack, saddling their horses as we speak."

Holt drained the last of his coffee and set his cup down on the mantelpiece above the fire. "I'll go have a talk with him. See if I can't make a dent."

"The children and I would be grateful if you do," she said. "Will hasn't always had a healthy respect for the law, but that was long ago. I just can't think of losing him. This place has already taken so much from us."

Holt offered her a smile as he stepped outside, but it did nothing to remove the concern lining her face.

Holt found Henderson outside the barn with Jack and Bob. Jack's mount was already saddled and hitched to the top rail of the corral while the young man tended to Holt's horse. The animals looked well-fed and rested. At least they were in good shape to make the quick ride back to town.

After bidding each other good morning, Holt asked Will if he could have a word with him in private.

But Henderson would hear none of it as he set the saddle across his horse's back. "I imagine my wife sent you out here to try to talk some sense into me. You can save your breath because I'm going no matter what you say."

"He's right," Bob said as he fussed with his saddle. "That man's more stubborn than a Missouri mule. Meaner too."

"As I'm from Missouri, I'll take that as a compliment," Henderson said.

But Holt was not so easily put off. "Be reasonable, Mr. Henderson. This isn't your fight. You and your family are doing something noble here. Something important. You're working the land and feeding your family. You're tending stock and putting down roots. Roots need tending if they're to take."

Henderson continued to fix his saddle. "My son and daughter are near enough grown to take care of my wife and babies if the need arises. But it won't come to that. I don't plan on dying on them if that's what's worrying you. I know all about those fellas. They don't know anything about me."

Holt did not give up. "Men like Mullen and the others don't amount to much when compared to men like you. Who cares if they took some clothes and some prized horses? We'll get them back for you in a couple of days. Men like me and Old Bob and even young Jack here do this work for a living. We're used to it."

"I wasn't always a farmer, Sheriff." Henderson adjusted the saddle and bent to buckle it beneath the barrel of his horse. "I've gone up against plenty of men like Mullen and his ilk before and I'm still kicking. And I'll be kicking still when I bring my property back. Clothes, horses, and some more in the bargain if I can lay my hands on it."

Holt was quickly beginning to doubt he could talk Henderson out of it. "Mullen and the others with him aren't men. They're wolves walking around on two legs. They don't care who they hurt or what they steal. They only know what they want or what they think they need and won't let anyone stand in their way." He gestured toward Bob and Jack. "We don't have anyone depending on us like you do. No one will miss us if we're gone. Your son and daughter might be able to keep this place running if something happens to you, but they're entitled to have a father and your wife a husband. She didn't marry you just to become a widow."

"She didn't marry a coward either." Henderson finished adjusting his saddle and picked up his rifle from the ground before sliding it into the saddle holster. "Save your breath for the ride ahead, Holt. You're just wasting it on me."

Old Bob stepped forward and placed his hand on the stock of Henderson's rifle. "Listen to him, son. I know what you're feeling. I've been there plenty of times myself. A bunch of low accounts came onto your land and took something that was rightfully yours. Something you tended to and cared for as if it was your own child. That ain't right and no one is trying to tell you it is. But let Holt and me run them down and lock them up so they can't do this to you or your family ever again. Going after them is up to the law, and Holt and me are the law. Even young Jack over there too."

Holt sensed a crack in Henderson and did his best to widen it. "He's right, Mr. Henderson. He's not right often, but he is now. All that gray hair of his ought to tell you he knows what he's talking about. Leave Mullen and the others to us. You've got more important concerns. And we'll see to it your horses are returned to you."

But Holt could tell by the look in the farmer's eyes that he had been wrong about the crack in his resolve. Their best attempts had failed.

"Last night my wife told you we came up here from Fort Worth. That's where I wound up after the war since there wasn't much to go back to in Missouri. It's where we met. I spent a fair amount of time in that town doing things I doubt either of you ever considered to survive. I didn't let anyone take from me then and I'll be hung if I'm going to let them do it now. A life's not much good without rules and I won't have my boy thinking his old man was content to allow a passel of thieves and murderers to just ride into his home and take what don't belong to them. I'm teaching him about more than just being a farmer. About more than just tending to livestock. I'm teaching these children how to live in this world. And you can't live unless you defend what you have."

He looked at Bob. "So, if you don't mind, take your hand off my rifle because I've got to finish getting ready."

Bob immediately let him go. "Sounds like you've made up your mind."

Henderson made sure his rifle was snug in the holster. "Mister, I made up my mind the second those men stepped foot on my property."

Holt, Old Bob, and Jack watched Henderson walk back into the barn.

"I told you he was stubborn," Jack reminded them.

"Yes, you surely did," Bob said, "but it didn't hurt to try. My conscience is clear no matter what happens to him."

Holt normally admired stubbornness, but not when there was so much to lose. He only hoped William Henderson did not learn that lesson the hard way.

CHAPTER 17

Mullen sat up in bed, glad to feel the warmth of the sun on his face for the first time in weeks.

The window in the jail was too small and high on the wall for him to get much sunlight each morning. He had to make do with whatever bled into the back of the jail when the door was open. Jack Turnbull had taken him outside to relieve himself a few times a day, but he hardly had time to enjoy the sun under such conditions.

He had never thought much about the sun until he had been in jail. Oh, he cared when it rose and its location in the sky, but only insofar as it affected his business. He had never enjoyed it for its own sake. For its own unique part in creation.

Jail had given Joe Mullen a special appreciation for much of what he had taken for granted for so long. Sunrises and sunsets. Good coffee and decent food. A warm comfortable bed. Money in his pocket and plenty of friends.

He'd once had all those things, of course, and knew he would have them again. Soon. He might have to dig himself out of the legal hole he was in before he regained what he lost, but he had built up from nothing before. He knew how to do it.

After stretching new energy into his limbs, he swung his

legs out of bed and looked down at the pile of bedclothes
in the far corner of his bedroom. He rubbed the sleep from
his eyes and remembered it was Hank Lassiter. He had left
the banker bound and gagged when he fell asleep. He had
thought there was no better way to prove a man was defeated
than to make him watch you sleep. Besides, with Sarabelle
locked in the cellar, he wanted to make sure the two were
kept far apart. If she managed to escape, it would be an
annoyance. If Lassiter got free, it would spell disaster for
his plans.

"Morning, Hank," Mullen said. "I trust you slept well."

The president of the Farmer and Miner's Bank muttered
a response ruined by the gag over his mouth. Lassiter had
been a fastidious dresser, almost too much so for Mullen's
tastes. He preferred expensive clothing and cigars that
showed the world his wealth. He was known for hosting
large dinners that remained the talk of the territory for weeks
afterward.

He wondered if any of the leading citizens of Devil's
Gulch would recognize the rumpled, frightened man in the
corner now. His normally coiffed hair looked like a rat's nest.
His collar gone. His shirt wrinkled and sweated through.
And the eyes that had often looked at the rest of the world
with such disdain blackened from the beating Mullen had
given him.

Lassiter continued to try to speak through his gag as
Mullen pulled on his robe. "That's the problem with you,
Hank. You're always looking to talk even when you have
nothing to say. I hope you won't hold what happened last
night against me. After all, Sarabelle is still my wife and it's
entirely in my rights to defend her honor. What would people
think of me if I let you swoop in like a hawk to steal her from
me while I was in prison?"

Mullen could tell from the tone of his muted mumblings
that Lassiter might be pleading for his life. He decided to let

him sweat a while longer. "I can't blame her for choosing you, though. You were always a bit of a dandy, though quite a wealthy and powerful one. Sarabelle has expensive tastes thanks to me."

Lassiter struggled to raise his bound hands to Mullen as if praying for his release.

Mullen sat at the end of his bed and wagged a finger at him. "And don't think I don't see why you had designs on her either. You could use her property and influence to your benefit. Why, in a year or so, you'd probably be one of the most dynamic couples in the territory. With your money and her drive, I'd say you might even become governor as soon as we become a state."

Mullen frowned when he realized Lassiter had begun to sob. "There's no reason for tears, Hank. I was cross with you last night, but we're beyond that now. You and I are friends again."

The banker looked up at him with hope in his swollen face.

"And friends do things for each other, don't they? They help out when fortune turns against them. And while you never once stopped by to visit me while I was rotting in jail, I don't hold it against you. But you can make it up to me."

Lassiter mumbled something through his gag and Mullen decided there was no harm in hearing him out. He stepped over and pulled down the gag. "What was it you were trying to say?"

"That you're a madman," Lassiter slurred. "I don't know how you managed to escape, but whatever you're planning now won't work. Every lawman in the territory is out looking for you at this very moment. Why, they probably already have the place surrounded."

"Do you really think so?" Mullen threw back his head and laughed. It was the first good, deep laugh he'd had in weeks. "Oh, Hank. It's people like you who are going to build this country. Your eternal optimism will serve you well. No one's looking for me yet. Later today, perhaps, but not right now."

Mullen took a knee beside his captive. "No one has us surrounded. No one even knows I'm free. Word of my release hasn't even reached Devil's Gulch yet, much less Golden City or Washington, D.C., not that I'd imagine they'd care much about me in Washington. The president has quite a few other more pressing matters before him these days."

"Maybe they don't know about you," Lassiter said, "but my bank is scheduled to open any minute now and I'm the one who opens it. When I'm not there and when I don't send word that I'm not coming, they'll raise an alarm. A few people knew I was coming here last night, and it won't take long for them to send someone out here to check on me. When they do—"

Mullen was beginning to get a headache and clapped his hand over the banker's mouth.

"No one knows you're here because you wouldn't risk the scandal. They won't come looking for you because they won't know the first place to look. But they will. Yes, Hank, they certainly will. Would you like to know why?"

He tightened his grip on Lassiter's face and forced him to nod.

"Because I'm going to tell them. That is, we're going to tell them together."

Lassiter cried out when Mullen grabbed his bound hands and began to drag him across the floor. He pulled him just high enough to drop him into the chair that stood before his wife's writing desk.

The banker began to fall off the chair, but Mullen jerked him into the seated position with a handful of hair. He made Lassiter jump when he brought his hand down flat on the desk. "There's a pen and ink and paper. I want you to write two letters for me. For us, really. One to that wretched weasel Norman Selwyn telling him I've got you captive."

Lassiter strained his neck to look up at him. "You want me to write that?"

"Of course. It's the truth and we have nothing to fear from the truth, do we? I want you to tell him I have you hostage and that I'll kill you unless he wires the governor and gets him to grant me a pardon."

"You're insane! He'll never—"

Mullen made him cry out with another tug of his hair. "Don't worry about what Selwyn does. Just worry about doing what I tell you. You're going to write that I don't want a cent, just a piece of paper with the governor's signature on it granting me a pardon. It must also clearly state that all of my holdings will remain mine." He pulled the paper closer to them. "Don't worry about remembering all that. I'll be right here to remind you."

Lassiter reached for the pen, but his hand was shaking too much, and he stopped. "Y-you said two letters. Who will get the second one?"

"That one is special. That one will go to my old friend Judge Cook. But Selwyn's first, as that one is the most important."

Mullen grabbed his wife's silver letter opener and held it to Lassiter's throat. "Prison has only served to make me more impatient and ill-tempered than you remember me, Hank. I advise you get started right now. We've quite a bit of business before us."

Once the notes were written, Mullen doubled Lassiter's gag and bindings and redeposited him in the same corner of the room where he had spent the previous night.

Mullen took Lassiter's letters downstairs, ignoring the pounding he heard coming from the door to the basement.

He had not been able to bear the idea of keeping her hands tied all night. She had such delicate wrists.

He stepped out onto the back porch. For once, he was glad to see his twenty men milling around not doing anything. He saw Geary and Gamble huddled away from the others. *Not much good could come of that.*

"Frank! Bart!" he called out to them. "I need you boys to saddle up some horses and ride over here. I've got something I need you to do for me."

The two men took hold of horses tied to a hitching rail and promptly rode over to the ranch house. Bart got there first. "What do you need us to do, sir?"

He handed him the note for Norman Selwyn, the bank manager. He handed the note for Judge Cook to Geary. "I'm giving each of you boys an assignment. It's perhaps the most important thing I've ever asked you to do, Bart."

"I've never let you down before, sir. I won't start now."

Mullen had heard a lot of promises over the past month or so. Most of them had come from his lawyer, Ty Arbour, about his freedom. Given his current predicament, he did not place much trust in promises, but Bart had always been a different sort. He was a capable man, so long as he was not asked to do too much. That was why Mullen knew he was perfect for this.

"Just give that to whoever is in charge at the bank. It's addressed to Norman Selwyn, but anyone will do. Make sure they understand it, then leave."

He looked at Geary. The big man looked like he was eager to please his new employer.

"Frank, that note is for Judge William Cook. You'll find him in his chamber upstairs at County Hall. You're going to need to be firm with him. I don't want you to kill him, but don't let him boss you around either. If he protests, make him come with you, but do what you can to make sure that isn't necessary. I hope news of Lassiter's imprisonment will be enough to quell any notions of bravery on his part."

Geary took the note and slipped it into his shirt pocket. "Sure, Joe, but what about the lawman in town? That Holt fella won't take too kindly to me just grabbing hold of a judge."

But Mullen had already considered that. The key part of his plan was the note to Selwyn. The cooperation of Lassiter's bank was vital to convincing the governor to offer him a pardon. Half of the leaders in the capital, including the governor, did business with Lassiter. He was counting on their willingness to protect the goose that laid the golden eggs that kept them rich.

Having Geary bring Cook to the ranch to assure he had Lassiter was just a dramatic gesture. Geary was liable to get himself killed in the process, which was acceptable. It would also allow Holt to feel he had stopped Mullen's plans. Let him think Mullen was irrational. He would use that belief to undo Holt once and for all.

He looked at both men. "I'll expect both of you back here within a couple of hours. Don't stop for a drink and don't talk to anyone. Is that clear?"

"Don't worry," Geary assured him. "I know just the right tone to take, especially with a judge. Leave it to me."

Bart looked less certain of himself as he joined the new man in climbing on his horse and riding toward Devil's Gulch.

Mullen watched them ride away, wondering what might await them there. The chances of both of them coming back alive were slim. But if only one of them succeeded, it would be enough to carry the day in his favor.

And if they failed, well, he had plenty more men.

CHAPTER 18

Frank Geary had not thought much of Devil's Gulch the first time he had been forced through it in Wheeler's prison wagon. His opinion had not changed now as he rode toward it a second time. The boardwalks were uneven. The buildings were crooked and already beginning to be reclaimed by the mud. The few people on the streets looked like they were stuck there. The surrounding lands were beautiful, and the mountains were majestic, but a man could not live on scenery. The town itself was a miserable and dank place. He'd be content to leave it to the rats and dirt.

He did not understand why Mullen had wanted to risk so much to come back here, but he knew the world looked different to a man who had a piece of it. Geary had never owned much in his life. Not as a boy on his family's farm in Ireland. Not in the bag he had brought with him across the Atlantic and not since. He had been to San Francisco and decided that was a city. Warm and sunny and full of life. It was a place he intended on seeing again once he felt he had repaid his debt to Mullen. It was the least he could do for the man who had kept him out of prison.

Geary kept his eyes moving as he and Bart rode through town toward their respective destinations. He was on the lookout for that cackling old prison cook and Sheriff Holt among the faces he passed. He had never seen Holt in action, but he knew the man by reputation. And having seen him himself when he was on the prison wagon, Geary could tell he was every bit as dangerous as he was supposed to be. He did not doubt Holt would kill him on sight if he recognized him.

The prison cook's cackling laugh and folksy demeanor on the trail had not fooled Geary. He had ridden too many miles with him and Wheeler to know Old Bob was no fool. He was always sure to hang a good distance behind the prison wagon, watching, and listening while he made like he was singing to himself. His food was good and had kept them alive, but all the complaints about his creaky bones and old age only served to remind Geary that there was more to the old codger than he let on. And he knew if anyone had tried to make a break for it during a meal, Old Bob's bullet would find them before Wheeler's gun cleared leather.

Which was why Geary was glad that Bart had decided to take the long way into town, only chancing being seen along Main Street when they were close enough to the bank and County Hall. The less anyone saw them, the better for all concerned.

After they tied their horses to the hitching rail and climbed down from the saddle, Bart said, "You take the judge and I'll take the bank. Be mindful of that old man. He's a spitfire when he's challenged, and you'll be challenging him now."

"That's too bad," Geary said as he headed toward the judge's chambers in County Hall. "So am I."

Geary could sense Bart was still looking at him as he entered the building. He did not like the ramrod. Then again, Geary had a natural distrust of anyone in authority and Bart was the top man at Mullen's ranch. The sooner he left for San Francisco, the better.

Geary had no idea if Mullen's scheme would turn out the way he had planned it or if it would get them both killed.

He was living on borrowed time anyway and anything beat another minute in the back of that rancid prison wagon. The prospect of spending the rest of his life behind bars did not interest him either. He would gladly take anything that came his way for this was a path of his choosing.

Geary was glad no one seemed to pay him special attention—much less recognize him—as he walked into Judge William Cook's chambers. There was no one in the office and Geary began to wonder if the judge might be elsewhere. A rattling cough from another room deeper in the office told him he was not alone.

He followed the cough and wound his way between desks and found a round man with a crown of white hair sitting behind a high, uneven stack of papers. Geary had been proud of the fact that he had taught himself to read but doubted he could ever sit in a place like this and spend so much time going over all those words.

Just about the only thing worse than reading would be having to listen to all those people talk to him so much. Lawyers loved to talk, whether they were saying anything or not.

"Yes, yes?" said the judge without looking up from his work. "I'm very busy so state your business or get out."

A quick glance around the office proved they were alone. Geary wanted to keep it that way and quietly shut the door.

Judge William Cook glared up at him from behind his rampart of paper. "I didn't tell you to shut that door. You'll open it this instant and get out."

"Not until I do what I'm here to do, Your Honor." Geary took the note from his shirt pocket and handed it to the judge. "Came here to deliver that to you directly. From your favorite citizen. He told me to wait for your answer, though I already know what it's going to be."

For the first time since he had barged into the office, Geary began to detect a bit of fear in the blustery old man.

A look in his eyes that showed he was beginning to grow concerned.

Judge Cook opened the note and replaced his spectacles on the end of his nose as he began to read.

Judging by Cook's expression, the judge did not like it one bit. "Is this really from Mullen? Is this some kind of sick joke?"

"You see me laughing, Judge? It's real enough. I brought it straight from his hand to yours directly."

"But that's impossible." Judge Cook tossed the note on his desk. "He was taken to the territorial prison. Marshal Wheeler hauled his worthless carcass away himself."

Geary cracked a smile. "I know all about Wheeler, Your Honor. I know that his wagon flipped over, and Wheeler died. Died bad too. I know all the men he was toting in the back escaped because, you see, I was one of them."

The judge looked as if he might let loose with a holler, but Geary drew his pistol and aimed it at him before he could make a sound. "That's right, Cook. I'm an escaped convict, too, and I've got as much to lose as Joe Mullen. But just because we're desperate doesn't mean we're stupid. Joe wants you to come out from behind that big desk and ride out to the ranch with me like he wrote. You'll do it now and you'll do it quiet, or you won't have to worry about anything anymore."

Cook whisked off his spectacles and slapped them against Mullen's note. "He must have lost his mind. I sentenced that man to spend the rest of his life behind bars. He'll kill me the moment he lays eyes on me."

"Maybe, but I'll kill you if you don't." Geary readjusted his grip on the pistol. "So quit fussing and let's go. Nice and quiet and slow. Act like I'm taking you for a nice meal, that is if you've got any nice restaurants in this dump."

But Judge Cook would not be hurried. "I'm not going anywhere until I know Hank Lassiter isn't at his bank. This could all be some kind of lie just to get me to ride to the middle of nowhere with you." He pointed up at Geary. "I've known Lassiter for almost ten years, and he's never missed the chance to open those doors personally. Not even when he was half crazed with scarlet fever. His bank is just up the boardwalk, only a few steps from here. If Mullen really is free and he really does have Lassiter, it'll be easy enough to prove. Then you have my word I'll go with you privately."

Geary had never considered himself a smart man, but he had common sense. Nothing the judge had said sounded unreasonable. He had seen the bank when he hitched his horse to the rail. It seemed close enough.

"Sounds fair so long as we get moving right now."

The judge began to stand when Geary thumbed back the hammer. "But don't go getting any foolish ideas that you can try to get away from me. I'll have this gun buried in your back the entire time. You try anything and you'll be trading those papers for a harp."

Judge Cook's eyes hardened as he looked down at Geary's gun, then back up into the face of the man holding it. "If you were a wise man, you'd give up this business right now. I can recommend leniency for you if you do. Might shave some years off that sentence of yours."

Geary laughed. "Thanks, pop, but I've already done that myself. Shaved them all off, right down the bare skin like the top of that bald head of yours. And I don't aim to go back neither." He wagged the gun toward the coat on the back of Cook's chair. "Now get moving."

Ty Arbour, Esquire, climbed the steps to Judge Cook's chambers to file some briefs with his cousin Les Patrick, who did double duty as the prosecutor and town clerk.

His newest client, Simon Smith, was scheduled to appear before the judge within the hour. Simon was a gambler who had pulled a knife on Ma McAdam at the Railhead Saloon the day before last. Despite that, Simon was harmless. Arbour had hoped Judge Cook would issue a summons and let him be on his way. But this was the third time he had appeared before the court for a similar offense, and the judge sought to make an example of him.

Arbour might have been the opposing counsel in Devil's Gulch, but he had never seen his cousin or Judge Cook as his enemies. The law was the law, and in his experience, it benefitted everyone eventually. Arbour had never bothered himself with the notion of whether his clients were guilty or innocent. He only cared about what could be proven and disproven in court. He knew he had his work cut out for him with the Smith case.

Arbour never minded going to the judge's chambers when the course of his duties called for it. He always looked forward to seeing his dour cousin and, if time allowed for it, bantering with old Judge Cook.

"Brass Billy," as he was known in certain parts of the territory, was a man of definite opinions about almost any subject at hand. Arbour found him easy to rile and very entertaining when he was.

Arbour had just reached the outer office when he heard Judge Cook speaking to someone in an odd tone before he heard a door slam.

That was strange. The judge preferred to shut the outer door that led to the hall rather than his office door. He said his office was too small for the door to be closed comfortably. Arbour had always thought he suffered from a mild fear of enclosed spaces.

The judge may have been a volatile man, but Arbour could never remember a time when he had slammed a door either. He preferred to keep a calm and dignified environment in his chambers. He encouraged spirited debate of the law, but these discussions rarely resulted in anger.

Arbour looked around the office but saw no sign of his cousin Les or anyone else. He set his client's paperwork on Les's desk and strained to hear the raised voices through the closed door to the judge's office.

He heard Judge Cook demand the door be opened and a man, whose voice was not Lester Patrick's, refuse to obey him.

Ty Arbour knew that something was seriously wrong, and Judge Cook was in dire trouble.

Since the judge forbade attorneys from coming to court with a pistol on their hip, Arbour was unarmed. He had seen his share of battle and blood in the late War between the States but trying to rescue the judge by himself in a cramped office would only make matters worse.

As he slowly backed out of the office, he thought about running to get John Holt. He'd know what to do. But Holt had left town the previous morning, leaving only Frank Peters in his place. And since Jack Turnbull was still missing, Arbour knew Judge Cook's life was in his hands.

Although Arbour did not have a gun, he knew where to get one.

He quietly closed the outer door to the judge's chambers to prevent anyone else from stumbling upon the scene and possibly getting themselves or Cook killed.

He raced back downstairs, looking for anyone who might be able to lend a hand. Anyone who might be armed. But the building was quiet, so he ran outside.

Once on the boardwalk, he looked for Lester or someone riding by with either a gun on their hip or a rifle, but it was the same merchants and laborers he saw walking through town every day. They would be of no help.

He looked to the jail in the hope that Holt might have come back to town, but the door was closed and there was no sign that anyone was inside. Peters had probably already crawled back into the bottle.

He thought about running back to his office to grab his

pistol, then rush back to County Hall. He knew that would be difficult, as his office was on the opposite end of town and the judge could be long dead by the time he got back.

It was only then that Ty remembered the bank had armed guards. They had hired on more men after the place had been robbed by the Turnbull boys several weeks before. If he could get one of them to help him, or at least lend him a pistol, he might be able to help Judge Cook.

CHAPTER 19

"This is outrageous," said Norman Selwyn, the manager of the Farmer and Miner's Bank. "I refuse to allow this institution to be blackmailed like this. How do I know you even have Mr. Lassiter?"

"That's his handwriting on the note. Who could've written it other than him?"

"Anyone," Selwyn countered. "Mr. Lassiter has a common handwriting."

Bart Gamble had not expected that kind of answer. He was not accustomed to dealing with men who did not answer to him. He was not even used to dealing with Mr. Mullen or his wife, who often gave him a free hand to do as he saw best. He had always preferred the company of livestock to people anyway.

But this business of riding into town and making threats was beyond him. He had always prided himself on being the top hand of the Mullen Ranch, which was no easy feat given the size of the place. He could run a cattle drive or push livestock from one field to another with hardly a thought. Strong-arming a banker was as beyond him as arguing with him.

"I was sent here to deliver a message and I delivered it," Bart said. "This ain't a holdup and I don't expect to go walking out of here with a couple of bags of gold. But I do expect you to send that telegram to the governor like Mr. Lassiter begged you to. If you don't, I can't say how long your boss will be in this world."

Selwyn crumpled the note into a ball. "You can be certain I will take up this matter with Judge Cook and Sheriff Holt before I so much as look in the direction of the telegraph office. And you may rest easy, Mr. Gamble, that during the course of my discussion with them, I'll be certain to swear out a warrant for your arrest!" The smaller man surprised him by getting to his feet and thrusting his finger at him. "This institution will not be threatened by you or Joe Mullen or anyone else."

As Bart backed away from Selwyn's desk, he could feel everyone in the bank looking at him. He remembered hearing some of the men at the ranch talking about the bank hiring extra guards since the robbery the previous month, but Bart saw no sign of them.

Selwyn only seemed emboldened by the attention. "And if Mullen decides to kill Mr. Lassiter, then it will only be another item at the end of a very long list for which Mullen will assuredly hang!"

The banker plucked his hat and coat from the coatrack beside his desk and stormed away.

Bart had not counted on a man who worked in a bank, much less one who wore glasses, to be so forceful. When he saw Selwyn was almost out the door, he decided it was time to get back to the ranch. He doubted Geary and Judge Cook would be ready to ride so soon, but he did not care. He could not report back to Mr. Mullen if he was locked in a jail cell.

Bart pushed past the employees and customers in his way as he reached the boardwalk. He spotted Selwyn between the bank and County Hall, talking to Ty Arbour. He recognized the lawyer as the man who had defended Mr. Mullen in his trial.

Bart was still deciding what to do when Arbour pointed at him. "You, Gamble. Don't move!"

Bart had never been good with a gun but knew how to handle one. He reached for his pistol to keep the attorney at bay, but Arbour was too fast for him.

He pushed Selwyn aside and ran at Bart.

Bart had just begun to clear leather when Arbour delivered a heavy right hand to his jaw. But Bart managed to remain on his feet until Arbour tackled him to the ground.

"Help him!" Selwyn yelled at the passersby who cleared out of the way of the scuffle. "Bart has a gun. Grab his gun, Ty! Grab it before he can."

As the attorney lunged for his gun hand, Bart slammed the butt against his temple. Arbour went slack and fell across him. Bart managed to roll him off to the side before scrambling to his feet.

He raised his pistol when he saw another man rushing to him. Bart did not take time to recognize the man before he fired. His bullet struck the man just below his right shoulder as he spun to the boardwalk and fell across Ty Arbour's back.

As Bart scrambled for his horse, he recognized the man he had just shot as Les Patrick, the town prosecutor. The knowledge only made Bart want to get out of town all that much faster.

He saw Selwyn begin to point at him wildly as people rushed to help the two fallen attorneys. "Don't let him get away. Joe Mullen has escaped! Bart Gamble has Mr. Lassiter! He's got Mr. Lassiter as a hostage!"

Despite the shooting, the crowd began to lose their fear. He quickly untied his mount's reins from the hitching rail before he practically leapt into the saddle and quickly brought his horse around. A few citizens had tried to approach him from behind but were easily knocked aside as the horse turned and broke into a gallop back toward the ranch.

Bart knew Mullen would be angry with him for coming back without Geary or Judge Cook, but Bart was beyond the point of caring. Geary had been in prison before. Bart had never even been locked up for being drunk and disorderly. Geary could fight his way out. He would kill if he had to. Bart had already shot one man out of desperation. He decided it would be his last.

As he raced away from town, Bart stole a quick glance behind him to see if anyone was following. He was glad to see everyone was huddled over the wounded lawyers. That was just fine by Bart.

He decided that, once he got back to the ranch, he would get the others to help fortify the place against the posse that would surely come after them. Later that night when his men were either asleep or standing watch, he would ready his horse and ride west.

He had been with Mullen for almost ten years. He was paid to tend to horses and cattle, not to be one of Mullen's gun hands. Mullen's activities in town had never extended as far as the ranch before, but now that they had, he wanted no part of it. The sooner he got away from the place, the better he would be.

Holt, Jack, Bob, and Will Henderson had just reached the outskirts of Devil's Gulch when they heard a shot ring out along Main Street.

Holt drew his revolver as he shouted to the others, "You three get back to the jail. I'll send for you if I need you."

He did not wait for a response before digging his heels into the side of his mount, sending the animal into a full gallop up Main Street. He sped by Le Café without looking to see if Jean was there or not.

He reined the horse to a sliding stop beside the large crowd that had gathered between County Hall and the bank. He peered over the heads of the crowd and saw Ty Arbour tending to Les Patrick, who was on the boardwalk bleeding from a large hole in his right shoulder.

"Hold on, cousin," the defense lawyer said as he clamped his hand over the wound. "Doc Klassen is on his way. He'll be here any minute."

Holt kept his pistol in hand as he looked over the street for the shooter. "What happened?"

Norman Selwyn answered for him. "Bart Gamble walked into the bank and handed me a note from Mr. Lassiter. It said Joe Mullen had Mr. Lassiter and Mrs. Mullen hostage. Said unless I wanted Lassiter back in pieces, that I should send a wire to the governor demanding a full pardon for Mullen. Said he was gonna have someone bring Judge Cook out to the ranch to verify it. I was on my way over to County Hall to discuss it with the judge when I ran into Ty. Him and Bart struggled, and when Les tried to help, Bart shot him."

Holt cursed. Joe Mullen had come home after all, just like Holt knew he would. If they had headed straight for town as Holt had wanted to do, he could have prevented this. No, he decided, he *would* have prevented it.

He decided to set his anger aside until he got the situation under control. Les looked pale, but Holt had seen men survive worse wounds. "How's Les faring, Ty?"

"He's strong," the attorney said without looking up. "But he'll do a lot better when Doc Klassen gets here. Looks like the bullet passed right through him."

Holt saw everything that could be done for Les until Klassen got there was being done. He focused on Norman Selwyn. "You said Bart Gamble delivered the note. That's Mullen's ramrod at the ranch, isn't it?"

"The very same," Selwyn confirmed. "Rode out of here like a bat out of hell just before you showed up. I'd bet he's got someone giving the judge the same bad time he gave me."

Holt looked at the edge of town in the hope he might catch a glimpse of Bart as he fled back to the ranch, but there was no sign of him. He was probably long gone by now and would not risk capture by sticking around town.

Holt decided he would deal with Bart another time and climbed down from the saddle. He tossed the reins to a young boy who stepped forward to take them. "Has anyone seen Judge Cook?"

Ty continued to keep pressure on his cousin's wound. "Heard him arguing with a man in his office and came down here to get help. That's when all of this trouble happened."

Holt held his pistol tight as he began to approach County Hall. He spotted a gray stallion hitched to the rail in front of the hall. To an untrained eye, it looked like either of the two horses next to it. Holt could tell by the animal's posture and muscles that this was a special animal. He checked under the saddle and saw a "WH" branded into the leather.

It was clearly William Henderson's horse and saddle, which meant that whoever had Judge Cook was probably one of the escaped convicts. And knowing Joe Mullen as well as he did, he would've sent the toughest man in his group to handle Judge Cook. From what Bob had told him, that meant it was Frank Geary.

"What do you want us to do, Sheriff?" one of the townsmen asked.

"I say we go up there and rush him!" another one called out. "He can't kill all of us before we get to him."

But Holt knew Geary would kill the judge if he had to. "I need you boys to stay out here and keep an eye on the street. There may be more of them in town. If you see Joe Mullen skulking around, raise a holler. I'm gonna check on the judge."

Holt waited for the men to spread out before he slowly walked into the County Hall. He wondered if Mayor Chapman was still in her office or if she had been out of the building when Geary showed up. If he had taken both the judge and the mayor hostage, it would be even more difficult to get them out alive.

Holt took a quick glance through the open doorway. Seeing that both the right and the left stairways were clear, he stepped inside.

He took the left staircase and began to climb them two at a time, careful not to make a sound. The building was always full of sound echoing from somewhere within it most days, but at that moment, an eerie quiet had settled over County Hall.

He kept looking up at the second landing as he ascended. It was not until he was halfway up when a large, muscular man stepped out into view. He had thick curly black hair and dark eyes. He was holding Judge Cook in front of him like a shield and steered the jurist by a thick arm around his neck.

Holt stifled a curse when he saw the judge was bleeding badly from a nasty gash on the left side of his head.

"That's far enough, mister," Geary warned as he pulled Judge Cook toward the right side of the staircase. "I take it by that star on your coat that you'd be John Holt?"

Holt stopped his ascent and began to track the man's movements with his pistol. "And I take it you're Frank Geary."

"You take it right, Holt," Geary sneered from behind the judge's head. "Sounds like you've already heard of me. I heard a shot just now. That your doing?"

Holt shook his head. "That was your friend Bart. Shot the town lawyer before he ran off back to the Mullen spread. Guess he's not as tough as you."

"Guess not," Geary said. "Sound like you've heard of me."

Holt decided to say anything to keep him talking and distracted. "Wheeler's cook has been singing your praises. He was especially impressed by how you killed his friend."

Geary cut loose with a nervous laugh. "Wheeler did that to himself. Served him right for bouncing us all over creation. If he'd been more careful, the wagon never would've flipped. If it hadn't, I'd be on my way to prison right now and you, me, and the judge never would've met."

Holt saw the cut on Judge Cook's head was still bleeding. "Bob also told me you were quite a handful, Geary. The man he described wasn't the kind to hide behind a bleeding old man. How about you turn him loose and let's talk this over."

Geary shook his head. "If that old cook told you anything, it's that I'm not dumb enough to throw down with the likes of you. I'd be dead as soon as you got a clear shot at me. I think I'll keep the judge right where he is." Geary squeezed Cook's neck until the older man cried out. "But I'll promise not to hurt him again if you toss your gun down the stairs for me. As a sign of good faith and all."

Holt had no intention of being unarmed. "Then there'd be nothing to keep you from killing me. But I'll make a deal with you. I'll holster my piece if you promise not to hurt him again."

"Shoot him, John!" Judge Cook called out. "Don't worry about me. Don't let him get out of here alive. He says he's working for Mullen!"

Geary was about to squeeze Cook's throat again, but Holt called out to him. "Don't hurt him. I'm putting my pistol away just like I promised." He slowly slid the gun into place and showed him both hands were empty. "See that? Now let's talk."

Geary tightened his grip around Cook's neck until the judge gurgled. "This old fella I've got here sure is a mouthy one. Mullen warned me about that." Geary smiled. "And I warned the judge here to speak to me nicely. Even cracked his head for him to show I meant business. He doesn't listen too good. Maybe I ought to hit him again to show I'm serious?"

"You hit him again and he's liable to pass out on you," Holt warned. "And the judge isn't exactly a feather. That's a lot of dead weight to lug down all those stairs. It'll be easier on you if you keep him awake."

Holt could tell Geary was barely hanging on to whatever sanity he had. He was trapped in County Hall with Holt and the judge with nowhere to go. He would come to that realization eventually, but not if Holt kept him talking. "But you don't have to talk to him anymore. I'm here now, so we can figure out a way to get you out of this alive."

"I'm already way ahead of you on that score, Sheriff, because here's what'll happen next. You're gonna call down there to your friends outside and tell them to fetch a wagon and two horses to pull it. They're going to leave it right out front so me and the judge can take it back to the ranch. I'll have a gun on His Honor the entire time, so if anyone takes a shot at me, including you, it'll cost this old boy his life."

Geary inclined his head down toward the front door of County Hall. "Go ahead. Might as well tell them now so it'll be waiting for us when we get down there. I don't aim to sit around waiting for one of those idiots to get brave and do something stupid."

Holt cupped his hands together and called down to them. "We need someone to get a wagon with a two-horse team. Move fast. We're coming out."

"See that?" Holt asked. "We're making progress."

Geary laughed. "We did no such thing. They're probably standing around out there like a bunch of scared chickens trying to figure out if you're serious. Well, when they see this gun I've got to the judge's head, they'll know how serious I am."

Judge Cook cried out again as Geary pulled him toward the stairs. "Quit your whining, old-timer. Just take these stairs one at a time, nice and easy. Wouldn't want you to fall, now, would we? With the hold I've got on your neck, it'll break just like a chicken's if you take a tumble."

Holt kept his hands in plain sight as he watched the two men slowly begin their descent. "Take it easy, you two. There's no rush. Just move nice and slow."

Sweat broke out on Geary's brow from the effort of moving Judge Cook down the stairs. "And don't think you're pulling any wool over my eyes, Sheriff. I know what you're up to here. You're just stringing me along to keep me calm while you wait for me to make a mistake so you can shoot me."

Just because Geary was right did not mean Holt had to admit it. "I put my gun away in a sign of good faith, remember? I came in here alone, not with a bunch of citizens looking to tear you to pieces. There's no reason for anyone to die here today. Not the judge and neither of us either."

"Lucky me," Geary said. "Of all the lawmen in the territory and I happen upon the nicest one. Don't make me laugh, Holt. It's almost insulting. Just make sure that gun stays where it is, even when we reach the wagon, because if I die, I'm taking the judge here with me."

Holt decided silence would be better. Geary had likely taken hostages before to get himself out of trouble. He knew someone would try to kill him the first chance they had.

Instead of arguing with him, Holt tried to confuse him. "Is Joe Mullen really back at the ranch?"

"All warm and cozy with his beloved and your banker." Geary and the judge had almost made it halfway down the staircase now. "And if you're working up to asking me if he'd really kill his wife and Lassiter, you can save your breath. If he doesn't get that pardon, he'll happily see them dead."

"What about you, Geary?" Holt asked.

"They've done nothing to me. I don't care if they live or die. I plan on taking off as soon as I've repaid my debt to Mullen."

"I'm not talking about that," Holt explained as he began to match Geary and the judge step for step. "Does he care if you live or die?"

Geary laughed again. "Holt, no one's cared about me except me my whole life. I don't expect Joe Mullen to be any different. You don't think I knew what I was getting into when I delivered his note for him? I knew the cards weren't in my favor, but I did it anyway because there wasn't a good reason to avoid it. I'm not looking to get killed, but I'm not afraid of it either. You'd do well to remember that when the judge and me climb into that wagon."

Holt tensed when Cook's feet tangled up in each other, but the arm Geary had locked around his throat helped him keep his balance.

"Careful, Your Honor. One more misstep like that and you're liable to break your blasted neck."

"Just take your time, Your Honor," Holt encouraged him from the opposite stairwell. "You're halfway down. Just a little more, then you reach the bottom. Go slow."

"But not too slow," Geary said into Judge Cook's ear. "You wouldn't want me to get impatient and toss you down the rest of the way, would you?"

"Scoundrel," the judge croaked, "Miserable criminal."

"You say the nicest things, old man. Now, mind your feet."

Holt and Geary both looked up the stairs when they heard a round being racked into a rifle.

Holt was surprised when he saw Frank Peters kneeling behind the top banister, aiming a Winchester down at Geary.

"That's far enough, convict." Peters's voice was surprisingly strong and clear. "This ends now. Throw up your hands and let Judge Cook go before I kill you."

Mrs. Chapman spoke from somewhere farther behind Peters. "Hold on tight, Judge. We'll get you out of this."

Holt's hand inched closer to the gun on his hip as Geary pressed himself flat against the wall and pivoted Judge Cook between him, Peters's rifle, and Holt. The judge was not a thin man, but it was difficult to use him as an effective shield from all angles.

"You'd best lower that rifle or I swear I'll kill him," Geary roared. "I'd sooner see him dead than give him up now."

Holt could not see Frank Peters well from his spot on the stairway. He could not tell if he was up to the task of shooting Geary. In all the stories he had heard about his predecessor, no one mentioned his skill with a gun.

"Don't shoot, Frank," Holt called up to him. "I've got the situation under control. Just let Geary and the judge continue on their way. I'm right here."

"You're there," Peters answered, "and you're not doing anything. You're just letting this crook dance out of here like he was in the Railhead."

Geary glanced over at Holt behind the cover of the judge. "This your idea of a joke, Sheriff?"

Holt held his left hand up toward Peters as if it was enough to hold him back while he waved his right for Geary to see. "Just look at me, Geary. I'm with you and I'm not going for my gun."

"Then who's that idiot upstairs?" Geary roared. "Looks like the town drunk to me."

Holt yelled back before Peters could respond. "He's nobody. Just someone who cleans the court. He thinks he's helping, but we don't need his help, do we Geary. We've got this all worked out between us, don't we?"

Holt's stomach ran cold when he saw the convict's eyes change. The realization that he was trapped came to life and he suddenly began to doubt his prospects of getting out alive. He stole a quick glance down the stairs and saw he was completely exposed at that angle, before turning his attention back up toward Peters.

Geary began to pull Judge Cook farther down the stairs as he yelled up at Peters, "You stay right where I can see you and no one gets hurt."

Holt could tell he was beginning to panic and knew now was as good a time as any to try to rescue the judge.

He quickly grabbed the banister as he shouted down toward the door. "No, Jack! Stay outside. He'll kill the judge!"

Geary tightened his grip on Judge Cook's neck as he pulled him around as cover between himself and the front door of County Hall.

Holt pulled his pistol and fired. All six shots struck Geary in the right side.

A single blast from Peters's rifle struck the convict in the back. Judge Cook grabbed on to the banister before the dead man's momentum forced him off his feet. Geary's body tumbled down the stairs until it came to a stop at the bottom landing.

Jack Turnbull rushed in through the front door, shotgun raised and ready to blast Geary again if needed.

"Don't shoot!" Holt called out to his deputy. "He's beyond killing."

Frank Peters and Mrs. Chapman ran down the stairs to tend to Judge Cook, who had managed to stand up when they reached him.

Jack kept people from entering County Hall while Holt ran up and over to the opposite staircase to help Peters steady the judge. "How bad is your head, Your Honor?"

Judge Cook pushed away Mrs. Chapman's handkerchief. "Stop fussing over me like I was a newborn. I'm fine. I don't want anyone seeing me like this. Keep the people out of here until I'm back in my chambers."

Holt and Peters each took one of the judge's arms and half carried him back upstairs as he ordered.

"Mind the door," Holt called down to Jack. "No one gets in here until I say otherwise."

Jack told him he would as Holt and Peters helped the judge with the mayor in tow.

Holt accidentally toppled one of the judge's towers of papers as he eased him back into his chair.

"Wonderful," the judge growled as papers spilled from his desk. "The wheels of justice grind to a halt once more due to Joe Mullen's interference. I have a hearing in thirty minutes."

Mrs. Chapman pushed past them and took a closer look at the cut on his head. "You don't have to do anything but sit there and be quiet. Your hearing and whatever poor old fool you were going to punish can wait another day, William. Your health is far more important."

Judge Cook tried to look around Mrs. Chapman as she tended to his wound. "I guess he must've hit me harder than I thought. I could've sworn I saw Frank Peters at the top of the stairs with a rifle."

"That was me, Your Honor," Peters assured him. "I came running when I heard the shot from outside. Lucky I was already here with Simon for his hearing."

"Who in God's name gave you that responsibility?" the judge asked. "And what were you doing with a rifle. Your hands shake so bad, you could've just as easily killed me instead."

Holt felt a sudden urge to protect Peters. "Frank was doing me a favor by keeping an eye on things while the prison cook and I rode out to check up on Wheeler. I guess I don't have to tell you what we found."

Mrs. Chapman held the handkerchief against the judge's cut. "Is Dan Wheeler dead?"

"Looks like the cook's bad feeling was right. The prison wagon rolled overtop of him and killed him. We found him on a hillside just a couple of hours out of town."

Judge Cook sank back into his chair as he held Mrs. Chapman's handkerchief to the side of his head. "Then Geary was telling the truth. Joe Mullen really has escaped.

And he probably has Hank Lassiter and Mrs. Mullen as hostages."

"Seems that way, Your Honor," Holt reluctantly agreed. "I heard Norm Selwyn on the street confirming that just before I rushed in here. Bart Gamble delivered a similar message to him demanding he ask the governor to pardon Mullen. Said it was in Lassiter's own handwriting."

"Mullen doesn't bluff, Your Honor," Frank Peters added. "If he's threatening to kill them, then that's what he'll do if he doesn't get what he wants."

Mrs. Chapman frowned at him. "Thank you, Frank. We can always rely on you to repeat the obvious."

Judge Cook waved them away from his desk. "This office is too small to have all of you people clustering around me like pigeons around a crust of bread. Get Les Patrick in here. He and I will get to the bottom of this."

Holt hated being the bearer of more bad news. "I'm afraid that's not possible, sir. Bart and Ty Arbour got into a fight before I came up here. Les tried to save his cousin but got shot for his trouble. They'd sent for Doc Klassen, and I expect he's tending to him now."

Judge Cook allowed the bloody handkerchief to drop to his desk. "Les Patrick has been shot? Will he make it?"

"Ty said the bullet went through his right shoulder," Holt told him. "It didn't look fatal, but any gunshot is bad."

Despite the gash to his head, Judge Cook began barking out orders. "Then don't waste time playing wet nurse to me. You two get down there and find out what happened. I want Les to receive any care he needs. And you, Madam Mayor, find Norm Selwyn and stop him from sending that telegram to the governor. We must get a handle on this situation before we even think about agreeing to Mullen's terms. If the governor gets involved, this matter will be out of our hands." When no one moved fast enough for him, he pounded his desk in frustration. "Go on! You've all got important work to do. This cut won't heal itself just by all of you looking at it."

As Holt, Peters, and Mrs. Chapman left the office to carry out their individual assignments, Holt feared the situation was already out of their control. Joe Mullen was calling the tune and they had no choice but to dance to it. For now.

CHAPTER 20

When Holt and Peters reached the boardwalk, they found Ty Arbour kneeling beside Les while Doc Klassen tended to his wounds.

"How's he holding up?" Holt asked the doctor.

Doc Klassen did not look up from his patient. "Still trying to get the bleeding under control. The bullet hit his shoulder blade and tumbled out his back. It managed to do quite a bit of damage along the way."

Klassen wrapped a tourniquet around the shoulder and tightened it, causing Les to cry out before he passed out. "I won't know the extent of the damage until I get him back to my office. That wagon's slow in getting here, so I'd appreciate it if you boys could lend a hand. His life depends on it."

Ty and Holt helped the doctor lift Les Patrick, while Frank Peters took his legs.

Before they got underway, Holt told Jack, "Stay here and don't let anyone into the County Hall. No one gets in, understand."

Jack said he did and took his spot next to the door.

Some of the men from town broke from the crowd to help clear a path for Les and those carrying him. Some ran ahead and formed a human corridor from the County Hall to Klassen's office just up the street.

Peters kicked open Klassen's door as they carried Les into the examining room and gently laid him on the table. Doc Klassen forced his way through the crowd and immediately got to work on the wound.

"Let me stay and help you, Doc," Ty told Klassen. "I picked up a thing or two about wounds during the war."

Klassen was clearly glad to have the help and directed Peters and Holt to clear the remaining townspeople out of his office. The crowd moved without incident, leaving Holt and Peters standing alone on the boardwalk in front of the office.

"You've seen more men shot than me, Holt," Peters said. "What do you think of his chances?"

Holt did not want to hazard a guess. "Depends on how deep the damage goes. Klassen said the bullet hit bone and traveled down and out through his back. Could've hit the lung or an artery. I'd say Les and the doctor are in for a long night of it."

"I was afraid you might say something like that. What do you want me to do?"

Now that Holt finally had a moment to think, something bothered him. "You didn't get that rifle from the courtroom, Frank. We both know that. Where'd you get it?"

Peters looked down at his boots. "I never gave up my keys to the jail when I went to work for Ma at the Railhead. Hauling Simon over here without a gun didn't feel right, so I used my keys to unlock the rifle rack at the jail and took down a Winchester. It was my gun anyway, John, so I didn't see the harm in it. Looks like I was right to bring it."

Holt knew he should have been cross with Peters for not having been honest with him, but there would be time for that later. "Lucky you did."

"You'd already plugged Geary plenty before I even got a shot off," Peters told him. "I don't think I've ever seen a man shoot like that before."

Holt knew this was no time for praise. There was still plenty of work to do. "Where'd you leave your rifle?"

"Up in Judge Cook's office. Why?"

"Because I want you to go back up there, fetch it, and come back down here to stand guard. This town's got plenty of busybodies and I don't want them pestering Doc and Ty while they're working on Les. I'll see to it that Jack relieves you at some point. And I'll ask Jean to run you over some coffee and food in a while."

"Thank you, John. This means the world to me."

"You can thank me by doing what I asked. And tell Jack to stay at the County Hall. I'll be over to talk to him when you get back."

Holt watched Peters head back to County Hall at a fast walk. He noticed a spring in the former sheriff's step that he had never seen before. Maybe Peters had not been exaggerating when he had asked Holt for a second chance that would save his life.

He only hoped Les Patrick could say the same to Dr. Klassen before too long.

After Peters returned with his rifle to stand guard at Doc Klassen's office, Holt went back to retrieve his horse from the hitching rail in front of County Hall. Jack Turnbull had closed the door to the hall and stood in front of it with his shotgun in both hands.

Like Peters, responsibility had clearly changed young Jack. He no longer looked like a kid with a star pinned to his shirt. He looked more like a deputy assigned an important task. Holt told him he would be back to see him soon before climbing into the saddle and riding his horse down Main Street to the jail.

He passed Earl Sibert and his men as they placed Frank Geary's body in the back of a buckboard.

The undertaker doffed his hat to the sheriff as he rode by. "Kindest wishes to you, Sheriff Holt. I only wish it was under better circumstances."

There was something about Sibert that always got under Holt's skin. Perhaps it was the nature of the man's work or his smarmy demeanor as he carried out his duties. "No need to hold up on planting that one, Earl. Might as well put him in the ground as soon as you're able. And there's no need to bother with any of that alchemy nonsense you use on your paying customers. I doubt the mayor's inclined to spend any more than the minimum before he's buried."

Sibert bowed his head as he placed his hat over his heart. "Thank you for the guidance, Sheriff. My men and I will be more than happy to carry out your wishes."

Holt fought off a shiver as he continued to ride down Main Street.

Once he reached the jail, Holt climbed down from the saddle and threw his reins around the hitching rail. He saw Geary's stolen horse tied up next to his own. Henderson had not wasted any time in claiming his property.

Holt went inside, expecting to find Old Bob and William Henderson waiting for him. He was disappointed to only see Henderson sitting behind his desk.

"Hope you don't mind me making myself at home," the farmer said. "Considering no one else was around, I didn't see the harm in it."

Holt could not have cared less. "Where's Bob?"

"When you rode off, Bob said he was going to head out to the Mullen spread. See if he wanted to read the ground to see what he was up against."

Holt could barely believe what he was hearing. "And you let him go out there alone?"

"Didn't see as I had cause to stop him," Henderson admitted. "In fact, the notion never entered my mind. He's a grown man, as he's fond of reminding us. Besides, I figured you'd be angry if we left this place unattended, so I decided to stay back."

"Not before you grabbed your horse, I see."

"My right as it's my property," Henderson reminded him.

"I might've been able to use you in the County Hall just now."

"You seemed to have it well in hand. Besides, Jack forbade anyone from going in after you, not that I exactly forced the matter. I was just as happy to collect my mount and lead him back here."

Holt decided that arguing with Henderson was pointless. He had not deputized the man and could not expect him to think like a lawman. That was about to change right now.

"Get on your feet, Henderson."

The farmer squinted up at him. "I don't like the sound of that, Sheriff."

"Get on your feet and raise your right hand. If you're going to hang around here, you're going to do it legally. That means I'm swearing you in right here and now."

Henderson sat farther back in his chair. "And what if I don't want to become your deputy."

"Then I can't guarantee you'll get all of your horses back," Holt said. "Would be a shame if the three you've got out at the Mullen spread somehow got spooked and ran off, wouldn't it?"

That drew Henderson to his feet, but he did not raise his right hand. "You've got a mean streak in you, mister."

Holt grinned. "The good people of Devil's Gulch didn't hire me for my kindness. Now get your right hand up. You've got an oath to take."

After Holt administered an oath he had made up on the spot, he went to the rifle rack and pulled down a box of bullets. He dumped out the spent bullets into his hand and put them in the top drawer of his desk. Devil's Gulch did not get a regular resupply of ammunition, though the general store offered to reload bullets at a fair price.

Henderson took his seat and watched Holt feed fresh rounds into his pistol. "You keep your pistol fully loaded. Mighty dangerous. I always keep one round empty, so it doesn't accidentally go off. Might cost me a toe or something."

"You're not me," Holt reminded him. "You're a farmer, remember?"

Henderson waited until Holt flicked the cylinder closed and had the gun back in its holster before asking, "Where are you off to now?"

"I'm heading out to fetch Bob back here. He's got no business being anywhere near the Mullen spread by himself. Mullen's not a fool and Bob's just as liable to wind up dead in a ditch like Wheeler."

Henderson made no effort to get up from his seat. "I'll be sure to keep an eye on things here."

"And your property, Henderson. I'd imagine the most dangerous place in town is between you and that stallion you've got hitched outside."

Henderson laughed. "You're a smart man, John Holt. Smarter than I gave you credit for."

Holt left him laughing as he climbed on his horse and rode out to the Mullen spread in search of Bob.

CHAPTER 21

Since seeing the prison cook in action on the trail, Holt had come to terms with the notion that he had never been much of a tracker. Not as good as Bob at least.

But Holt was far from a tenderfoot, and he knew how to read trail signs better than most men. Old Bob was not the only man in Devil's Gulch who could find a man in the wilderness.

Holt had only been in the area for a month, so he was not all that familiar with the land. But there was still plenty of sunshine left in the day for him to follow Bob's trail once he cleared the clutter of the land around town. Holt was not surprised to see it had diverged from the more well-traveled trail he had been following.

Bob's horse broke off to the left toward a rocky outcropping a fair distance away from the sprawling Mullen ranch. He decided the outcropping was too far away for Old Bob to see much, even if he happened to have a spyglass with him, but that was precisely where the tracks led him.

Holt found Bob's horse ground-hobbled near the outcropping and, after climbing down from the saddle, did the same to his horse. He found the older man at the edge of the outcropping, looking over the Mullen ranch. He was surprised to see him surveying the ground with a large pair of binoculars in his hand.

"Took you long enough to get here," Bob said without bothering to look at him. "I was beginning to think you got yourself shot in that ruckus up at the County Hall."

"Not likely," Holt said as he joined him on the outcropping. "Ran into an old friend of yours. Frank Geary took Judge Cook hostage."

"That so?" Bob worked the focus dial between the lenses. "You kill him?"

"Ask me a serious question."

"I take it Judge Cook sailed through it without a scratch."

"Geary busted him in the head, but he'll live. I was expecting you to show up, seeing as how Geary was your prisoner and all."

"You had it well in hand, Sheriff. Besides, I've been putting my time to better use right here." Bob shielded his binoculars from the sun as he observed the ranch. "Besides, that old mountain goat Cook is too mean to die, or at least allow the likes of Geary to finish him off. Who killed Geary, anyway? You or Jack?"

"Me," Holt told him. "Though Frank Peters finished him off."

The news was enough to make Bob lower his binoculars. "You don't say. Well, if that don't beat all? I didn't think Old Frank still had it in him. Good for him." The prison cook raised his glasses again and resumed looking over the ground. "Guess there's hope for that drunk yet."

Holt was glad to change the subject. "I didn't know you had binoculars with you. Could've mentioned that back when we were after Mullen."

"Didn't need them then," Bob told him. "The ground told me everything I needed to know. Up here is different. I only break these out for special occasions."

"Anything happen since you got here?"

"Saw a fella ride in here from the direction of town," Bob said. "He rode like his tail was on fire. I took that to mean he had something to do with what you were mixed up in."

"That was probably Bart Gamble. He's Mullen's top hand."

"He disappeared into the house about half an hour ago. His horse is still hitched out front. He hasn't come out since. I take it Mullen sent Geary to kidnap the judge."

"He's done more than that," Holt reported. "He's taken Hank Lassiter, the president of the bank, and Mullen's wife as hostages. He sent Bart to tell the bank manager to wire the governor to demand a pardon for himself in exchange for Lassiter's release. And he sent Geary to bring Judge Cook out here to see for himself that Mullen really had them."

"And Geary was dumb enough to do it." Bob shook his head in disbelief as he continued to watch the land. "Geary was always as strong as an ox but just as dumb. The world's better off without a man that stupid."

Holt joined Bob in looking out over the land. Even without the benefit of Bob's glasses, Holt could see why Mullen had been drawn to come back to it. There was a rugged beauty to the place. From area maps he had seen in town he knew Mullen's property stretched as far as the eye could see. It was enclosed on three sides by a ring of rocky outcroppings like the one he and Bob were on now. Only the land behind the ranch house was flat, which was where a sizable herd of horses roamed freely in a large bit of land surrounded by a wooden fence. Holt imagined Mullen kept his cattle in one of the distant fields that stretched out behind a sloping hill.

The house itself sat in the middle of a clearing. There was not so much as a pebble to offer a man cover for more than three hundred yards in any direction.

"Tough layout," Holt observed. "Mullen picked the worst place to build his house."

"Bad for us, but perfect for him." Bob handed Holt the binoculars and began to explain what he had seen.

"Looks like that fella you called Bart took a narrow path that runs through the rocks. Same kind of path is over to the left and it's the only other passable way I can see for miles. If Mullen gets enough plow horses to help him drag some trees over to block it, and I believe he will, the sides are too steep for our horses to get around."

Holt saw that too. "He's got plenty of mines up in these hills. He might save himself the trouble and just use dynamite to blow up the path."

"I saw some men over there earlier," Bob told him. "I imagine they're fixing to do exactly that."

A dull explosion echoed through the valley and, for a moment, Holt felt as though he was back in the war, standing on a rise as he surveyed a battle. The blast sounded like the roar of a cannon. But instead of seeing shrapnel and limbs flying through the air in a mist of blood, he saw a gentle trickle of rocks running down the rocky hillside.

"That'll be the farthest route going up," Bob said.

While Holt moved the binoculars to bring that area into view, another dull explosion rumbled beneath their feet.

Holt lowered his glasses and leaned over the side of a large rock. A similar trickle of stones rained down on the land beneath them. "And that's this trail done for."

"Like I said," Bob reminded him, "your Mr. Mullen is a smart man."

"He's not my anything," Holt said. "I guess that just leaves us with the flat land to the west of the house. It'll take us a long time to get around that far. The better part of a day."

"Less than that," Bob figured, "but it won't be easy going. Plenty of places for him to have men waiting to ambush us. If they're not ranch hands, then they'll be miners up in the hill. You told me he has claims all over those hills. I don't fancy letting myself get killed by a miner. It's bad luck in the hereafter."

Holt was about to ask him what he meant by that but decided the answer would only frustrate him. "Even if we managed to get down there, he's got a clear shot at anyone who comes within three hundred yards of the place."

"Nearer two hundred," Bob said, "but the result is still the same. Even at a gallop, we'd be dead before we got close."

The prison cook spat before standing up to take a final look at the scene. "Yes, sir. Joe Mullen has built himself a regular Alamo down there. We might get him if we had more men, but we won't get enough to hit this place. Half of them would break their necks trying to clear the rocks only to be shot dead when they got close."

Holt handed back the binoculars to him. "That means I'll have to go in at night. Tonight. Let's get back to town. I'd better get ready."

Bob took the binoculars and followed Holt down from the rocks. "Don't be a fool, Holt. You can't make that trip at night, especially tonight. He'll be waiting for us to do something like that."

"What makes you think we can wait?" Holt asked. "By now, Bart's already told him what happened in town. In a few hours when he realizes Geary's either been caught or killed, he'll get desperate. He might decide to kill Lassiter or his wife. Maybe even both of them. I can't risk that. Devil's Gulch and the surrounding county is my business, Bob. Not yours."

"He's not killing anyone," Bob explained. "If all he wanted was blood, he wouldn't have bothered sending those two into town with a list of demands. He would've killed them already."

Holt knew that made sense, but the alternative to doing something was to not do anything and he could not accept that. "So, what are we supposed to do? Just let him sit out there and come up with a way to kill us?"

"We buy time," Bob said. "He's not going anywhere and if he heads up into the hills where his mines are, we can't do much to stop him. And something tells me he's fixing to do exactly that. He knows that house is a fort, but it could just as easily become his tomb if we surround him. You were in the army, Holt. I don't need to tell you about the troubles with defending a fixed position, do I?"

No, Holt did not need Bob to explain it to him. And he knew Mullen would have probably already thought of that. He'd had plenty of time to think about such things during all the time he had spent alone in his cell. Plotting his revenge. Planning for the unlikely opportunity fate might give him to avenge himself.

He would not throw away his life on a whim. He had a plan and all of this could just be a clever distraction.

Bob placed a hand on Holt's shoulder, bringing him back to the present. "Let's head back to town and talk it over with the judge and the mayor. Let's find a way to buy ourselves some time while we come up with something that'll actually work. Maybe we can get some of the men in town to join us."

But Holt knew that was unlikely. Ma McAdam's boys would fight, especially if Joe Mullen was the prize. Joe had killed Hank Bostrom, the gang's former leader. He imagined Charlie Gardiner and the rest of the boys would like a piece of Joe's hide.

But Ma McAdam would not let her gun hands go cheaply, even if it meant killing Mullen. She had Tony Cassidy at the Blue Bottle on the run. She would want to keep the men in town so they could help her further stake her claim to Devil's Gulch.

Holt ran his hand across his mouth as his prospects for help quickly began to dim. No matter how he looked at it, they were facing a tough time ahead. He wanted to see Mullen brought to justice, but part of him wished he had ridden west where he would have become someone else's problem for a change.

"There you go brooding again," Bob said. "Let's you and me get back to town and get some food in our bellies. I do my best thinking on a full stomach."

He joined Bob in walking back to their horses.

"Come to think of it," Bob added, "I do my best thinking on a full jug, though it doesn't stay full for long once I get ahold of it. I just hope I don't have to fight that young Turnbull of yours for a bunk in the jail tonight. Don't know where Henderson will hang his hat. Probably in the livery. Farmers are strange about adapting to creature comforts and such."

"We'd all better get our fill of food and sleep," Holt said. "I have a feeling it'll have to last us for longer than we'd like."

Joe Mullen squinted through the spyglass, the only thing of value his father had left him before he died. "I can't believe it. Looks like they're getting on their horses and riding away."

"Of course they are," Sarabelle said from the spot where he had tired her on the couch. "You didn't expect them to charge the house across more than a mile of open ground in broad daylight, did you? They're not stupid, Joe."

Joe was beginning to regret his decision to allow her to come up from the cellar. "I think one of them is Holt. I can't see him clearly from this distance, but I can tell it's him by the way he moves. His arrogance carries clear across the land. There's another man with him, but I can't tell if it's Jack Turnbull or not."

"Doesn't matter who he's with as long as Holt is there.

He's not going to come riding in here to fetch you straight on, especially after he tracked Bart back here. And he was there to see you have your miners blow up the passes through the rock. They're onto you, Joe. And Holt's probably coming up with a way to kill you right now."

Joe knew that she was trying to get under his skin and refused to take the bait. He squinted into the distance at the places his miners had just blown up. Two of the passes had been obliterated by rubble. The third side remained unpassable, but he imagined a man could still make his way down that side if he was of a mind to.

Fortunately, Joe Mullen did not plan to wait around to find out. "Holt and the others might not be coming now, but they'll come for me in the next day or so. And when he does, I'll be waiting for him."

He grinned down at his wife, who flinched when he looked down at her. "Yes, ma'am. You just wait and see what I've got in store for John Holt and his friends."

Then he remembered Bart Gamble was still waiting for him in the kitchen. He imagined he was anxious to deliver bad news, but Mullen would put his mind at ease. Even if Geary had managed to find a way to get himself killed or captured, everything was still going according to Mullen's plan.

He left his wife on the couch and headed toward the kitchen. It was time to get busy unfolding the next part of his grand scheme and there was still much work to do.

CHAPTER 22

Mrs. Chapman scowled up at the map of Devil's Gulch she had asked Jack Turnbull to tack up on the wall of her office. "I had hoped the situation would look less dire if I saw it from afar. I'm afraid it doesn't look any better than it did across my desk."

It was as ugly a map as Holt had seen and he had seen more than his share of maps during the war. Seeing the layout for himself helped him read the map better, if it did not improve his outlook. "It doesn't look promising, I'll grant you that."

"The map's pretty accurate based on what I saw out there," Bob observed. "Even a bit more disheartening."

Holt looked at Jack, who had retreated to the back of the mayor's office. He knew the boy did not have much to contribute to the discussion but wanted to make sure he was paying attention. He was glad to see that he was.

"Well, Sheriff?" Mrs. Chapman asked him. "As acting mayor of this town, I'd like to know how you plan on getting Mullen out of there. But as someone who has come to see you as something of a friend, I'm not sure I want you to try."

Bob pushed himself out of his chair and walked over to the map. He traced the area in question with a gnarled finger. "Open land all around except for the boulders and gouges in the ground that cover three sides of the place. While we were out there a bit ago, Mullen had some of his miners take dynamite to the passes in the rocks. There's no way to get a horse down there now. That hems them in, but it keeps us out. It would've been dangerous to just charge in there before. Now it's impossible. Trying it in daylight is suicide and the ground's even more treacherous at night. He'll likely stake some of his men out there to keep an ear out for anyone trying it. I can't speak for his ranch hands, but based on the bodies Mullen has left behind, that leaves McCaffrey and Hardt from the prison wagon to back his play. Neither of them is as big or mean as Geary was, but they're both stone-cold killers and more than adequate with a knife. Hardt threw his lot in with some bad men in his time."

He moved his finger to the flat lands where the fields and corral were. "That leaves us to come at him from this direction. If the wind's against us, those mounts and cows he's got in the field will put up a fuss before we get within a quarter mile of the place."

Holt may not have been too familiar with the ground, but he knew it was even worse than it looked. "In order to get to him from that direction, we'll have to ride through Mullen's mines. And since he sent them to blow up the passes, they'll be waiting for us. He's got more than a dozen claims up there if that map's to be believed. Even if one miner spots us, they'll get word back to him that we're coming."

Mrs. Chapman's eyebrows rose. "But based on what you said, he'd be trapped. He won't have any way to get out of the house except to come your way."

Holt wished the matter was that simple. "Those hills are a labyrinth. We could easily lose him up there in the dark. He could ride within ten feet of us without us even knowing he was there. And even if we managed to hide from the miners, there's still a lot of open ground to cover in every direction."

The mayor folded her stubby arms across her ample bosom. "I don't know if I'm supposed to say this or not, but I've never been one to keep my mouth shut. I don't care if Joe Mullen escapes, gentlemen. In fact, I'd welcome it. He can take Lassiter and Sarabelle with him. Let him be someone else's problem for once. I know that might not sit well with your interests, Mr. Bob, but I'm not in the position to worry about the federal government's concerns just now."

"My right name is Robert Benjamin, ma'am," Bob told her, "but I suppose just plain Old Bob will do just fine for the purposes of this here discussion."

Mrs. Chapman was not fazed by the correction. "Unless your name is George Washington, it won't help us solve this Mullen problem." She cocked an eyebrow to Holt. "Have you given any thought to raising a posse to root him out of there?"

"Thought about it," Holt admitted, "but I don't think it'll do much good. Don't let the jury's decision to convict Mullen fool you. He's still got plenty of friends in town. And those who don't like him are scared of him. They've seen what he's done to people who cross him, and they won't want to risk him getting away again. He already escaped once. I can't blame them for being cautious."

But the mayor still had a point to make. "What about Ma McAdam's bunch? She's just hired on a bunch of gun hands. They're not afraid of Mullen and a bunch of ranch hands and miners. Those boys are always spoiling for a fight."

Holt had already thought about that too. "We could use them to comb through the mines, but someone could still get away and get word back to Mullen. Besides, I'd prefer to have them stay in town. If Mullen managed to somehow get past us, his next move is likely to be to come here. Might try to shoot up the place as he's trying to escape. I'd hate to have

Charlie Gardiner and his bunch out there with us when they could be of better use here."

She rose her fleshy chin in his direction. "You're not worried about the town, Holt. You're worried about me, aren't you?"

"I'm worried about the town, which includes you," Holt answered. "A desperate man is liable to pull down everything around him when he falls, and Joe Mullen certainly counts as a desperate man. You're as likely a target of his as Ma McAdam or Judge Cook. He already took a run at the judge and Norman Selwyn at the bank. It stands to reason that you're on his list, too, which is why I plan on having Frank Peters here to keep an eye on you."

Mrs. Chapman dropped her head into her hand. "Heaven help me. My life and the life of this town depend on a bunch of outlaws and an old drunk."

Jack piped up from the back of the room. "I'll be here too, ma'am. I'm no drunk."

Holt smiled to himself. The boy was catching on quick. He knew exactly what to say and when to say it.

"At least I have that going for me." Mrs. Chapman sighed heavily. "This entire discussion may become entirely moot anyway. Norman Selwyn has already wired the governor about Mullen's demands."

Holt's temper spiked. "Why'd he go and do a fool thing like that? I thought he was going to wait to talk it over with you first."

"So did I," the mayor said. "But after seeing Geary's resolve to bring Judge Cook to Mullen, Selwyn's own resolve faltered. He knows the land better than any of us since the bank holds mortgages on most of the properties in the county. He's already determined that we don't stand a chance against Mullen and his men. I received a telegram from the governor while you two were busy at the Mullen spread."

"Well?" Holt asked. "What did he say?"

"He's considering giving in to Mullen's demands. He's going to make his decision by this evening."

"He's what?" Old Bob snapped. "Why, if he does that, every important man in this territory will be fair game for the likes of Mullen!"

"Reserve your scorn for where it will be of use, Mr. Benjamin," she said. "You have no need to convince me. I replied that the idea he's even considering it is troubling. But there are other factors to consider here."

"Like what?" Holt asked. "Cowardice?"

"Practicality," the mayor answered him. "Lassiter's shareholders in the bank have known Joe Mullen for years. They're convinced they can reason with him. They believe a pardon is a small price to pay to assure Lassiter's safety. The governor also has quite a bit of money invested in Lassiter's other interests. A lot of important families do. They'll do anything to get Lassiter back to work, even if it means giving Mullen everything he wants."

Holt should have known better than to put his faith in a politician to do the right thing. "You said the governor's going to make a decision tonight. That doesn't leave us with much time."

"Time for what, exactly?" Mayor Chapman asked. "We can't act against him with the numbers we have. You just said so yourself. It's out of our hands, gentlemen. We will remain in town and await his orders. Whatever happens after that is on the governor's head, not ours."

Bob stepped back from the map. "Mullen is a convicted murderer who killed a deputy marshal while escaping from custody. His influence didn't do him any good when he was on trial and it shouldn't do him any good now."

208   *William W. Johnstone and J.A. Johnstone*

"You can't prove he killed Deputy Wheeler," she countered. "He'll say it was an accident and who's around to say otherwise. He escaped the wreckage, as anyone in his position might do in similar circumstances, and made his way back home. Yes, he took hostages, but if no harm comes to them, they'll be more than happy to turn a blind eye to that for the sake of their holdings." She looked up at Bob. "I'm not saying it's right, Deputy. I'm just reminding you of how things are. Wheeler was paid to risk his life. They'll write off what happened to him as a tragic accident. I'm not asking you to accept it or like it."

Holt and Bob began to protest, but she silenced them by raising her hand. "Nothing you say will change my mind, gentlemen. The matter rests entirely with the governor and his men. We have no choice but to hold fast and allow the tide to take us where it will."

As the rush of anger left him, Holt knew Mrs. Chapman was right. He had seen the power of politics during the war and when he had been in New Orleans. He knew the public good was quickly forgotten under the right circumstances. His general had called it "getting along and going along." One hand washed the other and it was up to men like Holt to dump out the dirty, bloody water. Far away from the prying eyes of the citizenry, of course.

Holt watched Bob trace the inside of his mouth with his tongue as if he was chewing over what he was about to say next. "You ordering Holt and Jack to do nothing, ma'am."

"For the moment, yes."

"Then I guess it's lucky for me I don't fall under your jurisdiction." Bob swiped his hat from the mayor's desk and pulled it on his head. "Dan Wheeler wasn't just my partner. He was a good friend, and I don't have enough friends to lose to the likes of Mullen. And every second that man and the others who killed him breathe free air is a slur against his memory. I won't stand for it."

Bob did not bother closing the door behind him after storming out into the hallway.

Mrs. Chapman did not look pleased as she told Holt, "You'd better throw a rope around him before he does something all of us will regret. We've already lost one federal man to Mullen. I won't want to explain to the governor how we lost two."

Holt motioned for Jack to leave with him. "I don't know how much use I'll be as I agree with him, but you have my word I'll try."

Mayor Chapman looked up at the map. "I suppose trying is the best any of us can hope for under the circumstances, Sheriff."

Holt and Jack managed to catch up to Bob just as he was about to enter the jail.

"Don't go trying to talk me out of it," the prison cook warned Holt as he barged into the jail. "Your words will have less effect on me than they did on keeping Henderson on his farm."

"No one's talking you out of anything," Holt yelled after him. "Just take a second to think."

But Bob did not stop. "That old lady back there is right. Joe Mullen and the others ain't a town concern. It's a federal one. I won't press you into service now. I'll handle it on my own."

"Don't be a fool, Bob." After Jack rushed into the jail, Holt shut it behind them. "If you go riding out there to bring Mullen in, you'll be dead before you get within a hundred yards of the place."

"I ain't so easy to kill." Bob pulled on his gray hair. "This just ain't for show, you know. I've learned a thing or two about surviving in my day."

But Holt could not afford to give up so easy. "And what

about Mullen's wife? What about Hank Lassiter? What if Mullen steps outside with a gun to Lassiter's head? What'll you do then?"

"I'll put him down and whatever happens to them or me happens. Wrong place at the wrong time, just like they're liable to say about what happened to Wheeler. Damn it, John. The three of us saw what happened to Dan on that hillside. That was no accident. But those fancy men in Golden City will make it sound that way because it suits them. I aim to make sure they don't have the chance. I don't want to see any harm come to that woman or the banker, but they knew what they were getting into when they joined up with Mullen. And we both know that banker wasn't up there to comfort Mrs. Mullen in her time of grief. If he dies, it's his fault, not mine."

Henderson remained sitting on the bed, cleaning his Winchester while he watched the two lawmen yell at each other. "I'll go."

Holt was prepared to continue arguing with Bob when the two men looked at the farmer. "Stay out of this, Henderson. You had your chance to listen to reason back at your farm."

"Is that what you call this? Reasoning?" Henderson grinned. "Just sounds like a whole lot of bickering if you ask me. Heard more reasoning from wild cats come mating season than I've heard from either of you just now. And if I wanted to sit around listening to arguing, I could have just stayed home with my family."

Holt was prepared to discount the farmer until Jack stepped in. "Let Mr. Henderson talk. I've found he doesn't speak unless he's got something to say."

Henderson smiled. "Like the Good Book says, 'And a child will lead them.'" He nodded toward Jack. "You're smarter than you look, Jack."

"I guess that'll have to depend on what you say next," Jack added.

Henderson set his rifle on the bed next to the cloth he had been using to wipe it down. "Holt, I got the impression from you that you were in the war."

"I was."

"Cavalry, I'd take it, judging by how you ride. Which side?"

Holt hoped this would not lead to another argument. "The Union."

"I was right again. Too bad I don't get some kind of prize. I was in the war, too, before I made my way down to Fort Worth. Rode with an outfit you might've heard of with a man named Quantrill."

Holt knew Jack had been right. Henderson might not have said much, but when he did, he said plenty. "Bill Quantrill. The Raiders."

"The very same," Henderson answered. "We weren't as fancy as you boys in blue, but we got the job done. We weren't much for fancy parades or marching, neither, but we did some damage."

Holt knew about Quantrill's bunch. "I didn't exactly spend the war peeling potatoes or digging latrines, Henderson."

"I don't think you did, but I doubt you ever had to fight like we did." He pointed at himself. "The way me and my boys fought. No artillery. No second lines to come up in support. Hardly any rations to speak of. We lived off the land."

"And off the men you killed," Holt added. "Union men."

"Didn't much matter to us who we were fighting, just that they were in the way," Henderson explained. "We had a knack for being able to sneak up on a place. Places that were better guarded by more men than Mullen or his bunch have up there on his ranch."

Henderson inclined his head to Bob. "I might not have

seen the place myself but judging by what Bob told me before the mayor called you boys in, I'd say this ranch house Mullen's got is out in the middle of nowhere. Easy lines of sight from four directions. I have that right?"

"You do," Bob told him.

"Figured as much. Glad all that farming hasn't cost me my edge. Sounds to me like the best way to hit the place is at night. If we go in there all together, even the four of us, chances are we'll tip our hand and wind up in a shooting match on unfamiliar ground."

"It's plain enough to see during the day," Bob said, "but I imagine it's a different story at night."

"All the more reason for me to go in alone. After dark. I'm going up there anyway to get my horses. Figured I might as well do some good while I'm at it."

Holt was not so certain. "It'll mean crossing the mines. Every man able will be listening for someone approaching."

"Sounds like a good reason why I should go in alone. It'll be easier for me to take my time and come in nice and slow. I expect it'll take me most of the night to do it right, but come morning, Joe Mullen will find me sitting at his breakfast table. All you have to do is tell me if you want me to kill him or pull him out of there."

"Kill him," Bob said.

"Alive," Holt said right after. "If possible. Holding him hostage is the only hope you'll have of getting out of there."

Henderson nodded once. The matter was decided. "Seeing as how I'll be doing the hard part, it sure would be nice if one of you boys was nearby with a couple of fresh horses. I'll likely have to hit the house on foot and I don't aim to walk all the way back to town."

"Don't worry," Holt said. "We'll be there."

Henderson slapped his knees as he stood. "Then it's settled." He reached behind him and pulled a bowie knife from the back of his pants. "Any of you boys have a stone I could sharpen this on? Seems like I'll be needing it this evening."

CHAPTER 23

As Bob knew the ground better than Holt, it made more sense for him to lead Henderson out toward the Mullen spread. They still had a few good hours of sunlight remaining, which would give the farmer a better chance to plot his way through the mining camps before coming around toward Mullen's house.

Once they were underway, Holt left Jack at the jail and walked over to Doc Klassen's office to check on Les. He was glad to see Frank Peters was still guarding the place. He had even moved a chair out onto the boardwalk from the doctor's waiting room to make himself more comfortable.

Peters stood as soon as he saw Holt approaching. "Afternoon, John. I've been standing watch all day, just like you told me."

"Any trouble?"

"Just a couple of curious people," Peters reported. "Lots of questions, but no one meant any harm. I've made sure no one interrupted Ralph or Ty while they're tending to Les."

Holt knew he had not asked Peters to do much but was glad to see he had been able to accomplish an easy assignment. He imagined he might have no choice but to rely on Peters before the Mullen mess was over.

"I'll be here for a while," Holt told him. "You'd best go

and get over to Jean's café. Get yourself something to eat and relax for a bit. Have her put it on my bill. Once you're done, head over to County Hall. I want you keeping an eye on the mayor until I tell you otherwise."

Peters picked up his chair and carried it back into the doctor's waiting room. "Want me to stay with her even when she goes home."

"Whether she likes it or not," Holt said. "I don't know if trouble's coming, but if Mullen comes back to town, I don't want her in danger. I'll send for you if I need you."

"Consider it done."

Holt paused to watch the former sheriff head off toward Le Café. He was looking for any hint of resentment in him. Any tic or movement that might confirm his worst suspicions that Peters was not up to the task at hand. But he was relieved to see he moved with purpose and confidence. And Holt began to hope Peters could be counted upon to do his best to keep Mayor Chapman alive.

Holt went inside and found Dr. Klassen and Ty Arbour sitting in his office adjacent to his examining room. Both men looked exhausted and barely acknowledged Holt's presence. Ty's right forearm was bandaged just above the elbow.

Holt did not remember Ty being wounded but might have missed it in all the confusion after Bart escaped. "How's Les doing?"

"Not as well as I had hoped by now," Dr. Klassen admitted. "It took me a while to find the source of the bleeding and even longer before I sewed it up. He lost a lot of blood in the process. Fortunately, Ty here was willing and able to allow me to perform a blood transfusion. It's risky, but he claims he has done it before with no ill effects for the patient."

Ty flexed his bandaged right arm. "The camp doctor used to take blood from me all the time back in the war. I just hope it helps Les get better." He seemed to remember something and cringed. "I just remembered what I was doing at County Hall in the first place. I was going to represent poor old Simon in court today."

Holt had almost forgotten about the gambler. "Don't worry. The judge kicked him loose. Told him to get out of town and to not come back for at least a year. Considering all that had just happened, Simon was only too glad to oblige."

Ty shrugged. "I'll chalk that up as a win."

"Not your only good deed for the day," Klassen remarked. "Your cousin would have surely died without that transfusion. Unfortunately, now all we can do is watch and wait to see how Les responds."

Holt envied them that. Their concerns were narrowed down to one man's condition. He had an entire county to worry about.

"You look worse than we do, John," Klassen noted. "How are things with the town? It was thoughtless of me not to ask earlier."

Holt had never been good at knowing how to break bad news well. "Mullen is behind all this. He escaped Dan Wheeler's prison wagon with four other men. He made his way back to his ranch and sent Bart Gamble to deliver a ransom demand to Norm Selwyn at the bank. He wanted to trade Hank Lassiter for a pardon from the governor."

"Good God," the doctor said. "He must have gone insane."

Holt continued. "He also sent one of the men who escaped with him, Frank Geary, to bring Judge Cook back to the ranch with him to confirm he had Lassiter so he could tell the governor about it. Me and Frank Peters killed him before he could do it, but you two already heard that part."

Ty rubbed a hand over his mouth. "I guess that's why I didn't recognize the strange voice I heard in the judge's chambers. Joe Mullen. That man sure knows how to cause trouble."

Dr. Klassen waved him quiet. "How did Mullen get away from the likes of Dan Wheeler?"

"Looks like there was an accident and the wagon rolled overtop of him," Holt said. "Jack Turnbull happened to be riding back to town and saw it right after it happened. Poor Dan didn't go quickly."

Holt watched a vacant look come over the doctor. "Dan Wheeler. Dead. If he can't stand up to Mullen, what chance do the rest of us have."

Holt knew Klassen had not meant to insult him, so he let it go. "We've got a couple of surprises cooking up for him as we speak."

But if Klassen had heard him, he did not show it. "Those miserable Mullens. The wife is just as bad as the husband."

Holt caught that. "What's that supposed to mean, Ralph?"

Klassen looked at the sheriff as if he had been woken from a dream. "Can I speak to you in private, John? It's important."

Holt might not have known Klassen for long, but he knew the kind of man he was. He had shown courage when the town lined up against him with Mullen. He had come running into a dangerous situation following Mayor Blair Chapman's shooting. He had never been secretive before.

"Sounds serious," Ty observed.

"That's because it is. No offense, Ty. I'd just prefer to speak to the sheriff in private. Do you mind stepping outside? It's only for a moment."

Holt motioned for the attorney to remain where he was. "No call to hide anything from him, Ralph. Judging by your demeanor right now, sounds like you could use an attorney's advice."

Ty Arbour said, "Anything you say will be held in the strictest confidence, Ralph. I wrote your will for you, so you're legally my client."

Holt watched Klassen sag in his chair. "I'm in debt to Tony Cassidy."

Holt and Arbour exchanged confused looks, with Ty saying, "Owing a man money isn't a crime."

"It's only a crime if he wants you to do something illegal to pay it off," Holt added. "He's asked you to do something, hasn't he?"

"That's just it," the doctor admitted. "It's not illegal. It's perfectly legal, at least I think it is." Klassen realized he was not making sense, so he blurted it out. "He'll forgive my debt if I run against Mrs. Chapman for mayor. He intends on putting me up against her and he guarantees I'll win." Klassen sat forward cradling his stomach. "He was waiting on the boardwalk for me last night. That's when he told me. He said he got the governor to approve a special election that'll happen in two weeks."

Holt saw Klassen's lower lip quiver. "I don't want the job, John. I certainly don't want to run against Elizabeth for it. But Cassidy's not giving me any choice. He's forcing my hand."

Klassen kept explaining himself, but Holt stopped listening. Pieces of a puzzle he had not known existed began to drop in place. The sound of them landing was like the explosions he had heard out at the Mullen ranch earlier that day.

He knew why the governor was considering Mullen's demands.

The election and Ralph Klassen's nomination had been an idea cooked up by Sarabelle Mullen and Tony Cassidy before Joe escaped. Holt doubted the governor cared one way or the other about Devil's Gulch itself, but Holt had heard rumors that Cassidy and Joe had friends in the capital. The governor had no problem granting such a request from friends.

And now that Joe Mullen had escaped detention, he was asking for a pardon. The governor would grant it because it would not cost him anything. In fact, he would profit from it.

Lassiter would be freed and would resume his duties.

Mullen would get his life and fortune back and continue to donate to the governor's causes. Mrs. Chapman and John Holt would be blamed for not acting quickly enough to stop the kidnapping, thus giving the governor no choice but to pardon Mullen. Cassidy would get the town back through Klassen's election, leaving Holt and Mrs. Chapman as the perfect scapegoats.

Holt punched the wall he had been leaning against as it all became clear to him. He did not think Cassidy or even the governor had planned all of this, but they were certainly taking advantage of the situation. And, as Holt had learned in the war, to know an enemy's motives was to know the enemy himself.

"What is it?" Ty Arbour asked him. "What's wrong?"

Holt knew it would take too long for him to explain, so he did not bother trying. "How well do you know the Mullen property?"

The attorney considered the question. "I know it well enough I suppose. I've been out there several times. The Mullens used to throw a party every spring. Why? You're not thinking of going out there are you?"

"No," Holt admitted. "I'm not thinking about it. I'm doing it and you're coming with me." He remembered Les Patrick and asked Klassen, "Can you spare him for a while, Doc?"

So much had happened over the past few moments that Klassen looked confused. "Yes, I suppose so. But you can't go riding out there, John. It's foolish."

Ty Arbour was already on his feet with his coat over his arm. "Whatever you need, John. You can count on me."

But Holt had other plans. "I'm not counting on you as much as I'm counting on your memory."

CHAPTER 24

Holt brought Arbour back to the mayor's office and found that she was not there. That was fine by Holt. He had come for the map, not the mayor.

He brought Arbour over to the map and pointed to the Mullen property. "You said you've been out there before, correct?"

Arbour nodded as he took in the map. "Yes, of course. From what I've seen of the place, this map looks accurate."

Holt was glad to hear that. "Does it jar your memory? Can you remember him ever taking you for a walk around the land while you were there at those parties? Did he ever tell you there was something special about the place? Not the view but about the land itself?"

"No, not really," Arbour admitted as he studied the map. "He never said anything about it. He told me why the house was special to him, but that's all. He told that story a lot, though. I'd bet everyone in town knows it."

Holt knew it might not be much, but it was something. "I don't know it. Try telling me."

"He said the house was where he had built his first shack when he came to Devil's Gulch," Arbour told him. "It was the site of his first mine. He said it hadn't yielded anything, but he didn't let that stop him from continuing the search.

He hit the mother lode of silver on the next shaft he started farther up in those rocks." Arbour's hand moved to the upper right edge of the map. "Up there somewhere. He said he built his house near his first mine to remind him to never give up."

Holt looked at the map again. He knew the answer had to be right in front of him. It had to be. He knew he was close. Joe Mullen was a literal man. He was not clever enough to speak in riddles or vague references. "Did he say he built the house on top of the old mine?"

"I remember someone asked him that once," Arbour recalled. "Someone's wife, but I don't remember who. He pointed to a section of the rock and said it had been over there but we couldn't see it. I remember looking, but I couldn't see it either."

Holt felt a cold sweat break out across his back. "Where did he point to, Ty? Close your eyes and think because this is important. Lives depend on what you say next."

Ty closed his eyes as he tried to summon a picture in his mind.

He placed his finger on the right side of the house. "He was standing there and he pointed to the rocky outcropping to his left, which would put it—"

"There." Holt pointed at the third outcropping. The only outcropping that Mullen's miners had not blown up earlier that afternoon.

"Yes," Ty decided. "I'm sure that's where it was because I remembered seeing a pile of rocks at the base of it and asked him if he had covered it up. He told me that the entrance was hidden, and those rocks had simply tumbled down the hill the previous winter."

Holt flicked the map with his finger. Now he saw the entire plan clearly. He had always known Mullen was too smart to have boxed himself in. He had blown up the two paths through the rocks because he did not need them. He already had an escape route ready. The old mine in the rocks must be it.

"Go back to your cousin," Holt told him as he rushed from the mayor's office. "You'll be better off there."

Arbour looked disappointed. "I thought you wanted me to go with you."

"I did," Holt yelled back. "That was before I knew where I was going."

Back at the jail, Holt split up the bullets he had just purchased at the general store between himself, Jack, and Bob.

"That was bothering me too," Bob said as he stuffed a box of bullets into his pocket. "I don't know Mullen, but I didn't think he'd cut himself off from a perfectly good escape route like that. And if he rode alongside the fields, he'd give up his biggest advantage. He'd be as exposed as we'd be coming in the opposite direction. Serves me right for not scouting that third wall closer. I should've known something was wrong when they didn't put the dynamite to it."

"Don't be so hard on yourself." Holt filled every loop on his belt with a bullet for his pistol, then dumped a handful of rounds into each of his coat pockets. "I was out there with you and I never thought to look either."

Jack loaded his shotgun and snapped it shut. "Too bad we couldn't have told Mr. Henderson about it before he rode off. Could've saved him the bother."

Holt did not think so. "If he sneaks through that side of the property, all the better. It'll keep Mullen's men on their toes. Give them something to shoot at other than us."

"And if it's us they see first?" Bob asked.

"Then they'll be shooting at us," Holt admitted. "But we'll have better cover than them in those rocks. And a nice mine to hide in if they get too close. It'll be like a turkey shoot if they come in after us and we won't be the turkeys."

"That's good," Bob said as he patted the rounds flat in his pocket. "I never did care much for the taste of turkey anyway. Stupid creatures. No taste to them, either, at least not in my experience."

Holt was glad they were ready to go so he did not have to fear being caught up in one of Bob's stories. "The problem with the mine is that we don't know exactly where it is. It's going on dark now and it'll be pitch black by the time we get close. We'll not only have to watch our footing but keep an eye out for the mine at the same time."

"Don't you go worrying about that," Bob said. "I'll be able to find it. Dark or no dark."

Jack laughed. "You planning on carrying a lantern with you? That could give Mullen's boys something to shoot at."

"A man doesn't have to see to find a mine, son. All he needs is this." He tapped his nose with a gnarled finger. "And a good set of these." He tugged on his earlobes.

Holt could tell a long explanation was coming, so he stepped outside and looked for Frank Peters. He saw him and Mrs. Chapman standing in front of County Hall and waved them to come over. He knew the jail would not be as comfortable as her own room, but it was much easier for Frank to defend it if the need arose, which also made it safer.

That did not mean the mayor was pleased about it and made sure to let her displeasure be known as soon as she got there. "Is all of this really necessary, Sheriff?"

"Let's hope it's not. And if that's the case, I'll be glad to offer you my apology in the morning."

As Mrs. Chapman entered the jail, Holt signaled Bob and Jack to come outside. He did not like all of his people being bunched up like this and was anxious to get underway while it was still bright enough to see the road.

Bob and Jack stepped out onto the boardwalk to start loading up their saddles, giving Holt time to give Frank a final bit of advice. "If something happens while we're gone, don't try to be a hero."

Frank Peters repeated what Holt had already told him three times that afternoon. "Keep the door shut, lock Mrs. Chapman in the cells, and lock the door. Shoot anyone who comes in who isn't you, Jack, or Bob."

"Or Henderson," Holt added. "That part might be important."

"Henderson," Frank said. "I remember. And thank you, John." He held out his hand to him. "Thank you for giving me this chance."

Holt was glad to see it was steady before he shook it. "You can thank me by doing what I said. Hopefully it won't come to anything, but if it does—"

"I'll be ready."

Holt ushered him inside and pulled the door shut as Peters threw the bolt from the other side.

He walked over to his horse and gave it a final look before climbing into the saddle.

Bob slid his Winchester into the saddle scabbard. "You sure leaving that drunk in charge of the mayor's a good idea?"

Holt was as sure of it as he could be. "He's not my first choice, but he's all I've got. There's something to be said for that."

"Guess it helps make the decision easier, doesn't it?" Jack observed.

"It certainly does." Holt pulled himself up into the saddle and backed his horse into the street. "Let's go, boys. We're burning daylight."

William Henderson stopped his horse at the edge of another mining camp.

It was already near dark, and this was the third camp he

had encountered. The first two had been easy to avoid. The miners were just coming back to the surface following a long day in constant darkness. Their eyes had not adjusted yet and they were too tired to be aware of their surroundings. He imagined Mullen had told them to be most watchful after the last of the sun's light disappeared behind the western horizon. Until then, the men would be busy cleaning up and enjoying their dinner. Henderson would use their distraction to his advantage and pass through without notice.

This one was tricky as the tents and shacks were spread out on either side of the trail he was using to snake his way through the hills and down toward the Mullen ranch. Cook fires had been started and the miners were beginning to linger around them for warmth. It was an especially warm night for early autumn, but there was a chill in the air.

Henderson was glad it was not summertime. The heat made men want to sleep outdoors, making his trek to the Mullen place even more of a challenge.

He kept his mount still as he listened to the sounds of the camp all around him. Muttered voices beneath canvas tents. Floorboards creaking in the shacks. Children being scolded by their parents. A giggle silenced by a slap.

These were the sounds he had come to read and understand when he had ridden with the Raiders. The subtle sounds of life that helped him avoid danger and live to fight another day. To carry on the battle for revenge against the men who had burned their land and killed their families not out of any loyalty to the Union, but out of the base desire to murder under the guise of patriotic duty.

Having already strapped down his rig tight before heading into the hills, Henderson urged his horse to step quietly through the edge of the camp. He did not fear a jangling bit or a rattling rifle betraying his position. He just hoped he was able to avoid being seen by a miner on their way back to their bed and meal.

He had just begun to think himself lucky when he heard a man call out to him from behind. "You, on the horse. State your business here."

Henderson stopped his horse and slowly turned around. "Evening, mister. I was just on my way to the next camp south of here."

"South?" The man's pink skin poked out from beneath the thin layer of coal dust on his face. He was roundish with stubby legs and a perpetual stoop of a man who had spent his life working chunks of ore out of the ground. He was undoubtedly strong, but hardly fast. "Which mine you working?"

Henderson had already thought of a story before he had even left the jail. He moved his horse closer. "Haven't started working it yet, mister. Wasn't told a name either. Just that it was off the top of the hill headed south. It's the first one I come to off this main trail here."

The miner was growing suspicious and took one step backward as Henderson's horse took another few steps toward him. "Who told you to look for a mine?"

"Why Mrs. Mullen herself," Henderson said. "Sarabelle Mullen. My wife and her are friends from way back. She wrote to her and told her I could find work at that claim."

"First I'm hearing about it," the round man told him. "What's your name?"

He saw no reason to lie as he was not known in this area. The horse was almost close enough. "Will Henderson. I farm a bit of land just south of here. Not a day's ride away. Crop's been poor this year, so I can use the extra money."

"Henderson," the man repeated as he backed into a tree, startling himself. "I didn't hear about any new man coming to work here and I'm the supervisor of this mine. I'd have known if someone—"

Henderson leapt from the horse as he pulled his blade. He fell on the miner just as his knife reached the end of its arc, burying itself in his heart. The impact as they both hit the ground buried the knife deeper, causing the man to gasp. His wide eyes staring wildly off to his right.

It was only then that Henderson noticed the pistol in his hand.

And with his dying breath, the miner squeezed the trigger. The single shot echoed like a thunderclap throughout the rocky land.

In one practiced motion he had honed dozens of times in battle, Henderson withdrew his blade as he got to his feet. One swipe of the blade across his pants cleared it as he slipped it back in its scabbard then climbed into the saddle with his left hand. In the span of less than five heartbeats, Henderson was back on the saddle and riding hard away from the camp.

He hunched low across his horse's neck as he dug his heels into the animal's flanks. The bay had spent many years on a farm, but like its rider, remembered how to flee the cries and shouts from surprised men in the darkness.

They darted through the trees as the panicked voices of miners filled the land behind him. And as if the first shot had left any doubt, someone began discharging a rifle.

Henderson knew that made it official. Mullen's miners knew he was coming and he still had more than halfway to go before he reached the flat land of the ranch.

Speed rather than stealth had become the order of his night.

CHAPTER 25

Joe Mullen stopped eating when he heard the shots.

McCaffrey and Hardt—rifles in hand—rushed into the dining room a moment later.

"You hear that?" McCaffrey asked him.

Hardt added, "Those are gunshots, Joe. Coming from the back of the house. Sound like they're still off a bit of ways."

Mullen did not bother to wipe his face as he got to his feet. None of his men were quick on the trigger. Not even the miners would shoot without good reason. Someone would get past them before they lost their nerve and shot blindly at shadows.

"You two best check the front of the house. I'll check the back."

The two escapees did as they were told while Mullen grabbed the rifle he had propped against the wall and moved at a crouch into the kitchen, where he had left Sarabelle and Lassiter bound and gagged in chairs. Mullen had drawn back the window coverings to make sure they could be seen. Anyone who had managed to get close enough to the house to see them might decide to take a shot at killing him. If they killed Lassiter, it would cost him his only bargaining chip, but would buy him precious seconds to ready himself.

Lassiter was his canary in the coal mine, an irony Mullen had rather enjoyed until he heard the rifle shots.

As he stole a quick glance outside, he was relieved to see several of his ranch hands were still in position in the dark. No one was firing, which meant the trouble was still up in the hills. He probably had plenty of time to make his escape.

Sarabelle had managed to work her gag free of her mouth and roared, "You hear that, Joe? That'll be Holt and his men coming for you. You think those half-blind fools up on the mountain are a match for a man like him? He's gonna get you, Joe. He's gonna run you down and string you up just like the frightened old stag you are."

She flinched when her husband wheeled to face her. His rifle was flush beneath her chin. He watched her shut her mouth as tight as her eyes as she waited for a blow or a shot.

He was glad to disappoint her. "Not on your life, Sarabelle dear. You'll be seeing me again real soon. I'll be back here before you know it, though you'll never know when."

She jumped when he spoke directly in her ear. "I hope you don't mind if I borrow your beau for a little while. I need him to help me out."

He withdrew from her as quickly as he had faced her and quickly undid the rope that had tied Lassiter's hands and feet to the chair. "Time for you to earn your keep, Hank."

He pulled the banker to his feet and shoved him toward the front room.

Lassiter made a feeble attempt to throw a punch, but Mullen easily sidestepped it and shouldered him off balance. Weak from days of having his hands and feet bound, Lassiter fell over.

"That'll be enough of that," Mullen said as he delivered a sharp kick to Lassiter's ribs. "I'm going to need you ready to move when I tell you to move. And if you pull anything like that again, I'll cripple you."

He snatched up Lassiter by the collar and hauled him into the front room.

"Can't see anyone out front," McCaffrey said.

Hardt said, "I checked the ridgeline and didn't see anything. Looks clear. Want me to make a play for the horses?"

Mullen decided now was the time to let them in on the rest of his plan. "I've gotten you boys this far, haven't I? I'm going to need you to trust me a bit farther. Think you can manage that?"

Both men said they would.

"Good, then follow right behind me. Keep your heads up and your eyes moving. Call out any movement you see but make sure you whisper. Don't shoot at it, either, unless they're right on us. Understand."

Again, both men said they understood, with McCaffrey adding, "What are we gonna do now, boss?"

Mullen threw Lassiter toward the front door. "Follow me and if you don't like small dark spaces, it'll be best if you keep it to yourself."

Holt looked up as he heard the echo of rifle fire rolling down the distant hillside.

Bob and Jack heard it too.

"That can't be good," Jack said as he joined the older men in ground-hobbling his horse. "Wonder if that's on account of Mr. Henderson."

Bob pulled his rifle from the saddle holster. "They ain't out shooting rabbits this time of night. That'll be Henderson sure enough."

Jack had clearly come to the same determination. "Hope they didn't get him."

Neither did Holt, but the sheriff knew all the hoping in the world would not change anything. Henderson had lost the element of surprise on the far side of Mullen's property, but he knew they had not been spotted yet along the rock line.

"Serves as a reminder for us to keep our heads down and our mouths shut while we move in," Holt whispered. "How's that nose of yours working, Bob? You sniff out the mine yet?"

He fell in behind the cook as the three of them crept toward the rocks. "Don't think I'll have to. I've got a feeling that weasel Mullen will lead us to his hole on his own before long."

Holt crouched next to him on a flat part of the outcropping. Even in the weak light of twilight, the new vantage point helped him appreciate the destruction the miners had carried out earlier that day.

Narrow paths had been dug out of two sides of the three rock outcroppings that surrounded the house. A path undoubtedly forged over the years by water led a meandering path down to the flat ground. He saw that path had been obliterated by rubble with the remnants of rocks blocking the path. Even on foot, the smaller stones would give way. Not only would it alert anyone in the house that someone was coming, but it also looked to break the leg of anyone trying to climb down quietly.

He was glad Bob had decided to come out there earlier in the day. If they had not known about the demolition, they might have found out too late and received only busted limbs and a bullet for their trouble.

He shifted his attention toward the ranch house when Bob quietly elbowed him in the shoulder. He saw the front door of the house had opened and he saw a shapeless mass of silhouettes spill outside.

There was still barely enough light left for Holt to see Bob hold up four fingers. He had counted four people leaving the ranch house. Holt knew one of them was bound to be Mullen. Another was probably Lassiter. The other two could have been the convicts or his ranch hands. Maybe Bart. Maybe Sarabelle Mullen. He decided trying to guess was pointless.

Holt remained still as he and Bob and Jack watched the shapes approach the rocky outcropping beneath him. One of the men tripped and fell to the ground. He heard Mullen's familiar voice cut loose with a stream of whispered curses as he shoved the man back to the two men behind him.

Holt pegged the clumsy one for Lassiter. The other two must have been men, since he doubted he would trust Sarabelle to watch his back or handle the prisoner.

Holt found he was holding his breath as Mullen led the small group up into the rocks. He climbed the path with ease and without benefit of a torch. He had obviously made the trip many times before. The three men behind him followed at a much slower pace, but still quicker than Holt would have liked.

He and Bob stretched their necks slowly over the ridge-line as Mullen led them close against the rock face. They saw him walk along a narrow path between the rocks until he disappeared about fifty feet beneath them.

They had reached Mullen's old mine.

After the last of them had disappeared inside for several seconds, Holt decided it was time to move. He had already spotted a few large rocks big enough to take his weight and, with his rifle in hand, lowered himself down to them. Bob and Jack followed him down.

Holt looked around and spotted a large rock just below him. He jumped down to it and landed quietly. He did not bother to check Bob's or Jack's progress. He was finding the way down for them all and did not want to risk being exposed for longer than he had to. There were still many men on the property with rifles. The quicker they reached the entrance of the mine, the safer they would be.

He moved to a rock on his left and spotted another one below him. He jumped down to it and slid the rest of the way down to the path that Mullen and his men had just taken. His back was sore from the hard edges that had dug into him on the last part of the way down, but he had made it without making a sound. He chanced a look back up at his companions and motioned which way they should take.

They followed Holt's direction, with Jack sliding down first, quickly followed by Bob.

The cook stifled a yelp when he landed and pawed at his back. Despite the failing light, Holt could see his hand was bloody.

Before Holt could say anything, the cook pushed past him and moved toward the entrance of the mine. Holt followed him with Jack bringing up the rear.

When Bob dropped to a crouch, Jack and Holt did the same.

Holt could see the flickering light of a torch coming from deep within the mine. Mullen and his men had made better time than Holt had thought or hoped they would.

Bob came back to them and whispered to Jack, "You think you could climb back up them rocks?"

Jack looked up at the way he had just come before whispering, "I guess I could find my way. But why?"

"Because we're gonna need them horses when we get to the end of this thing," Bob whispered.

Holt wished he had thought of that before they went down there. He whispered to his deputy, "Get the horses and follow these rocks for as long as you can. Move in a straight line. I don't know how far it'll go but keep going until you see flat land. If you can't make it down to us, stay up top and stay quiet. We'll find you when we reach the end. Got it?"

Jack said he did. Bob beckoned Holt to follow him and both of them set out in slow pursuit of Mullen through the darkness.

As Jack began to climb back up the very rocks he had just jumped down, he found himself wishing Bob and the sheriff had thought of the horses sooner. It was not that he minded climbing the rocks. He was not even tired. But he knew he was exposed every second he scaled the out-cropping.

He moved as slow and as sure as he had watched Holt move on the way down. He gently placed his shotgun against a rock before using both hands to pull himself up again. When he had reached the halfway point, he had gotten into a rhythm of movement.

He had just gotten a decent handhold on the rock above him when he was showered by bits of dust and rock. The report of a rifle sounded just after.

Jack's stomach ran cold. He had been spotted.

"Come quick!" a man below him and to his left cried out, "Someone's on the rocks."

Jack clamored up the rock and snatched his shotgun up as another bullet struck a good two feet behind him. He stole a quick glance above him to see how much farther he had to climb. He judged it to be about seven feet or so. Too far for him to risk it now that he had been seen.

He remained flat against the rocks as another shot rang out. No impact this time. The bullet must have sailed too high.

He heard another man's voice join the first one. "Where is he?"

"Can't see him now," the first man said. "But he's up there. About ten feet from the top."

Jack fought to keep from shaking as he gripped his shotgun tightly. The man had already come close to hitting him twice. He could just as easily guess the next shot and was bound to get lucky.

"You stay here," the second man said to the first. "I've got me an idea."

Jack knew he was as good as dead if he stayed there, but he was just as dead if he dared to move. He had no choice but to simply stand there like a statue until the men below made their move.

Jack did not chance even the quickest look around the rocky corner when he heard the scuff of the second man's boots on the ground. "This ought to shed some light on the situation."

Jack wondered what the men were planning, when he heard the first one say, "Wait a second. What do you think you're doing?"

"I'm gonna throw this up there," the second man told him.

"I've seen you rope," the first man said. "You've got a lousy arm. Give it to me. I'll do it."

"You?" the second man scoffed. "You throw a rope like my sister. You couldn't hit the side of those rocks. We've only got the one lamp. If I give it to you, you'll waste it."

Now Jack knew what the two men had in store for him. They were going to throw an oil lamp up at him and, when it shattered, hope it would light up his position. If the flaming oil did not burn him to death, their bullets would.

As the two men continued to argue about which one of them would throw the lamp, Jack chanced a quick look down at them. Each one had grabbed onto one side of a large oil lamp he had seen used on railroad cars. It was large and easy to see in the darkness.

It was also difficult to miss.

Jack brought his shotgun to his left shoulder, aimed down at the bickering men, and squeezed the trigger of both barrels.

The men screamed as much from the impact of the buckshot as they did from the burning oil from the shattered lamp. The liquid landed on their pants and shirts and boots. Jack watched them just long enough to see them throw themselves on the ground to douse the quickly spreading fire that threatened to consume them.

Knowing their screams of agony would bring more men to the spot, Jack knew it was time to get moving. He tossed his shotgun up to the next rock above him and scrambled to climb it. He heard more men beneath him kicking dirt and calling for the suffering men to be calm as he hauled himself up to and over the ledge. He had just managed to pull his shotgun away when bullets filled the air, peppering the same rocks he had just been on a few seconds before.

He stayed low as he ran for the horses. He could not afford to get shot now. The sheriff and Bob were counting on him.

CHAPTER 26

Holt had to keep his head low as he followed Bob through the pitch darkness of the mine. What little light they had received from Mullen's torch was long gone, so Holt knew the cook was moving on memory of what he had seen. Fortunately, the mine had been hewn from the rock in a relatively straight line. Narrower in some parts, lower in others, with only slight jogs to the left and right.

He had lost all sense of time since entering the cramped space. He imagined the absence of light was playing tricks on him. He found his mind drifting and had lost his sense of balance more than once. He had not fallen over, though he had been forced to steady himself against the rock walls several times.

It helped to be able to anchor his mind to something he could feel to keep his wits about him. He concentrated on the rock beneath his hands as he made sure to pick up his feet with every step. Even the slightest sound echoed, so one scrape of a boot would give them away. They were already boxed in with nowhere to go. It would not take a marksman to hit them in such spaces.

Holt stopped when he felt a hand on his face. Although he could not see him, he knew it had to be Bob. The confines of the mine were too close for it to have been anyone else.

Bob managed to more than whisper. "We're coming to a bend up ahead. Keep your eyes shut till I say."

Holt knew this was hardly the time to question him. It was too dark for him to see anything anyway, so he shut his eyes and continued following Bob as they felt their way through the mine.

After a few dozen additional steps, Holt sensed a wall in front of him. It was the bend in the mine that Bob had just mentioned. He quietly moved around with it to his right, conscious that the sudden shift in direction might slow Bob's pace. He did not want to risk walking into him and making noise.

Holt realized the mine snaked slightly back to the left and moved with it.

His body responded to the sound of gunmetal scraping rock before he made the decision to move. He dove hard into Bob's back, knocking the cook face-first before a rifle blast roared through the mine.

Holt slid over Bob's prone form and came to a stop on his elbows as the bullet ricocheted off the rock walls. He had landed ready to fire.

An unfamiliar voice echoed. "That's what you fools get for following us."

Holt did his best to aim at the sound, kept his rifle low, and squeezed the trigger. A man's bellow filled the air as Holt saw the wounded man's shot strike the ceiling.

Now that the element of surprise was lost, Holt got to his feet and moved quickly through the mine. He used his rifle as a guide to keep him from tripping over the man he had just shot.

He stopped when his barrel flicked what felt like a man's boot. Holt dropped to a knee and, because of the darkness, blindly felt for the man's neck. When he found it, he checked for a pulse, but the man was already dead.

Holt felt Bob tap him on the back. "Keep going. We can't lose them now."

Holt stepped over the body of the man he had just killed and got moving. The air was cooler in this part of the mine, and he could feel a hint of the night wind on his face. The space no longer felt as confined. He raised his arm as he broke into a trot and could not feel the ceiling.

He brought his rifle flush with his shoulder as he continued to move toward the mouth of the mine.

Holt had been in darkness so long that he was surprised when he was able to make out the exit set against the night sky. He broke to his left and took cover, ready to shoot anything that moved. Bob took the right and aimed outside. They remained crouched quietly and listened.

Holt quickly realized that Mullen and the others with him were long gone. A smoldering, discarded torch and fresh tracks on the ground were all they had left behind.

Bob cursed as he picked up the torch, thumbed a match alive, and set the wood aflame again. "That devil has all the luck, doesn't he?"

Holt stepped out from the mine but kept his eyes moving. The ground in front of the mine was flat and much of it was covered with overgrowth. He knew there was a chance that Mullen and the others were still out there waiting to ambush them. "He won't be moving as fast as he might have. I doubt he treated Lassiter well for the last couple of days and he's not used to being on horseback. He always preferred a wagon when he traveled."

Bob held the torch high and searched the area. "Where's Jack with those horses?"

Holt knew Jack would be along as soon as he was able. He had another question in mind. "Why'd you tell me to close my eyes back there?"

Bob did not stop looking over the ground. "We hit a jog in the wall. Made us slow our pace and made us easy targets. I didn't want us getting blinded by a gun blast if they shot at us. It was too dark to see much of anything anyway. Looks like I was right."

Holt imagined that maybe all of Bob's gray hair counted for something after all. "Good thing you were right."

The cook slowly straightened up. "Could've done without you flattening me like that. I think the bullet might've hurt less. That fella wasn't going to hit us with all that close rock around like it was."

"I hit him, didn't I?" Holt reminded him.

Bob grinned. "Yes, you did. Lucky shot."

They looked off to their right when they heard horses approaching from above. Bob remained standing while Holt moved to the overgrowth and took a knee.

"Put that torch down," Holt told him. "Could be one of Mullen's men."

"It's Jack with the horses," the cook said. "I can feel it in my bones."

Holt listened as the horses passed them, then heard smaller rocks that were kicked by hooves. They were coming down an incline beside the mine. He continued to track the noise until he saw Jack ride into a clearing where the two roads met. He was trailing their horses behind him by their reins.

"Sorry I couldn't get here sooner," Jack said. "The ground's awfully tricky in the dark."

Bob dropped the torch and walked toward the young deputy. "You did good, boy. You did really good."

Holt followed right behind him and climbed into the saddle just after Bob did. "There's only three of them now. We killed one of them back in the mine."

"Was it Mullen?" Jack asked hopefully.

Holt was sorry to have to disappoint him. "His face was too thin. But he's out there somewhere. We'll be seeing him soon enough."

"We will if you follow me," Bob said as he heeled his horse's flanks. "Let's go."

CHAPTER 27

As soon as Mullen heard the two shots from the mine, he knew McCaffrey was dead. One shot might have meant he had managed to kill Holt or anyone who might have been with him. But two shots so close together was bad news. A man only got one chance to kill John Holt and McCaffrey had flubbed it.

Mullen did not waste time mourning McCaffrey's passing as they rode through the mining camps. He had served his purpose when he thought he had heard movement behind them in the darkness of the mine. Sensed more than thought, Mullen imagined, for he had not heard a thing. He was glad McCaffrey had volunteered to stay behind and guard their retreat.

Mullen hoped the convict had wounded Holt. If he was injured, it might buy them even more valuable time as Mullen escaped with Hardt and his banker captive.

Mullen frowned back at the lagging horse upon which Lassiter rode. It served him right for having Bart pick out the mounts to stage at the mine exit should they need to escape. His foreman had always been a dependable man, but his troubles in town had obviously changed him. Mullen decided that if his plan went accordingly, he would need a new ramrod.

Mullen drew rein and allowed Lassiter to ride by before slapping the horse's rump, causing it to move with renewed speed. He was anxious to get to town under the cover of darkness. He would be able to take shortcuts through the mining camps he owned to get back to Devil's Gulch that much faster. He would make sure his miners delayed Holt for as long as possible.

He doubted they would be able to hold him indefinitely and he did not expect them to. None of them would be a patch for Holt and anyone riding with him. He just needed time to show Judge Cook and the Chapman widow that he had a gun to Hank Lassiter's head. He wanted them to see the look in his eyes so they would realize he meant to kill him unless he received that pardon from the governor. His efforts at diplomacy had failed. It was time for more direct action.

As he joined Lassiter and Hardt in riding through the dark forest, he realized he had not planned for what might happen after he received his pardon. He was usually a careful man who preferred to plot out his moves several steps in advance of taking them. But these were not usual times and Mullen was not the man he had once been. His conviction and time in jail had changed him and not for the better. He felt more reckless now and perhaps more desperate than ever before. He knew there was little chance of regaining the old life he had once enjoyed. If the governor caved to his demands, his political life would be finished.

But Mullen would deal with that if he had to. For now, he would have to hope the judge and the mayor would help secure his pardon when they laid eyes on the man Joe Mullen had become.

They reached a clearing in the wood and Hardt rode beside Lassiter's mount and pulled it to a halt.

Mullen was about to chastise him for the delay when the outlaw said, "Looks like we're coming up on some camps, boss. If those boys are out for blood as much as you say, then it might be a good idea if you ride out front. They're less apt to start blasting if they see you first."

Mullen found no fault in his logic. "Just keep an eye on Lassiter. Make sure he doesn't lag too far behind. We wouldn't want to lose him, would we?"

"Damn you, Joe Mullen," the banker spat. "Damn you for what you've done to me."

Lassiter cried out when Mullen grabbed hold of his neck and shook him. "You try anything to slow us up and I'll see to it that horse drags you. You don't have to be in good condition when I haul you before Cook and the Chapman woman. You just need to be alive. How alive you are at the time depends entirely on you."

Mullen released him with a shove and rode past him to take point. Behind him, he heard Hardt urge Lassiter's horse to get moving.

Despite all his worries, Mullen decided he was almost enjoying himself. He had spent too long rotting away in Holt's cell. His mind had grown dull as his mood darkened. Holt had done him a favor by putting him in Wheeler's prison wagon, though he had not known it at the time. And as he thought about it now, Mullen decided that things had gone remarkably well for him since. He had made his escape virtually unharmed save for the gash on his head. He had lost men along the way, but those had been manageable losses. He was about to ride through friendly mining camps full of men loyal to him. He would reach town before Holt and push the town leaders to do his bidding. He had the wind at his back and saw no reason why his luck would not continue.

He urged his horse to go faster as the sounds of a mining camp grew louder. Success was at hand.

* * *

Will Henderson stopped riding when he heard horses approaching from farther up the trail. He climbed down from the saddle and tethered his horse to a tree up the hillside. Rifle in hand, he moved to the rocks just off the trail and listened. He did not know who it might be, and given that he was in enemy territory, he could not risk discovery until he knew who was out there.

A man's voice was carried on the night wind. "Damn you, Joe Mullen. Damn you for what you've done to me."

Henderson tensed. Mullen had found a way to escape his ranch with at least one of his prisoners. Since it was a man's voice, he imagined it must be the banker. That was good. It meant Mullen would be traveling a mite slower than he probably liked. The pace would make it easier for Henderson to pounce.

He heard the horses get moving again and he grabbed hold of his knife. It was too dark for him to risk shooting at whomever crossed his path. He might hit Lassiter by mistake. Henderson did not care one way or the other but knew Holt would not be pleased about losing a hostage. He decided his knife was the best weapon at his disposal.

As the horses approached, Henderson left his rifle against the rock as he climbed out to get a perch from which he could leap. He felt the blood and excitement begin to race throughout his body. He had made such a move countless times before when he rode with Quantrill and his Raiders, but the excitement was always the same. Back then it had been to avenge all he had lost in Missouri. Now he would avenge a different kind of loss and he knew he was ready.

He waited until the first two riders passed before leaping from the rock at the third man. The horse screamed as Henderson crashed into the man, knocking the rider from his horse and riding him down to the ground.

Henderson rolled as soon as he hit the dirt and was back

on his feet before his target had a chance to regain himself. He lunged for the fallen man and felt the sharp pain of a bullet tearing through his left shoulder before he heard the shot. His momentum was stronger than impact and he reached out for the man he had set afoot.

He had not seen the hard right hand that connected with his jaw and sent him reeling backward. His heel hit a rock and he tumbled backward down a slight hill. He landed crooked and felt all the air escape his lungs in one forced breath.

Two more shots rang out as Henderson gasped for air. Seconds felt like hours as he struggled to will his lungs to work again.

"Looks like you got him, boss," Henderson heard a man say.

"Can you still ride?" Henderson took the voice for belonging to Mullen.

"It'll take more than that to finish me," the other man said. "Want me to go out there and make sure he's dead?"

"Get back on your horse," Mullen told him as he rode away. "We don't have a moment to lose."

Henderson tried to be still as he was finally able to draw in a decent breath. By the time he got to his feet and scrambled back up the incline, the three riders were long gone.

Will Henderson had failed.

His defeat was short-lived when he heard more riders coming approaching from the west. He imagined it was probably Holt and the others, but remained hidden behind a tree until he was sure. He saw Holt round the corner, pistol in hand as he rode.

Henderson tucked his knife into his belt and stepped out onto the trail. His empty hands raised. His left shoulder on fire from the gunshot would. "Don't shoot. It's just me."

Holt reined to a stop, as did Bob and Jack close behind him.

"We heard shots," Holt said. "That your doing?"

Henderson felt the hole in his shoulder and was glad to feel the bullet had passed clean through him. "Mullen and two others just rode by here and I tried to ambush them. Looks like they ambushed me."

"No wonder you lost the war." Holt did not seem to care about the farmer's embarrassment as he said to the others, "They're closer to Mullen than we thought. We can get them before they reach the mining camps."

Henderson kept blocking his path. "We're on the edge of the camps now, Sheriff. It's already too late."

"Get your horse and follow us." Holt turned to his men. "Get ready for a fight, boys. These miners will know we're coming and they're likely to try to stop us. Just ride through them as fast as you can. Shoot at anyone who shoots at you, but don't waste time trying to finish them off. We've got to get Mullen before he reaches town."

"This ain't my first taste of danger," Bob told him. "I was doing this before you were —"

But Holt had already dug his heels into his horse and charged down the trail before Bob could finish his thought.

"That boy is in an awful hurry to get himself shot at," Bob observed before pulling his gun and following Holt.

Jack remained behind. "You've been shot."

Henderson started going up the hillside to get his rifle. "I am and it ain't the first time."

"You fit to ride, Mr. Henderson?"

"Get going," Henderson told the young man as he moved amongst the rocks. "I'll be right behind you."

The boy did not waste any time joining the hunt. He admired Jack's youth and enthusiasm. His limber bones too. His were already beginning to ache and not just from the hole in his shoulder.

CHAPTER 28

Mullen braced for the impact of a bullet as he rode through the first camp. Men they had staked out along the trail had already called out that he was on his way, but it only took one nervous miner to ruin his plans.

He was glad to see five of them had spilled from their shacks and tents as he approached. All of them armed with either a rifle or a shotgun or shovels.

A short round miner he recognized smiled up at him. "Why, it really is you. I didn't believe it was true until this very moment."

"I'm alive, boys, but I won't be for long if Holt catches up to me. Think you can hold him up for a while?"

"We can do better than that." The miner hefted his shotgun. "We'll fill him full of holes and dump him down Old Betsy for his trouble. Nobody will ever find him there."

Mullen was glad the men were on his side. "Drinks on me for a week down at the Blue Bottle after all of this is done. And a raise in wages too!"

The men and their wives whooped and hollered in rejoicing as Mullen told Hardt, "Keep Lassiter close. We'll have some hard riding ahead. Don't want him taking a tumble from his horse, either by design or by accident."

He doffed his hat to more cheers from the miners as rifle

shots rang out behind him. That would be Holt and he was much closer than he would have preferred.

He stuck his hat back on his head as he brought his horse about and bolted into the night. Lassiter and Hardt were right behind him.

The night was quickly filled with shots and shouts as Mullen continued to race through the camps. He had taken to calling out, "It's Joe Mullen! Don't shoot!" as he rode.

It was enough to give the miners pause as he and the others sped by him. Each camp had been alerted to his approach by the sound of distant shooting and all gave a cheer as he darted by. He knew their loyalty only went as far as their wages, but at least they were putting up a fight. He could not have expected a better defense had he hired the Pinkertons to protect him.

As they rode through the last camp, he was glad to see more than thirty men waiting to defend him. He doubted they were good enough with the weapons they touted to stop a man of Holt's cunning, but at least he would not ride through the camps unchallenged.

He fought the urge to stop his horse as he broke clear of the rocks and saw Devil's Gulch spread out before him. Flickering oil lamps cast an uneasy glow along its crooked streets. The imperfect flames served as a beacon to him as if the town was calling him home. And Devil's Gulch was his home. It was his town, forged out of his own will and determination. He would sooner die than allow Holt or Sarabelle or anyone else to take it from him.

Just a little farther now. A little farther and the final phase of my plan will be set in motion.

He slowed his pace until he heard Lassiter and Hardt close the distance between them. "Hardt, draw your pistol and hold it on Mr. Lassiter for me until we get into town, then follow my lead."

"Already got him covered, boss," Hardt assured him. "And he knows it too."

Lassiter spoke over the echo of gunfire rising like an ill wind from the rocks behind them. "I don't know what you're planning, Mullen, but it won't work."

Mullen sneered at him. "Ye of little faith. You've always been a gambling man, Hank. So have I and I haven't lost yet."

He dug his heels into the horse's flanks and began his final descent toward town. Toward whatever destiny awaited him on the crooked wooden streets of Devil's Gulch.

He enjoyed watching all the townspeople who saw him back away as he led Hardt and Lassiter out of the alley. The Farmer and Miner's Bank loomed directly in front of him. The bell in the large clock in the tower high above him began to peal out past time as he approached. The bell sounded seven times. Seven o'clock on a cool autumn evening. He would have preferred to have been at home in front of his fire, digesting his supper as he tended to his accounts in his den. A glass of fine brandy at his elbow and a good Havana smoldering on its ashtray. Even a glass of whiskey at the Bottle would have been preferred above the task that now lay before him. He would have those things again and soon.

He climbed down from the saddle and hitched the reins to the rail in front of the bank as he had done countless times before in better days. He drew his pistol but kept it at his side as he climbed up onto the boardwalk and greeted the frightened onlookers as if he was a general just returned from a long, victorious battle.

"Good evening, ladies and gentlemen," he said with a bow as they backed farther away from them. "The rumors are, indeed, true and I have been freed from bondage. Just here

to conduct a little business is all before it becomes official
and legal."

He gestured toward Lassiter as Hardt pulled the banker
down from his horse. Hardt had grabbed a boy running by
and handed something to him before the kid continued running down Main Street. Mullen made a mental note to ask
him what it was about later.

"As you can see," Mullen continued, "I've even brought
Hank with me to help in my plight. I know I can count on all
of you for your support."

Hardt shoved Lassiter up the stairs and Mullen grabbed
him before he tripped.

Mullen laughed it off for the benefit of the crowd. "He's
fine, folks. Just a little winded from the hard ride down the
hill." He pulled Lassiter close and spoke directly into his
ear. "Get out your keys and open that door or I'll plug you
in the knee."

Lassiter fumbled the keys out of his pocket as Mullen
continued his address. "We're here for a meeting with Judge
Cook and the Chapman woman. Would one of you be kind
enough to tell them we're here? We'll be waiting for them
inside."

Lassiter finally got the bank door open and Mullen
stepped forward to put his foot in the door to keep the banker
from closing it behind him. "Thanks, Hank. Don't go anywhere. We need to get things ready to receive our guests."

"The only thing you're gonna receive is a bullet to the
belly," a man said from the thoroughfare.

Mullen looked up and squinted in the direction from
where the voice had come. It took him a few seconds to
recognize Frank Peters as the man holding a rifle aimed at
his chest.

"Frank Peters?" Mullen asked out loud. "Is that you?"

"It's Deputy Frank Peters to you, Mullen." He watched

his grip on the rifle tighten. "Now, step away from the door and let Hank lock it before I blow you off that porch."

Mullen's eyes shifted to Hardt, who was still on the ground between the horses. He had shifted his aim from Lassiter and was slowly moving to shoot Peters.

Mullen continued his distraction. "I can't decide if you're holding that rifle or if that rifle's holding you up. Holt might be a fool, but he's not fool enough to pin a star on your chest again."

"He did," Peters told him. "And I'm gonna stain that shirt of yours if you don't back away from that door like I told you."

Mullen sensed Lassiter was about to bolt deeper into the bank and grabbed his arm before he got around to doing it.

"You must be on quite a bender, Frank," Mullen said. "I'll tell you what I'll do. You were always good for a laugh. After I get settled here, I'll toss out a dollar for you. Buy yourself a drink. It looks like you're in dire need of one."

Peters licked his lips as he raised his aim. "I reckon I'm sober enough to drill you where you stand. Now—"

Hardt moved out from behind the horse and shot Peters. The deputy's rifle fired high as he staggered backward. The little outlaw might not have looked like much, but he was certainly fast.

Mullen kept his foot in the door and his grip on Lassiter as he fired twice. The two shots were enough to finally knock the big man down.

The townspeople cried out as they backed farther away from him, scattering among the shops and doorways around town.

Mullen lowered his smoking pistol. "I'm sure those aren't the only shots Frank's had all day, but they're sure to be his last." He beckoned Hardt up onto the boardwalk and told him to bring Lassiter inside. The outlaw had thought enough to take his rifle from the saddle before carrying out the task.

Mullen made a final address to the crowd. "That's all for

now, everyone. But be sure to come back in an hour to see the next show." Then, as if an afterthought, he said, "Oh, and don't forget to fetch the judge and the mayor. Hank will feel the brunt of it if you don't."

He stepped inside and shut the door behind him. He threw the heavy locks and bolt on the bank door. He leaned against it and allowed himself a smile.

I've made it. I've won. Victory is close. My freedom is at hand. I can almost taste it.

He realized Hardt and Lassiter were looking at him and the attention forced him to set aside his celebration. His plan was not finished and there was still a great deal of work to be done.

To Hardt, he said, "Stay here by the door. Keep an eye on that window over there and let me know if anyone tries anything stupid. If you see any sign of Holt or the others, call it out."

"You can count on me, boss," Hardt said as he took up his position, rifle in hand. "And if things go poorly, don't worry, I have a plan."

Mullen remembered Hardt grabbing that young boy in front of the bank before sending him on his way. "What did you say to that kid out there."

"All part of my plan," Hardt assured him. "Hopefully it won't come to anything."

Mullen was amused. "And here I was thinking all the planning was my job."

"It is," Hardt said. "But it can't hurt to have more than one plan, does it?"

Mullen decided he could not argue with him there. He only hoped he did not have to rely on the schemes of the smallish outlaw to survive.

Lassiter swallowed hard. "What do you have planned for me now?"

"The hard part is done, Hank." Mullen threw an arm

around the banker's shoulders and led him toward a chair at one of the clerk desks. "We're in the most secure building in town and there's no way anyone can get in here without us letting them. If Cook and the Chapman widow are as fond' of you as I suspect, they'll wire the governor and secure that pardon from the governor in exchange for your release."

"They'll never do that," Lassiter said with as much defiance as he could muster. "Holt won't let them. They'll see me dead first and then what'll you do?"

Mullen laughed as he pushed the banker down into a chair. "Don't trouble yourself with such details, Hank. Besides, I learned a long time ago that you can always count on a politician to do what's in their best interests before they think of the public good. And you make a lot of important people an awful lot of money. All I need is the governor's signature on a piece of paper. That's a small price to pay in exchange for the life of the goose that lays the golden egg, don't you think?"

Lassiter looked as if he wanted to continue the argument but thought better of it. He sagged in the chair instead. "I wish I'd stayed home that night instead of going to Sarabelle's house for dinner. I regret the day I ever laid eyes on that woman."

"You don't know the first thing about regret," Mullen said. "At least not yet." He leaned on the arms of the chair, forcing Lassiter as far back as possible. "But before all of this is over, you will. I promise you that."

Mullen laughed as he stood up. His cackle echoed in the empty bank. When he stopped, he heard gunfire raining down outside from the rocks above Devil's Gulch. The sound was louder now. Holt was making good time. He would reach town soon, or at least whatever was left of him.

Then the final piece of Mullen's plan would fall into place.

CHAPTER 29

Holt rode low across his horse's neck as the night filled with gun smoke.

The miners had put up a better defense than he had been expecting. They had hidden men along the trail to shoot at anyone who rode by. Mullen had done a good job of rallying them as he rode through.

Holt had been in this spot before and knew his best chance of survival was to stay low and ride hard. Returning fire was pointless and would only serve to make himself a target. Five of the miners had been foolish enough to step out into the road to block his path. He had dispatched them before any of them had managed to get off a shot.

He did not dare look behind him to see if Bob or Jack were still there. He was in no position to help them anyway amid the hail of gunfire coming from all sides.

As he rounded into the final camp, a miner cut loose with a rebel yell as he ran toward him blindly firing a pistol. All the shots went wide before Holt's horse barreled into him and knocked the man back into a roaring campfire.

He cleared the final camp and did not slow his pace until he saw the lights of Devil's Gulch in the distance. He opened the cylinder of his pistol and dumped out the empty rounds before quickly feeding fresh bullets into it.

He had just finished reloading when he heard riders behind him. He was glad to see it was only Bob, Jack, and Will Henderson.

"Any of you hit?" he asked them when they joined him.

"My horse took a bullet or two," Bob said as he and the others began loading their guns, "but he should make it as far as the town. It's still an awfully long walk from here."

Holt hated to hear about the horse, but it was unavoidable in battle. "What about you, Jack?"

"A couple of scratches here and there, but I'm fine. Not too sure about Mr. Henderson, though."

Holt moved his horse toward the farmer and saw he was bleeding badly on the left side. His shoulder was stained and so was the left side of his chest. "How bad is it?"

"Caught one in the shoulder back when I jumped Mullen's man," Henderson said. "Caught another one in the side as I rode by. Rifle, I think. It looks worse than it is. I'm fine."

Holt knew the farmer was far from fine, but there was nothing they could do about that now. "Looks like we didn't catch up to Mullen in time. He's probably already made it to town. Probably has himself holed up somewhere. The Blue Bottle is my guess. He and Cassidy were always close. We'll swing around to the end of town and approach from the jail. He won't risk going near Ma's men at the Railhead."

He did not wait for them to agree or finish reloading before moving off in that direction. He did not dwell on the fact that he had missed his chance to catch Mullen out in the open. The time for that had passed and all the wishing in the world would not change things. He was digging in now. Digging in good. He knew Holt was coming for him and he was getting ready. All Holt could do is let the matter play out and be ready if Mullen made a mistake.

He allowed the horse to move at a gentler pace now that they were clear of the camps. He had demanded a lot from the animal, perhaps too much, and he did not want to risk tiring it out completely before they reached town. Like Bob had observed, it was a long walk. Besides, there was no longer any reason to hurry. He only hoped that Peters had remained on the straight and narrow while Holt had been away. The former drunk might not be good for much, but he imagined he would need all the help he could get now that Mullen had made it to relative safety.

As soon as Holt entered town at the far end of Main Street, it was clear that Mullen had already made his presence known. People were huddled together in tight clusters along the boardwalk. The worry clear on their faces softened when they saw Holt riding past.

He was especially relieved to see Charlie Gardiner standing in front of the jail. His rifle propped up on the porch post he was leaning against.

"Evening, Sheriff," the former outlaw said as he touched the brim of his hat. "Sounds like you've had yourself quite a time of it."

Holt was in no mood for idle chatter as he climbed down from his horse. "Mullen here?"

Gardiner nodded up the street. "Mullen and Cecil Hardt got themselves all nice and snug up in the bank. They even thought to bring Hank Lassiter with him."

Holt had been hoping Mullen would have taken refuge in the saloon. It would've been easier for them to take him down that way. Choosing the bank complicated things. Holt figured he would just have to come up with a plan to watch him and react accordingly.

"I take it Peters is down at the bank."

"He was when they shot him. Now he's in the jail being tended to by Doc Klassen. You'd better get in there if you want to see him before he passes. He doesn't look too long for this world."

Holt cursed him for not telling him that in the beginning as he barged into the jail.

He found Peters as he had found Mayor Blair Chapman, bleeding on the bed behind his desk with Ralph Klassen crouched beside him. He looked up at Holt and slowly shook his head.

Peters struggled to lift his head from the pillow as Holt rushed to him. "Don't do that, Frank. Just lie still. It's going to be just fine. I'm back now."

"I . . . I was sober, John," Peters rasped. "Sober as a judge when it happened."

With all that had happened to him, Holt could hardly believe this was troubling the dying man. "I know that, Frank."

"I . . . I did my best, John. I tried, but he had another fella with him. They're in the bank now."

Holt took the man's hand and gripped it tight. "You don't have to worry about that now. Just lie still and let the doc here do his job. He'll have you patched up in no time, just like he did with Les."

Peters's lips quivered as he tried to say more, but his eyes grew wide as he seemed to glimpse whatever waited for him in his dying mind. And when those same eyes dimmed, a final breath escaped him. His body went slack, and Holt knew he was gone.

Klassen looked down at them. "He wouldn't let me give him any whiskey for the pain. Said he didn't want to smell of it when you got here."

Holt set the dead hand on Peters's chest and stood. "You see it happen?"

"No, but I had him brought here right after," Klassen said. "He was hit three times. Mullen and one of his men caught him. Heard he was steady, though."

Holt had seen men die worse. Frank Peters had not been a good man in life, but in death, he had been good enough. He only wished that counted for something.

Holt turned around when he heard Bob and Jack help Henderson into the jail.

Jack said, "Mr. Henderson here could sure use your help, Doc."

"Bring him into one of the cells in the back," Klassen directed him. "I'll tend to him there."

Holt decided he would not be of much use to Henderson in the cramped cell, so he went outside to talk to Gardiner some more. The outlaw was still leaning against the post as if he did not have a care in the world.

"You make it in time?"

Holt fought the urge to punch him. "No thanks to you."

Gardiner looked him up and down. "I didn't peg you for being one of those fellas who heaps praise on a man just because he winds up dead. Frank Peters was a drunk and a bully. Just because he got killed don't make him a saint."

"He died better than he lived," Holt said. "The rest of us should be so lucky."

"I don't aim to die at all," Gardiner said. "At least not tonight."

Holt decided he would only get aggravated, so he changed the subject. "Mullen say anything before he went into the bank?"

"Said all sorts of things," Gardiner told him, "not that I heard it personally. From what I've heard from those hens cackling in front of the Railhead, he was gassing on about getting that pardon from the governor he's been aiming for. Sounds to me like he might get it too. The mayor and Norm Selwyn are up in her office right now talking about it."

Holt knew he had learned as much as he was bound to get from Gardiner. It was time for him to hear it for himself. "You think you could hang around here for a while in case I need you?"

"I plan on being around. As for helping you, it depends on what you need doing."

"I wasn't planning on asking you to bake a cake for the church picnic."

"Didn't think you were," Gardiner said. "I'll be around if you need me. Just give a holler when you do."

Holt began walking up Main Street. "It won't be that subtle."

Holt turned when he heard a woman call his name and was glad to see Jean rushing across the thoroughfare to meet him.

She forgot about discretion as she threw her arms around him. "Thank God you're not hurt."

He felt some of the grit go out of him as he soaked in her embrace. "I'm fine, honey. Don't worry about me."

"But I *was* worried," she protested, "especially when I heard all those shots coming down from the hills like they were." She pulled away from him and looked him over. "Were you shot?"

He gently took her hands and eased them away from him. "I'm fine. One of my men got hit but I'm fine."

Her face relaxed just a little. "You heard Mullen's in the bank."

"Charlie told me. I'm on my way to talk it over with the mayor right now."

She slipped her arm around his. "Then I'm going with you. I don't plan on letting you out of my sight from now on."

But Holt did not want her anywhere near County Hall, much less the bank. "If you want to help me, the best thing you can do right now is run some coffee over to the jail. We've got a long night ahead of us and likely an even longer morning. Those men have had a tough time of it and your cooking will help it pass a bit better."

"I've already got my girls working on that," she told him. "Let me go with you. I'll keep an eye on things for you. He won't expect that coming from me."

Holt admired her bravery but could not afford it. "I can't

have you with me, Jean. Mullen knows about us. I don't want to risk him using you to get at me. I don't want you hurt. I've already got enough to worry about as it is."

"And what about me worrying about you?"

"I promised you I won't die on you, remember? And I always live up to my promises."

She was about to say something, but her voice cracked, and she threw her arms around him again. "Just don't go doing something stupid. I just found you. I don't plan on losing you."

Holt allowed himself to rest his chin on her head. He absorbed her concern. Her love. He would need it to sustain him in the fight ahead. "The only stupid thing I plan on doing is walking away from you now. Go help your girls with the food. Helping my men is the best way you can help me."

She released him and ran back across the thoroughfare. He hated to see her cry and hated himself for being the cause of it.

But he set his hatred aside as he walked toward the bank and County Hall beyond it.

CHAPTER 30

"Impregnable," Norman Selwyn said with a measure of pride as they sat in the mayor's office. "Mr. Lassiter built that bank to be impregnable and, by God, it is."

Holt was glad Mayor Chapman was not impressed. "It can't be too impregnable, Norm. The place was robbed recently, remember? By a couple of boys, as I remember. The Turnbulls, wasn't it?"

The bank president frowned. "That was only due to the carelessness of the guards. If they had been more careful with keeping the doors shut, the robbery would have been foiled. Many a bandit has tried to enter that building after hours and have gotten nothing but frustration for their troubles."

He raised a finger each time he discussed how secure the bank was. "The front door, while elegant, is cast iron with a thick wooden casing. You'd need a cannon to make a dent in it and it still wouldn't budge. Mr. Lassiter had it built in Chicago and shipped all the way here on special order."

"Bully for him," Holt said.

"Sneer all you want," Selwyn said, "but I'm not finished yet. The back door is also made of reinforced iron built into the framework. It's guaranteed to withstand a dynamite blast or the pull from an eight-horse team. And I'm not talking about just any horses, mind you. I'm talking about

Clydesdales. I saw a demonstration of it myself when Mr. Lassiter sent me to Chicago. Most impressive, sir. And bad news for you."

Holt was growing impatient. "It's got a big window in the front. Never saw glass that could stop a bullet."

Selwyn sat forward in his chair. "Glass that's four panes thick with wire netting between it. It might break eventually, but not from a stray bullet, nor from fifty such bullets. Not enough to allow you to hit anyone without tipping off Mullen of what you're doing. It's designed to withstand an assault from a Gatling gun. And that's not just conjecture, sir. I saw it with my own two eyes—"

"When Mr. Lassiter sent you to Chicago," Holt said, finishing the banker's thought for him.

Selwyn sank back in his chair. "I'm not fighting you, Sheriff. Merely telling you what you're up against. Joe Mullen picked the most secure building in town, perhaps even the territory, to hide in."

But Holt knew there was more to it than that. "Sounds to me like you're trying awfully hard to talk yourself into something. Like getting Mullen that pardon he's demanding."

"I don't see what other choice we have," Selwyn said. "There's no way for you to get into the bank to get him and no way for you to shoot him even if he stood in front of the window. Dynamite won't work and neither will bullets. And, if by some miracle you managed to get inside, all Mullen would have to do is go into the vault and pull the door behind him. It's designed to lock from the inside, a feature Mr. Lassiter demanded to be included in the design."

Holt figured Selwyn had seen that in his trip to Chicago, too, but decided not to find out for certain.

Mrs. Chapman broke the silence. "Too bad we can't force him into the vault and starve him out. That would be one way to end this."

Holt thought of something. "What about the roof?"

"There are no entrances to it from the outside and the clock tower is too high to scale. The only way to the top of it is by a ladder inside the tower. I suppose it could be done, of course. Perhaps the miners could help blow it up, in the unlikely event you could get any of them to help you, but you would lose any element of surprise."

Holt had no choice but to agree that Selwyn had painted a dire picture. There was no obvious way into the bank and no way to force Mullen out. Not without a great amount of effort that would most likely fail.

"Blowing up the tower is pointless," Holt said. "The street would be full of rubble and anyone on the roof would be hurt or killed before they could get clear. Even if we evacuated the town, it wouldn't be worth the effort."

Selwyn's eyebrows rose. "Hence my urging to give Mullen his pardon. I don't like it any more than either of you. It sets a horrible precedent, but I feel it's the only way we can avoid further bloodshed."

"And you get to keep your job," Holt said. "Let's not forget that part."

He had expected the banker to shy away from the jab and was surprised when he did not. "You get to keep your job, too, Sheriff. No one in this office is here out of the goodness of their heart and all of us seek to retain our positions after this crisis has passed. My job. Your job and the mayor's too. Not to mention Mr. Lassiter's life hangs in the balance."

Holt dropped his head into his hands and rubbed his temples. He hoped to get the blood flowing in his mind so he could find a way clear of this mess. But no matter how hard he thought about it, there was only one way to stop it.

"There's another way to bring all of this to a close. It won't be pretty, but it's all we've got."

Mrs. Chapman and Selwyn exchanged glances as they sat up straighter.

The mayor asked, "What do you propose, John?"
Holt lifted his head. "Me."

After he finished detailing his plan, he left the mayor and the banker alone to grumble about its prospects in private. He was surprised to find Judge Cook sitting on the stairs leading up to his office, smoking a cigar.

The man looked as if he had not slept in days and Holt imagined he had not. The bandage on his head had not been changed in all that time, though the judge did not seem to notice.

He looked up when he heard Holt's footsteps echo in the hall. "Guess you're wondering why I'm sitting out here like this."

"Not really."

"A lot of ugliness happened in my office," Cook said. "I don't like spending as much time in there as I used to. Besides, the place isn't the same with poor old Les still laid up like he is."

Holt had almost forgotten about Les Patrick. "I'm sure he'll pull through. Don't blame you for having bad memories of your office. What Geary did wasn't easy to forget."

"I guess fear is just another one of nature's rewards for getting old." He gestured toward the mayor's office. "Sounds to me like your meeting with Mrs. Chapman and Norm Selwyn didn't go so well."

Holt joined Cook by sitting on the stairs. He could not carry out his plan unless at least one of them was ready to help him. Judging by the amount of arguing he could still hear from the office it would be a while for either of them to warm up to it. He did not blame them. After all, he was asking them to step into harm's way and trust him with their lives.

"They'll see there's no other way to get Mullen out of that bank. I just need to let it sink in a little."

"From what I overheard from my perch out here, I think you're right. But they're also entitled to have their reservations."

"Guess that means you have reservations about me too," Holt concluded.

"Someone has to. You certainly don't. You're just about the most self-assured young man I've ever met. Your trouble is that you're every bit as good as you think you are. But you only need to be wrong once."

"I'm not wrong where Mullen is concerned," Holt said. "I know how to handle him and I will handle him if those two give me the chance."

"Frank Peters thought he could handle him too," the judge noted. "Once when he was sheriff. Mullen and his Vigilance Committee broke his spirit, which set him to drinking. He was done for even before he pulled off his badge and threw in with Ma McAdam. He went up against him again today. Look at where it got him. Shot to pieces in broad daylight just when he was trying to get back on his feet. Joe Mullen's like quicksand. Everything he touches gets pulled to the bottom with him. He'll do it to you, too, John, if you let him."

Holt did not like the direction their talk was taking. "Sounds to me like you think he should get his pardon."

"No. I've lived my entire life applying the rule of law the best way I knew how. But I'm not just the judge of Devil's Gulch. I also live here and as a citizen, I can't stand the number of good people he's used over the years. The lives he's destroyed. Judge Cook wants to see him swing from the gallows. But William Cook would like nothing better than to see him just go away."

Holt felt awkward about asking for the judge's help, but his plan would not work if he tried it alone. "If Mrs. Chapman and Selwyn turn me down, do you think you might be able to help? Mullen already thought you were important enough to send Geary to bring you out to the ranch before. You might be able to get him to come to the door now."

The judge wasted no time in turning him down flat. "Not a chance. I couldn't be party to what might be seen as an extrajudicial execution. Have you decided what might happen if your plan fails? What happens if Hank Lassiter gets killed because something goes wrong?"

Holt had already taken that into account. "Selwyn will take his place. If there's something this country's got plenty of, it's bankers and lawyers. And the only thing holding it together is the law. That's why we can't let Mullen get away with this or let this go on long enough for him to receive a pardon. I saw what happened when half a country decided the law didn't matter anymore. I spent four years of my life proving them wrong. I didn't endure all that just to give in to them now."

"Quite a speech, but no sale," Judge Cook said. "Bring him before me in a courtroom and I can all but assure he'll be found guilty and this time I'll see to it he hangs. But my powers are contained to the inside of my courtroom."

Holt's meeting with the mayor and Selwyn had already left him frustrated. Judge Cook's unwillingness to cooperate only added to it. "I'm not asking Judge Cook to do it. I'm asking Bill Cook, citizen."

"Both of them say no, but they wish you well."

Holt could tell his answer was final and decided against continuing the argument any further.

He looked up when he heard footsteps in the hall. Mayor Chapman and Mr. Selwyn looked as though they had made decisions of their own.

The mayor asked him, "Are you quite certain you can do it, John?"

"Yes, as long as you do exactly what I tell you to do when I tell you to do it."

Mr. Selwyn cleared his throat. "And all we have to do is stand there?"

"Stand there," Holt said, "and pray."

CHAPTER 31

At the Blue Bottle Saloon, Tony Cassidy was trying to decipher the truth of all that had happened from a group of regulars when Simpson, his bartender, beckoned him to come to the far end of the bar.

Cassidy reluctantly broke off from the men and joined Simpson at the back of the saloon. "This had better be important. I'm trying to find out what's going on out there. Or at least what they think is going on."

"I know, boss, but we've got trouble coming our way. Big trouble. One of the regulars just told me half the miners are coming off the mountain and into town right now."

Tony had not been expecting that. The events of the day had happened so quickly that he never had time to even consider it. "Half you say? How many is that? Fifty?"

"Fifty's near as he can figure," Simpson said. "Every one of them is armed too. Somebody must've gotten word to them that Mullen's in the bank. They plan on surrounding the bank to make sure Holt or somebody else doesn't try to kill Joe before he gets that pardon he's aiming for. Said they're willing to shut down the town if need be."

But Cassidy knew better. This was not a spontaneous outburst of support for their leader. Mullen had most likely paid off some of the mine's biggest rabble-rousers to stir up trouble in the camps. The gunfire he had heard coming from the hill earlier proved they had tried to defend Mullen from Holt once. They had planned it that way. It stood to reason that at least some of them would want to continue that fight here in town. He cursed himself for not thinking of it earlier.

Every second Mullen was alive cost Cassidy money under the new arrangement he had struck with Sarabelle Mullen. And if fifty miners went up against John Holt and his men, most of them would either be killed or too busted up to work. That would cost Tony Cassidy dearly.

Simpson interrupted his thoughts by saying, "This is mighty bad, boss. What do you want to do about it?"

"Shut your mouth for a moment and let me think." Cassidy turned away from him as he took stock of the situation. About what he could do about it.

He quickly realized there might be something he could do. Most of the miners—if not all of them—were regular customers of his every payday. He would probably know most of them. They would certainly know him.

Just as Cassidy knew that if they surrounded the bank, the odds would be in Mullen's favor. He might be able to get his pardon after all.

Cassidy knew of only one way he might be able to change their mind. He had used the tactic once to stir them up. It might work now to calm them down.

It was also the only weapon Tony Cassidy had at his disposal. He asked the bartender, "How close are they supposed to be?"

"Not far was all according to him."

Cassidy knew he did not have much time. If they reached town before he had the chance to head them off, his plan might not work.

"Get back behind the bar. Make sure you keep the

whiskey flowing and follow my lead. It'll cost us plenty, but not as much as it will if those fools get themselves killed. I'll be back when I can."

Cassidy ignored the questions and odd looks he drew from his customers as he rushed out of the saloon and into the street. And as each of them returned their attentions to their whiskey or beer, none of them could remember a time when they had seen Tony Cassidy move so fast or with such purpose.

They did not know it at the time, but they had never seen him fight for his future before.

Cassidy had no trouble spotting the men as they approached the town. The lit torches they held were like fireflies on a warm evening. Only that evening was far from warm. It was cold and damp. He only hoped he could find a way to keep it that way.

Some of the miners cheered when they saw Cassidy waiting to greet them in the middle of the thoroughfare. He judged Simpson's information was correct. There were about fifty or so men loaded into flatbed wagons and on horseback. It explained how they had been able to make it to town so quickly.

Tony was not surprised to see Nels Stewart driving the first wagon. The stocky Swede was always one of the loudest in the saloon when he got a few drinks into him. He was the last to buy a round but always more than willing to accept a free drink. He was known to consider himself something of an authority on mining, politics, and almost any other subject at hand.

"I'm afraid this ain't a social call, Tony," Stewart told him as he brought the wagon to a stop. "We're here on account of Joe."

"So am I." Cassidy made sure to speak loud enough so the rest of the miners could hear him. "As a matter of fact, he's sent me to welcome you boys to town and thank you for your loyalty."

A ripple of surprise and excitement went through the miners. Joe Mullen was a generous man who knew their worth.

Nels Stewart and a few others did not seem convinced. Cassidy knew these must have been the men Mullen had paid for their cooperation.

"Welcome us how?" Nels asked. "Mr. Mullen didn't say nothing about any appreciation to us."

"That's because I've just come back from talking to him over at the bank. He wanted me to tell you boys that he made it there safely and there's no way Holt or any of the other scoundrels were riding with him. There won't be any trouble for a while, and he hates the idea of you boys freezing for no reason. That's why he's been generous enough to pay me to let you boys drink your fill. Along with any other entertainment you boys might want."

Cassidy knew the quickest way to a miner's heart was through his liver, and the prospect of free whiskey and beer was too much for them to ignore. They threw up a cheer that Cassidy had not heard since news of Lee's surrender had reached him.

Stewart did not join the men. Neither did nine of the others. "This doesn't sound like Joe to me."

"Sure, it does," Cassidy said, keeping his voice loud enough for the men to hear. "The Vigilance Committee did it a month ago and it turned out well. He wants to bring the committee back and you boys are going to be the start of it." He played to the men. "I'm not trying to outshine you, Nels. If you want to keep these boys from good liquor on a cold night, I won't stop you."

The miners began spilling from the wagon before Nels or any of the others could stop them. They did not even try. They knew the most dangerous piece of land in the territory was between a miner and his drink.

Cassidy accepted the handshakes and pats on the back the men gave him as they rushed by and toward the welcoming glow of the Blue Bottle Saloon.

Nels Stewart and the eight other wagon drivers did not join them. Neither did the two men on horseback. They did not do much of anything except listen for Nels to tell them what he wanted to do next.

"What game are you playing here, Cassidy?" Nels asked him. "I know full well that Joe didn't tell you to do this."

"Why?" Cassidy asked. "Because he didn't tell you about it first? Since when has Joe Mullen asked the opinion of the men who work for him?" He laughed. "He hasn't been locked up long enough to change that much."

Nels stabbed a crooked finger down at Cassidy. "I'm gonna ride over to that bank and ask him personally. And if Mr. Mullins tells me this was all your doing, me and these boys are going to march right in there and hang you from the rafters."

Cassidy threw up his hands and backed away from the wagon. "You're more than welcome to try, Nels, though you'll find it's awfully crowded in there at the moment. And I don't think your boys will think too kindly of you pulling free drinks from their hands."

Nels balled his hands into fists before snapping the reins of the horses and driving them toward the bank.

Cassidy stood aside as he watched the eight wagons file by him. Each of the drivers looking more sour than the one before.

He turned and watched them as they rode toward the bank. His plan had worked, at least for the moment. Soon the men would be too drunk to care about why they had come to town. A few of them might get rowdy, but drunk men are less likely to be effective in a fight.

He was about to head back into his saloon when he saw the only man in town who might be able to upset his plans.

John Holt had stopped the wagons in front of County Hall.

CHAPTER 32

"Keep those wagons moving, Nels," Holt ordered him. "You can't park them on the street tonight."

"Says who?"

"Says me. And I won't say it again. We need to keep the thoroughfare clear while we clean up this mess at the bank. You can move them over to the livery. They have plenty of space for you there."

"You expect us to pay that old sourpuss to stow our wagons? Just so we can get a drink in town?"

"We both know you're not here to drink and you didn't come here by accident."

Nels raised his voice. "That's right, Sheriff. We didn't come here to drink. We came here to stand with our boss, the great Joe Mullen."

Holt was glad he was at least honest enough to admit it. "I'm sure he heard you and appreciates it. You've made your speech, now make your way out of here. The next time I see you better be on foot. And be sure to leave your guns in the wagon."

"Our guns?" Nels repeated. "You can't do that. You don't have the power to tell a man to do something like that."

Holt grew still. "I just did. And if I see you toting anything bigger than a spoon, I'm going to take it as a threat. And you boys don't want to threaten me, do you?"

He watched Nels brim with indignation. He could not blame him. Holt had just shown him up in front of his men. He had faced him down and stopped him in public. His pride was wounded and had this been any other man, he probably would have leapt at him from the wagon or gone for his guns.

But Holt knew full well that he was not any other man. He was John Holt and Nels Stewart knew what that meant. He had seen Holt square off against a crowd much larger than the nine men he had with him. He had heard of what Holt had done in the other towns he had tamed. In New Orleans and Junction City and Baxter Springs. Newton too.

Holt knew to someone like Nels, he was more than just a man. He was a stone-cold killer who would not think twice about cutting him down before going to work on the others. He had killed men more dangerous than Nels would ever be and the miner did not stand a chance against a force like that. A force as constant as the present threat of a cave-in down in the mines.

Which was why Holt was not surprised when Nels snapped the reins and led the wagons down Main Street to circle back to store them at the livery.

But he was surprised to see Tony Cassidy slowly approach him from the other side of the street. He was smart enough to keep his hands away from his sides as he did so.

"You are quite a man, Holt. I've never seen someone who could thwart a victory with so much flair as you."

"You're gonna keep talking yourself into a jail cell, Cassidy. What did you think you were doing by filling those men full of liquor?"

"Keeping them off the street and away from the bank is what. How long have you been standing there, Sheriff? You

see all the men who poured into my saloon just now. There's
near fifty of them, maybe a few less near as I can figure.
And right now, every single one of them is doing their best
to drink me dry. I've got Simpson and a couple of my gals
working up a sweat to do exactly that. They're not cowhands
or gunmen. They're hard-working boys who like to feel
numb for a while. To forget about risking their lives every
day to make another man rich. They'll lose interest in Joe's
cause quick enough once the liquor starts affecting them.
And they won't be in any hurry to protect him either."

Holt imagined Cassidy could find a way to justify anything he decided to do. "Whiskey lights a fire in a man's belly
worse than anything else."

"And it's up to me to make sure they're too drunk to be
effective. Not tonight, and not tomorrow when the shakes
and their sour stomachs take their toll."

Holt had not thought of that. And he could not think of
a reason why Cassidy was doing this except one. Only one
explanation made sense.

"You must've cut a fine deal with Sarabelle to be this
generous."

"Any agreement I have with her is my business," Cassidy
said. "Besides, you're not paying to pickle those boys. I am.
My reasons are my own."

"Just make sure they don't become mine or you'll find
yourself swinging from the same gallows as Mullen."

Cassidy laughed as he began to walk away. "Joe Mullen
will never hang, Sheriff. Not now. You'll have to kill him
yourself if you want to see him dead."

Holt allowed him to leave without another word because,
for once, he agreed with him.

Back at the jail, Ben, Jack, and Doc Klassen listened while
he told them about the miners.

"Fifty of them?" Jack said when Holt had finished. "And they're all in the Bottle right now?"

"All but ten," Holt said. "Nels Stewart is the ringleader of the group. Probably even took a couple of shots at us when we rode through the camps before. He didn't seem too anxious to try his luck with me head-on. Guess he's more of the indirect type."

Bob got up from his chair and paced the jail. "They shot at us and you just let them go as free as birds?"

"What else was I supposed to do?" Holt asked. "Cassidy had just gotten the rest of the miners into his saloon. Any gunplay would've brought them spilling out of there like a swarm of angry bees. He was right about filling them with whiskey. In another hour or two, they won't be any trouble. That's why I want you to hang around down there to keep an eye on things."

"I'd rather be helping you find a way into that bank and getting our hands on Mullen."

"Selwyn says that's impossible, and I tend to agree with him. Lassiter has big plans for this town and the best way to see those plans happen is to have a safe place for people to keep their money. And since we can't get in, we're going to have to find a way to get Mullen to come out."

"And just how do you figure we do that?" Bob wondered aloud. "Call him out? Challenge him to face you at ten spaces on Main Street? Mullen's too crafty for that."

"I've got something a bit more refined in mind." He decided there was no point in keeping his plan a secret from them, especially when he would be asking them to risk their lives to help him pull it off. "Mrs. Chapman and Mr. Selwyn have agreed to get Mullen to prove Lassiter is still alive by getting him to bring him to the door. And when he does, I'm going to kill him. It's as simple as that."

Ben, Jack, and Doc Klassen seemed to be waiting for Holt to say more, but that's all there was.

"That's it?" Bob asked. "That's your plan? Hoping he's foolish enough to stick his head out long enough for you to shoot him?"

"That's the plan, yeah."

Doc Klassen cleared his throat. "I know I'm not the one risking his neck here, but that doesn't sound like much of a plan to me, John."

"It's worked before," Holt told them. "It'll work here."

Even Jack did not seem to be impressed. "Mullen's got Hardt in there with him. Why wouldn't he just have him bring Mr. Lassiter to the door instead? Why would he risk you being able to take a shot at him?"

"Because I won't be toting a rifle. I'll only have my pistol. He won't expect me to be able to kill him with it, but that's what I'm going to do. I'm fast enough and good enough to do it. Like I said, I've done it before, and I can do it now."

Klassen was not convinced. "I've seen what you can do in tough situations, but that's a small margin of error, even for you."

Holt had already made up his mind. There was no reason to debate the matter any further.

Bob's mouth moved a bit before he finally managed to make a sound. "And what if you miss? Or let's say you do kill Mullen. What's to keep Hardt from just killing Lassiter after Mullen is dead?"

"Hardt doesn't need a pardon from the governor," Holt explained. "He doesn't want one and he won't get one. If he lets Lassiter go, we'll tell him he'll be allowed to take a bag full of cash with him and I'll let him leave town. He's greedy and stupid enough to take that deal. That's when you and I will hunt him down before he reaches the next town and kill him. Simple as that."

Holt had not known the prison cook for long, but he had never seen him so animated as he was now. "You call that a plan? He'll clear town like a bolt of lightning."

"On a tired old horse we'll leave for him to take at the back of the bank. He won't have any provisions and he's not likely to get any. You gas on enough about how good a tracker you are and this will be your chance to prove it."

"Letting a killer go isn't my way, Holt. And I ain't gonna let you do that. I aim to shoot Hardt before he ever gets near that horse."

Holt saw the cook was getting too worked up and decided to not let him get more riled up than he already was.

"I said that's what we were going to tell Hardt if things go that way," Holt reminded him. "But that's not going to happen. With Mullen dead, Hardt will be the only one left inside. A man is more apt to reason, especially one as scared and alone as Hardt will be. We'll take him as soon as he steps foot outside the bank. Or at least you will. I'll be out front distracting him if it comes to that."

Bob snatched his hat from a peg on the wall. "This is dangerous business, Holt, and you're sitting here playing games. There's something off about you, son. I knew it from the second I laid eyes on you. Come on, Jack. Let's you and me get some night air. It's too thick in here for my taste."

Jack looked at Holt for his approval, which the sheriff gave. He was glad the deputy had thought to take his shotgun with him before joining the cook on his stroll.

Holt grinned at Doc Klassen. "It was almost worth it just to get a rise out of Old Bob there."

"I wouldn't have done it that way," Klassen admitted. "He's a good man."

"He's too close to this," Holt said. "He's looking to avenge Wheeler's death. I need him to do what I tell him, or it might get all of us killed." He remembered the reason why Doc Klassen was there in the first place, so he asked, "How's Henderson coming along?"

"He was shot up pretty bad." Klassen gestured toward the map of Devil's Gulch on the wall. "His body's got more lines and scars than that map up there. I don't know how he's managed to live this long. Guess it's out of habit."

Holt welcomed some good news. "Too bad he won't be much use to us tonight. We could use the extra gun, though I guess I should be grateful that we're not facing fifty men. Who would've thought Cassidy would've done us a good turn for a change?"

He saw the doctor look at the floor. "Yeah. He sure is full of surprises."

Holt heard something strange in the doctor's voice. "What is it, Ralph?"

He watched Klassen wrestle with his own thoughts before saying, "I'm too ashamed to tell you."

Holt settled into his chair. He had a feeling this might take a while. "Sounds serious, so you should tell me just the same, especially since it's got you in such a state. I've never known you to be like this."

"Then I suppose you've never known me at all," he said. "I'll save us both a lot of time and hot air by getting directly to the point. I was a different man when I first came to town, and I got into debt with Cassidy. I've been paying him off slow and regular, but now he's decided to call in the debt."

"Can you pay it off?"

"I could, but it'd cost me all I have. He doesn't want money. He wants a service instead."

Holt imagined a man like Cassidy would. "What does he want you to do?"

Klassen rubbed his temples. "Run against Elizabeth Chapman for mayor. He claims he's gotten the governor's permission to hold an election in a couple of weeks."

Holt thought he had not heard him correctly. "You mean he contacted the governor before this mess with Mullen?"

"That's what he told me. I think it was through Sarabelle. I know she and Joe had a friendship with the governor long before Joe's downfall. If the rumors about her working with

Cassidy are true, then I suspect that's what they've been cooking up. Neither of them ever liked Mrs. Chapman anyway. I tried to get out of doing it, but he has a contract with my signature on it from when I needed money."

Given how he was acting, Holt had expected Klassen to have more dire news. "Maybe I'm just off a bit these days, but I fail to see the problem."

Klassen lowered his hands from his temples. "He's looking to put me in office instead of Elizabeth. I'd call that a problem."

"He's not giving you any choice about running, so don't fight it. If you win, you'll cancel your debt. If you lose, you cancel your debt. Tell him you'll do it as long as he tears it up. Then tell the mayor about it. This is politics, Ralph, not a cotillion. Etiquette doesn't apply here. Wait to talk to her about it until this Mullen nonsense is over. She'll understand. You're not doing this because you want to. You're doing it because Cassidy is making you. That puts a different face on it."

"You make it sound so . . . simple."

"Because it is," Holt told him. "I've seen lots of mayors come and go in my line of work. Most were relieved to be rid of the burden. And as soon as she knows you're being forced to do it, she'll decide what's best for you."

Holt watched the unease drain away from the doctor's face. "I thought you'd be angry about this."

"I might have been if I'd heard about it from someone else, but you lay out a convincing case. Whether you win or Elizabeth wins, this town will be in good hands. And I know neither of you will let the likes of Cassidy have their way."

"He's liable to force me to fire you," Klassen said.

"But you'll be mayor," Holt reminded him. "He can't really force you to do anything, can he? Especially if you get him to rip up that contract he has on you."

"He has ways," Klassen said. "You know that."

"And you have me." Holt got to his feet, eager to change the subject to more important matters. "I take it you left Les under Ty's care. How's he doing?"

Klassen acted as if he had been disturbed from a deep sleep. "I've tended to his wound the best way I know how. All we can do is wait to see if he develops a fever, much like Henderson in there, though his wounds were more manageable."

Holt decided a bit of fresh air might do the doctor some good. "Why don't you head back to your office and check on Les. In the meantime, see if you can't find Jack and send him back here. I want him to stay with Henderson while I take care of Mullen."

Klassen pulled on his coat. "You mean to do that now? I thought you'd wait until morning."

"I'm counting on Mullen to think the same thing, which is why now's the best time to do it. Stay in your office so I'll know where to find you if needed."

"I hope I won't be needed to tend to any wounds of yours, John."

Holt decided he could afford a smile for the doctor's benefit. "That makes two of us."

CHAPTER 33

Hank Lassiter had not realized he had fallen asleep at the clerk's desk until he was pulled up from his chair by Hardt.

"On your feet," the outlaw told him. "The boss wants to see you."

The smallish outlaw easily half dragged him toward the front door of the bank, where Joe Mullen was at the window peering outside.

"Sorry to wake you, Hank," Mullen said, "but something's stirring outside. I can feel it."

Lassiter was too tired to feel much of anything besides tired. He could not remember a time when he felt so weary in body and in spirit. "What makes you say that?"

"I just saw the Turnbull brat run back to the jail, then Holt stalking across the street," Mullen said. "Hardly gave this place a glance. He's up to something. I know it."

Lassiter had never bothered to try to comprehend the criminal mind, so he took Mullen at his word. "What does that have to do with me?"

Mullen laughed. "Haven't you been paying attention? It has everything to do with you. Or at least me having you. He's fixing to find a way to get you out of here alive. Probably putting the final touches on whatever he's planning with the Chapman witch." He looked at Hardt. "Best get to the back door and check it again. I wouldn't put it past them to have staked someone back there to keep an eye on it."

"They haven't," Hardt said as he went to carry out his task. "I told you I've got a plan, remember?"

Mullen did not seem impressed by whatever Hardt was talking about. "We all have plans. I've got plans of my own and they don't involve me winding up in another cell for my trouble." He smiled at Lassiter. "What about you, Hank? You have any plans? Concerning my wife, maybe."

Lassiter felt a new spike of fear course through his veins. "You can't hold that against me, Joe. We were just having supper together. It was as innocent as that. You saw it for yourself."

"I saw you were mighty comfortable in my dining room on my ranch eating off my plates."

He backhanded the banker, sending him flat on his backside. Mullen had struck him since taking him captive, but never quite that hard. He wondered if he might be reaching the end of this godless journey after all. He found himself beyond the point of caring.

And he found a new sense of bravery he did not think he possessed. "What did you expect her to do after your conviction? Sit alone in that big house and rot? She's still a young woman and she has considerable means. It's only natural that she'd want to prepare for her future."

Mullen resumed his watch of the window. "And you were only all too willing to help her, weren't you? Lay on the charm for the grieving woman. Maybe make a profit for yourself in the bargain?"

Lassiter knew there was no point in denying it. "You already have considerable holdings in the bank, Joe. I was trying to provide her with some guidance for her future is all."

"Don't recall you being so willing to help a poor woman. Or an ugly one."

"I won't deny a certain attraction between us, though I'm sure you're not so ignorant as to deny she's a beautiful woman."

Lassiter reacted too late when Mullen snatched him by the ruined collar and pulled him to his feet. "The only thing I'd like to deny is you another day of living. But since you're my only way out of this mess, I'll have to put that off for now."

He shoved the banker against the window. "Stand there until I tell you to move. It won't be long now."

Cecil Hardt went to the back door like Mullen had told him and tested the locks again. He had lost track of the number of times he had run through that exercise but decided it could never be enough. He imagined the next time he did it, it would be because Mullen's plan had fallen to pieces. He had done well by following Joe's orders until now, but this situation was different.

Everything that had happened up until now had happened fast. It had been unexpected. Rolling the prison wagon. Grabbing the Turnbull boy. Getting horses and clothes from the farmers. Heading to the ranch and even the escape had enjoyed the element of surprise.

Holt and his men had gotten lucky in finding them each time, but Joe had always managed to put enough distance between them and the law.

This was different. They had remained in one place for too long. The circumstances had been allowed to settle and Holt had been given too much time to come up with a plan. It was suicide to give a man like Holt time to think. He had heard he was dangerous enough when a problem jumped out at him. And Hardt had been in enough tight situations to know that Holt would not allow them to get out of this alive.

But Joe Mullen was not the only one in the bank who had spent his last day in prison. Hardt was getting on in the world. He'd be thirty in a month or so. He figured he had wasted about half his life behind bars and promised himself he would not die in prison.

And as he finished checking the last lock on the iron door, he prayed he would not have to. He prayed that boy delivered the message he had given him.

He checked to make sure Joe Mullen was not looking and was glad to see he was preoccupied with Lassiter and the street.

He gently tapped the barrel of his pistol three times on the iron door and held his breath.

He breathed again when he heard two knocks in reply.

The boy had come through. His plan was still in place. He only hoped he would not need it.

CHAPTER 34

Holt was glad he had called Bob away from the Blue Bottle Saloon so they could hear the bad news together. It saved him the trouble of repeating it.

"After much consideration," Mayor Chapman said from behind her desk, "Mr. Selwyn and I have decided we are ill-suited to help you trap Mullen. In light of all that has happened, we do not find it feasible."

Bob scowled at Selwyn, who refused to meet his glare. "Even you? You yellow dog."

The banker rallied and matched the prison cook's stare. "You saw all the miners in the Blue Bottle. If they had remained up in the hills, that would've been one thing. But I for one don't think Mrs. Chapman or I should risk being caught in the crossfire between Holt and a mob of drunken, half-crazed men bent on rescuing Mullen."

Bob began to argue, but Holt silenced him by raising his hand. "He's right. The miners being in town changes things. It's too dangerous."

Bob pulled off his hat and threw it on the floor in frustration. "I guess that throws your plan right into the gutter. I figure that's where it belongs. It wasn't much of a plan as plans go."

"Nothing's changed," Holt told them. "I'm still going through with it. I plan on drawing Mullen out on my own."

Mrs. Chapman got to her feet. "That won't be necessary, John. We've just received word from the governor. He has decided to grant Joe his pardon provided he allows Lassiter to leave the bank unharmed and he and his outlaw surrender without incident."

Holt had sensed that would be how it would go. Just once he would have liked to be pleasantly surprised by a politician. "Hardt get a pardon too?"

Mayor Chapman handed him a telegram. "The governor's office didn't say anything about Hardt. I'd imagine the pardon doesn't extend to him."

"At least that's something," Bob said as he scooped his hat from the floor. "Wheeler's memory will rest easy now."

Holt read the telegram before crumpling it into a ball and tossing it on the mayor's desk. "This doesn't change anything. I'm still going to try to draw him out."

Selwyn's eyes grew wide, "You can't do that. You don't have to do that. You read the telegram. We're giving in to Mullen's demands. He's free."

"A telegram's not the same as a pardon," Holt said. "And until I have one, it doesn't matter. Besides, Mullen won't come out of there without one and I wouldn't blame him. We could've had anyone send that telegram. And if I'd thought he would fall for it, I would've had one sent myself hours ago."

He pointed in the direction of the bank. "It'll be days before that pardon gets here, even with a team of men doing a lot of hard riding. I'm not going to allow him to hold this town hostage for a second longer than necessary. This ends and it ends tonight."

He watched Mayor Chapman's fleshy face redden at the challenge to her authority. "Sheriff Holt, I am ordering you to stop this madness now. You are not to approach that bank until morning when I deliver the news to Mullen personally. The miners in town won't be in any condition to render assistance by then."

"They're in no condition to do it now," Bob told her. "I reckon most of those boys are already well gone as it is. Sounds like Cassidy was right to fill them full of whiskey."

Holt had made his decision. "Bob, I'll need you to circle around the back. I don't want Mullen or Hardt trying to make an escape if things go poorly."

"I'd rather be out front with you," Bob said, "but I won't fight you on it, John."

The two lawmen had begun to leave the office when Selwyn grabbed Holt's arm. "This is suicide, Sheriff. If you won't think of yourself, consider the dire situation you're putting Mr. Lassiter in."

Holt looked down at Selwyn's grip on his arm. "You were concerned about danger a couple of minutes ago. Grabbing me isn't exactly safe either."

When the banker let him go, Holt held out his hand to the banker. "Your key to the front door. I'll be needing it. Don't worry, you'll get it back one way or the other."

Selwyn pulled out the ring of keys and handed him the one that opened the bank.

As Holt pocketed it and left her office, Mayor Chapman called out after him. "You've been warned, John. If you go through with this, it'll cost you your position."

But Holt did not stop. He knew allowing Mullen to remain in the bank would cost more than that.

When they left County Hall, Bob broke right while Holt went to the left. The bank was practically next door, but Bob went around the back the long way. He moved through a narrow alley between two buildings and pulled his pistol when he reached the corner.

The back of Main Street did not have any oil lamps to light the way. He allowed his eyes to grow accustomed to the darkness before chancing his first glance around the corner.

The only light was that which bled out from the windows at the back of the bank. They cast long, flickering shadows upon the hard ground. This part of town was rarely cleaned and Bob's eyes burned from the stench of trash and horse droppings allowed to accumulate there unattended.

He blinked his eyes clear and, after checking in front of him and behind him, saw he was alone in this forgotten part of town. He stepped out from the narrow alley and hugged the back wall of a building as he slowly closed the distance between himself and the bank.

He could hear Holt's voice carried along the night wind, though he could not make out what he was saying. Bob did not have to hear it to know the show had started.

Although he was sure he was alone back there, he moved along at a crouch. He reached the end of the building he had been using as cover when the sound of a crack reached his ears.

He knew he had not stepped on a stick, for nothing grew back here. He had not kicked a can or a bottle either. He had been too careful.

No, the sound he heard had come from in front of him. From the direction of the bank.

And it had not been a stick, but the unmistakable sound of a hammer being thumbed back.

Bob knew he had been wrong. He was not alone back here. Someone else was waiting in the darkness.

He cut loose with his pistol as night suddenly became alive with gunfire.

CHAPTER 35

Holt did not allow doubt to creep into his mind as he walked toward the front of the bank. The time for second-guessing had passed and the time for action was at hand. Thinking any other way might prove deadly and he was putting himself in enough danger as it was.

Only a few townspeople had decided to keep watch along the boardwalks. Most of the town had decided it was too cold to remain outside and, given the hour, probably thought nothing would happen until morning. Holt hoped that Joe Mullen had thought so too. He had surprised them enough since his escape. It was time for him to be thrown off for a change.

Holt sensed people moving behind him, undoubtedly off to the Blue Bottle Saloon to warn the miners something was about to happen. It only made him more anxious to get this over with.

"Joe Mullen!" Holt called out. "It's John Holt. I want to talk to you."

He thought he had seen someone move from the window, but assuming the glass was as thick as Selwyn had boasted, he did not fear a shot coming from there. If bullets could not reach anyone inside, he doubted they could strike him here.

He heard a mumbled voice he took to belong to Mullen, but could not make out what he was saying.

Just as he had planned.

"You can't hear me any better than I can hear you," Holt answered. "The door is too thick. You'll have to open it a crack if this is going to work."

He was surprised to hear the lock work so quickly. The door opened about six inches and he saw Hank Lassiter thrust into the space.

Mullen's sick cackle filled the air. "Guess you thought I'd be stupid enough to open the door and stand there myself, didn't you, Holt?"

The sheriff gauged his position. Just to the right of the open door from where Holt stood. "I suppose I can hear you clear enough now. But I never took you for a fool, Joe. No one did."

"You least of all, ain't that right, John. I showed you up plenty since this whole thing started, haven't I?"

Holt swallowed the bile that rose in his throat. *Just keep him talking.* "I suppose you did. Always one step ahead of me until now. But that ends tonight."

Lassiter's eyes were wide with terror as he silently mouthed the words, "Help me."

Holt held up his left hand and brought his fingers toward him as he mouthed, "Fall forward."

He knew there was no way Mullen could have seen this from behind the door and he gave no indication that he had. "Nothing ends tonight unless you've got that pardon for me. You might not be willing to listen to reason, but I'll bet he is. Especially since I've got a gun to his banker's head."

"He knows of your demands," Holt told him, "but I don't know what he's planning to do. We're not exactly on speaking terms."

"Then why are you wasting my time? Come back when

you have the pardon. Then we'll talk about what happens to old Hank here."

"Let him go?" Mullen laughed. "You expect me to do it just like that. Let the only reason why I'm still alive just walk out of here free as a bird."

"It won't cost you anything." Holt needed to goad him into showing his face. Everything depended on it. "You've picked the safest building in town. We can't go in there after you and you can't come out. Letting Lassiter go will show good faith on your part. It'll make it easier for the governor to pardon you. You'll still be locked in there with all the town's money. Isn't that enough?"

"It's not near enough," Mullen shouted back. "My freedom is worth more than that. Worth more than all the money in the world. The only way you're getting Lassiter is when I get my pardon. That's all."

Holt could feel he was losing whatever control he had of the situation. "You boys must be getting hungry in there. I know you didn't have time to grab provisions. Let Lassiter go and we'll make sure you get three meals a day. Whatever you want all at the county's expense."

"I had that kind of arrangement in your jail, remember?" Mullen yelled. "I don't aim to repeat it. If we're hungry, Lassiter's hungry. If you're willing to let him starve to death, that's on your head, not mine."

Holt decided none of his tactics were working and it was time to take a risk by goading him a bit harder. "Listen to reason, Mullen. You've already lost enough. Your good name. Your ranch. Your wife. No pardon in the world will—"

Mullen's head appeared in the space above Lassiter's. "You shut up about that thieving witch. . . ."

To John Holt, all sound died away and the rest of the town became nothing but a blur. All he could see was the wild eyes of Joe Mullen as he raged against the mention of his wife.

In one rapid, fluid motion, Holt drew his pistol, aimed, and fired.

The impact of the bullet snapped his head backward as he fell into the bank.

Lassiter fell forward and landed on all fours on the boardwalk. He quickly scrambled away as the bank door was slammed shut behind him.

He heard gunfire erupt from the back of the bank and knew Bob must have run into some trouble, but Holt had to tend to the banker first. He leapt onto the boardwalk and pulled Lassiter to his feet.

"Are you hurt?" Holt asked, paying particular attention to the top of the banker's head. That was the direction of where his bullet had gone.

"No, I'm fine," Lassiter said as he got to his feet.

Holt pushed him in the direction of the jail. "Head down to see Jack. He'll protect you."

Pistol and gunfire filled the air from behind the bank, and Holt knew he had to get back there. Bob must be in a mess of trouble.

Knowing it was unlikely Hardt could shoot him from inside the bank, Holt pulled the key from his pocket and slid it into the lock. He moved to the left side of the door and turned the key until the lock opened. He withdrew his hand and brought his left heel back to kick it all the way in. He waited for a shot, but it never came.

He dropped to a crouch and rounded through the open door. His pistol leading the way.

Hardt had already heard the first shot from the back alley when he began to shut the door. He had tried to grab Lassiter, but the man had fallen to the boardwalk just as Mullen was hit. He threw the locks and slid over to Mullen.

His hat was gone and his forehead was already a mess of

blood. He ran his hand over the wound and saw the deep gouge the bullet had plowed in the front of his skull. It was little more than a flesh wound, but the impact had rendered him unconscious and it would continue to bleed something awful. He imagined he had flinched when he heard the first shot from behind the bank. It had probably saved his life.

It was time for Hardt to put his plan into motion.

He grabbed hold of Mullen's collar and quickly dragged him toward the back door of the bank. He possessed more strength than people expected of a man his size, an ability which he put to good use now.

When they reached the back door, the gunfire had stopped and he heard pounding echoing through the bank. "If you're coming, best come now," came a muted shout from the other side. "It won't stay clear for long."

Hardt undid the locks with a practiced hand and pulled open the heavy door.

Charlie Gardiner reached in and helped pull the unconscious Mullen outside. "He looks dead."

"He ain't," Hardt said as they hauled him into the waiting wagon. "But we will be unless we get out of here."

"Good old Hardt," Charlie said as he scrambled for his horse. "Still as reckless as ever."

"Where are the others?" Hardt asked as he climbed onto the wagon box and took hold of the reins.

"Right behind us," Charlie said. "Just get going."

Hardt snapped the reins of the two-horse team and sped away into the darkness. He was normally not a trusting soul but knew he could count on the old Bostrom Gang to see him through to the finish. He had ridden with them for years and, even among outlaws, loyalty counted for something.

Holt swept the bank with his pistol, ready to shoot at anything that dared to move, but nothing did.

He looked at the spot on the floor where he expected to see Mullen. But all he saw was a pool of blood.

That did not make any sense to Holt. He had hit him. He knew it. He had seen him fall.

A cold wind reached him and caused the heavy front door to bang open. He looked in that direction and saw the back door of the bank swinging open as if mocking him.

"No," Holt said as he rushed to it. "That can't be."

He slid to a stop before blindly tumbling outside. He leaned against the doorjamb and looked to his left. He saw two men on the ground, one seeming to be tending to the other.

He darted to the left side of the doorway, his pistol ready. All he saw were the deep ruts of wagon wheels in the dirt trailing away from the bank.

Holt forgot himself and jumped out the back door. He peered into the darkness but saw nothing.

Mullen and Hardt had managed to escape.

He sagged against the bank. "That can't be. I shot him. I know I did."

"John!" Doc Klassen called out from behind him. "Get over here. Bob's been hit."

Holt snapped back to the present and holstered his pistol as he realized the men he had seen were Klassen tending to Bob. He dropped to a knee beside Klassen, who was already tying a tourniquet around Bob's left leg.

The prison cook howled in pain. "Forget about me, damn you. They're getting away. John, don't let them get away. They had a wagon waiting. Hardt and Mullen. Don't ask me who or how, but I saw it too late."

Holt thought about going, but Klassen grabbed his arm. "He'll bleed to death if I don't get to work on this wound right now and I can't move him by myself. I need you here."

Holt did not give pursuit a second thought as he helped Klassen lift the bellowing cook and carried him in the direction of Klassen's office. "I came out here when I saw Bob pass by my back window. I saw he was hit and knocked him to the ground."

"Took me out of the fight is more like it," Bob seethed through gritted teeth as they reached the back door of Klassen's office. "I could've stopped them, John. I had them dead to rights."

The two men ignored him as they lugged him into the cramped hallway and into the part of the office Klassen called home. They set him on the dining room table as Klassen quickly shoved the dishes and silverware off the tabletop so Bob could lie outstretched.

"Go tell Ty I need him in here now," Klassen commanded Holt. "There's a tray next to Les in the next room. Bring those in with him."

"Already ahead of you," Ty said as he entered the kitchen carrying the tray. "Glad all those years of law school are being put to good use."

Holt backed away from the men as they began to cut away Bob's pants leg, much to the protests of the patient. He decided there was nothing more he could do there.

He needed answers. And knew of only one place where he might find them.

CHAPTER 36

Holt ignored Jack's questions when he barged into the jail. He continued to ignore them when he pulled down his Winchester and stormed back out again. He had not needed to check if it was loaded. He knew it was.

He knew Jack was following him as he headed toward the one place in town from where he knew he could get answers to all that had happened that evening.

He only paused when he reached the Railhead Saloon to listen for any sound that might tell him what was awaiting him inside. He heard the muted sounds of men while they gambled. The occasional clicking of poker chips. The piano was silent.

"What is it, boss?" Jack whispered. "I heard shooting. Did you get Mullen?"

Holt pushed through the door and stood inside. The butt of his rifle on his hip. He looked over the crowd for any sign of Gardiner or the others.

All he saw was Ma McAdam alone at a table beside the bar. She knew he was there, but could not look at him.

Holt's grip on his rifle tightened. She knew.

To Jack, Holt said, "Clear out this place. Ma and I need to talk."

The young deputy did not have much trouble in convincing the gamblers to leave. The look on Holt's face had provided enough encouragement.

Jack followed the last of them outside, leaving only Holt and McAdam in the saloon.

"Where are they?" he asked her. "And don't lie to me."

She drained her glass of whiskey and quickly poured herself another. "Gone is all I know. Heard them riding off a few minutes ago, but I guess you already figured that out. It's why you're here." She finally raised her bloodshot eyes to look at him. "How did you know?"

"Hardt," Holt said, managing to somehow keep his voice under control. "When I saw Charlie Gardiner out in front of the jail earlier, he told me Mullen and Hardt were holed up in the bank with Lassiter. I never told him who was with Mullen, so how did he know it was Hardt? I didn't pay it any mind until I found they'd gotten away clear. Had a wagon waiting for them and everything. Hardt and Gardiner knew each other from before, didn't they?"

Ma drew in a ragged breath as she nodded. "I didn't find that out until I saw them getting ready to ride out right before everything happened."

That did not make Holt feel any better. "You didn't tell me. You should have."

She rose her head as she swallowed. "He threatened to kill me if I did. Had me locked in my room until they were ready to leave and by then it was already too late. He said he'd kill me if I told you. You didn't see the look in his eye when he said it, John. He would've killed me. He looked at me like I was nothing. Like I was less than nothing. After all this. After all I gave him. After all it cost me. I thought he had come to regard me as something more."

Holt could not care less about her broken heart. "Guess you know how poor Frank felt all these years."

"Ah, yes. Poor Frank." She lifted her glass and toasted his memory. "At least he's at peace."

"Where are they?" Holt asked her. "You must have an idea."

She refilled her glass. "I don't and you know I wouldn't tell you if I did. These hills are full of hideouts and old mines bandits have been using since before the war. I imagine you'll be able to find them there, should you have the mind to look, which I imagine you do."

Holt gritted his teeth. "I'll find them. And I'll kill them when I do."

Ma shut her eyes and her chin quivered from emotion. "Yes, I imagine you will. Did you kill Mullen?"

Holt lowered his rifle. "I thought I did. But Hardt took him with him, so I don't know for certain."

"Well, if you didn't, I know you will. Everyone knows John Holt always gets his man."

Holt decided he had learned all he could from the madam. It was best to let her battle her own ghosts in peace. "Not yet," he said as he left the saloon. "But soon."

Over the next week, life in Devil's Gulch had settled back into an easy rhythm. A light snow had coated the ground following the events at the bank, which served to quell some of the unease that might have otherwise threatened the town.

Les Patrick had been given a hero's welcome as he hobbled out of Doc Klassen's office. His cousin Ty had done his best to keep people from slapping Les on the back out of fear of reopening his stitches. Holt had heard he had insisted on catching up on the paperwork that had piled up during his absence. Judge Cook had brought the files to him personally.

Henderson was still suffering from his wounds, but after a lengthy argument with Doc Klassen, decided that he was healthy enough to go back home, provided his son would come to fetch him with a wagon. Holt had sent Jack out to the farm to deliver the message and the two young men had returned with the wagon.

Holt saw the farmer's mood brighten as Jack and his boy helped him from the jail to the sight of the four stallions he had lost tethered to the back of the wagon.

"Figured that would make you smile, Pa," Tom said as he helped his father get situated in the flatbed. "Jack rode out to Mullen's ranch with me and helped me bring them back. The ranch hands had them separated and waiting for us."

"I had a word with them," Holt said, preferring to leave it at that.

Henderson hid some embarrassment as he propped himself up. "Sorry I was more trouble than I planned on, Holt. Guess I've gone and become a farmer after all."

"You're still a Raider in my book, Henderson. No one can take that away from you."

The two men shook hands as Tom climbed up into the wagon box.

"You know where to find me if you need me," Henderson told him as Tom drove the wagon back to the farm.

Holt was glad he did. Men with Henderson's grit were tough to find in Devil's Gulch. Anywhere, really.

Jack stood beside him as he waved at the Hendersons until they rounded the corner out of town. Holt could not help but be reminded of the time he had bid Marshal Dan Wheeler goodbye a little more than a week before. Had it only been a week? It felt like years ago.

Since the events at the bank, Jack had done a good job of keeping his questions to a minimum, but now that Henderson was gone, a veil seemed to have been lifted on the young man's curiosity.

"Is what they're saying about Doc Klassen true?" the deputy asked. "Is he really running against Mrs. Chapman?"

Holt knew it was more than true. In fact, Cassidy and his people had wasted little time making hay of the situation. They blamed Mrs. Chapman for her inability to capture Joe Mullen or keep him from causing havoc in the town. They said a stronger mayor would have made an outlaw like Mullen think twice before daring to come back to town.

Those same people claimed Klassen was a hero who risked his life to save Bob from the clutches of the Bostrom Gang, and also blamed Mrs. Chapman for allowing those outlaws to remain in town.

Holt knew it was all nonsense, but no one had bothered to ask his opinion.

"It's true," Holt told him. "Don't think the old girl has much fight left in her. She hasn't spoken much to me since it happened. I think part of her hopes Ralph wins. Can't say as I blame her. Mullen has caused her nothing but trouble." He frowned at the thought of it. "I guess he still is."

Jack leaned against the porch post and picked at a splinter of wood with his nail. "Doc Klassen says Bob might lose his leg if the infection gets any worse."

Holt knew Klassen was concerned about how the old prison cook might take being left a cripple for the rest of his days. But Holt knew Bob had at least one good fight left in him. He would never let the loss of a leg keep him from bringing Mullen and Hardt to justice. "I'm no doctor and neither are you. Best if we just let that play out as it will. No sense fretting about it. We'll just handle it when it happens."

Jack stopped picking at the wood. "We going to start looking for Mullen and the Bostrom Boys?"

Holt lifted his head and looked out at the mountains that surrounded Devil's Gulch. He knew they were out there somewhere. Mullen might be alive, but he would be a burden to them if he was. He did not know why Hardt had bothered taking him from the bank, but he planned on finding that out for himself soon enough.

"We'll find them, boy. We'll find them soon. That much I can promise you."

Jack wiped his hands on his shirt. "And I'll be with you when you do. I ain't riding off again. I can promise you that."

"Good, because I need you." He patted his deputy on the back and motioned for him to go ahead of him. "Let's go see if Jean has Bob's supper ready. You know how ornery he gets when he's hungry."

Jack sprinted across the thoroughfare while Holt stayed back to lock the jail. He paused before he closed it, seeing the inside of the place in a new light. He saw the bed he slept on most nights. The same bed Blair Chapman and Frank Peters had died in. He saw back to the cells where Will Henderson had recuperated and where Joe Mullen had rotted away.

He gripped the handle tightly as he recalled all the pain and blood that had been spilled over Mullen. The lives that had been lost.

The losses John Holt would avenge and soon.

He pulled the door shut and locked it. For now, it was better to concentrate on what was, not what would be.

They say you can't teach an old dog new tricks.
But old cowboys? That's a different story—especially
when those cowboys are trail-hardened cattlemen like
Casey Tubbs and Levi Doolin. When these longtime
buddies learn that their bosses are getting out of the
beef business, there's nothing left to do now but deliver the
last two thousand cows to Abilene and collect their pay.
Except for one problem. Their bosses' lawyer is skipping
town with all the workers' cash, which means Tubbs
and Doolin have one last job to do—steal it back.

Sure, pulling off a robbery is a new challenge
for these old boys. But they've learned a lot of tricks over
the years, and once they pull off the perfect crime—
and get away with it—Tubbs and Doolin start thinking
they may have missed their calling in life. This could be
the start of a whole new career . . . as outlaws.

So begins the wild, wild story of two old cowboys who are
one step ahead of the law—and the young U.S. marshal
who's determined to catch them. . . .

National Bestselling Authors
William W. Johnstone
and J.A. Johnstone

OLD COWBOYS NEVER DIE
A Thrilling New Series of the American Frontier

On sale now, wherever Pinnacle Books are sold.

Live Free. Read Hard.
www.williamjohnstone.net

CHAPTER 1

"Well, I reckon that about ties a knot in it," Casey Tubbs announced as he joined the little group of eight men sprawled on their bedrolls around the chuckwagon. "any coffee left in that pot, Smiley"

"Yeah," Smiley said, and poured a cup for him.

Like the rest of the crew, Smiley was anxious to hear what Casey had found out when he went to look for Ronald Dorsey. They had driven the last of the two thousand cows into the holding pens at the Abilene rail yards. Dorsey, a lawyer for Whitmore Brothers Cattle Company, was responsible for collecting the money when the cattle were sold. He was also the man who would pay the crew their wages.

"Did you find Dorsey?" Smiley asked. "Yep, I found him," Casey said.

"Well, what did he say?" Eli Doolin asked impatiently. "When are we gonna get paid?"

"He said he figured it all up and we owe the company money for our horses and such," Casey said.

"Damn it, Casey," Eli said, "when's he gonna pay us?" Eli, along with Casey, was one of the older cowhands for Whitmore Brothers. The two of them had been working cattle together for so long that each one knew when the other was joking. The rest of the crew, all but two were young men in their teens, anxiously waited to hear what Casey had found out.

"Dorsey said the payroll was deposited in the First Cattleman's Bank under each man's name. We have to go to the bank to draw our money out. And the damn bank's closed now, so we'll have to wait till tomorrow mornin' to get our money." His statement was met with a chorus of groans and complaints. Every man was eager to have money in his pocket tonight. It had not been a particularly long drive. But every drive was hard work, pushing ornery cows across a dusty prairie, driving them all day, watching them all night. The pay was forty dollars a month, so a drive this short wouldn't put much money in their pockets. It had only taken a couple of days longer than two months. But it was enough time for them to want to "see the elephant" and ride home broke but happy after a night in Abilene.

Eli got up from his blanket and walked over to talk to Casey. "Why the hell didn't he just hold the payroll and pay us tonight? They've always paid us before," he said to him. "All the years before this, when John Whitmore was running things, we got our money the same time he got his."

"Well, this year, thanks to the way Mr. Dorsey handles it, we'll rest up tonight so we can light up Abilene tomorrow, good and proper. You still got grub to cook on that wagon, don't you, Smiley?"

"I sure do," Smiley said, "and I'm supposed to get some money to feed us on the way back home."

"There you go, boys," Eli declared. "You'll have a good meal in your belly on top of a good night's rest when you attack Abilene tomorrow." He looked then at Davey Springer, youngest of the crew at the age of fifteen—and this, his first cattle drive. "This way, you'll be able to brag about it when you get back home. You can tell 'em you didn't spend all the little bit of money you made until the second night you were in Abilene." Still looking directly at Davey, he said, "You'd best be careful if you fancy one of those little gals that makes her livin' gazin' at the ceilin'. You reach in your pocket and her hand will already be in there, countin' your change."

"You talk like you ain't gonna go into town with the rest of us, Eli," Sam Dunn, an experienced drover at the age of eighteen, remarked.

"Oh, I'll be goin' in with you," Eli said. "Both Me and Casey, I expect. But when you young bucks head for the saloons and the dancehalls, we'll most likely find us a good supper and a drink of likker afterward. Right, Casey?" Casey nodded in reply. "You see, I've left too many a little dance-hall gal with a broken heart when I had to tell her I couldn't stay with her. I don't fancy breakin' any more hearts."

His remarks received the mocking he expected. "Maybe when you and Casey finish your supper, you can look for a dancehall where the old ladies are all rollin' around in their wheelchairs," Sam suggested.

"That's a right interestin' proposition," Casey commented. "I like the sound of that."

The jawing back and forth continued right through supper, and for a while afterward, because there was nothing else to do. Dorsey sold the remuda, as well as the cattle, so there were no horses to take care of except the one you kept to ride back home.

There was no reason to roll out of their blankets early the next morning. The bank didn't open until nine o'clock, which to a cowhand seemed more like noon. Smiley was up early as usual, however, to fix breakfast. They were all standing by the front door of the bank when one of the tellers came to open it. He hesitated when he saw the nine cowhands waiting there. Evidently surmising that they could break the door down, he proceeded to open it. They filed in and lined up at the teller's window.

"Good morning," the teller greeted Casey, who was the first in his line. "What can I help you with?"

"You can help me with my lack of spendin' money," Casey said cheerfully. He gestured with his hand at the men standing behind him. "The nine of us work for the Whitmore Brothers Cattle Company. We brought a herd of cows up here that were sold yesterday. And Mr. Ronald Dorsey deposited the payroll for us in your bank so each one of us could pick up our money this mornin'. My name's Casey Tubbs." He stood there waiting for the teller to do whatever he was going to do to give him his money.

The teller could only respond with an expression of complete puzzlement. He had no knowledge of any payroll the bank was holding. "I'm sorry, Mr. Tubbs, I'll have to get Mr. Skidmore to help you. I'm afraid I don't know anything about your payroll." When he saw Casey's immediate reaction, he said, "I'll be right back. Mr. Skidmore will know about it, I'm sure." He left the cage and hurried back to the bank president's office.

In a few minutes, the teller returned with the president following. Casey didn't like the expression on the president's face. It was one of concern, instead of confidence. "Mr. Tubbs," he said, "I'm Malcolm Skidmore. I'm the president of this bank. There seems to be some confusion about some payroll money?"

"This is the First Cattleman's Bank, ain't it?" Casey asked. When Skidmore acknowledged that, Casey asked, "You did have a Mr. Ronald Dorsey in here yesterday to cash a check for the sale of Whitmore Brothers Cattle Company's herd of two thousand cows, right?"

"Yes, we did," Skidmore said.

"Then there ain't no confusion," Casey declared confidently.

But Skidmore still showed plenty. "The check was honored and the cash was picked up by a special messenger before we opened this morning to be put on the train for Chicago. Those were Mr. Dorsey's instructions."

"But there was most likely a separate sum of money that was the *payroll only*," Casey stressed. "That was supposed to be left here in the bank for us to pick up this morning."

"I'm afraid there's been some misunderstanding," Skidmore said. "Mr. Dorsey said nothing about any payroll. He wanted the entire amount of the money from the sale put on the train to Chicago." Seeing the instant shock of all nine men, he quickly sought to explain his position. "Please understand, the bank is in no way involved with Mr. Dorsey's decision on how the money was to be paid. He had a legitimate check and we honored it. Then, as is often the case with a large sum of cash, the customer wishes to have it transported in the safety of the mail car on the train. In that case, we are happy to provide a guard to accompany the customer to the train station, as we did this morning with Mr. Dorsey before the bank opened."

"So you're tellin' us that the money we worked for went to Chicago this mornin' with Ronald Dorsey?" Eli asked.

Skidmore turned to answer him. "I'm afraid so," he said. "At least it will. That train isn't scheduled to leave here until nine forty-five."

Eli turned to look at Casey. They were both thinking the same thing. "We ain't got much time to find that double-crossin' lawyer," he said.

"No we ain't," Casey said, "let's get goin'!" They headed straight for the door, and Smiley and the six younger men followed.

Outside, they gathered around the three older men, looking for answers. "Whadda we gonna do, Casey?" Sam Dunn asked, plainly bewildered.

Casey looked at the lot of them, all as bewildered as Sam. He made an instant decision. "Me and Eli will take care of it.

Smiley, you boys go on back by the creek where we camped and wait for us there. We'll meet you back there."

Too confused to offer any other suggestions, they dutifully climbed on their horses and went back to the place they had camped the night just passed. Casey and Eli headed for the train station at a gallop.

The train was still sitting in the station and still taking on passengers when they pulled their horses to a stop beside what appeared to be the mail car. The intention was to find Ronald Dorsey, so they climbed on the train and entered the passenger car behind the mail car. Since Casey was the only one who had actually talked to him, he led the way as they hurried down the aisle, looking left and right for Dorsey. Not seeing him in the first car, they went into the next car and looked for him with the same results. The same happened in the third car, where they bumped into the conductor.

"Can I help you gentlemen?"

"No," Eli said. "We're just lookin' for somebody. We'll look in the next car."

"That's the caboose," the conductor said.

"Oh, well, I reckon we'll look again in them other cars," Eli said.

"Can I see your tickets?" The conductor was now concerned with the two desperate-looking men.

"We left 'em with our suitcases up in the first car," Casey said, and started back up the aisle, Eli went right behind him. The conductor just stood there for a moment before deciding he'd better follow them and get a look at their tickets, if they actually had tickets.

They hurried back up the aisles with still no sign of Ronald Dorsey. When they got to the door they had first entered, they stopped to decide what to do. "I'm afraid I'm going to have to ask you gentlemen to get off the train, unless you can show me your tickets."

Ignoring his ultimatum, Casey asked, "What's in that next car?"

"That's the mail car," the conductor said. "You can't go in there." Casey ignored him and went to the door, but found it locked. "You can't go in the mail car," the conductor repeated, now past concern and approaching panic. Still, he tried to maintain his posture of authority. "Now, both of you, off the train, unless you show me a ticket."

"Here's my ticket," Eli said, and pulled his Colt .45 from his holster and jammed it in the conductor's back. "You'd best come up with a key to that door right quick. We ain't got time to argue with you."

"Yes, sir," the conductor said right away, abandoning all pretense of authority. "But it won't open if he's slid the bolt on the other side." He fumbled with his ring of keys until he found one for the mail car. With one hand on the back of the conductor's collar and the other holding the gun against his back, Eli pushed him through the door when it opened.

A startled mail guard looked up from a small desk and asked, "What's goin' on, John?" A second later, he realized what was happening and he started to bolt upright from his chair, only to flop back down when he saw Casey, also holding a gun. Regaining a portion of his valor, he had to exclaim, "Right here? In the station? You must be out of your mind."

"What's your name?" Casey demanded.

"Wesley Logan," he said, staring at the revolver aimed at him.

"Well, I'm gonna make this real easy for you, Wesley," Casey continued. "All you have to do is follow my orders and we'll soon be gone. First thing is to reach over with your left hand and pull that pistol outta your holster and lay it on the floor. Be real careful, Wesley, I druther not have to shoot you." When Wesley laid the revolver on the floor, Casey said, "Kick it over here." Wesley did so and Eli picked it up.

"We're here for one sack of money that belongs to the Whitmore Brothers Cattle Company," Casey continued then. "The sooner you give us that sack, the sooner we'll be out of here."

Wesley looked confused. He glanced down at a ledger on his desk, then back up at Casey. "We don't have any bag for Whitmore Brothers," he said.

"How 'bout one for Ronald Dorsey?" Eli asked.

Wesley checked his ledger again and said, "We've got one for him." So Casey asked how much was in the bag. "Fifty thousand," Wesley said.

"Whaddaya think?" Casey asked Eli. "I ain't tried to figure it up."

"We could take two thousand and that oughta cover it," Eli suggested. They hadn't taken the time to figure out exactly what the total should be for the whole crew.

Casey nodded his agreement. To Wesley then, he said, "Open that bag and count out two thousand dollars."

"I can't open it," Wesley said. "It has a lock on it, and Ronald Dorsey has the key."

"Get the damn bag," Casey ordered, "we're wastin' time here." Wesley jumped to follow his demand. Casey followed him to a cabinet and held his gun on him while he opened it and pulled out a canvas bag. As Wesley had said, it had a lock on it.

Eli didn't wait. He stepped forward and stabbed the bag with his skinning knife, and left the knife sticking in the bag. He told Wesley to cut a hole big enough for him to pull the money out. "Reach in there and count out two thousand"— he paused and looked at Casey and shrugged—"three thousand dollars. Hurry up," he ordered when he felt the train jerk as if about to start. "Put it in one of them bags." He pointed to a stack of empty mail sacks on the floor. Wesley kept pulling money out of the hole in the bag until he had counted out three thousand dollars. He paused then and looked up at Eli to see if he was going to tell him to stop. "Three thousand," Eli said. "That's all we came for. Hand me my knife." Wesley dutifully extended the knife toward him. "Turn it around, handle first, you bloomin' idiot."

"Oops, sorry," Wesley uttered, and turned the knife around. With their guns still trained on the two railroad men, Eli and Casey backed up to the door. "I wanna thank you fellers for not makin' us have to shoot one of ya." He looked at Eli and said, "Come on, partner, we gotta hit the north road outta here." They backed out the door and jumped off the train just as the wheels started to turn over. In the saddle, they dashed away from the station at a gallop, expecting to hear shouts of alarm at any second, but hearing none.

Back in the mail car, John and Wesley were both amazed to still be standing. It was the first train robbery for both and Wesley was still holding the ripped bag. "There's gonna be hell to pay for this," he said, staring at the bag and the ragged tear in its side.

"They were two desperate-lookin' men," John, the conductor, said. "With all the money in this car, I wonder why they didn't want it all. There's fifty thousand dollars in that one bag, and all they took was three thousand."

"Yeah, don't make sense, does it?" Wesley said, still staring at the bag. "They coulda took more and this fellow, Dorsey, wouldn't know the difference. Makes just as much sense if they had took an even five thousand."

"That's a fact," John said. "I'm glad there was two of us witnesses to the holdup, so we can tell 'im what happened. And I expect we'd better report it right away. That fellow, Dorsey, is riding in the caboose. I let him ride back there because he said he had a fear of riding in open passenger cars. He's gonna be fit to be tied when we tell him what happened."

"Right," Wesley agreed, "we'd best get goin'." He reached

in the hole again and pulled out two thousand more and gave John half.

Approaching the south end of town, the two train robbers continued their escape at a fast lope. When it appeared there was no one chasing them, they reined their horses back to a walk and Eli pulled up beside Casey.

"What the hell were you talkin' about when we left back there and you said we gotta hit the north road? What's the north road?"

"There's gotta be some road outta here headin' north," Casey said. "So I said that in case they get up a posse to come after us. Wesley and John can tell 'em we were goin' out the north road."

Eli just looked at him and shook his head slowly. "We need to stop and figure our money out before we get back to the camp." Neither one was good at arithmetic, so they dismounted beside the road, and with the road as a blackboard and a stick as their chalk, they figured the split of the money. They finally resorted to moving off the road and into the trees, so they could divide the money in nine little piles. When they were finished, they returned to their camp and the seven anxious souls awaiting them. They all got up to crowd around the two, excited to see Eli holding a sack.

"Boys," Casey announced, "we're happy to tell you that you will all get your wages for two months' work, as the honorable Ronald Dorsey promised. Plus, you're each gettin' a one-hundred-dollar bonus for the delay in receivin' your wages." That brought forth a cheer from the young cowhands.

"What about the money for my supplies?" Smiley asked.
"You got that, too," Casey said to him, "more than they'll actually cost. We all got what was owed us, plus the bonus."
"You musta found ol' Dorsey," Smiley said. "Where'd you find him?"

"We maybe oughta chip in some of our money to you

and Eli," Sam Dunn suggested. "We wouldn'ta got a nickel, if you hadn't gone after Dorsey to get it."

Casey and Eli looked at each other to see who was going to explain the special circumstances around the crew's payday. Finally Eli volunteered. "Boys, there are some special conditions that come along with your payoff. It's best that you head straight back to Texas, and don't go into Abilene tonight to spend your money." He immediately captured everyone's attention. "You see, we never caught up with Ronald Dorsey. We caught up with the money he got for the sale of the cattle we drove up here. It was on a train that just left here for Chicago."

"You robbed a train?" Davey Springer asked.

"I guess you could call it that," Casey said to him. "But it seems only fair. We just took what was rightfully our money and left the rest in Dorsey's bag. If he had been honest with us, he wouldn't have had that money to take to Chicago in the first place. That was ours, and me and Eli just went to get it back."

"That does seem fair," Smiley remarked, "but the Union Pacific Railroad ain't likely to see it that way. You had to break into the mail car to get the money, didn't you?"

"We had to persuade the conductor to unlock the door, so we could get in the car," Casey said. "But we didn't break down no doors, or destroy no railroad property, did we, Eli?" He paused, then said, "Except for that money sack you had to cut open with your knife."

"That weren't railroad property," Eli reasoned. "That belonged to Ronald Dorsey."

"That don't make no difference," Smiley insisted. He was genuinely worried about the two old cowhands. "How'd you persuade the conductor to let you in the mail car?"

Casey looked toward Eli again, but saw no tendency to answer the question, so he said, "We told him they had something that belonged to us in there."

"And he just unlocked the door for you?" Smiley asked. "That was pretty much what happened," Casey said.

After a pause, he added, " 'Course, when Eli stuck his .44 into the conductor's back, he knew we weren't just wastin' his time."

Smiley shook his head, scarcely able to believe what the two of them were telling him. "I swear, Casey, you're talkin' about armed robbery of the Union Pacific Railroad. It don't matter if it was for that little bit of money. You're gonna have Union Pacific detectives lookin' for you, for sure."

"I hope they take the north road to start lookin'," Eli mumbled to himself. Then he announced, "If any of you don't want your share of the money, we'll be glad to take it back." No one opted to return the tainted money, including Smiley, which was of no surprise to Casey or Eli.

Given the special circumstances that insured their pay, plus bonuses, the rest of the crew were in agreement with Casey and Eli's recommendation to leave Kansas at once and return to Texas. All the younger hands were planning to ride the grub line in hopes of finding permanent employment with some of the bigger ranches. The coming winter would be a little easier on their efforts with the extra money Casey and Eli had procured for them. Each man thanked the two for their sacrifice on their behalf and promised to never tell where they got the money.

Smiley was the only one of them who had a place to go. He had already agreed to go to work for another rancher in North Texas he had worked for before. He was replacing an old cook who was making his last trip to market that year. That left the two train robbers to decide what to do.

CHAPTER 2

"I swear, Eli, I don't know if I'm ready to start out on the grub line again," Casey confessed. "I started out in this business as a wrangler for Sid Williams down in Mason County. I was the same age Davey Springer is, fifteen years old. That was thirty-some years ago, and it seems more like a hundred. Maybe I'll change my mind, but right now, I don't wanna push another herd of half-crazy cows across another storm-swollen river or chase another stampede in the middle of a thunderstorm."

"I reckon I know how you feel," Eli said. "I was a few years older than Davey when I got into this business, but I've been doin' it about the same number of years as you have. If Whitmore hadn't shut down, I expect I woulda signed on again for next year, just because there ain't nothin' else I can do but work cows."

"Right now, I'm gonna set right here on this creek bank and drink the rest of that pot of coffee Smiley made," Casey declared. "I didn't see a sign of anybody noticin' us when we rode away from that train, so I don't really expect to see any posse makin' up in Abilene to come lookin' for us." He looked at Smiley, a dozen yards away, still packing up his chuck wagon, and yelled, "You ain't ready to throw that coffee out, are you, Smiley?"

"Nope," Smiley yelled back. "I'm fixin' to have myself some apple pie with a cup of this coffee. I've got enough of that pie left to make about three servings, if you're interested." He waited for the reaction he was betting on.

"Hell yeah," Eli yelled. "That was damn good pie." Smiley always brought dried fruit of some kind on every cattle drive. And he had the talent to roll out some dough crust and fry it in lard for a treat once in a while.

Eli and Casey went over to the chuckwagon, and Smiley filled their cups with the last of the coffee and gave them each a serving of pie. "I didn't say nothin' about this till after the other boys had gone 'cause I didn't have enough to feed everybody. Besides, you two deserve a special treat for goin' after that money. I just hope to hell you don't see your names up on the post office wall."

"I don't think we've got much to worry about," Casey said. "We didn't tell them two what our names were."

"A railroad detective might be asking about men lookin' to find new outfits to ride for," Smiley speculated, "since they do know that Whitmore shut down, and that's who you were ridin' for."

"I thought about that, too," Casey said. "That's another reason not to ride the grub line this winter."

They finished up the pie and coffee, and Eli and Casey cleaned their plates in the creek while Smiley washed out the coffeepot. When he was packed up and ready to go, he asked if they were going to head back to the old Whitmore Brothers Ranch.

"I ain't decided yet," Casey told him, and Eli said he hadn't, either.

"Well, I'll see you when I see you," Smiley said, and shook hands with each of them. "Take care of yourselves. You're the only outlaws I know that I can call friends." They enjoyed a good chuckle over that and wished him well. He climbed up into the wagon seat and started out after the younger hands. He figured he'd catch up to them when they got hungry.

The two friends remained there for a long while, talking about what they could possibly do to earn a living if they didn't try to find another cattle outfit to sign on with. They found themselves caught in a canyon between too young to stop working and too old to start out fresh on some other occupation. The only thing they could think of where they might make a living was prospecting for gold or silver, which neither of them knew anything about.

"At least we've got a little money to tide us over the winter," Eli said, "thanks to the generosity of Ronald Dorsey."

"I think he would agree that as many years as we worked in cattle, we deserved a decent retirement packge," Casey joked. After they paid the men their due wages, plus a hundred dollar bonus, he and Eli came away with over eight hundred dollars each. It was a sum they were unaccustomed to having in their pockets. "'Course, now that we don't have Smiley to count on, we're gonna have to buy some supplies, plus pots and pans, a coffeepot, everything we'll need to live. Hell, we're gonna need a packhorse to carry all our possibles, too." He looked at Eli then before suggesting, "It'd be a lot cheaper if we was to partner up. Then we wouldn't have to buy two of everything."

"I was kinda hopin' you'd think of that," Eli responded, and extended his hand. Casey shook it and the partnership was formed. "Too bad we can't celebrate our partnership with a good supper and a drink of likker."

"I've been thinkin' about that a little more, too," Casey said. "And I don't see why we don't just ride on into Abilene and have supper at the hotel. The only people who saw us take that money are on the train headin' east right now. There ain't nobody in Abilene that knows who we are, except the bank people, and there's a good chance nobody even knows that robbery happened yet. Hell, we can stay in the hotel tonight and buy all our supplies right here tomorrow mornin'."

"Now that I think about it, I believe you're right. Let's do it."

There was only one hotel in Abilene, and it was not hard to find. Called Drovers Cottage, it towered over everything else in town, standing three stories tall. Lavishly decorated for a hotel in a cattle town, it had a large dining room, a billiard room, and a saloon. Casey and Eli decided there could be no better place to celebrate their partnership, so they walked up to the desk and informed the clerk that they desired a room for the night. They were told there was a room available, since most of the cattle owners and buyers had checked out that day. They considered that another sign that things were happening in their favor, since they decided to partner up. The desk clerk took a close look at the two obvious cowhands and informed them that the room rent would have to be paid in advance. He was quite surprised when there was no objection to the price, and both men readily peeled off a couple of bills from a sizable roll. After they were given a key to a room on the second floor, they put their horses in the hotel's stable and took their saddlebags and rifles up to the room.

Taking advantage of every luxury afforded them, they made use of the hotel's washroom to take a bath and shave. All slicked up and wearing clean underwear, they were ready for supper, so they went into the dining room, where they were met by a young man who called himself the maître d'hôtel and asked how he could help them.

"We're wantin' to eat supper," Eli told him. "Reckon there's somebody here to tell us where we can set down?"

"Sir, that's what I do," the young man said.

"Well, do it then, sonny. We're about to starve to death," Eli said.

"May I ask you to remove your firearms?" the young man responded.

"Is that what everybody else is doin'?" Casey asked. "Or just folks like us that ain't wearin' no evenin' coat?" The young man said it was asked of everyone, so Casey and Eli unbuckled their gun belts and held the weapons out to him. He backed away as if they might go off at any second. Then he pointed to a table where there were a couple of pistols already deposited.

After they left their weapons, the young man led them through the busy dining room, past several empty tables, to the back corner of the large room and sat them at a small table right by the kitchen door.

"Your waiter will be here shortly," the young man said, then did a rapid about-face.

"Damned if he ain't a fussy one," Eli remarked when the maître d'hôtel walked back to his post in the doorway of the dining room.

"Yeah," Casey agreed, "but he must notta been as fussy as he acts. He gave us the best table in the place, right next to the kitchen door."

They were somewhat relieved when their waiter came to the table. "Howdy, fellows, my name's Carl. What can I get you to drink while you're deciding what you want to eat?" They both said coffee, so he said, "I'll go get your coffee while you decide if you're gonna have pork chops or stewed chicken. I don't expect you want beef."

"You're right about that, Carl," Casey said. "I ain't had nothin' but beef for over two months. I'm goin' with the pork chops."

"Me too," Eli said.

"I'll go tell the cook," Carl responded, "and I'll be right back with your coffee." He popped back into the kitchen.

"Ol' Carl's all right," Eli remarked. "If he'da been as finicky as that first feller, I mighta said let's go find some-place else to eat."

In the kitchen, the cook commented to the waiter, "Got yourself a couple of cowboys right off the trail, ain'tcha, Carl?"

"Yeah, Bruce always sticks me with the trail hands that haven't ever been in a nice dining room before. It's good and it's bad. They don't usually complain about the food, but they ain't ever heard about tipping the waiter."

They enjoyed a fine supper with excellent service by Carl; so much so, they decided to make him a present of a couple of dollars to let him know they appreciated the attention. When they told him they were guests in the hotel, he told them they could pay cash for their dining-room charge, or it could be added to their hotel bill. Casey winked at Eli and said, "Let's just add it to the room bill." They had already paid for their room; they just might decide to skip the bill for the dinner, since it was too much, even if it was good.

"I reckon we're ready for that drink of likker now," Eli announced, so they left the dining room and went into the saloon. They noticed a few men in the saloon wearing guns, so they promptly put theirs back on. One man, in particular, caught their attention. Standing at the end of the bar, a tall, somber-looking man, with long, dark hair down to his shoulders and a mustache that hung down to his chin, was idling over a drink of whiskey on the bar before him. He was well armed, wearing two revolvers high on his hips.

"What'll you have, fellows?" the bartender asked. "What's that feller down at the other end of the bar drinkin'?" Casey asked.

"Bill?" the bartender responded. "He don't drink nothin' but rye whiskey."

"I'll have the same as he's havin'," Casey said. "He looks like he's all business and he's ready for trouble, wearin' a pair of pistols. Do we need 'em in here? Looks pretty peaceful to me."

The bartender chuckled. "He's the reason it is peaceful in here. He's the town marshal. You mighta heard of him, 'Wild Bill' Hickok." He waited, but didn't get the reaction he expected from the two of them.

"The name sounds familiar, but I don't recall where I heard it," Casey said.

"Where are you fellows from?" the bartender had to ask then.

"Texas," Casey said. "I reckon we oughta get out where the people are once in a while." When the bartender moved down the bar to wait on another customer, Casey chuckled and said, "Here we are havin' a drink with Wild Bill Hickok, and he don't even know he's drinkin' with two desperate train robbers. I'm thinkin' the least we can do is buy the marshal a drink."

"What for?" Eli wanted to know.

"So we can say we done it, in case he's famous sometime," Casey said. "We can afford it, and it might bring us good luck."

"It's your money," Eli commented. They had another drink before deciding to call it quits for the night.

They paid the bartender, and since Hickok was still standing there, staring at half a shot in his glass, Casey said, "Here's something for another drink for Marshal Hickok." He dropped a couple of quarters on the bar.

"Who will I tell him paid for the drink?" the bartender asked.

"Tell him just a couple of tired old cowboys," Casey said, "who want him to keep up the good work."

With full stomachs and heads with enough alcohol buzz

to tell them it was time to get to bed, they went back to their room. After a solid night's sleep, they woke up early the following morning ready to get started with the rest of their lives. Since it was too early for the dining room to open for breakfast, they decided to go to the stable and get their horses saddled and ready to go. There was no one in the stable. The fellow who showed them which stalls to put them in the night before was not there. Eli spotted him going to the back door of the kitchen. *Probably gets some breakfast before they open up for business,* he thought. He started to call out to him to tell him they wanted their horses now, but decided not to interfere with the man's breakfast. When he walked back into the stable, he found Casey pulling the cinch tight on his horse's belly, but staring at the little gathering of horses in the corral.

"You know," Casey said when Eli picked up his saddle, "there's some decent-lookin' horses in that corral yonder, and we're needin' a good packhorse."

"I don't know if they've got any horses for sale," Eli said. "Don't you suppose all those horses belong to the guests or the hotel employees?"

"That would be my guess," Casey agreed, "but I never said anything about buyin' a horse. We keep buyin' things and we're gonna be runnin' outta money. Besides, we're already outlaws, ain't we? Won't hurt to put us down for a little bit more."

"Well, in that case, I expect we'd best decide on which one we want and not waste any more time around this hotel," Eli said. "I like the look of that sorrel with the stripe down his face. Whaddaya think?"

"Suits me. Let's look him over and make sure he's in good shape. We don't wanna cheat ourselves," Casey said. "If we're gonna steal a horse, let's steal a good one. You look him over and I'll take another look in the tack room. There just might be a packsaddle in there. Save us the cost of buyin' one." A few minutes later, he came back out, holding up a packsaddle for Eli to see. "Is that our horse?" he asked, nodding toward the sorrel.

"Looks okay to me," Eli said as he tightened his saddle cinch. "Let's see how he likes that packsaddle." The horse proved to be very gentle and showed no objection to the saddle at all. "Danged if I don't believe this ain't the first one he's seen."

"Might be his," Casey said with a chuckle.

"I expect we'd best get goin'," Eli said. "It's startin' to get light, and we don't know how fast that feller that works in the stable eats."

They climbed up in their saddles and filed out the back door of the stable, with Eli leading the packhorse. Their departure was blocked from view by the stables, so Harry Blanchard wasn't aware of the hotel's loss of a horse belonging to one of their guests. Pausing at the bottom of the kitchen steps, he swallowed hard and released a loud belch of satisfaction before returning to the horses in his care.

The two newly minted outlaws, after discussing the best place to buy the supplies they needed, as well as a place to get some breakfast, decided they were pushing their luck to remain in Abilene. They had heard there was another town close by that was rapidly establishing itself as a trade center and a cattle town to rival Abilene. At this point, that seemed their best choice. Salina was a little town about six miles east of the point where the Saline River joined the Smoky Hill River. It was only a little over half a day's ride from Abilene. Neither man had ever been to Salina, but they knew if they followed the Union Pacific Railroad tracks west, they couldn't miss it. And from the looks of the road running along beside the tracks, there was quite a bit of travel between the two towns.

They arrived in the middle of the morning, too early for dinner and too late for breakfast. Entering the town from the east, they rode past the railroad station before coming to a building that proclaimed itself to be SALINA MERCHANDISE. They decided they might as well take care of their supplies first, so they tied their horses at the rail out front and went inside. "Mornin'," greeted a rather stocky man, with thick gray hair cropped off short. "What can I help you fellows with this mornin'?"

"We'll be needing quite a bit of stuff," Casey said. "We were over in Abilene last night and the shed we put all our possibles in caught fire, burned up everything we had. So I hope you're feelin' like dealin' this mornin'. If not, we'll spend our money somewhere else." He glanced at Eli, who had a hint of a grin on his face. So he turned quickly back to the man behind the counter before he caused Eli to chuckle.

"You fellows ain't been in my store before, and I'm guessin' you ain't ever been to Salina before, either. Otherwise, you'd know there ain't no other place near here where you can get everything you most likely need. My name's Jim Lawrence, and if you ask around, folks will tell you that I always work with the farmers and ranchers around this part of the county as fair and square as I can. That's the reason this store is as big as it is, so why don't you tell me what you need? And I'll give you the best price I can afford. How's that?"

Casey looked at Eli again and laughed. "Can't ask for much more than that, can we? We've also got some tired and thirsty horses, and we're gonna take a little time comin' up with everything we need." He shook his head. "I mean, everything we had to make camp got ruined. We couldn't even stop for breakfast. Didn't have anything to cook and nothing to cook it in. So, why don't we turn our horses out by that creek back of your store and let 'em rest up while we're dealin'?"

"That sounds like a good idea," Jim said. "You boys do that and I'll sharpen up my pencil whenever you're ready."

They took the saddles off their horses and turned them loose to go to the creek. As a precaution, they hobbled their new packhorse in case he decided he'd go back to his previous owner. Casey was riding a gray gelding named Smoke, while Eli favored a bay that he called Biscuit. When they were working on a cattle drive, they actually used from ten to twelve different horses. The work was too hard to ride only one horse all day, so they were changed often. But every cowhand had a personal favorite that he counted as his horse. The horse knew he belonged to that cowhand, so it was unnecessary to hobble Smoke or Biscuit. They would naturally stay close to their masters. Knowing that, Casey and Eli left the horses by the creek and returned to the store, where Jim Lawrence was waiting to do business. There was a cheerful-looking woman standing beside him when they went back inside.

"Gentlemen, this is my wife, Mae. She's wantin' to know if you could use a cup of fresh, hot coffee. I heard you say you couldn't even cook any breakfast this mornin', and she put on a fresh pot while you were out taking care of your horses. It'll give you a chance to taste the coffee we sell, and I expect you'll need a good coffee grinder, too, unless you rather beat 'em to death with a hammer and a sack."

"Why, that would be mighty neighborly of you, Miz Lawrence," Casey said. "A cup of hot coffee would taste mighty good right now, wouldn't it, Eli?"

"It surely would," Eli said.

"It would be my pleasure," Mae said. "How do you take your coffee? Sugar or some milk? We've got some milk cooling in the spring box."

"No, thank you, ma'am," Casey said. "We take it black, just like it comes outta the bean." She went to the kitchen to fetch the coffee, and they started calling out the items they were in need of. They started with a coffeepot and a grinder, since that was the topic of the discussion just ended.

As things came to mind, they called off items at random, things they might need, like a hand ax, a spade, a pot, a frying pan, spoons, cups and plates, cooking utensils. All of these were placed on the counter before even getting to the food items. In the middle of all this ordering, Mae Lawrence came in with three cups of fresh coffee. The three men paused to enjoy the coffee, and it was Casey who commented first. "Ma'am, I've gotta tell you, you sure make a fine cup of coffee. I don't know if I've ever had a better cup, or even one as good as this one."

His comment caused Mae to smile as Jim winked at her. "Thank you, sir," Mae responded. "I'd like to take all the credit, but I think more of it will have to go to the coffee itself."

"We ran a little test on you," her husband explained then. "That coffee is a special roasted coffee called Arbuckles'. Fellow named John Arbuckle roasts the beans, mixed with a couple of secret ingredients that hold the flavor in. So his beans don't go stale after the bag has been open for a while. He packs it in one-pound bags, and I just got a shipment of it from back east on the train this week." He paused to let that sink in before continuing. "Now, there ain't nothin' wrong with the roasted beans I've been sellin' ever since we opened this store here. But I just wanted you to try out the Arbuckles' to see how you liked it. You may be thinkin' it's good, but not worth payin' more, but we're only talkin' about two cents a pound over my regular beans."

Eli had to laugh. "Danged if that ain't a sneaky way to sell coffee." He turned to his partner and asked, "Whaddaya think, Casey? You wanna buy some fancy coffee?"

"Why not?" Casey said. "We're startin' out this winter with everything new. Might as well try some Arbuckles'. This whole season is gonna be our Arbuckle season." He looked at the pile of merchandise stacked on the counter already and was prompted to comment. "I believe we're gonna need another packhorse."

"Maybe not," Eli said, "but Smoke and Biscuit might have to give the sorrel a hand." He grinned at Jim then and remarked, "I expect we'd best settle for what we've got there on the counter."

"Right," Jim said, and grinned back at him, although the grin was forced. For the thought just struck him that whole transaction seemed to be overly amusing to the two strangers, as if it was a joke. And he suddenly wondered if he was being played for a fool and their form of payment might be in the Colt Single Action Army revolvers each man wore. All the conversation seemed to stop, and both men set their coffee cups on the counter while he added up the cost. When he had totaled it and checked his arithmetic, he was reluctant to announce the figure. "Looks like it comes to ninety-two dollars and sixty cents. We can round it off to ninety dollars."

"Dang," Eli commented, "we might have to find a bank to rob. Does that include the two cups of coffee?"

Jim responded with a sickly smile and nodded.

Eli looked at Casey then and said, "That's forty-five apiece," and reached in his pocket for the money. When Casey did the same, Jim almost reacted with a sigh of relief, but turned it into a genuine smile of appreciation.

By the time they finished buying a new outfit, it was getting along toward the noon hour. And while they were going about packing their purchases efficiently on their new packhorse, they asked Jim if there was a decent place in town to eat dinner. Jim recommended the saloon. "It's called O'Malley's," he said. "He does a pretty good dinner and supper business. He's got a cook named Kati . . ." He paused then and took a quick peek to make sure Mae was not in earshot before he continued. ". . . who can outcook any woman in the county."

Visit our website at
KensingtonBooks.com
to sign up for our newsletters, read
more from your favorite authors, see
books by series, view reading group
guides, and more!

BOOK CLUB

BETWEEN THE CHAPTERS

Become a Part of Our
Between the Chapters Book Club
Community and Join the Conversation

Betweenthechapters.net